DATE DUE

$4.11

1963-64

The New York Edition of Henry James

THE NOVELS AND TALES OF
HENRY JAMES

New York Edition

VOLUME IV

THE PORTRAIT OF A LADY

VOLUME II

HENRY JAMES

NEW YORK

CHARLES SCRIBNER'S SONS

THE PORTRAIT OF A LADY

VOLUME II

THE PORTRAIT OF A LADY

XXVIII

On the morrow, in the evening, Lord Warburton went again to see his friends at their hotel, and at this establishment he learned that they had gone to the opera. He drove to the opera with the idea of paying them a visit in their box after the easy Italian fashion; and when he had obtained his admittance — it was one of the secondary theatres — looked about the large, bare, ill-lighted house. An act had just terminated and he was at liberty to pursue his quest. After scanning two or three tiers of boxes he perceived in one of the largest of these receptacles a lady whom he easily recognised. Miss Archer was seated facing the stage and partly screened by the curtain of the box; and beside her, leaning back in his chair, was Mr. Gilbert Osmond. They appeared to have the place to themselves, and Warburton supposed their companions had taken advantage of the recess to enjoy the relative coolness of the lobby. He stood a while with his eyes on the interesting pair; he asked himself if he should go up and interrupt the harmony. At last he judged that Isabel had seen him, and this accident determined him. There should be no marked holding off. He took his way to the upper regions and on the staircase met Ralph Touchett slowly descending, his hat at the

I

inclination of ennui and his hands where they usually were.

"I saw you below a moment since and was going down to you. I feel lonely and want company," was Ralph's greeting.

"You've some that's very good which you've yet deserted."

"Do you mean my cousin? Oh, she has a visitor and does n't want me. Then Miss Stackpole and Bantling have gone out to a café to eat an ice — Miss Stackpole delights in an ice. I did n't think *they* wanted me either. The opera's very bad; the women look like laundresses and sing like peacocks. I feel very low."

"You had better go home," Lord Warburton said without affectation.

"And leave my young lady in this sad place? Ah no, I must watch over her."

"She seems to have plenty of friends."

"Yes, that's why I must watch," said Ralph with the same large mock-melancholy.

"If she does n't want you it's probable she does n't want me."

"No, you're different. Go to the box and stay there while I walk about."

Lord Warburton went to the box, where Isabel's welcome was as to a friend so honourably old that he vaguely asked himself what queer temporal province she was annexing. He exchanged greetings with Mr. Osmond, to whom he had been introduced the day before and who, after he came in, sat blandly apart and silent, as if repudiating competence in the subjects of allusion now probable. It struck her second visitor that Miss Archer had, in operatic conditions, a radiance, even a slight exaltation; as she was, however, at all times a keenly-glancing, quickly-moving, completely animated young woman, he may have been mistaken on this point. Her talk with him moreover pointed to presence of mind; it expressed a kindness so ingenious and deliberate as to indicate that she was in undisturbed possession of her faculties. Poor Lord Warburton had moments of bewilderment. She had discouraged him, formally, as much as a woman could; what business had she then with such arts and such felicities, above all with such tones of reparation — preparation? Her voice had tricks of sweetness, but why play them on *him?* The others came back; the bare, familiar, trivial opera began again. The box was large, and there was room for him to remain if he would sit a little behind and in the dark. He did so for half an hour, while Mr. Osmond remained in front, leaning forward, his elbows on his knees, just behind Isabel. Lord Warburton heard nothing, and from his gloomy corner saw nothing but the clear profile of this young lady defined against the dim illumination of the house. When there was another interval no one moved. Mr. Osmond talked to Isabel, and Lord Warburton kept his corner. He did so but for a short time, however; after which he got up and bade good-night to the ladies. Isabel said nothing to detain him, but it did n't prevent his being puzzled again. Why should she mark so one of his values — quite the wrong one — when she would have nothing to do with another, which was quite the right? He was angry with himself for being puzzled, and then angry for being angry. Verdi's music did little to comfort him, and he left the theatre and walked homeward, without knowing his way, through the tortuous, tragic streets of Rome, where heavier sorrows than his had been carried under the stars.

"What's the character of that gentleman?" Osmond asked of Isabel after he had retired.

"Irreproachable — don't you see it?"

"He owns about half England; that's his character," Henrietta remarked. "That's what they call a free country!"

"Ah, he's a great proprietor? Happy man!" said Gilbert Osmond.

"Do you call that happiness — the ownership of wretched human beings?" cried Miss Stackpole. "He owns his tenants and has thousands of them. It's pleasant to own something, but inanimate objects are enough for me. I don't insist on flesh and blood and minds and consciences."

"It seems to me you own a human being or two," Mr. Bantling suggested jocosely. "I wonder if Warburton orders his tenants about as you do me."

"Lord Warburton's a great radical," Isabel said. "He has very advanced opinions."

"He has very advanced stone walls. His park's enclosed by a gigantic iron fence, some thirty miles round," Henrietta announced for the information of Mr. Osmond. "I should like him to converse with a few of our Boston radicals."

"Don't they approve of iron fences?" asked Mr. Bantling.

"Only to shut up wicked conservatives. I always feel as if I were talking to *you* over something with a neat top-finish of broken glass."

"Do you know him well, this unreformed reformer?" Osmond went on, questioning Isabel.

"Well enough for all the use I have for him."

"And how much of a use is that?"

"Well, I like to like him."

"'Liking to like'—why, it makes a passion!" said Osmond.

"No"—she considered—"keep that for liking to *dis*like."

"Do you wish to provoke me then," Osmond laughed, "to a passion for *him?*"

She said nothing for a moment, but then met the light question with a disproportionate gravity. "No, Mr. Osmond; I don't think I should ever dare to provoke you. Lord Warburton, at any rate," she more easily added, "is a very nice man."

"Of great ability?" her friend enquired.

"Of excellent ability, and as good as he looks."

"As good as he's good-looking do you mean? He's very good-looking. How detestably fortunate! —to be a great English magnate, to be clever and handsome into the bargain, and, by way of finishing off, to enjoy your high favour! That's a man I could envy."

Isabel considered him with interest. "You seem to me to be always envying some one. Yesterday it was the Pope; to-day it's poor Lord Warburton."

"My envy's not dangerous; it would n't hurt a mouse. I don't want to destroy the people — I only want to *be* them. You see it would destroy only myself."

"You'd like to be the Pope?" said Isabel.

"I should love it — but I should have gone in for it earlier. But why" — Osmond reverted — "do you speak of your friend as poor?"

"Women — when they are very, very good — sometimes pity men after they've hurt them; that's their great way of showing kindness," said Ralph. joining in the conversation for the first time and with a cynicism so transparently ingenious as to be virtually innocent.

"Pray, have I hurt Lord Warburton?" Isabel asked, raising her eyebrows as if the idea were perfectly fresh.

"It serves him right if you have," said Henrietta while the curtain rose for the ballet.

Isabel saw no more of her attributive victim for the next twenty-four hours, but on the second day after the visit to the opera she encountered him in the gallery of the Capitol, where he stood before the lion of the collection, the statue of the Dying Gladiator. She had come in with her companions, among whom, on this occasion again, Gilbert Osmond had his place, and the party, having ascended the staircase, entered the first and finest of the rooms. Lord Warburton addressed her alertly enough, but said in a moment that he was leaving the gallery. "And I'm leaving Rome," he added. "I must bid you goodbye." Isabel, inconsequently enough, was now sorry to hear it. This was perhaps because she had ceased to be afraid of his renewing his suit; she was thinking of something else. She was on the point of naming her regret, but she checked herself and simply wished him a happy journey; which made him look at her rather unlightedly. "I'm afraid you'll think me very 'volatile.' I told you the other day I wanted so much to stop."

"Oh no; you could easily change your mind."

"That's what I have done."

"*Bon voyage* then."

"You're in a great hurry to get rid of me," said his lordship quite dismally.

"Not in the least. But I hate partings."

"You don't care what I do," he went on pitifully.

Isabel looked at him a moment. "Ah," she said, "you're not keeping your promise!"

He coloured like a boy of fifteen. "If I'm not, then it's because I can't; and that's why I'm going."

"Good-bye then."

"Good-bye." He lingered still, however. "When shall I see you again?"

Isabel hesitated, but soon, as if she had had a happy inspiration: "Some day after you're married."

"That will never be. It will be after you are."

"That will do as well," she smiled.

"Yes, quite as well. Good-bye."

They shook hands, and he left her alone in the glorious room, among the shining antique marbles. She sat down in the centre of the circle of these presences, regarding them vaguely, resting her eyes on their beautiful blank faces; listening, as it were, to

7

their eternal silence. It is impossible, in Rome at least, to look long at a great company of Greek sculptures without feeling the effect of their noble quietude; which, as with a high door closed for the ceremony, slowly drops on the spirit the large white mantle of peace. I say in Rome especially, because the Roman air is an exquisite medium for such impressions. The golden sunshine mingles with them, the deep stillness of the past, so vivid yet, though it is nothing but a void full of names, seems to throw a solemn spell upon them. The blinds were partly closed in the windows of the Capitol, and a clear, warm shadow rested on the figures and made them more mildly human. Isabel sat there a long time, under the charm of their motionless grace, wondering to what, of their experience, their absent eyes were open, and how, to our ears, their alien lips would sound. The dark red walls of the room threw them into relief; the polished marble floor reflected their beauty. She had seen them all before, but her enjoyment repeated itself, and it was all the greater because she was glad again, for the time, to be alone. At last, however, her attention lapsed, drawn off by a deeper tide of life. An occasional tourist came in, stopped and stared a moment at the Dying Gladiator, and then passed out of the other door, creaking over the smooth pavement. At the end of half an hour Gilbert Osmond reappeared, apparently in advance of his companions. He strolled toward her slowly, with his hands behind him and his usual enquiring, yet not quite appealing smile. "I'm surprised to find you alone, I thought you had company."

8

"So I have — the best." And she glanced at the Antinous and the Faun.

"Do you call them better company than an English peer?"

"Ah, my English peer left me some time ago." She got up, speaking with intention a little dryly.

Mr. Osmond noted her dryness, which contributed for him to the interest of his question. "I'm afraid that what I heard the other evening is true: you're rather cruel to that nobleman."

Isabel looked a moment at the vanquished Gladiator. "It's not true. I'm scrupulously kind."

"That's exactly what I mean!" Gilbert Osmond returned, and with such happy hilarity that his joke needs to be explained. We know that he was fond of originals, of rarities, of the superior and the exquisite; and now that he had seen Lord Warburton, whom he thought a very fine example of his race and order, he perceived a new attraction in the idea of taking to himself a young lady who had qualified herself to figure in his collection of choice objects by declining so noble a hand. Gilbert Osmond had a high appreciation of this particular patriciate; not so much for its distinction, which he thought easily surpassable, as for its solid actuality. He had never forgiven his star for not appointing him to an English dukedom, and he could measure the unexpectedness of such conduct as Isabel's. It would be proper that the woman he might marry should have done something of that sort.

XXIX

RALPH TOUCHETT, in talk with his excellent friend, had rather markedly qualified, as we know, his recognition of Gilbert Osmond's personal merits; but he might really have felt himself illiberal in the light of that gentleman's conduct during the rest of the visit to Rome. Osmond spent a portion of each day with Isabel and her companions, and ended by affecting them as the easiest of men to live with. Who would n't have seen that he could command, as it were, both tact and gaiety?—which perhaps was exactly why Ralph had made his old-time look of superficial sociability a reproach to him. Even Isabel's invidious kinsman was obliged to admit that he was just now a delightful associate. His good-humour was imperturbable, his knowledge of the right fact, his production of the right word, as convenient as the friendly flicker of a match for your cigarette. Clearly he was amused — as amused as a man could be who was so little ever surprised, and that made him almost applausive. It was not that his spirits were visibly high — he would never, in the concert of pleasure, touch the big drum by so much as a knuckle: he had a mortal dislike to the high, ragged note, to what he called random ravings. He thought Miss Archer sometimes of too precipitate a readiness. It was pity she had that fault, because if she had not had it she would really have had none; she would have been as smooth to his general need of her as handled ivory to the palm. If he was not personally loud, however, he was deep, and during these closing days of the Roman May he knew a complacency that matched with slow irregular walks under the pines of the Villa Borghese, among the small sweet meadow-flowers and the mossy marbles. He was pleased with everything; he had never before been pleased with so many things at once. Old impressions, old enjoyments, renewed themselves; one evening, going home to his room at the inn, he wrote down a little sonnet to which he prefixed the title of "Rome Revisited." A day or two later he showed this piece of correct and ingenious verse to Isabel, explaining to her that it was an Italian fashion to commemorate the occasions of life by a tribute to the muse.

He took his pleasures in general singly; he was too often — he would have admitted that — too sorely aware of something wrong, something ugly; the fertilising dew of a conceivable felicity too seldom descended on his spirit. But at present he was happy — happier than he had perhaps ever been in his life, and the feeling had a large foundation. This was simply the sense of success — the most agreeable emotion of the human heart. Osmond had never had too much of it; in this respect he had the irritation of satiety, as he knew perfectly well and often reminded himself. "Ah no, I've not been spoiled; certainly I've not been spoiled," he used inwardly to repeat. "If I do succeed before I die I shall thoroughly have earned it." He was too apt to reason as if "earning" this boon consisted above all of covertly aching for it and might be confined to that exercise. Absolutely void of it, also, his career had not been; he might indeed have suggested to a spectator here and there that he was resting on vague laurels. But his triumphs were, some of them, now too old; others had been too easy. The present one had been less arduous than might have been expected, but had been easy — that is had been rapid — only because he had made an altogether exceptional effort, a greater effort than he had believed it in him to make. The desire to have something or other to show for his "parts" — to show somehow or other — had been the dream of his youth; but as the years went on the conditions attached to any marked proof of rarity had affected him more and more as gross and detestable; like the swallowing of mugs of beer to advertise what one could "stand." If an anonymous drawing on a museum wall had been conscious and watchful it might have known this peculiar pleasure of being at last and all of a sudden identified — as from the hand of a great master — by the so high and so unnoticed fact of style. His "style" was what the girl had discovered with a little help; and now, beside herself enjoying it, she should publish it to the world without his having any of the trouble. She should do the thing *for* him, and he would not have waited in vain.

Shortly before the time fixed in advance for her departure this young lady received from Mrs. Touchett a telegram running as follows: "Leave Florence 4th June for Bellaggio, and take you if you have not other views. But can't wait if you dawdle in Rome."

The dawdling in Rome was very pleasant, but Isabel had different views, and she let her aunt know she would immediately join her. She told Gilbert Osmond that she had done so, and he replied that, spending many of his summers as well as his winters in Italy, he himself would loiter a little longer in the cool shadow of Saint Peter's. He would not return to Florence for ten days more, and in that time she would have started for Bellaggio. It might be months in this case before he should see her again. This exchange took place in the large decorated sitting-room occupied by our friends at the hotel; it was late in the evening, and Ralph Touchett was to take his cousin back to Florence on the morrow. Osmond had found the girl alone; Miss Stackpole had contracted a friendship with a delightful American family on the fourth floor and had mounted the interminable staircase to pay them a visit. Henrietta contracted friendships, in travelling, with great freedom, and had formed in railway-carriages several that were among her most valued ties. Ralph was making arrangements for the morrow's journey, and Isabel sat alone in a wilderness of yellow upholstery. The chairs and sofas were orange; the walls and windows were draped in purple and gilt. The mirrors, the pictures had great flamboyant frames; the ceiling was deeply vaulted and painted over with naked muses and cherubs. For Osmond the place was ugly to distress; the false colours, the sham splendour were like vulgar, bragging, lying talk. Isabel had taken in hand a volume of Ampere, presented, on their arrival in Rome, by Ralph; but though she held it in her lap with her finger vaguely kept in the place she was not impatient to pursue her study. A lamp covered with a drooping veil of pink tissue-paper burned on the table beside her and diffused a strange pale rosiness over the scene.

"You say you'll come back; but who knows?" Gilbert Osmond said. "I think you're much more likely to start on your voyage round the world. You're under no obligation to come back; you can do exactly what you choose; you can roam through space."

"Well, Italy's a part of space," Isabel answered. "I can take it on the way."

"On the way round the world? No, don't do that. Don't put us in a parenthesis — give us a chapter to ourselves. I don't want to see you on your travels. I'd rather see you when they're over. I should like to see you when you're tired and satiated," Osmond added in a moment. "I shall prefer you in that state."

Isabel, with her eyes bent, fingered the pages of M. Ampère. "You turn things into ridicule without seeming to do it, though not, I think, without intending it. You've no respect for my travels — you think them ridiculous."

"Where do you find that?"

She went on in the same tone, fretting the edge of her book with the paper-knife. "You see my ignorance, my blunders, the way I wander about as if the world belonged to me, simply because — because it has been put into my power to do so. You don't think a woman ought to do that. You think it bold and ungraceful."

"I think it beautiful," said Osmond. "You know

my opinions — I've treated you to enough of them. Don't you remember my telling you that one ought to make one's life a work of art? You looked rather shocked at first; but then I told you that it was exactly what you seemed to me to be trying to do with your own."

She looked up from her book. "What you despise most in the world is bad, is stupid art."

"Possibly. But yours seem to me very clear and very good."

"If I were to go to Japan next winter you would laugh at me," she went on.

Osmond gave a smile — a keen one, but not a laugh, for the tone of their conversation was not jocose. Isabel had in fact her solemnity; he had seen it before. "You have an imagination that startles one!"

"That's exactly what I say. You think such an idea absurd."

"I would give my little finger to go to Japan; it's one of the countries I want most to see. Can't you believe that, with my taste for old lacquer?"

"I have n't a taste for old lacquer to excuse me," said Isabel.

"You've a better excuse — the means of going. You're quite wrong in your theory that I laugh at you. I don't know what has put it into your head."

"It would n't be remarkable if you did think it ridiculous that I should have the means to travel when you've not; for you know everything, and I know nothing."

"The more reason why you should travel and

learn," smiled Osmond. "Besides," he added as if it were a point to be made, "I don't know everything."

Isabel was not struck with the oddity of his saying this gravely; she was thinking that the pleasantest incident of her life — so it pleased her to qualify these too few days in Rome, which she might musingly have likened to the figure of some small princess of one of the ages of dress overmuffled in a mantle of state and dragging a train that it took pages or historians to hold up — that this felicity was coming to an end. That most of the interest of the time had been owing to Mr. Osmond was a reflexion she was not just now at pains to make; she had already done the point abundant justice. But she said to herself that if there were a danger they should never meet again, perhaps after all it would be as well. Happy things don't repeat themselves, and her adventure wore already the changed, the seaward face of some romantic island from which, after feasting on purple grapes, she was putting off while the breeze rose. She might come back to Italy and find him different — this strange man who pleased her just as he was; and it would be better not to come than run the risk of that. But if she was not to come the greater the pity that the chapter was closed; she felt for a moment a pang that touched the source of tears. The sensation kept her silent, and Gilbert Osmond was silent too; he was looking at her. "Go everywhere," he said at last, in a low, kind voice; "do everything; get everything out of life. Be happy — be triumphant."

"What do you mean by being triumphant?"

"Well, doing what you like."

"To triumph, then, it seems to me, is to fail! Doing all the vain things one likes is often very tiresome."

"Exactly," said Osmond with his quiet quickness. "As I intimated just now, you'll be tired some day." He paused a moment and then he went on: "I don't know whether I had better not wait till then for something I want to say to you."

"Ah, I can't advise you without knowing what it is. But I'm horrid when I'm tired," Isabel added with due inconsequence.

"I don't believe that. You're angry, sometimes — that I can believe, though I've never seen it. But I'm sure you're never 'cross.'"

"Not even when I lose my temper?"

"You don't lose it — you find it, and that must be beautiful." Osmond spoke with a noble earnestness. "They must be great moments to see."

"If I could only find it now!" Isabel nervously cried.

"I'm not afraid; I should fold my arms and admire you. I'm speaking very seriously." He leaned forward, a hand on each knee; for some moments he bent his eyes on the floor. "What I wish to say to you," he went on at last, looking up, "is that I find I'm in love with you."

She instantly rose. "Ah, keep that till I *am* tired!"

"Tired of hearing it from others?" He sat there raising his eyes to her. "No, you may heed it now or never, as you please. But after all I must say it now." She had turned away, but in the movement she had stopped herself and dropped her gaze upon him. The two remained a while in this situation, exchanging a

17

long look — the large, conscious look of the critical hours of life. Then he got up and came near her, deeply respectful, as if he were afraid he had been too familiar. "I'm absolutely in love with you."

He had repeated the announcement in a tone of almost impersonal discretion, like a man who expected very little from it but who spoke for his own needed relief. The tears came into her eyes: this time they obeyed the sharpness of the pang that suggested to her somehow the slipping of a fine bolt — backward, forward, she could n't have said which. The words he had uttered made him, as he stood there, beautiful and generous, invested him as with the golden air of early autumn; but, morally speaking, she retreated before them — facing him still — as she had retreated in the other cases before a like encounter. "Oh don't say that, please," she answered with an intensity that expressed the dread of having, in this case too, to choose and decide. What made her dread great was precisely the force which, as it would seem, ought to have banished all dread — the sense of something within herself, deep down, that she supposed to be inspired and trustful passion. It was there like a large sum stored in a bank — which there was a terror in having to begin to spend. If she touched it, it would all come out.

"I have n't the idea that it will matter much to you," said Osmond. "I've too little to offer you. What I have — it 's enough for me; but it 's not enough for you. I 've neither fortune, nor fame, nor extrinsic advantages of any kind. So I offer nothing. I only tell you because I think it can't offend you, and some day

or other it may give you pleasure. It gives me pleasure, I assure you," he went on, standing there before
her, considerately inclined to her, turning his hat,
which he had taken up, slowly round with a movement which had all the decent tremor of awkwardness
and none of its oddity, and presenting to her his firm,
refined, slightly ravaged face. "It gives me no pain,
because it's perfectly simple. For me you'll always
be the most important woman in the world."

Isabel looked at herself in this character — looked
intently, thinking she filled it with a certain grace.
But what she said was not an expression of any such
complacency. "You don't offend me; but you ought
to remember that, without being offended, one may
be incommoded, troubled." "Incommoded:" she
heard herself saying that, and it struck her as a ridiculous word. But it was what stupidly came to her.

"I remember perfectly. Of course you're surprised
and startled. But if it's nothing but that, it will pass
away. And it will perhaps leave something that I
may not be ashamed of."

"I don't know what it may leave. You see at all
events that I'm not overwhelmed," said Isabel with
rather a pale smile. "I'm not too troubled to think.
And I think that I'm glad we're separating — that
I leave Rome to-morrow."

"Of course I don't agree with you there."

"I don't at all *know* you," she added abruptly; and
then she coloured as she heard herself saying what
she had said almost a year before to Lord Warburton.

"If you were not going away you'd know me
better."

"I shall do that some other time."

"I hope so. I'm very easy to know."

"No, no," she emphatically answered — "there you're not sincere. You're not easy to know; no one could be less so."

"Well," he laughed, "I said that because I know myself. It may be a boast, but I do."

"Very likely; but you're very wise."

"So are you, Miss Archer!" Osmond exclaimed.

"I don't feel so just now. Still, I'm wise enough to think you had better go. Good-night."

"God bless you!" said Gilbert Osmond, taking the hand which she failed to surrender. After which he added: "If we meet again you'll find me as you leave me. If we don't I shall be so all the same."

"Thank you very much. Good-bye."

There was something quietly firm about Isabel's visitor; he might go of his own movement, but would n't be dismissed. "There's one thing more. I have n't asked anything of you — not even a thought in the future; you must do me that justice. But there's a little service I should like to ask. I shall not return home for several days; Rome's delightful, and it's a good place for a man in my state of mind. Oh, I know you're sorry to leave it; but you're right to do what your aunt wishes."

"She does n't even wish it!" Isabel broke out strangely.

Osmond was apparently on the point of saying something that would match these words, but he changed his mind and rejoined simply: "Ah well, it's proper you should go with her, very proper. Do everything that's proper; I go in for that. Excuse my being so patronising. You say you don't know me, but when you do you'll discover what a worship I have for propriety."

"You're not conventional?" Isabel gravely asked.

" I like the way you utter that word! No, I'm not conventional: I'm convention itself. You don't understand that?" And he paused a moment, smiling. "I should like to explain it." Then with a sudden, quick, bright naturalness, "Do come back again," he pleaded. "There are so many things we might talk about."

She stood there with lowered eyes. "What service did you speak of just now?"

"Go and see my little daughter before you leave Florence. She's alone at the villa; I decided not to send her to my sister, who hasn't at all my ideas. Tell her she must love her poor father very much," said Gilbert Osmond gently.

"It will be a great pleasure to me to go," Isabel answered. "I'll tell her what you say. Once more good-bye."

On this he took a rapid, respectful leave. When he had gone she stood a moment looking about her and seated herself slowly and with an air of deliberation. She sat there till her companions came back, with folded hands, gazing at the ugly carpet. Her agitation — for it had not diminished — was very still, very deep. What had happened was something that for a week past her imagination had been going forward to meet; but here, when it came, she stopped — that sublime principle somehow broke down. The working of this young lady's spirit was strange, and I can only give it to you as I see it, not hoping to make it seem altogether natural. Her imagination, as I say, now hung back: there was a last vague space it could n't cross — a dusky, uncertain tract which looked ambiguous and even slightly treacherous, like a moorland seen in the winter twilight. But she was to cross it yet.

XXX

SHE returned on the morrow to Florence, under her
cousin's escort, and Ralph Touchett, though usually
restive under railway discipline, thought very well
of the successive hours passed in the train that hur-
ried his companion away from the city now distinguished by Gilbert Osmond's preference — hours
that were to form the first stage in a larger scheme
of travel. Miss Stackpole had remained behind;
she was planning a little trip to Naples, to be carried out with Mr. Bantling's aid. Isabel was to have
three days in Florence before the 4th of June, the
date of Mrs. Touchett's departure, and she determined to devote the last of these to her promise to
call on Pansy Osmond. Her plan, however, seemed
for a moment likely to modify itself in deference to
an idea of Madame Merle's. This lady was still at
Casa Touchett; but she too was on the point of
leaving Florence, her next station being an ancient
castle in the mountains of Tuscany, the residence
of a noble family of that country, whose acquaintance (she had known them, as she said, "forever")
seemed to Isabel, in the light of certain photographs
of their immense crenellated dwelling which her
friend was able to show her, a precious privilege.
She mentioned to this fortunate woman that Mr. Osmond had asked her to take a look at his daughter,

23

but did n't mention that he had also made her a declaration of love.

"*Ah, comme cela se trouve!*" Madame Merle exclaimed. "I myself have been thinking it would be a kindness to pay the child a little visit before I go off."

"We can go together then," Isabel reasonably said: "reasonably" because the proposal was not uttered in the spirit of enthusiasm. She had prefigured her small pilgrimage as made in solitude; she should like it better so. She was nevertheless prepared to sacrifice this mystic sentiment to her great consideration for her friend.

That personage finely meditated. "After all, why should we both go; having, each of us, so much to do during these last hours?"

"Very good; I can easily go alone."

"I don't know about your going alone — to the house of a handsome bachelor. He has been married — but so long ago!"

Isabel stared. "When Mr. Osmond's away what does it matter?"

"They don't know he's away, you see."

"They? Whom do you mean?"

"Every one. But perhaps it does n't signify."

"If you were going why should n't I?" Isabel asked.

"Because I'm an old frump and you're a beautiful young woman."

"Granting all that, you've not promised."

"How much you think of your promises!" said the elder woman in mild mockery.

"I think a great deal of my promises. Does that surprise you?"

"You're right," Madame Merle audibly reflected. "I really think you wish to be kind to the child."

"I wish very much to be kind to her."

"Go and see her then; no one will be the wiser. And tell her I'd have come if you had n't. Or rather," Madame Merle added, "*don't* tell her. She won't care."

As Isabel drove, in the publicity of an open vehicle, along the winding way which led to Mr. Osmond's hill-top, she wondered what her friend had meant by no one's being the wiser. Once in a while, at large intervals, this lady, whose voyaging discretion, as a general thing, was rather of the open sea than of the risky channel, dropped a remark of ambiguous quality, struck a note that sounded false. What cared Isabel Archer for the vulgar judgements of obscure people? and did Madame Merle suppose that she was capable of doing a thing at all if it had to be sneakingly done? Of course not: she must have meant something else — something which in the press of the hours that preceded her departure she had not had time to explain. Isabel would return to this some day; there were sorts of things as to which she liked to be clear. She heard Pansy strumming at the piano in another place as she herself was ushered into Mr. Osmond's drawing-room; the little girl was "practising," and Isabel was pleased to think she performed this duty with rigour. She immediately came in, smoothing down her frock, and did the honours of her father's house with a wide-eyed earnestness of courtesy. Isabel sat there half an hour, and Pansy rose to the occasion as the small, winged fairy in the pantomime soars by the aid of the dissimulated wire — not chattering, but conversing, and showing the same respectful interest in Isabel's affairs that Isabel was so good as to take in hers. Isabel wondered at her; she had never had so directly presented to her nose the white flower of cultivated sweetness. How well the child had been taught, said our admiring young woman; how prettily she had been directed and fashioned; and yet how simple, how natural, how innocent she had been kept! Isabel was fond, ever, of the question of character and quality, of sounding, as who should say, the deep personal mystery, and it had pleased her, up to this time, to be in doubt as to whether this tender slip were not really all-knowing. Was the extremity of her candour but the perfection of self-consciousness? Was it put on to please her father's visitor, or was it the direct expression of an un-spotted nature? The hour that Isabel spent in Mr. Osmond's beautiful empty, dusky rooms — the win-dows had been half-darkened, to keep out the heat, and here and there, through an easy crevice, the splendid summer day peeped in, lighting a gleam of faded colour or tarnished gilt in the rich gloom — her interview with the daughter of the house, I say, effectually settled this question. Pansy was really a blank page, a pure white surface, successfully kept so; she had neither art, nor guile, nor temper, nor talent — only two or three small exquisite in-stincts: for knowing a friend, for avoiding a mistake, for taking care of an old toy or a new frock. Yet to be so tender was to be touching withal, and she could be felt as an easy victim of fate. She would have no will, no power to resist, no sense of her own importance; she would easily be mystified, easily crushed: her force would be all in knowing when and where to cling. She moved about the place with her visitor, who had asked leave to walk through the other rooms again, where Pansy gave her judgement on several works of art. She spoke of her prospects, her occupations, her father's intentions; she was not egotistical, but felt the propriety of supplying the information so distinguished a guest would naturally expect.

"Please tell me," she said, "did papa, in Rome, go to see Madame Catherine? He told me he would if he had time. Perhaps he had not time. Papa likes a great deal of time. He wished to speak about my education; it isn't finished yet, you know. I don't know what they can do with me more; but it appears it's far from finished. Papa told me one day he thought he would finish it himself; for the last year or two, at the convent, the masters that teach the tall girls are so very dear. Papa's not rich, and I should be very sorry if he were to pay much money for me, because I don't think I'm worth it. I don't learn quickly enough, and I have no memory. ,For what I'm told, yes — especially when it's pleasant; but not for what I learn in a book. There was a young girl who was my best friend, and they took her away from the convent, when she was fourteen, to make — how do you say it in English? — to make a *dot*. You don't say it in English? I hope it is n't wrong; I only mean they wished to keep the money to marry her. I don't know whether it is for that that papa wishes to keep the money — to marry *me*. It costs so much to marry!" Pansy went on with a sigh; "I think papa might make that economy. At any rate I 'm too young to think about it yet, and I don't care for any gentleman; I mean for any but him. If he were not my papa I should like to marry him; I would rather be his daughter than the wife of — of some strange person. I miss him very much, but not so much as you might think, for I 've been so much away from him. Papa has always been principally for holidays. I miss Madame Catherine almost more; but you must not tell him that. You shall not see him again? I 'm very sorry, and he 'll be sorry too. Of every one who comes here I like you the best. That 's not a great compliment, for there are not many people. It was very kind of you to come to-day — so far from your house; for I 'm really as yet only a child. Oh, yes, I 've only the occupations of a child. When did *you* give them up, the occupations of a child? I should like to know how old you are, but I don't know whether it 's right to ask. At the convent they told us that we must never ask the age. I don't like to do anything that 's not expected; it looks as if one had not been properly taught. I myself — I should never like to be taken by surprise. Papa left directions for everything. I go to bed very early. When the sun goes off that side I go into the garden. Papa left strict orders that I was not to get scorched. I always enjoy the view;

the mountains are so graceful. In Rome, from the convent, we saw nothing but roofs and bell-towers. I practise three hours. I don't play very well. You play yourself? I wish very much you'd play something for me; papa has the idea that I should hear good music. Madame Merle has played for me several times; that's what I like best about Madame Merle; she has great facility. I shall never have facility. And I've no voice — just a small sound like the squeak of a slate-pencil making flourishes."

Isabel gratified this respectful wish, drew off her gloves and sat down to the piano, while Pansy, standing beside her, watched her white hands move quickly over the keys. When she stopped she kissed the child good-bye, held her close, looked at her long. "Be very good," she said; "give pleasure to your father."

"I think that's what I live for," Pansy answered. "He has not much pleasure; he's rather a sad man."

Isabel listened to this assertion with an interest which she felt it almost a torment to be obliged to conceal. It was her pride that obliged her, and a certain sense of decency; there were still other things in her head which she felt a strong impulse, instantly checked, to say to Pansy about her father; there were things it would have given her pleasure to hear the child, to make the child, say. But she no sooner became conscious of these things than her imagination was hushed with horror at the idea of taking advantage of the little girl — it was of this she would have accused herself — and of exhaling into that air where he might still have a subtle sense for it any breath of her charmed state. She had come — she had come;

but she had stayed only an hour. She rose quickly from the music-stool; even then, however, she lingered a moment, still holding her small companion, drawing the child's sweet slimness closer and looking down at her almost in envy. She was obliged to confess it to herself — she would have taken a passionate pleasure in talking of Gilbert Osmond to this innocent, diminutive creature who was so near him. But she said no other word; she only kissed Pansy once again. They went together through the vestibule, to the door that opened on the court; and there her young hostess stopped, looking rather wistfully beyond. "I may go no further. I've promised papa not to pass this door."

"You're right to obey him; he'll never ask you anything unreasonable."

"I shall always obey him. But when will you come again?"

"Not for a long time, I'm afraid."

"As soon as you can, I hope. I'm only a little girl," said Pansy, "but I shall always expect you." And the small figure stood in the high, dark doorway, watching Isabel cross the clear, grey court and disappear into the brightness beyond the big *portone*, which gave a wider dazzle as it opened.

XXXI

ISABEL came back to Florence, but only after several months; an interval sufficiently replete with incident. It is not, however, during this interval that we are closely concerned with her; our attention is engaged again on a certain day in the late spring-time, shortly after her return to Palazzo Crescentini and a year from the date of the incidents just narrated. She was alone on this occasion, in one of the smaller of the numerous rooms devoted by Mrs. Touchett to social uses, and there was that in her expression and attitude which would have suggested that she was expecting a visitor. The tall window was open, and though its green shutters were partly drawn the bright air of the garden had come in through a broad interstice and filled the room with warmth and perfume. Our young woman stood near it for some time, her hands clasped behind her; she gazed abroad with the vagueness of unrest. Too troubled for attention she moved in a vain circle. Yet it could not be in her thought to catch a glimpse of her visitor before he should pass into the house, since the entrance to the palace was not through the garden, in which stillness and privacy always reigned. She wished rather to forestall his arrival by a process of conjecture, and to judge by the expression of her face this attempt gave her plenty to do. Grave she found herself, and positively more weighted, as by the experience of the lapse of the year she had spent in seeing the world. She had ranged, she would have said, through space and surveyed much of mankind, and was therefore now, in her own eyes, a very different person from the frivolous young woman from Albany who had begun to take the measure of Europe on the lawn at Gardencourt a couple of years before. She flattered herself she had harvested wisdom and learned a great deal more of life than this light-minded creature had even suspected. If her thoughts just now had inclined themselves to retrospect, instead of fluttering their wings nervously about the present, they would have evoked a multitude of interesting pictures. These pictures would have been both landscapes and figure-pieces; the latter, however, would have been the more numerous. With several of the images that might have been projected on such a field we are already acquainted. There would be for instance the conciliatory Lily, our heroine's sister and Edmund Ludlow's wife, who had come out from New York to spend five months with her relative. She had left her husband behind her, but had brought her children, to whom Isabel now played with equal munificence and tenderness the part of maiden-aunt. Mr. Ludlow, toward the last, had been able to snatch a few weeks from his forensic triumphs and, crossing the ocean with extreme rapidity, had spent a month with the two ladies in Paris before taking his wife home. The little Ludlows had not yet, even from the American point of view, reached the proper tourist-age; so that while her sister was with her Isabel had confined her movements to a narrow circle. Lily and the babies had joined her in Switzerland in the month of July, and they had spent a summer of fine weather in an Alpine valley where the flowers were thick in the meadows and the shade of great chestnuts made a resting-place for such upward wanderings as might be undertaken by ladies and children on warm afternoons. They had afterwards reached the French capital, which was worshipped, and with costly ceremonies, by Lily, but thought of as noisily vacant by Isabel, who in these days made use of her memory of Rome as she might have done, in a hot and crowded room, of a phial of something pungent hidden in her handkerchief.

Mrs. Ludlow sacrificed, as I say, to Paris, yet had doubts and wonderments not allayed at that altar; and after her husband had joined her found further chagrin in his failure to throw himself into these speculations. They all had Isabel for subject; but Edmund Ludlow, as he had always done before, declined to be surprised, or distressed, or mystified, or elated, at anything his sister-in-law might have done or have failed to do. Mrs. Ludlow's mental motions were sufficiently various. At one moment she thought it would be so natural for that young woman to come home and take a house in New York —the Rossiters', for instance, which had an elegant conservatory and was just round the corner from her own; at another she could n't conceal her surprise at the girl's not marrying some member of one of the great aristocracies. On the whole, as I have said, she had fallen from high communion with the probabilities. She had taken more satisfaction in Isabel's accession of fortune than if the money had been left to herself; it had seemed to her to offer just the proper setting for her sister's slightly meagre, but scarce the less eminent figure. Isabel had developed less, however, than Lily had thought likely — development, to Lily's understanding, being somehow mysteriously connected with morning-calls and evening-parties. Intellectually, doubtless, she had made immense strides; but she appeared to have achieved few of those social conquests of which Mrs. Ludlow had expected to admire the trophies. Lily's conception of such achievements was extremely vague; but this was exactly what she had expected of Isabel — to give it form and body. Isabel could have done as well as she had done in New York; and Mrs. Ludlow appealed to her husband to know whether there was any privilege she enjoyed in Europe which the society of that city might not offer her. We know ourselves that Isabel had made conquests — whether inferior or not to those she might have effected in her native land it would be a delicate matter to decide; and it is not altogether with a feeling of complacency that I again mention that she had not rendered these honourable victories public. She had not told her sister the history of Lord Warburton, nor had she given her a hint of Mr. Osmond's state of mind; and she had had no better reason for her silence than that she did n't wish to speak. It was more romantic to say nothing, and, drinking deep, in secret, of romance, she was as little disposed to ask poor Lily's advice as she would have been to close that rare volume forever. But Lily knew nothing of these discriminations, and could only pronounce her sister's career a strange anti-climax —

an impression confirmed by the fact that Isabel's silence about Mr. Osmond, for instance, was in direct proportion to the frequency with which he occupied her thoughts. As this happened very often it sometimes appeared to Mrs. Ludlow that she had lost her courage. So uncanny a result of so exhilarating an incident as inheriting a fortune was of course perplexing to the cheerful Lily; it added to her general sense that Isabel was not at all like other people.

Our young lady's courage, however, might have been taken as reaching its height after her relations had gone home. She could imagine braver things than spending the winter in Paris — Paris had sides by which it so resembled New York, Paris was like smart, neat prose — and her close correspondence with Madame Merle did much to stimulate such flights. She had never had a keener sense of freedom, of the absolute boldness and wantonness of liberty, than when she turned away from the platform at the Euston Station on one of the last days of November, after the departure of the train that was to convey poor Lily, her husband and her children to their ship at Liverpool. It had been good for her to regale; she was very conscious of that; she was very observant, as we know, of what was good for her, and her effort was constantly to find something that was good enough. To profit by the present advantage till the latest moment she had made the journey from Paris with the unenvied travellers. She would have accompanied them to Liverpool as well, only Edmund Ludlow had asked her, as a favour, not to do so; it made Lily so fidgety and she asked such impossible questions. Isabel watched the train move away; she kissed her hand to the elder of her small nephews, a demonstrative child who leaned dangerously far out of the window of the carriage and made separation an occasion of violent hilarity, and then she walked back into the foggy London street. The world lay before her — she could do whatever she chose. There was a deep thrill in it all, but for the present her choice was tolerably discreet; she chose simply to walk back from Euston Square to her hotel. The early dusk of a November afternoon had already closed in; the street-lamps, in the thick, brown air, looked weak and red; our heroine was unattended and Euston Square was a long way from Piccadilly. But Isabel performed the journey with a positive enjoyment of its dangers and lost her way almost on purpose, in order to get more sensations, so that she was disappointed when an obliging policeman easily set her right again. She was so fond of the spectacle of human life that she enjoyed even the aspect of gathering dusk in the London streets — the moving crowds, the hurrying cabs, the lighted shops, the flaring stalls, the dark, shining dampness of everything. That evening, at her hotel, she wrote to Madame Merle that she should start in a day or two for Rome. She made her way down to Rome without touching at Florence — having gone first to Venice and then proceeded southward by Ancona. She accomplished this journey without other assistance than that of her servant, for her natural protectors were not now on the ground. Ralph Touchett was spending the winter at Corfu, and Miss Stackpole, in the September previous, had been recalled to America by a telegram from the *Interviewer*. This journal offered its brilliant correspondent a fresher field for her genius than the mouldering cities of Europe, and Henrietta was cheered on her way by a promise from Mr. Bantling that he would soon come over to see her. Isabel wrote to Mrs. Touchett to apologise for not presenting herself just yet in Florence, and her aunt replied characteristically enough. Apologies, Mrs. Touchett intimated, were of no more use to her than bubbles, and she herself never dealt in such articles. One either did the thing or one did n't, and what one "would" have done belonged to the sphere of the irrelevant, like the idea of a future life or of the origin of things. Her letter was frank, but (a rare case with Mrs. Touchett) not so frank as it pretended. She easily forgave her niece for not stopping at Florence, because she took it for a sign that Gilbert Osmond was less in question there than formerly. She watched of course to see if he would now find a pretext for going to Rome, and derived some comfort from learning that he had not been guilty of an absence.

Isabel, on her side, had not been a fortnight in Rome before she proposed to Madame Merle that they should make a little pilgrimage to the East. Madame Merle remarked that her friend was restless, but she added that she herself had always been consumed with the desire to visit Athens and Constantinople. The two ladies accordingly embarked on this expedition, and spent three months in Greece, in Turkey, in Egypt. Isabel found much to interest her in these countries, though Madame Merle continued to remark that even among the most classic sites, the scenes most calculated to suggest repose and reflexion, a certain incoherence prevailed in her. Isabel travelled rapidly and recklessly; she was like a thirsty person draining cup after cup. Madame Merle meanwhile, as lady-in-waiting to a princess circulating *incognita*, panted a little in her rear. It was on Isabel's invitation she had come, and she imparted all due dignity to the girl's uncountenanced state. She played her part with the tact that might have been expected of her, effacing herself and accepting the position of a companion whose expenses were profusely paid. The situation, however, had no hardships, and people who met this reserved though striking pair on their travels would not have been able to tell you which was patroness and which client. To say that Madame Merle improved on acquaintance states meagrely the impression she made on her friend, who had found her from the first so ample and so easy. At the end of an intimacy of three months Isabel felt she knew her better; her character had revealed itself, and the admirable woman had also at last redeemed her promise of relating her history from her own point of view — a consummation the more desirable as Isabel had already heard it related from the point of view of others. This history was so sad a one (in so far as it concerned the late M. Merle, a positive adventurer, she might say, though originally so plausible, who had taken advantage, years before, of her youth and of an inexperience in which doubtless those who knew her only now would find it difficult to believe); it abounded so in startling and lamentable incidents that her companion wondered a person so *éprouvée* could have kept so much of her freshness, her interest in life. Into this freshness of Madame Merle's she obtained a considerable insight; she seemed to see it as professional, as slightly mechanical, carried about in its case like the fiddle of the virtuoso, or blanketed and bridled like the "favourite" of the jockey. She liked her as much as ever, but there was a corner of the curtain that never was lifted; it was as if she had remained after all something of a public performer, condemned to emerge only in character and in costume. She had once said that she came from a distance, that she belonged to the "old, old" world, and Isabel never lost the impression that she was the product of a different moral or social clime from her own, that she had grown up under other stars.

She believed then that at bottom she had a different morality. Of course the morality of civilised persons has always much in common; but our young woman had a sense in her of values gone wrong or, as they said at the shops, marked down. She considered, with the presumption of youth, that a morality differing from her own must be inferior to it; and this conviction was an aid to detecting an occasional flash of cruelty, an occasional lapse from candour, in the conversation of a person who had raised delicate kindness to an art and whose pride was too high for the narrow ways of deception. Her conception of human motives might, in certain lights, have been acquired at the court of some kingdom in decadence, and there were several in her list of which our heroine had not even heard. She had not heard of everything, that was very plain; and there were evidently things in the world of which it was not advantageous to hear. She had once or twice had a positive scare; since it so affected her to have to exclaim, of her friend, "Heaven forgive her, she does n't understand me!" Absurd as it may seem this discovery operated as a shock, left her with a vague dismay in which there was even an element of foreboding. The dismay of course subsided, in the light of some sudden proof of Madame Merle's remarkable intelligence; but it stood for a high-water-mark in the ebb and flow of confidence. Madame Merle had once declared her belief that when a friendship ceases to grow it immediately begins to decline — there being no point of equilibrium between liking more and liking less. A stationary affection, in other words, was impossible — it must move one way or the other. However that might be, the girl had in these days a thousand uses for her sense of the romantic, which was more active than it had ever been. I do not allude to the impulse it received as she gazed at the Pyramids in the course of an excursion from Cairo, or as she stood among the broken columns of the Acropolis and fixed her eyes upon the point designated to her as the Strait of Salamis; deep and memorable as these emotions had remained. She came back by the last of March from Egypt and Greece and made another stay in Rome. A few days after her arrival Gilbert Osmond descended from Florence and remained three weeks, during which the fact of her being with his old friend Madame Merle, in whose house she had gone to

lodge, made it virtually inevitable that he should
see her every day. When the last of April came she
wrote to Mrs. Touchett that she should now rejoice
to accept an invitation given long before, and went
to pay a visit at Palazzo Crescentini, Madame Merle
on this occasion remaining in Rome. She found her
aunt alone; her cousin was still at Corfu. Ralph,
however, was expected in Florence from day to day,
and Isabel, who had not seen him for upwards of
a year, was prepared to give him the most affectionate welcome.

XXXII

It was not of him, nevertheless, that she was thinking while she stood at the window near which we found her a while ago, and it was not of any of the matters I have rapidly sketched. She was not turned to the past, but to the immediate, impending hour. She had reason to expect a scene, and she was not fond of scenes. She was not asking herself what she should say to her visitor; this question had already been answered. What he would say to her — that was the interesting issue. It could be nothing in the least soothing — she had warrant for this, and the conviction doubtless showed in the cloud on her brow. For the rest, however, all clearness reigned in her; she had put away her mourning and she walked in no small shimmering splendour. She only felt older — ever so much, and as if she were "worth more" for it, like some curious piece in an antiquary's collection. She was not at any rate left indefinitely to her apprehensions, for a servant at last stood before her with a card on his tray. "Let the gentleman come in," she said, and continued to gaze out of the window after the footman had retired. It was only when she had heard the door close behind the person who presently entered that she looked round.

Caspar Goodwood stood there — stood and received a moment, from head to foot, the bright, dry gaze with which she rather withheld than offered a greeting. Whether his sense of maturity had kept pace with Isabel's we shall perhaps presently ascertain; let me say meanwhile that to her critical glance he showed nothing of the injury of time. Straight, strong and hard, there was nothing in his appearance that spoke positively either of youth or of age; if he had neither innocence nor weakness, so he had no practical philosophy. His jaw showed the same voluntary cast as in earlier days; but a crisis like the present had in it of course something grim. He had the air of a man who had travelled hard; he said nothing at first, as if he had been out of breath. This gave Isabel time to make a reflexion: "Poor fellow, what great things he's capable of, and what a pity he should waste so dreadfully his splendid force! What a pity too that one can't satisfy everybody!" It gave her time to do more — to say at the end of a minute: "I can't tell you how I hoped you would n't come!"

"I've no doubt of that." And he looked about him for a seat. Not only had he come, but he meant to settle.

"You must be very tired," said Isabel, seating herself, and generously, as she thought, to give him his opportunity.

"No, I'm not at all tired. Did you ever know me to be tired?"

"Never; I wish I had! When did you arrive?"

"Last night, very late; in a kind of snail-train they call the express. These Italian trains go at about the rate of an American funeral."

"That's in keeping — you must have felt as if you were coming to bury me!" And she forced a smile of encouragement to an easy view of their situation. She had reasoned the matter well out, making it perfectly clear that she broke no faith and falsified no contract; but for all this she was afraid of her visitor. She was ashamed of her fear; but she was devoutly thankful there was nothing else to be ashamed of. He looked at her with his stiff insistence, an insistence in which there was such a want of tact; especially when the dull dark beam in his eye rested on her as a physical weight.

"No, I did n't feel that; I could n't think of you as dead. I wish I could!" he candidly declared.

"I thank you immensely."

"I 'd rather think of you as dead than as married to another man."

"That's very selfish of you!" she returned with the ardour of a real conviction. "If you 're not happy yourself others have yet a right to be."

"Very likely it 's selfish; but I don't in the least mind your saying so. I don't mind anything you can say now — I don't feel it. The cruellest things you could think of would be mere pin-pricks. After what you 've done I shall never feel anything — I mean anything but that. That I shall feel all my life."

Mr. Goodwood made these detached assertions with dry deliberateness, in his hard, slow American tone, which flung no atmospheric colour over propositions intrinsically crude. The tone made Isabel angry rather than touched her; but her anger perhaps was fortunate, inasmuch as it gave her a further reason for controlling herself. It was under the pressure of this control that she became, after a little, irrelevant. "When did you leave New York?"

He threw up his head as if calculating. "Seventeen days ago."

"You must have travelled fast in spite of your slow trains."

"I came as fast as I could. I'd have come five days ago if I had been able."

"It would n't have made any difference, Mr. Goodwood," she coldly smiled.

"Not to you — no. But to me."

"You gain nothing that I see."

"That's for me to judge!"

"Of course. To me it seems that you only torment yourself." And then, to change the subject, she asked him if he had seen Henrietta Stackpole. He looked as if he had not come from Boston to Florence to talk of Henrietta Stackpole; but he answered, distinctly enough, that this young lady had been with him just before he left America. "She came to see you?" Isabel then demanded.

"Yes, she was in Boston, and she called at my office. It was the day I had got your letter."

"Did you tell her?" Isabel asked with a certain anxiety.

"Oh no," said Caspar Goodwood simply; "I did n't want to do that. She'll hear it quick enough; she hears everything."

"I shall write to her, and then she'll write to me and scold me," Isabel declared, trying to smile again.

Caspar, however, remained sternly grave. "I guess she'll come right out," he said.

"On purpose to scold me?"

"I don't know. She seemed to think she had not seen Europe thoroughly."

"I'm glad you tell me that," Isabel said. "I must prepare for her."

Mr. Goodwood fixed his eyes for a moment on the floor; then at last, raising them, "Does she know Mr. Osmond?" he enquired.

"A little. And she doesn't like him. But of course I don't marry to please Henrietta," she added. It would have been better for poor Caspar if she had tried a little more to gratify Miss Stackpole; but he didn't say so; he only asked, presently, when her marriage would take place. To which she made answer that she didn't know yet. "I can only say it will be soon. I've told no one but yourself and one other person — an old friend of Mr. Osmond's."

"Is it a marriage your friends won't like?" he demanded.

"I really haven't an idea. As I say, I don't marry for my friends."

He went on, making no exclamation, no comment, only asking questions, doing it quite without delicacy. "Who and what then is Mr. Gilbert Osmond?"

"Who and what? Nobody and nothing but a very good and very honourable man. He's not in business," said Isabel. "He's not rich; he's not known for anything in particular."

She disliked Mr. Goodwood's questions, but she said to herself that she owed it to him to satisfy him as far as possible. The satisfaction poor Caspar exhibited was, however, small; he sat very upright, gazing at her. "Where does he come from? Where does he belong?"

She had never been so little pleased with the way he said "belawng." "He comes from nowhere. He has spent most of his life in Italy."

"You said in your letter he was American. Has n't he a native place?"

"Yes, but he has forgotten it. He left it as a small boy."

"Has he never gone back?"

"Why should he go back?" Isabel asked, flushing all defensively. "He has no profession."

"He might have gone back for his pleasure. Does n't he like the United States?"

"He does n't know them. Then he's very quiet and very simple — he contents himself with Italy."

"With Italy and with you," said Mr. Goodwood with gloomy plainness and no appearance of trying to make an epigram. "What has he ever done?" he added abruptly.

"That I should marry him? Nothing at all," Isabel replied while her patience helped itself by turning a little to hardness. "If he had done great things would you forgive me any better? Give me up, Mr. Goodwood; I'm marrying a perfect nonentity. Don't try to take an interest in him. You can't."

"I can't appreciate him; that's what you mean. And you don't mean in the least that he's a perfect nonentity. You think he's grand, you think he's great, though no one else thinks so."

Isabel's colour deepened; she felt this really acute of her companion, and it was certainly a proof of the aid that passion might render perceptions she had never taken for fine. "Why do you always come back to what others think? I can't discuss Mr. Osmond with you."

"Of course not," said Caspar reasonably. And he sat there with his air of stiff helplessness, as if not only this were true, but there were nothing else that they might discuss.

"You see how little you gain," she accordingly broke out — "how little comfort or satisfaction I can give you."

"I did n't expect you to give me much."

"I don't understand then why you came."

"I came because I wanted to see you once more — even just as you are."

"I appreciate that; but if you had waited a while, sooner or later we should have been sure to meet, and our meeting would have been pleasanter for each of us than this."

"Waited till after you're married? That's just what I did n't want to do. You'll be different then."

"Not very. I shall still be a great friend of yours. You'll see."

"That will make it all the worse," said Mr. Goodwood grimly.

"Ah, you're unaccommodating! I can't promise to dislike you in order to help you to resign yourself."

"I should n't care if you did!"

Isabel got up with a movement of repressed impatience and walked to the window, where she remained a moment looking out. When she turned round her visitor was still motionless in his place. She came toward him again and stopped, resting her hand on the back of the chair she had just quitted. "Do you mean you came simply to look at me? That's better for you perhaps than for me."

"I wished to hear the sound of your voice," he said.

"You've heard it, and you see it says nothing very sweet."

"It gives me pleasure, all the same." And with this he got up.

She had felt pain and displeasure on receiving early that day the news he was in Florence and by her leave would come within an hour to see her. She had been vexed and distressed, though she had sent back word by his messenger that he might come when he would. She had not been better pleased when she saw him; his being there at all was so full of heavy implications. It implied things she could never assent to — rights, reproaches, remonstrance, rebuke, the expectation of making her change her purpose. These things, however, if implied, had not been expressed; and now our young lady, strangely enough, began to resent her visitor's remarkable self-control. There was a dumb misery about him that irritated her; there was a manly staying of his hand that made her heart beat faster. She felt her agitation rising, and she said to herself that she was angry in the way a woman is angry when she has been in the wrong. She was not in the wrong; she had fortunately not that bitterness to swallow; but, all the same, she wished he would denounce her a little. She had wished his visit would be short; it had no purpose, no propriety; yet now that he seemed to be turning away she felt a sudden horror of his leaving her without uttering a word that would give her an opportunity to defend herself more than she had done in writing to him a month before, in a few carefully chosen words, to announce her engagement. If she were not in the wrong, however, why should she desire to defend herself? It was an excess of generosity on Isabel's part to desire that Mr. Goodwood should be angry. And if he had not meanwhile held himself hard it might have made him so to hear the tone in which she suddenly exclaimed, as if she were accusing him of having accused her: "I've not deceived you! I was perfectly free!"

"Yes, I know that," said Caspar.

"I gave you full warning that I'd do as I chose."

"You said you'd probably never marry, and you said it with such a manner that I pretty well believed it."

She considered this an instant. "No one can be more surprised than myself at my present intention."

"You told me that if I heard you were engaged I was not to believe it," Caspar went on. "I heard it twenty days ago from yourself, but I remembered what you had said. I thought there might be some mistake, and that's partly why I came."

"If you wish me to repeat it by word of mouth, that's soon done. There's no mistake whatever."

"I saw that as soon as I came into the room."

"What good would it do you that I should n't marry?" she asked with a certain fierceness.

"I should like it better than this."

"You're very selfish, as I said before."

"I know that. I'm selfish as iron."

"Even iron sometimes melts! If you'll be reasonable I'll see you again."

"Don't you call me reasonable now?"

"I don't know what to say to you," she answered with sudden humility.

"I shan't trouble you for a long time," the young man went on. He made a step towards the door, but he stopped. "Another reason why I came was that I wanted to hear what you would say in explanation of your having changed your mind."

Her humbleness as suddenly deserted her. "In explanation? Do you think I'm bound to explain?"

He gave her one of his long dumb looks. "You were very positive. I did believe it."

"So did I. Do you think I could explain if I would?"

"No, I suppose not. Well," he added, "I've done what I wished. I've seen you."

"How little you make of these terrible journeys," she felt the poverty of her presently replying.

"If you're afraid I'm knocked up — in any such way as that—you may be at your ease about it." He turned away, this time in earnest, and no hand-shake, no sign of parting, was exchanged between them.

At the door he stopped with his hand on the knob. "I shall leave Florence to-morrow," he said without a quaver.

"I'm delighted to hear it!" she answered passionately. Five minutes after he had gone out she burst into tears.

XXXIII

HER fit of weeping, however, was soon smothered, and the signs of it had vanished when, an hour later, she broke the news to her aunt. I use this expression because she had been sure Mrs. Touchett would not be pleased; Isabel had only waited to tell her till she had seen Mr. Goodwood. She had an odd impression that it would not be honourable to make the fact public before she should have heard what Mr. Goodwood would say about it. He had said rather less than she expected, and she now had a somewhat angry sense of having lost time. But she would lose no more; she waited till Mrs. Touchett came into the drawing-room before the mid-day breakfast, and then she began. "Aunt Lydia, I've something to tell you."

Mrs. Touchett gave a little jump and looked at her almost fiercely. "You need n't tell me; I know what it is."

"I don't know how you know."

"The same way that I know when the window's open — by feeling a draught. You're going to marry that man."

"What man do you mean?" Isabel enquired with great dignity.

"Madame Merle's friend — Mr. Osmond."

"I don't know why you call him Madame Merle's friend. Is that the principal thing he's known by?"

"If he's not her friend he ought to be — after what

53

she has done for him!" cried Mrs. Touchett. "I should n't have expected it of her; I 'm disappointed."

"If you mean that Madame Merle has had anything to do with my engagement you 're greatly mistaken," Isabel declared with a sort of ardent coldness.

"You mean that your attractions were sufficient, without the gentleman's having had to be lashed up ? You 're quite right. They 're immense, your attractions, and he would never have presumed to think of you if she had n't put him up to it. He has a very good opinion of himself, but he was not a man to take trouble. Madame Merle took the trouble *for* him."

"He has taken a great deal for himself!" cried Isabel with a voluntary laugh.

Mrs. Touchett gave a sharp nod. "I think he must, after all, to have made you like him so much."

"I thought he even pleased *you*."

"He did, at one time; and that's why I 'm angry with him."

"Be angry with me, not with him," said the girl.

"Oh, I 'm always angry with you; that's no satisfaction! Was it for this that you refused Lord Warburton ?"

"Please don't go back to that. Why should n't I like Mr. Osmond, since others have done so ?"

" Others, at their wildest moments, never wanted to marry him. There's nothing *of* him," Mrs. Touchett explained.

"Then he can't hurt me," said Isabel.

"Do you think you 're going to be happy ? No one's happy, in such doings, you should know."

"I shall set the fashion then. What does one marry for?"

"What *you* will marry for, heaven only knows. People usually marry as they go into partnership — to set up a house. But in your partnership you'll bring everything."

"Is it that Mr. Osmond isn't rich? Is that what you're talking about?" Isabel asked.

"He has no money; he has no name; he has no importance. I value such things and I have the courage to say it; I think they're very precious. Many other people think the same, and they show it. But they give some other reason."

Isabel hesitated a little. "I think I value everything that's valuable. I care very much for money, and that's why I wish Mr. Osmond to have a little."

"Give it to him then; but marry some one else."

"His name's good enough for me," the girl went on. "It's a very pretty name. Have I such a fine one myself?"

"All the more reason you should improve on it. There are only a dozen American names. Do you marry him out of charity?"

"It was my duty to tell you, Aunt Lydia, but I don't think it's my duty to explain to you. Even if it were I shouldn't be able. So please don't remonstrate; in talking about it you have me at a disadvantage. I can't talk about it."

"I don't remonstrate, I simply answer you: I must give some sign of intelligence. I saw it coming, and I said nothing. I never meddle."

"You never do, and I'm greatly obliged to you. You've been very considerate."

"It was not considerate — it was convenient," said Mrs. Touchett. "But I shall talk to Madame Merle."

"I don't see why you keep bringing her in. She has been a very good friend to me."

"Possibly; but she has been a poor one to me."

"What has she done to you?"

"She has deceived me. She had as good as promised me to prevent your engagement."

"She couldn't have prevented it."

"She can do anything; that's what I've always liked her for. I knew she could play any part; but I understood that she played them one by one. I didn't understand that she would play two at the same time."

"I don't know what part she may have played to you," Isabel said; "that's between yourselves. To me she has been honest and kind and devoted."

"Devoted, of course; she wished you to marry her candidate. She told me she was watching you only in order to interpose."

"She said that to please you," the girl answered; conscious, however, of the inadequacy of the explanation.

"To please me by deceiving me? She knows me better. Am I pleased to-day?"

"I don't think you're ever much pleased," Isabel was obliged to reply. "If Madame Merle knew you would learn the truth what had she to gain by insincerity?"

"She gained time, as you see. While I waited for her to interfere you were marching away, and she was really beating the drum."

"That's very well. But by your own admission you saw I was marching, and even if she had given the alarm you would n't have tried to stop me."

"No, but some one else would."

"Whom do you mean?" Isabel asked, looking very hard at her aunt.

Mrs. Touchett's little bright eyes, active as they usually were, sustained her gaze rather than returned it. "Would you have listened to Ralph?"

"Not if he had abused Mr. Osmond."

"Ralph does n't abuse people; you know that perfectly. He cares very much for you."

"I know he does," said Isabel; "and I shall feel the value of it now, for he knows that whatever I do I do with reason."

"He never believed you would do this. I told him you were capable of it, and he argued the other way."

"He did it for the sake of argument," the girl smiled. "You don't accuse him of having deceived you; why should you accuse Madame Merle?"

"He never pretended he'd prevent it."

"I'm glad of that!" cried Isabel gaily. "I wish very much," she presently added, "that when he comes you'd tell him first of my engagement."

"Of course I'll mention it," said Mrs. Touchett. "I shall say nothing more to you about it, but I give you notice I shall talk to others."

"That's as you please. I only meant that it's

rather better the announcement should come from you than from me."

"I quite agree with you; it's much more proper!" And on this the aunt and the niece went to breakfast, where Mrs. Touchett, as good as her word, made no allusion to Gilbert Osmond. After an interval of silence, however, she asked her companion from whom she had received a visit an hour before.

"From an old friend — an American gentleman," Isabel said with a colour in her cheek.

"An American gentleman of course. It's only an American gentleman who calls at ten o'clock in the morning."

"It was half-past ten; he was in a great hurry; he goes away this evening."

"Could n't he have come yesterday, at the usual time?"

"He only arrived last night."

"He spends but twenty-four hours in Florence?" Mrs. Touchett cried. "He's an American gentleman truly."

"He is indeed," said Isabel, thinking with perverse admiration of what Caspar Goodwood had done for her.

Two days afterward Ralph arrived; but though Isabel was sure that Mrs. Touchett had lost no time in imparting to him the great fact, he showed at first no open knowledge of it. Their prompted talk was naturally of his health; Isabel had many questions to ask about Corfu. She had been shocked by his appearance when he came into the room; she had forgotten how ill he looked. In spite of Corfu he looked very ill to-day, and she wondered if he were really worse or if she were simply disaccustomed to living with an invalid. Poor Ralph made no nearer approach to conventional beauty as he advanced in life, and the now apparently complete loss of his health had done little to mitigate the natural oddity of his person. Blighted and battered, but still responsive and still ironic, his face was like a lighted lantern patched with paper and unsteadily held; his thin whisker languished upon a lean cheek; the exorbitant curve of his nose defined itself more sharply. Lean he was altogether, lean and long and loose-jointed; an accidental cohesion of relaxed angles. His brown velvet jacket had become perennial; his hands had fixed themselves in his pockets; he shambled and stumbled and shuffled in a manner that denoted great physical helplessness. It was perhaps this whimsical gait that helped to mark his character more than ever as that of the humorous invalid — the invalid for whom even his own disabilities are part of the general. joke. They might well indeed with Ralph have been the chief cause of the want of seriousness marking his view of a world in which the reason for his own continued presence was past finding out. Isabel had grown fond of his ugliness; his awkwardness had become dear to her. They had been sweetened by association; they struck her as the very terms on which it had been given him to be charming. He was so charming that her sense of his being ill had hitherto had a sort of comfort in it; the state of his health had seemed not a limitation, but a kind of intellectual advantage; it absolved him from all professional and official emotions and left him the luxury of being exclusively personal. The personality so resulting was delightful; he had remained proof against the staleness of disease; he had had to consent to be deplorably ill, yet had somehow escaped being formally sick. Such had been the girl's impression of her cousin; and when she had pitied him it was only on reflection. As she reflected a good deal she had allowed him a certain amount of compassion; but she always had a dread of wasting that essence — a precious article, worth more to the giver than to any one else. Now, however, it took no great sensibility to feel that poor Ralph's tenure of life was less elastic than it should be. He was a bright, free, generous spirit, he had all the illumination of wisdom and none of its pedantry, and yet he was distressfully dying.

Isabel noted afresh that life was certainly hard for some people, and she felt a delicate glow of shame as she thought how easy it now promised to become for herself. She was prepared to learn that Ralph was not pleased with her engagement; but she was not prepared, in spite of her affection for him, to let this fact spoil the situation. She was not even prepared, or so she thought, to resent his want of sympathy; for it would be his privilege — it would be indeed his natural line — to find fault with any step she might take toward marriage. One's cousin always pretended to hate one's husband; that was traditional, classical; it was a part of one's cousin's always pretending to adore one. Ralph was nothing if not critical; and though she would certainly, other things being equal, have been as glad to marry to please him as to please any one, it would be absurd to regard as important that her choice should square with his views. What were his views after all? He had pretended to believe she had better have married Lord Warburton; but this was only because she had refused that excellent man. If she had accepted him Ralph would certainly have taken another tone; he always took the opposite. You could criticise any marriage; it was the essence of a marriage to be open to criticism. How well she herself, should she only give her mind to it, might criticise this union of her own! She had other employment, however, and Ralph was welcome to relieve her of the care. Isabel was prepared to be most patient and most indulgent. He must have seen that, and this made it the more odd he should say nothing. After three days had elapsed without his speaking our young woman wearied of waiting; dislike it as he would, he might at least go through the form. We, who know more about poor Ralph than his cousin, may easily believe that during the hours that followed his arrival at Palazzo Crescentini he had privately gone through many forms. His mother had literally greeted him with the great news, which had been even more sensibly chilling than Mrs. Touchett's maternal kiss. Ralph was shocked and humiliated; his calculations had been false and the person in the world in whom he was most interested was lost. He drifted about the house like a rudderless vessel in a rocky stream, or sat in the garden of the palace on a great cane chair, his long legs extended, his head thrown back and his hat pulled over his eyes. He felt cold about the heart; he had never liked anything less. What could he do, what could he say? If the girl were irreclaimable could he pretend to like it? To attempt to reclaim her was permissible only if the attempt should succeed. To try to persuade her of anything sordid or sinister in the man to whose deep art she had succumbed would be decently discreet only in the event of her being persuaded. Otherwise he should simply have damned himself. It cost him an equal effort to speak his thought and to dissemble; he could neither assent with sincerity nor protest with hope. Meanwhile he knew — or rather he supposed — that the affianced pair were daily renewing their mutual vows. Osmond at this moment showed himself little at Palazzo Crescentini; but Isabel met him every day elsewhere, as she was free to do after their engagement had been made public. She had taken a carriage by the month, so as not to be indebted to her aunt for the means of pursuing a course of which Mrs. Touchett disapproved, and she drove in the morning to the Cascine. This suburban wilderness, during the early hours, was void of all intruders, and our young lady, joined by her lover in its quietest part, strolled with him a while through the grey Italian shade and listened to the nightingales.

XXXIV

ONE morning, on her return from her drive, some half-hour before luncheon, she quitted her vehicle in the court of the palace and, instead of ascending the great staircase, crossed the court, passed beneath another archway and entered the garden. A sweeter spot at this moment could not have been imagined. The stillness of noontide hung over it, and the warm shade, enclosed and still, made bowers like spacious caves. Ralph was sitting there in the clear gloom, at the base of a statue of Terpsichore — a dancing nymph with taper fingers and inflated draperies in the manner of Bernini; the extreme relaxation of his attitude suggested at first to Isabel that he was asleep. Her light footstep on the grass had not roused him, and before turning away she stood for a moment looking at him. During this instant he opened his eyes; upon which she sat down on a rustic chair that matched with his own. Though in her irritation she had accused him of indifference she was not blind to the fact that he had visibly had something to brood over. But she had explained his air of absence partly by the languor of his increased weakness, partly by worries connected with the property inherited from his father — the fruit of eccentric arrangements of which Mrs. Touchett disapproved and which, as she had told Isabel, now encountered opposition from the other partners in the bank. He ought to have gone to England, his mother said, instead of coming to Florence; he had not been there for months, and took no more interest in the bank than in the state of Patagonia.

"I'm sorry I waked you," Isabel said; "you look too tired."

"I feel too tired. But I was not asleep. I was thinking of you."

"Are you tired of that?"

"Very much so. It leads to nothing. The road's long and I never arrive."

"What do you wish to arrive at?" she put to him, closing her parasol.

"At the point of expressing to myself properly what I think of your engagement."

"Don't think too much of it," she lightly returned.

"Do you mean that it's none of my business?"

"Beyond a certain point, yes."

"That's the point I want to fix. I had an idea you may have found me wanting in good manners. I've never congratulated you."

"Of course I've noticed that. I wondered why you were silent."

"There have been a good many reasons. I'll tell you now," Ralph said. He pulled off his hat and laid it on the ground; then he sat looking at her. He leaned back under the protection of Bernini, his head against his marble pedestal, his arms dropped on either side of him, his hands laid upon the rests of his wide chair. He looked awkward, uncomfortable; he hesitated long. Isabel said nothing; when people were embarrassed she was usually sorry for them, but she was determined not to help Ralph to utter

a word that should not be to the honour of her high
decision. "I think I've hardly got over my surprise,"
he went on at last. "You were the last person I expected to see caught."

"I don't know why you call it caught."

"Because you're going to be put into a cage."

"If I like my cage, that need n't trouble you," she
answered.

"That's what I wonder at; that's what I've been
thinking of."

"If you've been thinking you may imagine how
I've thought! I'm satisfied that I'm doing well."

"You must have changed immensely. A year ago
you valued your liberty beyond everything. You
wanted only to see life."

"I've seen it," said Isabel. "It does n't look to me
now, I admit, such an inviting expanse."

"I don't pretend it is; only I had an idea that you
took a genial view of it and wanted to survey the
whole field."

"I've seen that one can't do anything so general.
One must choose a corner and cultivate that."

"That's what I think. And one must choose as
good a corner as possible. I had no idea, all winter,
while I read your delightful letters, that you were
choosing. You said nothing about it, and your silence
put me off my guard."

"It was not a matter I was likely to write to you
about. Besides, I knew nothing of the future. It has
all come lately. If you had been on your guard, however," Isabel asked, "what would you have done?"

"I should have said 'Wait a little longer.'"

"Wait for what?"

"Well, for a little more light," said Ralph with rather an absurd smile, while his hands found their way into his pockets.

"Where should my light have come from? From you?"

"I might have struck a spark or two."

Isabel had drawn off her gloves; she smoothed them out as they lay upon her knee. The mildness of this movement was accidental, for her expression was not conciliatory. "You're beating about the bush, Ralph. You wish to say you don't like Mr. Osmond, and yet you're afraid."

"'Willing to wound and yet afraid to strike'? I'm willing to wound *him*, yes — but not to wound you. I'm afraid of you, not of him. If you marry him it won't be a fortunate way for me to have spoken."

"*If* I marry him! Have you had any expectation of dissuading me?"

"Of course that seems to you too fatuous."

"No," said Isabel after a little; "it seems to me too touching."

"That's the same thing. It makes me so ridiculous that you pity me."

She stroked out her long gloves again. "I know you've a great affection for me. I can't get rid of that."

"For heaven's sake don't try. Keep that well in sight. It will convince you how intensely I want you to do well."

"And how little you trust me!"

There was a moment's silence; the warm noontide seemed to listen. "I trust you, but I don't trust him," said Ralph.

She raised her eyes and gave him a wide, deep look. "You've said it now, and I'm glad you've made it so clear. But you'll suffer by it."

"Not if you're just."

"I'm very just," said Isabel. "What better proof of it can there be than that I'm not angry with you? I don't know what's the matter with me, but I'm not. I was when you began, but it has passed away. Perhaps I ought to be angry, but Mr. Osmond wouldn't think so. He wants me to know everything; that's what I like him for. You've nothing to gain, I know that. I've never been so nice to you, as a girl, that you should have much reason for wishing me to remain one. You give very good advice; you've often done so. No, I'm very quiet; I've always believed in your wisdom," she went on, boasting of her quietness, yet speaking with a kind of contained exaltation. It was her passionate desire to be just; it touched Ralph to the heart, affected him like a caress from a creature he had injured. He wished to interrupt, to reassure her; for a moment he was absurdly inconsistent; he would have retracted what he had said. But she gave him no chance; she went on, having caught a glimpse, as she thought, of the heroic line and desiring to advance in that direction. "I see you've some special idea; I should like very much to hear it. I'm sure it's disinterested; I feel that. It seems a strange thing to argue about, and of course I ought to tell you definitely that if you expect to dissuade me

you may give it up. You'll not move me an inch;
it's too late. As you say, I'm caught. Certainly
it won't be pleasant for you to remember this, but
your pain will be in your own thoughts. I shall
never reproach you."

"I don't think you ever will," said Ralph. "It's
not in the least the sort of marriage I thought you'd
make."

"What sort of marriage was that, pray?"

"Well, I can hardly say. I had n't exactly a positive view of it, but I had a negative. I did n't think
you'd decide for — well, for *that* type."

"What's the matter with Mr. Osmond's type,
if it be one? His being so independent, so individual, is what *I* most see in him," the girl declared.
"What do you know against him? You know him
scarcely at all."

"Yes," Ralph said, "I know him very little, and
I confess I have n't facts and items to prove him a
villain. But all the same I can't help feeling that
you're running a grave risk."

"Marriage is always a grave risk, and his risk's
as grave as mine."

"That's his affair! If he's afraid, let him back
out. I wish to God he would."

Isabel reclined in her chair, folding her arms
and gazing a while at her cousin. "I don't think I
understand you," she said at last coldly. "I don't
know what you're talking about."

"I believed you'd marry a man of more importance."

Cold, I say, her tone had been, but at this a colour

like a flame leaped into her face. "Of more importance to whom? It seems to me enough that one's
husband should be of importance to one's self!"

Ralph blushed as well; his attitude embarrassed
him. Physically speaking he proceeded to change
it; he straightened himself, then leaned forward,
resting a hand on each knee. He fixed his eyes on
the ground; he had an air of the most respectful
deliberation. "I'll tell you in a moment what I
mean," he presently said. He felt agitated, intensely
eager; now that he had opened the discussion he
wished to discharge his mind. But he wished also
to be superlatively gentle.

Isabel waited a little — then she went on with
majesty. "In everything that makes one care for
people Mr. Osmond is pre-eminent. There may be
nobler natures, but I've never had the pleasure of
meeting one. Mr. Osmond's is the finest I know; he's
good enough for me, and interesting enough, and
clever enough. I'm far more struck with what he has
and what he represents than with what he may lack."

"I had treated myself to a charming vision of
your future," Ralph observed without answering
this; "I had amused myself with planning out a
high destiny for you. There was to be nothing of
this sort in it. You were not to come down so easily
or so soon."

"Come down, you say?"

"Well, that renders my sense of what has happened to you. You seemed to me to be soaring far
up in the blue — to be, sailing in the bright light,
over the heads of men. Suddenly some one tosses

up a faded rosebud — a missile that should never have reached you — and straight you drop to the ground. It hurts me," said Ralph audaciously, "hurts me as if I had fallen myself!"

The look of pain and bewilderment deepened in his companion's face. "I don't understand you in the least," she repeated. "You say you amused yourself with a project for my career — I don't understand that. Don't amuse yourself too much, or I shall think your're doing it at my expense."

Ralph shook his head. "I'm not afraid of your not believing that I've had great ideas for you."

"What do you mean by my soaring and sailing?" she pursued. "I've never moved on a higher plane than I'm moving on now. There's nothing higher for a girl than to marry a — a person she likes," said poor Isabel, wandering into the didactic.

"It's your liking the person we speak of that I venture to criticise, my dear cousin. I should have said that the man for you would have been a more active, larger, freer sort of nature." Ralph hesitated, then added: "I can't get over the sense that Osmond is somehow — well, small." He had uttered the last word with no great assurance; he was afraid she would flash out again. But to his surprise she was quiet; she had the air of considering.

"Small?" She made it sound immense.

"I think he's narrow, selfish. He takes himself so seriously!"

"He has a great respect for himself; I don't blame him for that," said Isabel. " It makes one more sure to respect others."

Ralph for a moment felt almost reassured by her reasonable tone. "Yes, but everything is relative; one ought to feel one's relation to things — to others. I don't think Mr. Osmond does that."

"I've chiefly to do with his relation to me. In that he's excellent."

"He's the incarnation of taste," Ralph went on, thinking hard how he could best express Gilbert Osmond's sinister attributes without putting himself in the wrong by seeming to describe him coarsely. He wished to describe him impersonally, scientifically. "He judges and measures, approves and condemns, altogether by that."

"It's a happy thing then that his taste should be exquisite."

"It's exquisite, indeed, since it has led him to select you as his bride. But have you ever seen such a taste — a really exquisite one — ruffled?"

"I hope it may never be my fortune to fail to gratify my husband's."

At these words a sudden passion leaped to Ralph's lips. "Ah, that's wilful, that's unworthy of you! You were not meant to be measured in that way — you were meant for something better than to keep guard over the sensibilities of a sterile dilettante!"

Isabel rose quickly and he did the same, so that they stood for a moment looking at each other as if he had flung down a defiance or an insult. But "You go too far," she simply breathed.

"I've said what I had on my mind — and I've said it because I love you!"

Isabel turned pale: was he too on that tiresome

71

list ? She had a sudden wish to strike him off. "Ah then, you're not disinterested!"

"I love you, but I love without hope," said Ralph quickly, forcing a smile and feeling that in that last declaration he had expressed more than he intended.

Isabel moved away and stood looking into the sunny stillness of the garden; but after a little she turned back to him. "I'm afraid your talk then is the wildness of despair! I don't understand it — but it doesn't matter. I'm not arguing with you; it's impossible I should; I've only tried to listen to you. I'm much obliged to you for attempting to explain," she said gently, as if the anger with which she had just sprung up had already subsided. "It's very good of you to try to warn me, if you're really alarmed; but I won't promise to think of what you've said: I shall forget it as soon as possible. Try and forget it yourself; you've done your duty, and no man can do more. I can't explain to you what I feel, what I believe, and I wouldn't if I could." She paused a moment and then went on with an inconsequence that Ralph observed even in the midst of his eagerness to discover some symptom of concession. "I can't enter into your idea of Mr. Osmond; I can't do it justice, because I see him in quite another way. He's not important — no, he's not important; he's a man to whom importance is supremely indifferent. If that's what you mean when you call him 'small,' then he's as small as you please. I call that large — it's the largest thing I know. I won't pretend to argue with you about a person I'm going to marry," Isabel repeated. "I'm not in the least concerned to defend Mr. Osmond; he's not so weak as to need my defence. I should think it would seem strange even to yourself that I should talk of him so quietly and coldly, as if he were any one else. I wouldn't talk of him at all to any one but you; and you, after what you've said — I may just answer you once for all. Pray, would you wish me to make a mercenary marriage — what they call a marriage of ambition? I've only one ambition — to be free to follow out a good feeling. I had others once, but they've passed away. Do you complain of Mr. Osmond because he's not rich? That's just what I like him for. I've fortunately money enough; I've never felt so thankful for it as to-day. There have been moments when I should like to go and kneel down by your father's grave: he did perhaps a better thing than he knew when he put it into my power to marry a poor man — a man who has borne his poverty with such dignity, with such indifference. Mr. Osmond has never scrambled nor struggled — he has cared for no worldly prize. If that's to be narrow, if that's to be selfish, then it's very well. I'm not frightened by such words, I'm not even displeased; I'm only sorry that you should make a mistake. Others might have done so, but I'm surprised that *you* should. You might know a gentleman when you see one — you might know a fine mind. Mr. Osmond makes no mistakes! He knows everything, he understands everything, he has the kindest, gentlest, highest spirit. You've got hold of some false idea. It's a pity, but I can't help it; it regards you more than me." Isabel

paused a moment, looking at her cousin with an
eye illumined by a sentiment which contradicted
the careful calmness of her manner — a mingled
sentiment, to which the angry pain excited by his
words and the wounded pride of having needed to
justify a choice of which she felt only the nobleness
and purity, equally contributed. Though she paused
Ralph said nothing; he saw she had more to say.
She was grand, but she was highly solicitous; she
was indifferent, but she was all in a passion. "What
sort of a person should you have liked me to marry?"
she asked suddenly. "You talk about one's soaring
and sailing, but if one marries at all one touches
the earth. One has human feelings and needs, one
has a heart in one's bosom, and one must marry
a particular individual. Your mother has never
forgiven me for not having come to a better understanding with Lord Warburton, and she's horrified
at my contenting myself with a person who has none
of his great advantages — no property, no title,
no honours, no houses, nor lands, nor position, nor
reputation, nor brilliant belongings of any sort.
It's the total absence of all these things that pleases
me. Mr. Osmond's simply a very lonely, a very
cultivated and a very honest man — he's not a pro-
digious proprietor."

Ralph had listened with great attention, as if
everything she said merited deep consideration;
but in truth he was only half thinking of the things she
said, he was for the rest simply accommodating himself to the weight of his total impression — the impression of her ardent good faith. She was wrong,

but she believed; she was deluded, but she was dismally consistent. It was wonderfully characteristic of her that, having invented a fine theory about Gilbert Osmond, she loved him not for what he really possessed, but for his very poverties dressed out as honours. Ralph remembered what he had said to his father about wishing to put it into her power to meet the requirements of her imagination. He had done so, and the girl had taken full advantage of the luxury. Poor Ralph felt sick; he felt ashamed. Isabel had uttered her last words with a low solemnity of conviction which virtually terminated the discussion, and she closed it formally by turning away and walking back to the house. Ralph walked beside her, and they passed into the court together and reached the big staircase. Here he stopped and Isabel paused, turning on him a face of elation — absolutely and perversely of gratitude. His opposition had made her own conception of her conduct clearer to her. "Shall you not come up to breakfast?" she asked.

"No; I want no breakfast; I'm not hungry."

"You ought to eat," said the girl; "you live on air."

"I do, very much, and I shall go back into the garden and take another mouthful. I came thus far simply to say this. I told you last year that if you were to get into trouble I should feel terribly sold. That's how I feel to-day."

"Do you think I'm in trouble?"

"One's in trouble when one's in error."

"Very well," said Isabel; "I shall never complain

of my trouble to you!" And she moved up the staircase.

Ralph, standing there with his hands in his pockets, followed her with his eyes; then the lurking chill of the high-walled court struck him and made him shiver, so that he returned to the garden to breakfast on the Florentine sunshine.

XXXV

ISABEL, when she strolled in the Cascine with her
lover, felt no impulse to tell him how little he was
approved at Palazzo Crescentini. The discreet opposition offered to her marriage by her aunt and
her cousin made on the whole no great impression
upon her; the moral of it was simply that they disliked Gilbert Osmond. This dislike was not alarm-
ing to Isabel; she scarcely even regretted it; for
it served mainly to throw into higher relief the fact,
in every way so honourable, that she married to
please herself. One did other things to please other
people; one did this for a more personal satisfaction; and Isabel's satisfaction was confirmed by her
lover's admirable good conduct. Gilbert Osmond
was in love, and he had never deserved less than
during these still, bright days, each of them num-
bered, which preceded the fulfilment of his hopes, the
harsh criticism passed upon him by Ralph Touchett.
The chief impression produced on Isabel's spirit by
this criticism was that the passion of love separated
its victim terribly from every one but the loved object. She felt herself disjoined from every one she
had ever known before — from her two sisters, who
wrote to express a dutiful hope that she would be
happy, and a surprise, somewhat more vague, at
her not having chosen a consort who was the hero
of a richer accumulation of anecdote; from Henrietta,

who, she was sure, would come out, too late, on purpose to remonstrate; from Lord Warburton, who would certainly console himself, and from Caspar Goodwood, who perhaps would not; from her aunt, who had cold, shallow ideas about marriage, for which she was not sorry to display her contempt; and from Ralph, whose talk about having great views for her was surely but a whimsical cover for a personal disappointment. Ralph apparently wished her not to marry at all — that was what it really meant — because he was amused with the spectacle of her adventures as a single woman. His disappointment made him say angry things about the man she had preferred even to him: Isabel flattered herself that she believed Ralph had been angry. It was the more easy for her to believe this because, as I say, she had now little free or unemployed emotion for minor needs, and accepted as an incident, in fact quite as an ornament, of her lot the idea that to prefer Gilbert Osmond as she preferred him was perforce to break all other ties. She tasted of the sweets of this preference, and they made her conscious, almost with awe, of the invidious and remorseless tide of the charmed and possessed condition, great as was the traditional honour and imputed virtue of being in love. It was the tragic part of happiness; one's right was always made of the wrong of some one else.

The elation of success, which surely now flamed high in Osmond, emitted meanwhile very little smoke for so brilliant a blaze. Contentment, on his part, took no vulgar form; excitement, in the most self-conscious of men, was a kind of ecstasy of self-control. This disposition, however, made him an admirable lover; it gave him a constant view of the smitten and dedicated state. He never forgot himself, as I say; and so he never forgot to be graceful and tender, to wear the appearance — which presented indeed no difficulty — of stirred senses and deep intentions. He was immensely pleased with his young lady; Madame Merle had made him a present of incalculable value. What could be a finer thing to live with than a high spirit attuned to softness? For would not the softness be all for one's self, and the strenuousness for society, which admired the air of superiority? What could be a happier gift in a companion than a quick, fanciful mind which saved one repetitions and reflected one's thought on a polished, elegant surface? Osmond hated to see his thought reproduced literally — that made it look stale and stupid; he preferred it to be freshened in the reproduction even as "words" by music. His egotism had never taken the crude form of desiring a dull wife; this lady's intelligence was to be a silver plate, not an earthen one — a plate that he might heap up with ripe fruits, to which it would give a decorative value, so that talk might become for him a sort of served dessert. He found the silver quality in this perfection in Isabel; he could tap her imagination with his knuckle and make it ring. He knew perfectly, though he had not been told, that their union enjoyed little favour with the girl's relations; but he had always treated her so completely as an independent person that it hardly seemed necessary to express regret for the attitude of her family. Nevertheless, one morning, he made an abrupt allusion to it. "It's the difference in our fortune they don't like," he said. "They think I'm in love with your money."

"Are you speaking of my aunt — of my cousin?" Isabel asked. "How do you know what they think?"

"You've not told me they're pleased, and when I wrote to Mrs. Touchett the other day she never answered my note. If they had been delighted I should have had some sign of it, and the fact of my being poor and you rich is the most obvious explanation of their reserve. But of course when a poor man marries a rich girl he must be prepared for imputations. I don't mind them; I only care for one thing — for your not having the shadow of a doubt. I don't care what people of whom I ask nothing think — I'm not even capable perhaps of wanting to know. I've never so concerned myself, God forgive me, and why should I begin to-day, when I have taken to myself a compensation for everything? I won't pretend I'm sorry you're rich; I'm delighted. I delight in everything that's yours — whether it be money or virtue. Money's a horrid thing to follow, but a charming thing to meet. It seems to me, however, that I've sufficiently proved the limits of my itch for it: I never in my life tried to earn a penny, and I ought to be less subject to suspicion than most of the people one sees grubbing and grabbing. I suppose it's their business to suspect — that of your family; it's proper on the whole they should. They'll like me better some day; so will you, for that matter. Meanwhile my business is not to make myself bad blood, but simply to be thankful for life and love." "It has made me better, loving you," he said on another occasion; "it has made me wiser and easier and — I won't pretend to deny — brighter and nicer and even stronger. I used to want a great many things before and to be angry I did n't have them. Theoretically I was satisfied, as I once told you. I flattered myself I had limited my wants. But I was subject to irritation; I used to have morbid, sterile, hateful fits of hunger, of desire. Now I'm really satisfied, because I can't think of anything better. It's just as when one has been trying to spell out a book in the twilight and suddenly the lamp comes in. I had been putting out my eyes over the book of life and finding nothing to reward me for my pains; but now that I can read it properly I see it's a delightful story. My dear girl, I can't tell you how life seems to stretch there before us — what a long summer afternoon awaits us. It's the latter half of an Italian day — with a golden haze, and the shadows just lengthening, and that divine delicacy in the light, the air, the landscape, which I have loved all my life and which you love to-day. Upon my honour, I don't see why we should n't get on. We've got what we like — to say nothing of having each other. We've the faculty of admiration and several capital convictions. We're not stupid, we're not mean, we're not under bonds to any kind of ignorance or dreariness. You're remarkably fresh, and I'm remarkably well-seasoned. We've my poor child to amuse us; we'll try and make up some little life for her. It's all soft and mellow — it has the Italian colouring."

They made a good many plans, but they left themselves also a good deal of latitude; it was a matter of course, however, that they should live for the present in Italy. It was in Italy that they had met, Italy had been a party to their first impressions of each other, and Italy should be a party to their happiness. Osmond had the attachment of old acquaintance and Isabel the stimulus of new, which seemed to assure her a future at a high level of consciousness of the beautiful. The desire for unlimited expansion had been succeeded in her soul by the sense that life was vacant without some private duty that might gather one's energies to a point. She had told Ralph she had "seen life" in a year or two and that she was already tired, not of the act of living, but of that of observing. What had become of all her ardours, her aspirations, her theories, her high estimate of her independence and her incipient conviction that she should never marry? These things had been absorbed in a more primitive need — a need the answer to which brushed away numberless questions, yet gratified infinite desires. It simplified the situation at a stroke, it came down from above like the light of the stars, and it needed no explanation. There was explanation enough in the fact that he was her lover, her own, and that she should be able to be of use to him. She could surrender to him with a kind of humility, she could marry him with a kind of pride; she was not only taking, she was giving.

He brought Pansy with him two or three times

to the Cascine — Pansy who was very little taller than a year before, and not much older. That she would always be a child was the conviction expressed by her father, who held her by the hand when she was in her sixteenth year and told her to go and play while he sat down a little with the pretty lady. Pansy wore a short dress and a long coat; her hat always seemed too big for her. She found pleasure in walking off, with quick, short steps, to the end of the alley, and then in walking back with a smile that seemed an appeal for approbation. Isabel approved in abundance, and the abundance had the personal touch that the child's affectionate nature craved. She watched her indications as if for herself also much depended on them — Pansy already so represented part of the service she could render, part of the responsibility she could face. Her father took so the childish view of her that he had not yet explained to her the new relation in which he stood to the elegant Miss Archer. "She does n't know," he said to Isabel; "she does n't guess; she thinks it perfectly natural that you and I should come and walk here together simply as good friends. There seems to me something enchantingly innocent in that; it 's the way I like her to be. No, I 'm not a failure, as I used to think; I 've succeeded in two things. I 'm to marry the woman I adore, and I 've brought up my child, as I wished, in the old way."

He was very fond, in all things, of the "old way"; that had struck Isabel as one of his fine, quiet, sincere notes. "It occurs to me that you 'll not know whether you 've succeeded until you 've told her," she said. "You must see how she takes your news. She may be horrified — she may be jealous."

"I'm not afraid of that; she's too fond of you on her own account. I should like to leave her in the dark a little longer — to see if it will come into her head that if we're not engaged we ought to be."

Isabel was impressed by Osmond's artistic, the plastic view, as it somehow appeared, of Pansy's innocence — her own appreciation of it being more anxiously moral. She was perhaps not the less pleased when he told her a few days later that he had communicated the fact to his daughter, who had made such a pretty little speech — "Oh, then I shall have a beautiful sister!" She was neither surprised nor alarmed; she had not cried, as he expected.

"Perhaps she had guessed it," said Isabel.

"Don't say that; I should be disgusted if I believed that. I thought it would be just a little shock; but the way she took it proves that her good manners are paramount. That's also what I wished. You shall see for yourself; to-morrow she shall make you her congratulations in person."

The meeting, on the morrow, took place at the Countess Gemini's, whither Pansy had been conducted by her father, who knew that Isabel was to come in the afternoon to return a visit made her by the Countess on learning that they were to become sisters-in-law. Calling at Casa Touchett the visitor had not found Isabel at home; but after our young woman had been ushered into the Countess's drawing-room Pansy arrived to say that her aunt would presently appear. Pansy was spending the day with that lady, who thought her of an age to begin to learn how to carry herself in company. It was Isabel's view that the little girl might have given lessons in deportment to her relative, and nothing could have justified this conviction more than the manner in which Pansy acquitted herself while they waited together for the Countess. Her father's decision, the year before, had finally been to send her back to the convent to receive the last graces, and Madame Catherine had evidently carried out her theory that Pansy was to be fitted for the great world.

"Papa has told me that you've kindly consented to marry him," said this excellent woman's pupil. "It's very delightful; I think you'll suit very well."

"You think I shall suit *you?*"

"You'll suit me beautifully; but what I mean is that you and papa will suit each other. You're both so quiet and so serious. You're not so quiet as he — or even as Madame Merle; but you're more quiet than many others. He should not for instance have a wife like my aunt. She's always in motion, in agitation — to-day especially; you'll see when she comes in. They told us at the convent it was wrong to judge our elders, but I suppose there's no harm if we judge them favourably. You'll be a delightful companion for papa."

"For you too, I hope," Isabel said.

"I speak first of him on purpose. I've told you already what I myself think of you; I liked you from the first. I admire you so much that I think it will be a good fortune to have you always before me. You'll be my model; I shall try to imitate you though I'm afraid it will be very feeble. I'm very glad for papa — he needed something more than me. Without you I don't see how he could have got it. You'll be my stepmother, but we must n't use that word. They're always said to be cruel; but I don't think you'll ever so much as pinch or even push me. I'm not afraid at all."

"My good little Pansy," said Isabel gently, "I shall be ever so kind to you." A vague, inconsequent vision of her coming in some odd way to need it had intervened with the effect of a chill.

"Very well then, I've nothing to fear," the child returned with her note of prepared promptitude. What teaching she had had, it seemed to suggest — or what penalties for non-performance she dreaded!

Her description of her aunt had not been incorrect; the Countess Gemini was further than ever from having folded her wings. She entered the room with a flutter through the air and kissed Isabel first on the forehead and then on each cheek as if according to some ancient prescribed rite. She drew the visitor to a sofa and, looking at her with a variety of turns of the head, began to talk very much as if, seated brush in hand before an easel, she were applying a series of considered touches to a composition of figures already sketched in. "If you expect me to congratulate you I must beg you to excuse me. I don't suppose you care if I do or not; I believe you're supposed not to care — through being so clever — for all sorts of ordinary things. But I care myself if I tell fibs; I never tell them unless there's something rather good

86

to be gained. I don't see what's to be gained with you
— especially as you would n't believe me. I don't
make professions any more than I make paper flowers
or flouncey lampshades — I don't know how. My
lampshades would be sure to take fire, my roses and
my fibs to be larger than life. I'm very glad for my
own sake that you're to marry Osmond; but I won't
pretend I'm glad for yours. You're very brilliant —
you know that's the way you're always spoken of;
you're an heiress and very good-looking and original,
not *banal;* so it's a good thing to have you in the
family. Our family's very good, you know; Osmond
will have told you that; and my mother was rather
distinguished — she was called the American Corinne.
But we're dreadfully fallen, I think, and perhaps
you'll pick us up. I've great confidence in you; there
are ever so many things I want to talk to you about.
I never congratulate any girl on marrying; I think
they ought to make it somehow not quite so awful a
steel trap. I suppose Pansy ought n't to hear all this;
but that's what she has come to me for — to acquire
the tone of society. There's no harm in her knowing
what horrors she may be in for. When first I got an
idea that my brother had designs on you I thought
of writing to you, to recommend you, in the strongest
terms, not to listen to him. Then I thought it would
be disloyal, and I hate anything of that kind. Besides, as I say, I was enchanted for myself; and after
all I'm very selfish. By the way, you won't respect
me, not one little mite, and we shall never be intimate.
I should like it, but you won't. Some day, all the
same, we shall be better friends than you will believe

at first. My husband will come and see you, though, as you probably know, he's on no sort of terms with Osmond. He's very fond of going to see pretty women, but I'm not afraid of you. In the first place I don't care what he does. In the second, you won't care a straw for him; he won't be a bit, at any time, your affair, and, stupid as he is, he'll see you're not his. Some day, if you can stand it, I'll tell you all about him. Do you think my niece ought to go out of the room? Pansy, go and practise a little in my boudoir."

"Let her stay, please," said Isabel. "I would rather hear nothing that Pansy may not!"

XXXVI

ONE afternoon of the autumn of 1876, toward dusk, a young man of pleasing appearance rang at the door of a small apartment on the third floor of an old Roman house. On its being opened he enquired for Madame Merle; whereupon the servant, a neat, plain woman, with a French face and a lady's maid's manner, ushered him into a diminutive drawing-room and requested the favour of his name. "Mr. Edward Rosier," said the young man, who sat down to wait till his hostess should appear.

The reader will perhaps not have forgotten that Mr. Rosier was an ornament of the American circle in Paris, but it may also be remembered that he sometimes vanished from its horizon. He had spent a portion of several winters at Pau, and as he was a gentleman of constituted habits he might have continued for years to pay his annual visit to this charming resort. In the summer of 1876, however, an incident befell him which changed the current not only of his thoughts, but of his customary sequences. He passed a month in the Upper Engadine and encountered at Saint Moritz a charming young girl. To this little person he began to pay, on the spot, particular attention: she struck him as exactly the household angel he had long been looking for. He was never precipitate, he was nothing if not discreet, so he forbore for the present to declare his passion; but it seemed to him when they parted — the young lady to go down into Italy and her admirer to proceed to Geneva, where he was under bonds to join other friends — that he should be romantically wretched if he were not to see her again. The simplest way to do so was to go in the autumn to Rome, where Miss Osmond was domiciled with her family. Mr. Rosier started on his pilgrimage to the Italian capital and reached it on the first of November. It was a pleasant thing to do, but for the young man there was a strain of the heroic in the enterprise. He might expose himself, unseasoned, to the poison of the Roman air, which in November lay, notoriously, much in wait. Fortune, however, favours the brave; and this adventurer, who took three grains of quinine a day, had at the end of a month no cause to deplore his temerity. He had made to a certain extent good use of his time; he had devoted it in vain to finding a flaw in Pansy Osmond's composition. She was admirably finished; she had had the last touch; she was really a consummate piece. He thought of her in amorous meditation a good deal as he might have thought of a Dresden-china shepherdess. Miss Osmond, indeed, in the bloom of her juvenility, had a hint of the rococo which Rosier, whose taste was predominantly for that manner, could not fail to appreciate. That he esteemed the productions of comparatively frivolous periods would have been apparent from the attention he bestowed upon Madame Merle's drawing-room, which, although furnished with specimens of every style, was especially rich in articles of the last two centuries. He had immediately put a glass into one eye and looked round; and then "By Jove, she has some jolly good things!" he had yearningly murmured. The room was small and densely filled with furniture; it gave an impression of faded silk and little statuettes which might totter if one moved. Rosier got up and wandered about with his careful tread, bending over the tables charged with knick-knacks and the cushions embossed with princely arms. When Madame Merle came in she found him standing before the fireplace with his nose very close to the great lace flounce attached to the damask cover of the mantel. He had lifted it delicately, as if he were smelling it.

"It's old Venetian," she said; "it's rather good."

"It's too good for this; you ought to wear it."

"They tell me you have some better in Paris, in the same situation."

"Ah, but I can't wear mine," smiled the visitor.

"I don't see why you shouldn't! I've better lace than that to wear."

His eyes wandered, lingeringly, round the room again. "You've some very good things."

"Yes, but I hate them."

"Do you want to get rid of them?" the young man quickly asked.

"No, it's good to have something to hate: one works it off!"

"I love my things," said Mr. Rosier as he sat there flushed with all his recognitions. "But it's not about them, nor about yours, that I came to talk to you." He paused a moment and then, with greater softness: "I care more for Miss Osmond than for all the *bibelots* in Europe!"

Madame Merle opened wide eyes. "Did you come to tell me that?"

"I came to ask your advice."

She looked at him with a friendly frown, stroking her chin with her large white hand. "A man in love, you know, does n't ask advice."

"Why not, if he's in a difficult position? That's often the case with a man in love. I've been in love before, and I know. But never so much as this time — really never so much. I should like particularly to know what you think of my prospects. I'm afraid that for Mr. Osmond I'm not — well, a real collector's piece."

"Do you wish me to intercede?" Madame Merle asked with her fine arms folded and her handsome mouth drawn up to the left.

"If you could say a good word for me I should be greatly obliged. There will be no use in my troubling Miss Osmond unless I have good reason to believe her father will consent."

"You're very considerate; that's in your favour. But you assume in rather an off-hand way that *I* think you a prize."

"You've been very kind to me," said the young man. "That's why I came."

"I'm always kind to people who have good Louis Quatorze. It's very rare now, and there's no telling what one may get by it." With which the left-hand corner of Madame Merle's mouth gave expression to the joke.

But he looked, in spite of it, literally apprehensive and consistently strenuous. "Ah, I thought you liked me for myself!"

"I like you very much; but, if you please, we won't analyse. Pardon me if I seem patronising, but I think you a perfect little gentleman. I must tell you, however, that I've not the marrying of Pansy Osmond."

"I did n't suppose that. But you've seemed to me intimate with her family, and I thought you might have influence."

Madame Merle considered. "Whom do you call her family?"

"Why, her father; and — how do you say it in English? — her *belle-mère*."

"Mr. Osmond's her father, certainly; but his wife can scarcely be termed a member of her family. Mrs. Osmond has nothing to do with marrying her."

"I'm sorry for that," said Rosier with an amiable sigh of good faith. "I think Mrs. Osmond would favour me."

"Very likely — if her husband does n't."

He raised his eyebrows. "Does she take the opposite line from him?"

"In everything. They think quite differently."

"Well," said Rosier, "I'm sorry for that; but it's none of my business. She's very fond of Pansy."

"Yes, she's very fond of Pansy."

"And Pansy has a great affection for her. She has told me how she loves her as if she were her own mother."

"You must, after all, have had some very intimate talk with the poor child," said Madame Merle. "Have you declared your sentiments?"

"Never!" cried Rosier, lifting his neatly-gloved hand. "Never till I've assured myself of those of the parents."

"You always wait for that? You've excellent principles; you observe the proprieties."

"I think you're laughing at me," the young man murmured, dropping back in his chair and feeling his small moustache. "I did n't expect that of you, Madame Merle."

She shook her head calmly, like a person who saw things as she saw them. "You don't do me justice. I think your conduct in excellent taste and the best you could adopt. Yes, that's what I think."

"I would n't agitate her — only to agitate her; I love her too much for that," said Ned Rosier.

"I'm glad, after all, that you've told me," Madame Merle went on. "Leave it to me a little; I think I can help you."

"I said you were the person to come to!" her visitor cried with prompt elation.

"You were very clever," Madame Merle returned more dryly. "When I say I can help you I mean once assuming your cause to be good. Let us think a little if it is."

"I'm awfully decent, you know," said Rosier earnestly. "I won't say I've no faults, but I'll say I've no vices."

"All that's negative, and it always depends, also,

on what people call vices. What's the positive side? What's the virtuous? What have you got besides your Spanish lace and your Dresden teacups?"

"I've a comfortable little fortune — about forty thousand francs a year. With the talent I have for arranging, we can live beautifully on such an income."

"Beautifully, no. Sufficiently, yes. Even that depends on where you live."

"Well, in Paris. I would undertake it in Paris."

Madame Merle's mouth rose to the left. "It would n't be famous; you'd have to make use of the teacups, and they'd get broken."

"We don't want to be famous. If Miss Osmond should have everything pretty it would be enough. When one's as pretty as she one can afford — well, quite cheap *faience*. She ought never to wear anything but muslin — without the sprig," said Rosier reflectively.

"Would n't you even allow her the sprig? She'd be much obliged to you at any rate for that theory."

"It's the correct one, I assure you; and I'm sure she'd enter into it. She understands all that; that's why I love her."

"She's a very good little girl, and most tidy — also extremely graceful. But her father, to the best of my belief, can give her nothing."

Rosier scarce demurred. "I don't in the least desire that he should. But I may remark, all the same, that he lives like a rich man."

"The money's his wife's; she brought him a large fortune."

"Mrs. Osmond then is very fond of her step-daughter; she may do something."

"For a love-sick swain you have your eyes about you!" Madame Merle exclaimed with a laugh.

"I esteem a *dot* very much. I can do without it, but I esteem it."

"Mrs. Osmond," Madame Merle went on, "will probably prefer to keep her money for her own children."

"Her own children? Surely she has none."

"She may have yet. She had a poor little boy, who died two years ago, six months after his birth. Others therefore may come."

"I hope they will, if it will make her happy. She's a splendid woman."

Madame Merle failed to burst into speech. "Ah, about her there's much to be said. Splendid as you like! We've not exactly made out that you're a *parti*. The absence of vices is hardly a source of income."

"Pardon me, I think it may be," said Rosier quite lucidly.

"You'll be a touching couple, living on your innocence!"

"I think you underrate me."

"You're not so innocent as that? Seriously," said Madame Merle, "of course forty thousand francs a year and a nice character are a combination to be considered. I don't say it's to be jumped at, but there might be a worse offer. Mr. Osmond, however, will probably incline to believe he can do better."

"*He* can do so perhaps; but what can his daughter

do ? She can't do better than marry the man she loves. For she does, you know," Rosier added eagerly.

"She does — I know it."

"Ah," cried the young man, "I said you were the person to come to."

"But I don't know how *you* know it, if you have n't asked her," Madame Merle went on.

"In such a case there's no need of asking and telling; as you say, we're an innocent couple. How did *you* know it?"

"I who am not innocent? By being very crafty. Leave it to me; I'll find out for you."

Rosier got up and stood smoothing his hat. "You say that rather coldly. Don't simply find out how it is, but try to make it as it should be."

"I'll do my best. I'll try to make the most of your advantages."

"Thank you so very much. Meanwhile then I'll say a word to Mrs. Osmond."

"*Gardez-vous-en bien!*" And Madame Merle was on her feet. "Don't set her going, or you'll spoil everything."

Rosier gazed into his hat; he wondered whether his hostess *had* been after all the right person to come to. "I don't think I understand you. I'm an old friend of Mrs. Osmond, and I think she would like me to succeed."

"Be an old friend as much as you like; the more old friends she has the better, for she does n't get on very well with some of her new. But don't for the present try to make her take up the cudgels for you. Her husband may have other views, and, as a person who wishes her well, I advise you not to multiply points of difference between them."

Poor Rosier's face assumed an expression of alarm; a suit for the hand of Pansy Osmond was even a more complicated business than his taste for proper transitions had allowed. But the extreme good sense which he concealed under a surface suggesting that of a careful owner's "best set" came to his assistance. "I don't see that I'm bound to consider Mr. Osmond so very much!" he exclaimed.

"No, but you should consider *her*. You say you're an old friend. Would you make her suffer?"

"Not for the world."

"Then be very careful, and let the matter alone till I've taken a few soundings."

"Let the matter alone, dear Madame Merle? Remember that I'm in love."

"Oh, you won't burn up! Why did you come to me, if you're not to heed what I say?"

"You're very kind; I'll be very good," the young man promised. "But I'm afraid Mr. Osmond's pretty hard," he added in his mild voice as he went to the door.

Madame Merle gave a short laugh. "It has been said before. But his wife isn't easy either."

"Ah, she's a splendid woman!" Ned Rosier repeated, for departure.

He resolved that his conduct should be worthy of an aspirant who was already a model of discretion; but he saw nothing in any pledge he had given Madame Merle that made it improper he should keep himself in spirits by an occasional visit to Miss

Osmond's home. He reflected constantly on what his adviser had said to him, and turned over in his mind the impression of her rather circumspect tone. He had gone to her *de confiance*, as they put it in Paris; but it was possible he had been precipitate. He found difficulty in thinking of himself as rash — he had incurred this reproach so rarely; but it certainly was true that he had known Madame Merle only for the last month, and that his thinking her a delightful woman was not, when one came to look into it, a reason for assuming that she would be eager to push Pansy Osmond into his arms, gracefully arranged as these members might be to receive her. She had indeed shown him benevolence, and she was a person of consideration among the girl's people, where she had a rather striking appearance (Rosier had more than once wondered how she managed it) of being intimate without being familiar. But possibly he had exaggerated these advantages. There was no particular reason why she should take trouble for him; a charming woman was charming to every one, and Rosier felt rather a fool when he thought of his having appealed to her on the ground that she had distinguished him. Very likely — though she had appeared to say it in joke — she was really only thinking of his *bibelots*. Had it come into her head that he might offer her two or three of the gems of his collection? If she would only help him to marry Miss Osmond he would present her with his whole museum. He could hardly say so to her outright; it would seem too gross a bribe. But he should like her to believe it.

It was with these thoughts that he went again to Mrs. Osmond's, Mrs. Osmond having an "evening" — she had taken the Thursday of each week — when his presence could be accounted for on general principles of civility. The object of Mr. Rosier's well-regulated affection dwelt in a high house in the very heart of Rome; a dark and massive structure overlooking a sunny *piazzetta* in the neighbourhood of the Farnese Palace. In a palace, too, little Pansy lived — a palace by Roman measure, but a dungeon to poor Rosier's apprehensive mind. It seemed to him of evil omen that the young lady he wished to marry, and whose fastidious father he doubted of his ability to conciliate, should be immured in a kind of domestic fortress, a pile which bore a stern old Roman name, which smelt of historic deeds, of crime and craft and violence, which was mentioned in "Murray" and visited by tourists who looked, on a vague survey, disappointed and depressed, and which had frescoes by Caravaggio in the *piano nobile* and a row of mutilated statues and dusty urns in the wide, nobly-arched loggia overhanging the damp court where a fountain gushed out of a mossy niche. In a less preoccupied frame of mind he could have done justice to the Palazzo Roccanera; he could have entered into the sentiment of Mrs. Osmond, who had once told him that on settling themselves in Rome she and her husband had chosen this habitation for the love of local colour. It had local colour enough, and though he knew less about architecture than about Limoges enamels he could see that the proportions of the windows and even the details of the cornice had quite

the grand air. But Rosier was haunted by the conviction that at picturesque periods young girls had
been shut up there to keep them from their true loves,
and then, under the threat of being thrown into convents, had been forced into unholy marriages. There
was one point, however, to which he always did justice when once he found himself in Mrs. Osmond's
warm, rich-looking reception-rooms, which were on
the second floor. He acknowledged that these people were very strong in "good things." It was a taste
of Osmond's own — not at all of hers; this she had
told him the first time he came to the house, when,
after asking himself for a quarter of an hour whether
they had even better "French" than he in Paris, he
was obliged on the spot to admit that they had, very
much, and vanquished his envy, as a gentleman
should, to the point of expressing to his hostess his
pure admiration of her treasures. He learned from
Mrs. Osmond that her husband had made a large
collection before their marriage and that, though
he had annexed a number of fine pieces within the
last three years, he had achieved his greatest finds at
a time when he had not the advantage of her advice.
Rosier interpreted this information according to
principles of his own. For "advice" read "cash,"
he said to himself; and the fact that Gilbert Osmond
had landed his highest prizes during his impecunious
season confirmed his most cherished doctrine — the
doctrine that a collector may freely be poor if he be
only patient. In general, when Rosier presented himself on a Thursday evening, his first recognition was
for the walls of the saloon; there were three or four

objects his eyes really yearned for. But after his talk with Madame Merle he felt the extreme seriousness of his position; and now, when he came in, he looked about for the daughter of the house with such eagerness as might be permitted a gentleman whose smile, as he crossed a threshold, always took everything comfortable for granted.

XXXVII

Pansy was not in the first of the rooms, a large apartment with a concave ceiling and walls covered with old red damask; it was here Mrs. Osmond usually sat — though she was not in her most customary place to-night — and that a circle of more especial intimates gathered about the fire. The room was flushed with subdued, diffused brightness; it contained the larger things and — almost always — an odour of flowers. Pansy on this occasion was presumably in the next of the series, the resort of younger visitors, where tea was served. Osmond stood before the chimney, leaning back with his hands behind him; he had one foot up and was warming the sole. Half a dozen persons, scattered near him, were talking together; but he was not in the conversation; his eyes had an expression, frequent with them, that seemed to represent them as engaged with objects more worth their while than the appearances actually thrust upon them. Rosier, coming in unannounced, failed to attract his attention; but the young man, who was very punctilious, though he was even exceptionally conscious that it was the wife, not the husband, he had come to see, went up to shake hands with him. Osmond put out his left hand, without changing his attitude.

"How d' ye do? My wife's somewhere about."

"Never fear; I shall find her," said Rosier cheerfully.

Osmond, however, took him in; he had never in his life felt himself so efficiently looked at. "Madame Merle has told him, and he does n't like it," he privately reasoned. He had hoped Madame Merle would be there, but she was not in sight; perhaps she was in one of the other rooms or would come later. He had never especially delighted in Gilbert Osmond, having a fancy he gave himself airs. But Rosier was not quickly resentful, and where politeness was concerned had ever a strong need of being quite in the right. He looked round him and smiled, all without help, and then in a moment, "I saw a jolly good piece of Capo di Monte to-day," he said.

Osmond answered nothing at first; but presently, while he warmed his boot-sole, " I don't care a fig for Capo di Monte! " he returned.

"I hope you 're not losing your interest ? "

"In old pots and plates ? Yes, I 'm losing my interest."

Rosier for an instant forgot the delicacy of his position. "You 're not thinking of parting with a — a piece or two ? "

"No, I 'm not thinking of parting with anything at all, Mr. Rosier," said Osmond, with his eyes still on the eyes of his visitor.

"Ah, you want to keep, but not to add," Rosier remarked brightly.

"Exactly. I 've nothing I wish to match."

Poor Rosier was aware he had blushed; he was distressed at his want of assurance. "Ah, well, I have!" was all he could murmur; and he knew his murmur was partly lost as he turned away. He took his course to the adjoining room and met Mrs. Osmond coming out of the deep doorway. She was dressed in black velvet; she looked high and splendid, as he had said, and yet oh so radiantly gentle! We know what Mr. Rosier thought of her and the terms in which, to Madame Merle, he had expressed his admiration. Like his appreciation of her dear little stepdaughter it was based partly on his eye for decorative character, his instinct for authenticity; but also on a sense for uncatalogued values, for that secret of a " lustre " beyond any recorded losing or rediscovering, which his devotion to brittle wares had still not disqualified him to recognise. Mrs. Osmond, at present, might well have gratified such tastes. The years had touched her only to enrich her; the flower of her youth had not faded, it only hung more quietly on its stem. She had lost something of that quick eagerness to which her husband had privately taken exception — she had more the air of being able to wait. Now, at all events, framed in the gilded doorway, she struck our young man as the picture of a gracious lady. "You see I'm very regular," he said. "But who should be if I'm not ? "

"Yes, I've known you longer than any one here. But we must n't indulge in tender reminiscences. I want to introduce you to a young lady."

"Ah, please, what young lady ? " Rosier was immensely obliging; but this was not what he had come for.

"She sits there by the fire in pink and has no one to speak to."

Rosier hesitated a moment. "Can't Mr. Osmond speak to her? He's within six feet of her."

Mrs. Osmond also hesitated. "She's not very lively, and he does n't like dull people."

"But she's good enough for me? Ah now, that's hard!"

"I only mean that you've ideas for two. And then you're so obliging."

"So is your husband."

"No, he's not — to me." And Mrs. Osmond vaguely smiled.

"That's a sign he should be doubly so to other women."

"So I tell him," she said, still smiling.

"You see I want some tea," Rosier went on, looking wistfully beyond.

"That's perfect. Go and give some to my young lady."

"Very good; but after that I'll abandon her to her fate. The simple truth is I'm dying to have a little talk with Miss Osmond."

"Ah," said Isabel, turning away, "I can't help you there!"

Five minutes later, while he handed a tea-cup to the damsel in pink, whom he had conducted into the other room, he wondered whether, in making to Mrs. Osmond the profession I have just quoted, he had broken the spirit of his promise to Madame Merle. Such a question was capable of occupying this young man's mind for a considerable time. At last, however, he became — comparatively speaking — reckless; he cared little what promises he might break. The fate to which he had threatened to abandon the damsel in pink proved to be none so terrible; for Pansy Osmond, who had given him the tea for his companion — Pansy was as fond as ever of making tea — presently came and talked to her. Into this mild colloquy Edward Rosier entered little; he sat by moodily, watching his small sweetheart. If we look at her now through his eyes we shall at first not see much to remind us of the obedient little girl who, at Florence, three years before, was sent to walk short distances in the Cascine while her father and Miss Archer talked together of matters sacred to elder people. But after a moment we shall perceive that if at nineteen Pansy has become a young lady she does n't really fill out the part; that if she has grown very pretty she lacks in a deplorable degree the quality known and esteemed in the appearance of females as style; and that if she is dressed with great freshness she wears her smart attire with an undisguised appearance of saving it — very much as if it were lent her for the occasion. Edward Rosier, it would seem, would have been just the man to note these defects; and in point of fact there was not a quality of this young lady, of any sort, that he had not noted. Only he called her qualities by names of his own — some of which indeed were happy enough. "No, she's unique — she's absolutely unique," he used to say to himself; and you may be sure that not for an instant would he have admitted to you that she was wanting in style. Style? Why, she had the style of a little princess; if you could n't see it you had no eye. It was not modern, it was not conscious, it would produce no impression in Broadway; the small, serious damsel, in her stiff little dress, only looked like an Infanta of Velasquez. This was enough for Edward Rosier, who thought her delightfully old-fashioned. Her anxious eyes, her charming lips, her slip of a figure, were as touching as a childish prayer. He had now an acute desire to know just to what point she liked him — a desire which made him fidget as he sat in his chair. It made him feel hot, so that he had to pat his forehead with his handkerchief; he had never been so uncomfortable. She was such a perfect *jeune fille*, and one could n't make of a *jeune fille* the enquiry requisite for throwing light on such a point. A *jeune fille* was what Rosier had always dreamed of — a *jeune fille* who should yet not be French, for he had felt that this nationality would complicate the question. He was sure Pansy had never looked at a newspaper and that, in the way of novels, if she had read Sir Walter Scott it was the very most. An American *jeune fille* — what could be better than that? She would be frank and gay, and yet would not have walked alone, nor have received letters from men, nor have been taken to the theatre to see the comedy of manners. Rosier could not deny that, as the matter stood, it would be a breach of hospitality to appeal directly to this unsophisticated creature; but he was now in imminent danger of asking himself if hospitality were the most sacred thing in the world. Was not the sentiment that he entertained for Miss Osmond of infinitely greater importance? Of greater

importance to him — yes; but not probably to the
master of the house. There was one comfort; even
if this gentleman had been placed on his guard by
Madame Merle he would not have extended the
warning to Pansy; it would not have been part of his
policy to let her know that a prepossessing young man
was in love with her. But he *was* in love with her, the
prepossessing young man; and all these restrictions
of circumstance had ended by irritating him. What
had Gilbert Osmond meant by giving him two fingers
of his left hand ? If Osmond was rude, surely he himself might be bold. He felt extremely bold after the
dull girl in so vain a disguise of rose-colour had responded to the call of her mother, who came in to say,
with a significant simper at Rosier, that she must
carry her off to other triumphs. The mother and
daughter departed together, and now it depended
only upon him that he should be virtually alone with
Pansy. He had never been alone with her before; he
had never been alone with a *jeune fille*. It was a great
moment; poor Rosier began to pat his forehead again.
There was another room beyond the one in which
they stood — a small room that had been thrown
open and lighted, but that, the company not being
numerous, had remained empty all the evening. It
was empty yet; it was upholstered in pale yellow;
there were several lamps; through the open door it
looked the very temple of authorised love. Rosier
gazed a moment through this aperture; he was afraid
that Pansy would run away, and felt almost capable
of stretching out a hand to detain her. But she. lingered where the other maiden had left them, making

no motion to join a knot of visitors on the far side of
the room. For a little it occurred to him that she was
frightened — too frightened perhaps to move; but a
second glance assured him she was not, and he then
reflected that she was too innocent indeed for that.
After a supreme hesitation he asked her if he might
go and look at the yellow room, which seemed so attractive yet so virginal. He had been there already
with Osmond, to inspect the furniture, which was of
the First French Empire, and especially to admire the
clock (which he did n't really admire), an immense
classic structure of that period. He therefore felt that
he had now begun to manœuvre.

"Certainly, you may go," said Pansy; "and if
you like I 'll show you." She was not in the least
frightened.

"That 's just what I hoped you 'd say; you 're so
very kind," Rosier murmured.

They went in together; Rosier really thought the
room very ugly, and it seemed cold. The same idea
appeared to have struck Pansy. "It 's not for winter
evenings; it 's more for summer," she said. "It 's
papa's taste; he has so much."

He had a good deal, Rosier thought; but some of
it was very bad. He looked about him; he hardly
knew what to say in such a situation. "Does n't Mrs.
Osmond care how her rooms are done? Has she no
taste?" he asked.

"Oh yes, a great deal; but it 's more for literature,"
said Pansy — "and for conversation. But papa cares
also for those things. I think he knows everything."

Rosier was silent a little. "There 's one thing I 'm

sure he knows!" he broke out presently. "He knows
that when I come here it's, with all respect to him,
with all respect to Mrs. Osmond, who's so charming
— it's really," said the young man, "to see you!"

"To see me?" And Pansy raised her vaguely-
troubled eyes.

"To see you; that's what I come for," Rosier repeated, feeling the intoxication of a rupture with
authority.

Pansy stood looking at him, simply, intently, openly;
a blush was not needed to make her face more modest.
"I thought it was for that."

"And it was not disagreeable to you?"

"I could n't tell; I did n't know. You never told
me," said Pansy.

"I was afraid of offending you."

"You don't offend me," the young girl murmured,
smiling as if an angel had kissed her.

"You like me then, Pansy?" Rosier asked very
gently, feeling very happy.

"Yes — I like you."

They had walked to the chimney-piece where the
big cold Empire clock was perched; they were well
within the room and beyond observation from without. The tone in which she had said these four words
seemed to him the very breath of nature, and his only
answer could be to take her hand and hold it a moment. Then he raised it to his lips. She submitted,
still with her pure, trusting smile, in which there was
something ineffably passive. She liked him — she
had liked him all the while; now anything might
happen! She was ready — she had been ready al-

ways, waiting for him to speak. If he had not spoken she would have waited for ever; but when the word came she dropped like the peach from the shaken tree. Rosier felt that if he should draw her toward him and hold her to his heart she would submit without a murmur, would rest there without a question. It was true that this would be a rash experiment in a yellow Empire *salottino*. She had known it was for her he came, and yet like what a perfect little lady she had carried it off!

"You're very dear to me," he murmured, trying to believe that there was after all such a thing as hospitality.

She looked a moment at her hand, where he had kissed it. "Did you say papa knows?"

"You told me just now he knows everything."

"I think you must make sure," said Pansy.

"Ah, my dear, when once I'm sure of *you!*" Rosier murmured in her ear; whereupon she turned back to the other rooms with a little air of consistency which seemed to imply that their appeal should be immediate.

The other rooms meanwhile had become conscious of the arrival of Madame Merle, who, wherever she went, produced an impression when she entered. How she did it the most attentive spectator could not have told you, for she neither spoke loud, nor laughed profusely, nor moved rapidly, nor dressed with splendour, nor appealed in any appreciable manner to the audience. Large, fair, smiling, serene, there was something in her very tranquillity that diffused itself, and when people looked round it was because of a sudden quiet. On this occasion she had done the quietest thing she could do; after embracing Mrs. Osmond, which was more striking, she had sat down on a small sofa to commune with the master of the house. There was a brief exchange of commonplaces between these two — they always paid, in public, a certain formal tribute to the commonplace — and then Madame Merle, whose eyes had been wandering, asked if little Mr. Rosier had come this evening.

"He came nearly an hour ago — but he has disappeared," Osmond said.

"And where's Pansy?"

"In the other room. There are several people there."

"He's probably among them," said Madame Merle.

"Do you wish to see him?" Osmond asked in a provokingly pointless tone.

Madame Merle looked at him a moment; she knew each of his tones to the eighth of a note. "Yes, I should like to say to him that I've told you what he wants, and that it interests you but feebly."

"Don't tell him that. He'll try to interest me more — which is exactly what I don't want. Tell him I hate his proposal."

"But you don't hate it."

"It does n't signify; I don't love it. I let him see that, myself, this evening; I was rude to him on purpose. That sort of thing's a great bore. There's no hurry."

"I'll tell him that you'll take time and think it over."

"No, don't do that. He'll hang on."

"If I discourage him he'll do the same."

"Yes, but in the one case he'll try to talk and explain — which would be exceedingly tiresome. In the other he'll probably hold his tongue and go in for some deeper game. That will leave me quiet. I hate talking with a donkey."

"Is that what you call poor Mr. Rosier?"

"Oh, he's a nuisance — with his eternal majolica."

Madame Merle dropped her eyes; she had a faint smile. "He's a gentleman, he has a charming temper; and, after all, an income of forty thousand francs!"

"It's misery — 'genteel' misery," Osmond broke in. "It's not what I've dreamed of for Pansy."

"Very good then. He has promised me not to speak to her."

"Do you believe him?" Osmond asked absent-mindedly.

"Perfectly. Pansy has thought a great deal about him; but I don't suppose you consider that that matters."

"I don't consider it matters at all; but neither do I believe she has thought of him."

"That opinion's more convenient," said Madame Merle quietly.

"Has she told you she's in love with him?"

"For what do you take her? And for what do you take me?" Madame Merle added in a moment.

Osmond had raised his foot and was resting his slim ankle on the other knee; he clasped his ankle in his hand familiarly — his long, fine forefinger and thumb could make a ring for it — and gazed a while before him. "This kind of thing does n't find me unprepared. It 's what I educated her for. It was all for this — that when such a case should come up she should do what I prefer."

"I 'm not afraid that she 'll not do it."

"Well then, where 's the hitch ?"

"I don't see any. But, all the same, I recommend you not to get rid of Mr. Rosier. Keep him on hand; he may be useful."

"I can't keep him. Keep him yourself."

"Very good; I 'll put him into a corner and allow him so much a day." Madame Merle had, for the most part, while they talked, been glancing about her; it was her habit in this situation, just as it was her habit to interpose a good many blank-looking pauses. A long drop followed the last words I have quoted; and before it had ended she saw Pansy come out of the adjoining room, followed by Edward Rosier. The girl advanced a few steps and then stopped and stood looking at Madame Merle and at her father.

"He has spoken to her," Madame Merle went on to Osmond.

Her companion never turned his head. "So much for your belief in his promises. He ought to be horse-whipped."

"He intends to confess, poor little man!"

Osmond got up; he had now taken a sharp look at his daughter. "It does n't matter," he murmured, turning away.

Pansy after a moment came up to Madame Merle with her little manner of unfamiliar politeness. This lady's reception of her was not more intimate; she simply, as she rose from the sofa, gave her a friendly smile.

"You're very late," the young creature gently said.

"My dear child, I'm never later than I intend to be."

Madame Merle had not got up to be gracious to Pansy; she moved toward Edward Rosier. He came to meet her and, very quickly, as if to get it off his mind, "I've spoken to her!" he whispered.

"I know it, Mr. Rosier."

"Did she tell you?"

"Yes, she told me. Behave properly for the rest of the evening, and come and see me to-morrow at a quarter past five." She was severe, and in the manner in which she turned her back to him there was a degree of contempt which caused him to mutter a decent imprecation.

He had no intention of speaking to Osmond; it was neither the time nor the place. But he instinctively wandered toward Isabel, who sat talking with an old lady. He sat down on the other side of her; the old lady was Italian, and Rosier took for granted she understood no English. "You said just now you would n't help me," he began to Mrs. Osmond. "Perhaps you'll feel differently when you know — when you know —!"

Isabel met his hesitation. "When I know what?"

"That she's all right."

"What do you mean by that?"

"Well, that we've come to an understanding."

"She's all wrong," said Isabel. "It won't do."

Poor Rosier gazed at her half-pleadingly, half-angrily; a sudden flush testified to his sense of injury. "I've never been treated so," he said. "What is there against me, after all? That's not the way I'm usually considered. I could have married twenty times."

"It's a pity you did n't. I don't mean twenty times, but once, comfortably," Isabel added, smiling kindly. "You're not rich enough for Pansy."

"She does n't care a straw for one's money."

"No, but her father does."

"Ah yes, he has proved that!" cried the young man.

Isabel got up, turning away from him, leaving her old lady without ceremony; and he occupied himself for the next ten minutes in pretending to look at Gilbert Osmond's collection of miniatures, which were neatly arranged on a series of small velvet screens. But he looked without seeing; his cheek burned; he was too full of his sense of injury. It was certain that he had never been treated that way before; he was not used to being thought not good enough. He knew how good he was, and if such a fallacy had not been so pernicious he could have laughed at it. He searched again for Pansy, but she had disappeared, and his main desire was now to get out of the house. Before doing so he spoke once more to Isabel; it was not agreeable to him to reflect that he had just said a rude thing to her — the only point that would now justify a low view of him.

"I referred to Mr. Osmond as I should n't have

done, a while ago," he began. "But you must remember my situation."

"I don't remember what you said," she answered coldly.

"Ah, you're offended, and now you'll never help me."

She was silent an instant, and then with a change of tone: "It's not that I won't; I simply can't!" Her manner was almost passionate.

"If you *could*, just a little, I'd never again speak of your husband save as an angel."

"The inducement's great," said Isabel gravely — inscrutably, as he afterwards, to himself, called it; and she gave him, straight in the eyes, a look which was also inscrutable. It made him remember somehow that he had known her as a child; and yet it was keener than he liked, and he took himself off.

XXXVIII

HE went to see Madame Merle on the morrow, and to his surprise she let him off rather easily. But she made him promise that he would stop there till something should have been decided. Mr. Osmond had had higher expectations; it was very true that as he had no intention of giving his daughter a portion such expectations were open to criticism or even, if one would, to ridicule. But she would advise Mr. Rosier not to take that tone; if he would possess his soul in patience he might arrive at his felicity. Mr. Osmond was not favourable to his suit, but it would n't be a miracle if he should gradually come round. Pansy would never defy her father, he might depend on that; so nothing was to be gained by precipitation. Mr. Osmond needed to accustom his mind to an offer of a sort that he had not hitherto entertained, and this result must come of itself — it was useless to try to force it. Rosier remarked that his own situation would be in the meanwhile the most uncomfortable in the world, and Madame Merle assured him that she felt for him. But, as she justly declared, one could n't have everything one wanted; she had learned that lesson for herself. There would be no use in his writing to Gilbert Osmond, who had charged her to tell him as much. He wished the matter dropped for a few weeks and would himself write when he should have anything to communicate that it might please Mr. Rosier to hear.

"He does n't like your having spoken to Pansy. Ah, he does n't like it at all," said Madame Merle.

"I'm perfectly willing to give him a chance to tell me so!"

"If you do that he'll tell you more than you care to hear. Go to the house, for the next month, as little as possible, and leave the rest to me."

"As little as possible? Who's to measure the possibility?"

"Let me measure it. Go on Thursday evenings with the rest of the world, but don't go at all at odd times, and don't fret about Pansy. I'll see that she understands everything. She's a calm little nature; she'll take it quietly."

Edward Rosier fretted about Pansy a good deal, but he did as he was advised, and awaited another Thursday evening before returning to Palazzo Roccanera. There had been a party at dinner, so that though he went early the company was already tolerably numerous. Osmond, as usual, was in the first room, near the fire, staring straight at the door, so that, not to be distinctly uncivil, Rosier had to go and speak to him.

"I'm glad that you can take a hint," Pansy's father said, slightly closing his keen, conscious eyes.

"I take no hints. But I took a message, as I supposed it to be."

"You took it? Where did you take it?"

It seemed to poor Rosier he was being insulted, and he waited a moment, asking himself how much a true lover ought to submit to. "Madame Merle gave me, as I understood it, a message from you —

to the effect that you declined to give me the opportunity I desire, the opportunity to explain my wishes
to you." And he flattered himself he spoke rather
sternly.

"I don't see what Madame Merle has to do with
it. Why did you apply to Madame Merle?"

"I asked her for an opinion — for nothing more.
I did so because she had seemed to me to know you
very well."

"She does n't know me so well as she thinks," said
Osmond.

"I'm sorry for that, because she has given me
some little ground for hope."

Osmond stared into the fire a moment. "I set a
great price on my daughter."

"You can't set a higher one than I do. Don't I
prove it by wishing to marry her?"

"I wish to marry her very well," Osmond went on
with a dry impertinence which, in another mood,
poor Rosier would have admired.

"Of course I pretend she'd marry well in marrying me. She could n't marry a man who loves her
more — or whom, I may venture to add, she loves
more."

"I'm not bound to accept your theories as to whom
my daughter loves" — and Osmond looked up with
a quick, cold smile.

"I'm not theorising. Your daughter has spoken."

"Not to me," Osmond continued, now bending
forward a little and dropping his eyes to his boot-toes.

"I have her promise, sir!" cried Rosier with the
sharpness of exasperation.

As their voices had been pitched very low before, such a note attracted some attention from the company. Osmond waited till this little movement had subsided; then he said, all undisturbed: "I think she has no recollection of having given it."

They had been standing with their faces to the fire, and after he had uttered these last words the master of the house turned round again to the room. Before Rosier had time to reply he perceived that a gentleman — a stranger — had just come in, unannounced, according to the Roman custom, and was about to present himself to his host. The latter smiled blandly, but somewhat blankly; the visitor had a handsome face and a large, fair beard, and was evidently an Englishman.

"You apparently don't recognise me," he said with a smile that expressed more than Osmond's.

"Ah yes, now I do. I expected so little to see you."

Rosier departed and went in direct pursuit of Pansy. He sought her, as usual, in the neighbouring room, but he again encountered Mrs. Osmond in his path. He gave his hostess no greeting — he was too righteously indignant, but said to her crudely: "Your husband's awfully cold-blooded."

She gave the same mystical smile he had noticed before. "You can't expect every one to be as hot as yourself."

"I don't pretend to be cold, but I'm cool. What has he been doing to his daughter?"

"I've no idea."

"Don't you take any interest?" Rosier demanded with his sense that she too was irritating.

For a moment she answered nothing; then, "No!" she said abruptly and with a quickened light in her eyes which directly contradicted the word.

"Pardon me if I don't believe that. Where's Miss Osmond?"

"In the corner, making tea. Please leave her there."

Rosier instantly discovered his friend, who had been hidden by intervening groups. He watched her, but her own attention was entirely given to her occupation. "What on earth has he done to her?" he asked again imploringly. "He declares to me she has given me up."

"She has not given you up," Isabel said in a low tone and without looking at him.

"Ah, thank you for that! Now I'll leave her alone as long as you think proper!"

He had hardly spoken when he saw her change colour, and became aware that Osmond was coming toward her accompanied by the gentleman who had just entered. He judged the latter, in spite of the advantage of good looks and evident social experience, a little embarrassed. "Isabel," said her husband, "I bring you an old friend."

Mrs. Osmond's face, though it wore a smile, was, like her old friend's, not perfectly confident. "I'm very happy to see Lord Warburton," she said. Rosier turned away and, now that his talk with her had been interrupted, felt absolved from the little pledge he had just taken. He had a quick impression that Mrs. Osmond would n't notice what he did.

Isabel in fact, to do him justice, for some time quite ceased to observe him. She had been startled;

she hardly knew if she felt a pleasure or a pain. Lord Warburton, however, now that he was face to face with her, was plainly quite sure of his own sense of the matter; though his grey eyes had still their fine original property of keeping recognition and attestation strictly sincere. He was " heavier " than of yore and looked older; he stood there very solidly and sensibly.

"I suppose you did n't expect to see me," he said; "I 've but just arrived. Literally, I only got here this evening. You see I 've lost no time in coming to pay you my respects. I knew you were at home on Thursdays."

"You see the fame of your Thursdays has spread to England," Osmond remarked to his wife.

"It 's very kind of Lord Warburton to come so soon; we 're greatly flattered," Isabel said.

"Ah well, it 's better than stopping in one of those horrible inns," Osmond went on.

"The hotel seems very good; I think it 's the same at which I saw you four years since. You know it was here in Rome that we first met; it 's a long time ago. Do you remember where I bade you good-bye ? " his lordship asked of his hostess. "It was in the Capitol, in the first room."

"I remember that myself," said Osmond. "I was there at the time."

"Yes, I remember you there. I was very sorry to leave Rome — so sorry that, somehow or other, it became almost a dismal memory, and I 've never cared to come back till to-day. But I knew you were living here," her old friend went on to Isabel, " and I assure you I've often thought of you. It must be a charming place to live in," he added with a look, round him, at her established home, in which she might have caught the dim ghost of his old ruefulness.

"We should have been glad to see you at any time," Osmond observed with propriety.

"Thank you very much. I have n't been out of England since then. Till a month ago I really supposed my travels over."

"I've heard of you from time to time," said Isabel, who had already, with her rare capacity for such inward feats, taken the measure of what meeting him again meant for her.

"I hope you 've heard no harm. My life has been a remarkably complete blank."

"Like the good reigns in history," Osmond suggested. He appeared to think his duties as a host now terminated — he had performed them so conscientiously. Nothing could have been more adequate, more nicely measured, than his courtesy to his wife's old friend. It was punctilious, it was explicit, it was everything but natural — a deficiency which Lord Warburton, who, himself, had on the whole a good deal of nature, may be supposed to have perceived. "I 'll leave you and Mrs. Osmond together," he added. "You have reminiscences into which I don't enter."

"I 'm afraid you lose a good deal!" Lord Warburton called after him, as he moved away, in a tone which perhaps betrayed overmuch an appreciation of his generosity. Then the visitor turned on Isabel the deeper, the deepest, consciousness of his look, which gradually became more serious. "I'm really very glad to see you."

"It's very pleasant. You're very kind."

"Do you know that you're changed — a little?"

She just hesitated. "Yes — a good deal."

"I don't mean for the worse, of course; and yet how can I say for the better?"

"I think I shall have no scruple in saying that to *you*," she bravely returned.

"Ah well, for me — it's a long time. It would be a pity there should n't be something to show for it." They sat down and she asked him about his sisters, with other enquiries of a somewhat perfunctory kind. He answered her questions as if they interested him, and in a few moments she saw — or believed she saw — that he would press with less of his whole weight than of yore. Time had breathed upon his heart and, without chilling it, given it a relieved sense of having taken the air. Isabel felt her usual esteem for Time rise at a bound. Her friend's manner was certainly that of a contented man, one who would rather like people, or like her at least, to know him for such. "There's something I must tell you without more delay," he resumed. "I've brought Ralph Touchett with me."

"Brought him with you?" Isabel's surprise was great.

"He's at the hotel; he was too tired to come out and has gone to bed."

"I'll go to see him," she immediately said.

"That's exactly what I hoped you'd do. I had an idea you had n't seen much of him since your marriage, that in fact your relations were a — a little more formal. That's why I hesitated — like an awkward Briton."

"I'm as fond of Ralph as ever," Isabel answered. "But why has he come to Rome?" The declaration was very gentle, the question a little sharp.

"Because he's very far gone, Mrs. Osmond."

"Rome then is no place for him. I heard from him that he had determined to give up his custom of wintering abroad and to remain in England, indoors, in what he called an artificial climate."

"Poor fellow, he does n't succeed with the artificial! I went to see him three weeks ago, at Gardencourt, and found him thoroughly ill. He has been getting worse every year, and now he has no strength left. He smokes no more cigarettes! He had got up an artificial climate indeed; the house was as hot as Calcutta. Nevertheless he had suddenly taken it into his head to start for Sicily. I did n't believe in it — neither did the doctors, nor any of his friends. His mother, as I suppose you know, is in America, so there was no one to prevent him. He stuck to his idea that it would be the saving of him to spend the winter at Catania. He said he could take servants and furniture, could make himself comfortable, but in point of fact he has n't brought anything. I wanted him at least to go by sea, to save fatigue; but he said he hated the sea and wished to stop at Rome. After that, though I thought it all rubbish, I made up my mind to come with him. I'm acting as — what do you call it in America? — as a kind of moderator. Poor Ralph's very moderate now. We left England a fortnight ago, and he has been very bad on the way. He can't keep warm, and the further south we come the more he feels the cold. He has got rather a good man, but I'm afraid he's beyond human help. I wanted him to take with him some clever fellow — I mean some sharp young doctor; but he would n't hear of it. If you don't mind my saying so, I think it was a most extraordinary time for Mrs. Touchett to decide on going to America."

Isabel had listened eagerly; her face was full of pain and wonder. "My aunt does that at fixed periods and lets nothing turn her aside. When the date comes round she starts; I think she'd have started if Ralph had been dying."

"I sometimes think he *is* dying," Lord Warburton said.

Isabel sprang up. "I'll go to him then now."

He checked her; he was a little disconcerted at the quick effect of his words. "I don't mean I thought so to-night. On the contrary, to-day, in the train, he seemed particularly well; the idea of our reaching Rome — he's very fond of Rome, you know — gave him strength. An hour ago, when I bade him good-night, he told me he was very tired, but very happy. Go to him in the morning; that's all I mean. I did n't tell him I was coming here; I did n't decide to till after we had separated. Then I remembered he had told me you had an evening, and that it was this very Thursday. It occurred to me to come in and tell you he's here, and let you know you had perhaps better not wait for him to call. I think he said he had n't written to you." There was no need of Isabel's declaring that she would act upon Lord Warburton's information; she looked, as she sat there, like a winged creature held back. "Let alone that I wanted to see you for myself," her visitor gallantly added.

"I don't understand Ralph's plan; it seems to me very wild," she said. "I was glad to think of him between those thick walls at Gardencourt."

"He was completely alone there; the thick walls were his only company."

"You went to see him; you've been extremely kind."

"Oh dear, I had nothing to do," said Lord Warburton.

"We hear, on the contrary, that you're doing great things. Every one speaks of you as a great statesman, and I'm perpetually seeing your name in the *Times*, which, by the way, does n't appear to hold it in reverence. You're apparently as wild a radical as ever."

"I don't feel nearly so wild; you know the world has come round to me. Touchett and I have kept up a sort of parliamentary debate all the way from London. I tell him he 's the last of the Tories, and he calls me the King of the Goths — says I have, down to the details of my personal appearance, every sign of the brute. So you see there 's life in him yet."

Isabel had many questions to ask about Ralph, but she abstained from asking them all. She would see for herself on the morrow. She perceived that after a little Lord Warburton would tire of that subject — he had a conception of other possible topics. She was more and more able to say to herself that he had recovered, and, what is more to the point, she was able to say it without bitterness. He had been for her, of old, such an image of urgency, of insistence, of something to be resisted and reasoned with, that his reappearance at first menaced her with a new trouble. But she was now reassured; she could see he only wished to live with her on good terms, that she was to understand he had forgiven her and was incapable of the bad taste of making pointed allusions. This was not a form of revenge, of course; she had no suspicion of his wishing to punish her by an exhibition of disillusionment; she did him the justice to believe it had simply occurred to him that she would now take a good-natured interest in knowing he was resigned. It was the resignation of a healthy, manly nature, in which sentimental wounds could never fester. British politics had cured him; she had known they would. She gave an envious thought to the happier lot of men, who are always free to plunge into the healing waters of action. Lord Warburton of course spoke of the past, but he spoke of it without implications; he even went so far as to allude to their former meeting in Rome as a very jolly time. And he told her he had been immensely interested in hearing of her marriage and that it was a great pleasure for him to make Mr. Osmond's acquaintance — since he could hardly be said to have made it on the other occasion. He had not written to her at the time of that passage in her history, but he did n't apologise to her for this. The only thing he implied was that they were old friends, intimate friends. It was very much as an intimate friend that he said to her, suddenly, after a short pause which he had occupied in smiling, as he looked about him, like a person amused, at a provincial entertainment, by some innocent game of guesses —

"Well now, I suppose you're very happy and all that sort of thing?"

Isabel answered with a quick laugh; the tone of his remark struck her almost as the accent of comedy. "Do you suppose if I were not I'd tell you?"

"Well, I don't know. I don't see why not."

"I do then. Fortunately, however, I'm very happy."

"You've got an awfully good house."

"Yes, it's very pleasant. But that's not my merit — it's my husband's."

"You mean he has arranged it?"

"Yes, it was nothing when we came."

"He must be very clever."

"He has a genius for upholstery," said Isabel.

"There's a great rage for that sort of thing now. But you must have a taste of your own."

"I enjoy things when they're done, but I've no ideas. I can never propose anything."

"Do you mean you accept what others propose?"

"Very willingly, for the most part."

"That's a good thing to know. I shall propose to you something."

"It will be very kind. I must say, however, that I've in a few small ways a certain initiative. I should like for instance to introduce you to some of these people."

"Oh, please don't; I prefer sitting here. Unless it be to that young lady in the blue dress. She has a charming face."

131

"The one talking to the rosy young man? That's my husband's daughter."

"Lucky man, your husband. What a dear little maid!"

"You must make her acquaintance."

"In a moment — with pleasure. I like looking at her from here." He ceased to look at her, however, very soon; his eyes constantly reverted to Mrs. Osmond. "Do you know I was wrong just now in saying you had changed?" he presently went on. "You seem to me, after all, very much the same."

"And yet I find it a great change to be married," said Isabel with mild gaiety.

"It affects most people more than it has affected you. You see I have n't gone in for that."

"It rather surprises me."

"You ought to understand it, Mrs. Osmond. But I do want to marry," he added more simply.

"It ought to be very easy," Isabel said, rising — after which she reflected, with a pang perhaps too visible, that she was hardly the person to say this. It was perhaps because Lord Warburton divined the pang that he generously forbore to call her attention to her not having contributed then to the facility.

Edward Rosier had meanwhile seated himself on an ottoman beside Pansy's tea-table. He pretended at first to talk to her about trifles, and she asked him who was the new gentleman conversing with her stepmother.

"He's an English lord," said Rosier. "I don't know more."

"I wonder if he 'll have some tea. The English are so fond of tea."

"Never mind that; I 've something particular to say to you."

"Don't speak so loud — every one will hear," said Pansy.

"They won't hear if you continue to look that way: as if your only thought in life was the wish the kettle would boil."

"It has just been filled; the servants never know!" — and she sighed with the weight of her responsibility.

"Do you know what your father said to me just now? That you did n't mean what you said a week ago."

"I don't mean everything I say. How can a young girl do that? But I mean what I say to *you*."

"He told me you had forgotten me."

"Ah no, I don't forget," said Pansy, showing her pretty teeth in a fixed smile.

"Then everything 's just the very same?"

"Ah no, not the very same. Papa has been terribly severe."

"What has he done to you?"

"He asked me what *you* had done to me, and I told him everything. Then he forbade me to marry you."

"You need n't mind that."

"Oh yes, I must indeed. I can't disobey papa."

"Not for one who loves you as I do, and whom you pretend to love?"

She raised the lid of the tea-pot, gazing into this

vessel for a moment; then she dropped six words into its aromatic depths. "I love you just as much."

"What good will that do me?"

"Ah," said Pansy, raising her sweet, vague eyes, "I don't know that."

"You disappoint me," groaned poor Rosier.

She was silent a little; she handed a tea-cup to a servant. "Please don't talk any more."

"Is this to be all my satisfaction?"

"Papa said I was not to talk with you."

"Do you sacrifice me like that? Ah, it's too much!"

"I wish you'd wait a little," said the girl in a voice just distinct enough to betray a quaver.

"Of course I'll wait if you'll give me hope. But you take my life away."

"I'll not give you up — oh no!" Pansy went on.

"He'll try and make you marry some one else."

"I'll never do that."

"What then are we to wait for?"

She hesitated again. "I'll speak to Mrs. Osmond and she'll help us." It was in this manner that she for the most part designated her stepmother.

"She won't help us much. She's afraid."

"Afraid of what?"

"Of your father, I suppose."

Pansy shook her little head. "She's not afraid of any one. We must have patience."

"Ah, that's an awful word," Rosier groaned; he was deeply disconcerted. Oblivious of the customs of good society, he dropped his head into his hands and, supporting it with a melancholy grace, sat staring at the carpet. Presently he became aware of a good deal of movement about him and, as he looked up, saw Pansy making a curtsey — it was still her little curtsey of the convent — to the English lord whom Mrs. Osmond had introduced.

XXXIX

It will probably not surprise the reflective reader that Ralph Touchett should have seen less of his cousin since her marriage than he had done before that event — an event of which he took such a view as could hardly prove a confirmation of intimacy. He had uttered his thought, as we know, and after this had held his peace, Isabel not having invited him to resume a discussion which marked an era in their relations. That discussion had made a difference — the difference he feared rather than the one he hoped. It had not chilled the girl's zeal in carrying out her engagement, but it had come dangerously near to spoiling a friendship. No reference was ever again made between them to Ralph's opinion of Gilbert Osmond, and by surrounding this topic with a sacred silence they managed to preserve a semblance of reciprocal frankness. But there was a difference, as Ralph often said to himself — there was a difference. She had not forgiven him, she never would forgive him: that was all he had gained. She thought she had forgiven him; she believed she did n't care; and as she was both very generous and very proud these convictions represented a certain reality. But whether or no the event should justify him he would virtually have done her a wrong, and the wrong was of the sort that women remember best. As Osmond's wife she could never again be his friend. If in this character she

should enjoy the felicity she expected, she would have
nothing but contempt for the man who had attempted,
in advance, to undermine a blessing so dear; and if
on the other hand his warning should be justified the
vow she had taken that he should never know it would
lay upon her spirit such a burden as to make her hate
him. So dismal had been, during the year that followed his cousin's marriage, Ralph's prevision of the
future; and if his meditations appear morbid we
must remember he was not in the bloom of health.
He consoled himself as he might by behaving (as he
deemed) beautifully, and was present at the ceremony
by which Isabel was united to Mr. Osmond, and
which was performed in Florence in the month of June.
He learned from his mother that Isabel at first had
thought of celebrating her nuptials in her native land,
but that as simplicity was what she chiefly desired
to secure she had finally decided, in spite of Osmond's
professed willingness to make a journey of any length,
that this characteristic would be best embodied in
their being married by the nearest clergyman in the
shortest time. The thing was done therefore at the
little American chapel, on a very hot day, in the presence only of Mrs. Touchett and her son, of Pansy
Osmond and the Countess Gemini. That severity in
the proceedings of which I just spoke was in part the
result of the absence of two persons who might have
been looked for on the occasion and who would have
lent it a certain richness. Madame Merle had been
invited, but Madame Merle, who was unable to leave
Rome, had written a gracious letter of excuses. Henrietta Stackpole had not been invited, as her depart-

ure from America, announced to Isabel by Mr. Goodwood, was in fact frustrated by the duties of her profession; but she had sent a letter, less gracious than
Madame Merle's, intimating that, had she been able
to cross the Atlantic, she would have been present
not only as a witness but as a critic. Her return to
Europe had taken place somewhat later, and she had
effected a meeting with Isabel in the autumn, in Paris,
when she had indulged — perhaps a trifle too freely
— her critical genius. Poor Osmond, who was chiefly
the subject of it, had protested so sharply that Henrietta was obliged to declare to Isabel that she had
taken a step which put a barrier between them. "It
is n't in the least that you 've married — it is that you
have married *him*," she had deemed it her duty to
remark; agreeing, it will be seen, much more with
Ralph Touchett than she suspected, though she had
few of his hesitations and compunctions. Henrietta's
second visit to Europe, however, was not apparently
to have been made in vain; for just at the moment
when Osmond had declared to Isabel that he really
must object to that newspaper-woman, and Isabel
had answered that it seemed to her he took Henrietta
too hard, the good Mr. Bantling had appeared upon
the scene and proposed that they should take a run
down to Spain. Henrietta's letters from Spain had
proved the most acceptable she had yet published,
and there had been one in especial, dated from the
Alhambra and entitled 'Moors and Moonlight,' which
generally passed for her masterpiece. Isabel had been
secretly disappointed at her husband's not seeing his
way simply to take the poor girl for funny. She even

wondered if his sense of fun, or of the funny — which would be his sense of humour, would n't it? — were by chance defective. Of course she herself looked at the matter as a person whose present happiness had nothing to grudge to Henrietta's violated conscience. Osmond had thought their alliance a kind of monstrosity; he could n't imagine what they had in common. For him, Mr. Bantling's fellow tourist was simply the most vulgar of women, and he had also pronounced her the most abandoned. Against this latter clause of the verdict Isabel had appealed with an ardour that had made him wonder afresh at the oddity of some of his wife's tastes. Isabel could explain it only by saying that she liked to know people who were as different as possible from herself. "Why then don't you make the acquaintance of your washerwoman?" Osmond had enquired; to which Isabel had answered that she was afraid her washerwoman would n't care for her. Now Henrietta cared so much.

Ralph had seen nothing of her for the greater part of the two years that had followed her marriage; the winter that formed the beginning of her residence in Rome he had spent again at San Remo, where he had been joined in the spring by his mother, who afterwards had gone with him to England, to see what they were doing at the bank — an operation she could n't induce him to perform. Ralph had taken a lease of his house at San Remo, a small villa which he had occupied still another winter; but late in the month of April of this second year he had come down to Rome. It was the first time since her marriage that

he had stood face to face with Isabel; his desire to see
her again was then of the keenest. She had written
to him from time to time, but her letters told him
nothing he wanted to know. He had asked his mother
what she was making of her life, and his mother had
simply answered that she supposed she was making
the best of it. Mrs. Touchett had not the imagination
that communes with the unseen, and she now pretended to no intimacy with her niece, whom she rarely
encountered. This young woman appeared to be
living in a sufficiently honourable way, but Mrs.
Touchett still remained of the opinion that her marriage had been a shabby affair. It had given her no
pleasure to think of Isabel's establishment, which
she was sure was a very lame business. From time
to time, in Florence, she rubbed against the Countess
Gemini, doing her best always to minimise the con-
tact; and the Countess reminded her of Osmond,
who made her think of Isabel. The Countess was less
talked of in these days; but Mrs. Touchett augured
no good of that: it only proved how she had been
talked of before. There was a more direct suggestion of Isabel in the person of Madame Merle; but
Madame Merle's relations with Mrs. Touchett had
undergone a perceptible change. Isabel's aunt had
told her, without circumlocution, that she had played
too ingenious a part; and Madame Merle, who never
quarrelled with any one, who appeared to think no
one worth it, and who had performed the miracle of
living, more or less, for several years with Mrs. Touchett and showing no symptom of irritation — Madame Merle now took a very high tone and declared

that this was an accusation from which she could n't stoop to defend herself. She added, however (without stooping), that her behaviour had been only too simple, that she had believed only what she saw, that she saw Isabel was not eager to marry and Osmond not eager to please (his repeated visits had been nothing; he was boring himself to death on his hill-top and he came merely for amusement). Isabel had kept her sentiments to herself, and her journey to Greece and Egypt had effectually thrown dust in her companion's eyes. Madame Merle accepted the event — she was unprepared to think of it as a scandal; but that she had played any part in it, double or single, was an imputation against which she proudly protested. It was doubtless in consequence of Mrs. Touchett's attitude, and of the injury it offered to habits consecrated by many charming seasons, that Madame Merle had, after this, chosen to pass many months in England, where her credit was quite unimpaired. Mrs. Touchett had done her a wrong; there are some things that can't be forgiven. But Madame Merle suffered in silence; there was always something exquisite in her dignity.

Ralph, as I say, had wished to see for himself; but while engaged in this pursuit he had yet felt afresh what a fool he had been to put the girl on her guard. He had played the wrong card, and now he had lost the game. He should see nothing, he should learn nothing; for him she would always wear a mask. His true line would have been to profess delight in her union, so that later, when, as Ralph phrased it, the bottom should fall out of it, she might have the pleasure of saying to him that he had been a goose. He would gladly have consented to pass for a goose in order to know Isabel's real situation. At present, however, she neither taunted him with his fallacies nor pretended that her own confidence was justified; if she wore a mask it completely covered her face. There was something fixed and mechanical in the serenity painted on it; this was not an expression, Ralph said—it was a representation, it was even an advertisement. She had lost her child; that was a sorrow, but it was a sorrow she scarcely spoke of; there was more to say about it than she could say to Ralph. It belonged to the past, moreover; it had occurred six months before and she had already laid aside the tokens of mourning. She appeared to be leading the life of the world; Ralph heard her spoken of as having a "charming position." He observed that she produced the impression of being peculiarly enviable, that it was supposed, among many people, to be a privilege even to know her. Her house was not open to every one, and she had an evening in the week to which people were not invited as a matter of course. She lived with a certain magnificence, but you needed to be a member of her circle to perceive it; for there was nothing to gape at, nothing to criticise, nothing even to admire, in the daily proceedings of Mr. and Mrs. Osmond. Ralph, in all this, recognised the hand of the master; for he knew that Isabel had no faculty for producing studied impressions. She struck him as having a great love of movement, of gaiety, of late hours, of long rides, of fatigue; an eagerness to be entertained, to be interested, even to be bored, to make acquaintances, to see people who were talked about, to explore the neighbourhood of Rome, to enter into relation with certain of the mustiest relics of its old society. In all this there was much less discrimination than in that desire for comprehensiveness of development on which he had been used to exercise his wit. There was a kind of violence in some of her impulses, of crudity in some of her experiments, which took him by surprise: it seemed to him that she even spoke faster, moved faster, breathed faster, than before her marriage. Certainly she had fallen into exaggerations — she who used to care so much for the pure truth; and whereas of old she had a great delight in good-humoured argument, in intellectual play (she never looked so charming as when in the genial heat of discussion she received a crushing blow full in the face and brushed it away as a feather), she appeared now to think there was nothing worth people's either differing about or agreeing upon. Of old she had been curious, and now she was indifferent, and yet in spite of her indifference her activity was greater than ever. Slender still, but lovelier than before, she had gained no great maturity of aspect; yet there was an amplitude and a brilliancy in her personal arrangements that gave a touch of insolence to her beauty. Poor human-hearted Isabel, what perversity had bitten her? Her light step drew a mass of drapery behind it; her intelligent head sustained a majesty of ornament. The free, keen girl had become quite another person; what he saw was the fine lady who was supposed to represent something. What did Isabel represent? Ralph asked himself; and he could only answer by saying that she represented Gilbert Osmond. "Good heavens, what a function!" he then woefully exclaimed. He was lost in wonder at the mystery of things.

He recognised Osmond, as I say; he recognised him at every turn. He saw how he kept all things within limits; how he adjusted, regulated, animated their manner of life. Osmond was in his element; at last he had material to work with. He always had an eye to effect, and his effects were deeply calculated. They were produced by no vulgar means, but the motive was as vulgar as the art was great. To surround his interior with a sort of invidious sanctity, to tantalise society with a sense of exclusion, to make people believe his house was different from every other, to impart to the face that he presented to the world a cold originality — this was the ingenious effort of the personage to whom Isabel had attributed a superior morality. "He works with superior material," Ralph said to himself; "it's rich abundance compared with his former resources." Ralph was a clever man; but Ralph had never — to his own sense — been so clever as when he observed, *in petto*, that under the guise of caring only for intrinsic values Osmond lived exclusively for the world. Far from being its master as he pretended to be, he was its very humble servant, and the degree of its attention was his only measure of success. He lived with his eye on it from morning till night, and the world was so stupid it never suspected the trick. Everything he did was *pose* — *pose* so subtly considered that if one were not on the lookout one mistook it for impulse. Ralph had never met a man who lived so much in the land of consideration. His tastes, his studies, his accomplishments, his collections, were all for a purpose. His life on his hill-top at Florence had been the conscious attitude of years. His solitude, his ennui, his love for his daughter, his good manners, his bad manners, were so many features of a mental image constantly present to him as a model of impertinence and mystification. His ambition was not to please the world, but to please himself by exciting the world's curiosity and then declining to satisfy it. It had made him feel great, ever, to play the world a trick. The thing he had done in his life most directly to please himself was his marrying Miss Archer; though in this case indeed the gullible world was in a manner embodied in poor Isabel, who had been mystified to the top of her bent. Ralph of course found a fitness in being consistent; he had embraced a creed, and as he had suffered for it he could not in honour forsake it. I give this little sketch of its articles for what they may at the time have been worth. It was certain that he was very skilful in fitting the facts to his theory — even the fact that during the month he spent in Rome at this period the husband of the woman he loved appeared to regard him not in the least as an enemy.

For Gilbert Osmond Ralph had not now that importance. It was not that he had the importance of a friend; it was rather that he had none at all. He was Isabel's cousin and he was rather unpleasantly ill — it was on this basis that Osmond treated with him. He made the proper enquiries, asked about his health, about Mrs. Touchett, about his opinion of winter climates, whether he were comfortable at his hotel. He addressed him, on the few occasions of their meeting, not a word that was not necessary; but his manner had always the urbanity proper to conscious success in the presence of conscious failure. For all this, Ralph had had, toward the end, a sharp inward vision of Osmond's making it of small ease to his wife that she should continue to receive Mr. Touchett. He was not jealous — he had not that excuse; no one could be jealous of Ralph. But he made Isabel pay for her old-time kindness, of which so much was still left; and as Ralph had no idea of her paying too much, so when his suspicion had become sharp, he had taken himself off. In doing so he had deprived Isabel of a very interesting occupation: she had been constantly wondering what fine principle was keeping him alive. She had decided that it was his love of conversation; his conversation had been better than ever. He had given up walking; he was no longer a humorous stroller. He sat all day in a chair — almost any chair would serve, and was so dependent on what you would do for him that, had not his talk been highly contemplative, you might have thought he was blind. The reader already knows more about him than Isabel was ever to know, and the reader may therefore be given the key to the mystery. What kept Ralph alive was simply the fact that he had not yet seen enough of the person in the world in whom he was most interested: he was not yet satisfied. There was more to come; he could n't make up his mind to lose that. He wanted to see what she would make of her husband — or what her husband would make of her. This was only the first act of the drama, and he was determined to sit out the performance. His determination had held good; it had kept him going some eighteen months more, till the time of his return to Rome with Lord Warburton. It had given him indeed such an air of intending to live indefinitely that Mrs. Touchett, though more accessible to confusions of thought in the matter of this strange, unremunerative — and unremunerated — son of hers than she had ever been before, had, as we have learned, not scrupled to embark for a distant land. If Ralph had been kept alive by suspense it was with a good deal of the same emotion — the excitement of wondering in what state she should˙find him — that Isabel mounted to his apartment the day after Lord Warburton had notified her of his arrival in Rome.

She spent an hour with him; it was the first of several visits. Gilbert Osmond called on him punctually, and on their sending their carriage for him Ralph came more than once to Palazzo Roccanera. A fortnight elapsed, at the end of which Ralph announced to Lord Warburton that he thought after all he would n't go to Sicily. The two men had been dining together after a day spent by the latter in ranging about the Campagna. They had left the table, and Warburton, before the chimney, was lighting a cigar, which he instantly removed from his lips.

"Won't go to Sicily? Where then will you go?"

"Well, I guess I won't go anywhere," said Ralph, from the sofa, all shamelessly.

"Do you mean you'll return to England?"

"Oh dear no; I'll stay in Rome."

"Rome won't do for you. Rome's not warm enough."

"It will have to do. I'll make it do. See how well I've been."

Lord Warburton looked at him a while, puffing a cigar and as if trying to see it. "You've been better than you were on the journey, certainly. I wonder how you lived through that. But I don't understand your condition. I recommend you to try Sicily."

"I can't try," said poor Ralph. "I've done trying. I can't move further. I can't face that journey. Fancy me between Scylla and Charybdis! I don't want to die on the Sicilian plains—to be snatched away, like Proserpine in the same locality, to the Plutonian shades."

"What the deuce then did you come for?" his lordship enquired.

"Because the idea took me. I see it won't do. It really does n't matter where I am now. I've exhausted all remedies, I've swallowed all climates. As I'm here I'll stay. I have n't a single cousin in Sicily — much less a married one."

"Your cousin's certainly an inducement. But what does the doctor say?"

"I have n't asked him, and I don't care a fig. If I die here Mrs. Osmond will bury me. But I shall not die here."

"I hope not." Lord Warburton continued to smoke

reflectively. "Well, I must say," he resumed, "for myself I'm very glad you don't insist on Sicily. I had a horror of that journey."

"Ah, but for you it need n't have mattered. I had no idea of dragging you in my train."

"I certainly did n't mean to let you go alone."

"My dear Warburton, I never expected you to come further than this," Ralph cried.

"I should have gone with you and seen you settled," said Lord Warburton.

"You're a very good Christian. You're a very kind man."

"Then I should have come back here."

"And then you'd have gone to England."

"No, no; I should have stayed."

"Well," said Ralph, "if that's what we are both up to, I don't see where Sicily comes in!"

His companion was silent; he sat staring at the fire. At last, looking up, "I say, tell me this," he broke out; "did you really mean to go to Sicily when we started?"

"Ah, *vous m'en demandez trop!* Let me put a question first. Did you come with me quite — platonically?"

"I don't know what you mean by that. I wanted to come abroad."

"I suspect we've each been playing our little game."

"Speak for yourself. I made no secret whatever of my desiring to be here a while."

"Yes, I remember you said you wished to see the Minister of Foreign Affairs."

"I've seen him three times. He's very amusing."

"I think you've forgotten what you came for," said Ralph.

"Perhaps I have," his companion answered rather gravely.

These two were gentlemen of a race which is not distinguished by the absence of reserve, and they had travelled together from London to Rome without an allusion to matters that were uppermost in the mind of each. There was an old subject they had once discussed, but it had lost its recognised place in their attention, and even after their arrival in Rome, where many things led back to it, they had kept the same half-diffident, half-confident silence.

"I recommend you to get the doctor's consent, all the same," Lord Warburton went on, abruptly, after an interval.

"The doctor's consent will spoil it. I never have it when I can help it."

"What then does Mrs. Osmond think?" Ralph's friend demanded.

"I've not told her. She'll probably say that Rome's too cold and even offer to go with me to Catania. She's capable of that."

"In your place I should like it."

"Her husband won't like it."

"Ah well, I can fancy that; though it seems to me you're not bound to mind his likings. They're his affair."

"I don't want to make any more trouble between them," said Ralph.

"Is there so much already?"

"There's complete preparation for it. Her going

off with me would make the explosion. Osmond is n't fond of his wife's cousin."

"Then of course he'd make a row. But won't he make a row if you stop here?"

"That's what I want to see. He made one the last time I was in Rome, and then I thought it my duty to disappear. Now I think it's my duty to stop and defend her."

"My dear Touchett, your defensive powers —!" Lord Warburton began with a smile. But he saw something in his companion's face that checked him. "Your duty, in these premises, seems to me rather a nice question," he observed instead.

Ralph for a short time answered nothing. "It's true that my defensive powers are small," he returned at last; "but as my aggressive ones are still smaller Osmond may after all not think me worth his gunpowder. At any rate," he added, "there are things I'm curious to see."

"You're sacrificing your health to your curiosity then?"

"I'm not much interested in my health, and I'm deeply interested in Mrs. Osmond."

"So am I. But not as I once was," Lord Warburton added quickly. This was one of the allusions he had not hitherto found occasion to make.

"Does she strike you as very happy?" Ralph enquired, emboldened by this confidence.

"Well, I don't know; I've hardly thought. She told me the other night she was happy."

"Ah, she told *you*, of course," Ralph exclaimed, smiling.

"I don't know that. It seems to me I was rather the sort of person she might have complained to."

"Complained? She'll never complain. She has done it — what she *has* done — and she knows it. She'll complain to you least of all. She's very careful."

"She need n't be. I don't mean to make love to her again."

"I'm delighted to hear it. There can be no doubt at least of *your* duty."

"Ah no," said Lord Warburton gravely; "none!"

"Permit me to ask," Ralph went on, "whether it's to bring out the fact that you don't mean to make love to her that you're so very civil to the little girl?"

Lord Warburton gave a slight start; he got up and stood before the fire, looking at it hard. "Does that strike you as very ridiculous?"

"Ridiculous? Not in the least, if you really like her."

"I think her a delightful little person. I don't know when a girl of that age has pleased me more."

"She's a charming creature. Ah, she at least is genuine."

"Of course there's the difference in our ages — more than twenty years."

"My dear Warburton," said Ralph, "are you serious?"

"Perfectly serious — as far as I've got."

"I'm very glad. And, heaven help us," cried Ralph, "how cheered-up old Osmond will be!"

His companion frowned. "I say, don't spoil it. I should n't propose for his daughter to please *him*."

"He'll have the perversity to be pleased all the same."

"He's not so fond of me as that," said his lordship.

"As that? My dear Warburton, the drawback of your position is that people need n't be fond of you at all to wish to be connected with you. Now, with me in such a case, I should have the happy confidence that they loved me."

Lord Warburton seemed scarcely in the mood for doing justice to general axioms — he was thinking of a special case. "Do you judge she'll be pleased?"

"The girl herself? Delighted, surely."

"No, no; I mean Mrs. Osmond."

Ralph looked at him a moment. "My dear fellow, what has she to do with it?"

"Whatever she chooses. She's very fond of Pansy."

"Very true — very true." And Ralph slowly got up. "It's an interesting question — how far her fondness for Pansy will carry her." He stood there a moment with his hands in his pockets and rather a clouded brow. "I hope, you know, that you're very — very sure. The deuce!" he broke off. "I don't know how to say it."

"Yes, you do; you know how to say everything."

"Well, it's awkward. I hope you're sure that among Miss Osmond's merits her being — a — so near her stepmother is n't a leading one?"

"Good heavens, Touchett!" cried Lord Warburton angrily, "for what do you take me?"

XL

Isabel had not seen much of Madame Merle since her marriage, this lady having indulged in frequent absences from Rome. At one time she had spent six months in England; at another she had passed a portion of a winter in Paris. She had made numerous visits to distant friends and gave countenance to the idea that for the future she should be a less inveterate Roman than in the past. As she had been inveterate in the past only in the sense of constantly having an apartment in one of the sunniest niches of the Pincian — an apartment which often stood empty — this suggested a prospect of almost constant absence; a danger which Isabel at one period had been much inclined to deplore. Familiarity had modified in some degree her first impression of Madame Merle, but it had not essentially altered it; there was still much wonder of admiration in it. That personage was armed at all points; it was a pleasure to see a character so completely equipped for the social battle. She carried her flag discreetly, but her weapons were polished steel, and she used them with a skill which struck Isabel as more and more that of a veteran. She was never weary, never overcome with disgust; she never appeared to need rest or consolation. She had her own ideas; she had of old exposed a great many of them to Isabel, who knew also that under an appearance of extreme self-control her highly-cultivated friend concealed a rich sensibility. But her will was mistress of her life; there was something gallant in the way she kept going. It was as if she had learned the secret of it — as if the art of life were some clever trick she had guessed. Isabel, as she herself grew older, became acquainted with revulsions, with disgusts; there were days when the world looked black and she asked herself with some sharpness what it was that she was pretending to live for. Her old habit had been to live by enthusiasm, to fall in love with suddenly-perceived possibilities, with the idea of some new adventure. As a younger person she had been used to proceed from one little exaltation to the other: there were scarcely any dull places between. But Madame Merle had suppressed enthusiasm; she fell in love now-a-days with nothing; she lived entirely by reason and by wisdom. There were hours when Isabel would have given anything for lessons in this art; if her brilliant friend had been near she would have made an appeal to her. She had become aware more than before of the advantage of being like that — of having made one's 'self a firm surface, a sort of corselet of silver.

But, as I say, it was not till the winter during which we lately renewed acquaintance with our heroine that the personage in question made again a continuous stay in Rome. Isabel now saw more of her than she had done since her marriage; but by this time Isabel's needs and inclinations had considerably changed. It was not at present to Madame Merle that she would have applied for instruction; she had lost the desire to know this lady's clever trick. If she had troubles she must keep them to herself, and if life was difficult it would not make it easier to confess herself beaten. Madame Merle was doubtless of great use to herself and an ornament to any circle; but was she — would she be — of use to others in periods of refined embarrassment? The best way to profit by her friend — this indeed Isabel had always thought — was to imitate her, to be as firm and bright as she. She recognised no embarrassments, and Isabel, considering this fact, determined for the fiftieth time to brush aside her own. It seemed to her too, on the renewal of an intercourse which had virtually been interrupted, that her old ally was different was almost detached — pushing to the extreme a certain rather artificial fear of being indiscreet. Ralph Touchett, we know, had been of the opinion that she was prone to exaggeration, to forcing the note — was apt, in the vulgar phrase, to overdo it. Isabel had never admitted this charge — had never indeed quite understood it; Madame Merle's conduct, to her perception, always bore the stamp of good taste, was always "quiet." But in this matter of not wishing to intrude upon the inner life of the Osmond family it at last occurred to our young woman that she overdid a little. That of course was not the best taste; that was rather violent. She remembered too much that Isabel was married; that she had now other interests; that though she, Madame Merle, had known Gilbert Osmond and his little Pansy very well, better almost than any one, she was not after all of the inner circle. She was on her guard; she never spoke of their affairs till she was asked, even pressed — as when her opinion was wanted; she had a dread of seeming to meddle. Madame Merle was as candid as we know, and one day she candidly expressed this dread to Isabel.

"I *must* be on my guard," she said; "I might so easily, without suspecting it, offend you. You would be right to be offended, even if my intention should have been of the purest. I must not forget that I knew your husband long before you did; I must not let that betray me. If you were a silly woman you might be jealous. You 're not a silly woman; I know that perfectly. But neither am I; therefore I 'm determined not to get into trouble. A little harm 's very soon done; a mistake 's made before one knows it. Of course if I had wished to make love to your husband I had ten years to do it in, and nothing to prevent; so it is n't likely I shall begin to-day, when I 'm so much less attractive than I was. But if I were to annoy you by seeming to take a place that does n't belong to me, you would n't make that reflection; you 'd simply say I was forgetting certain differences. I 'm determined not to forget them. Certainly a good friend is n't always thinking of that; one does n't suspect one's friends of injustice. I don't suspect you, my dear, in the least; but I suspect human nature. Don't think I make myself uncomfortable; I 'm not always watching myself. I think I sufficiently prove it in talking to you as I do now. All I wish to say is, however, that if you were to be jealous — that 's the form it would take — I should be sure to think it was a little my fault. It certainly would n't be your husband's."

Isabel had had three years to think over Mrs. Touchett's theory that Madame Merle had made Gilbert Osmond's marriage. We know how she had at first received it. Madame Merle might have made Gilbert Osmond's marriage, but she certainly had not made Isabel Archer's. That was the work of — Isabel scarcely knew what: of nature, providence, fortune, of the eternal mystery of things. It was true her aunt's complaint had been not so much of Madame Merle's activity as of her duplicity: she had brought about the strange event and then she had denied her guilt. Such guilt would not have been great, to Isabel's mind; she could n't make a crime of Madame Merle's having been the producing cause of the most important friendship she had ever formed. This had occurred to her just before her marriage, after her little discussion with her aunt and at a time when she was still capable of that large inward reference, the tone almost of the philosophic historian, to her scant young annals. If Madame Merle had desired her change of state she could only say it had been a very happy thought. With her, moreover, she had been perfectly straightforward; she had never concealed her high opinion of Gilbert Osmond. After their union Isabel discovered that her husband took a less convenient view of the matter; he seldom consented to finger, in talk, this roundest and smoothest bead of their social rosary.

"Don't you like Madame Merle?" Isabel had once said to him. "She thinks a great deal of you."

"I 'll tell you once for all," Osmond had answered. "I liked her once better than I do to-day. I 'm tired of her, and I'm rather ashamed of it. She's so almost unnaturally good! I'm glad she's not in Italy; it makes for relaxation — for a sort of moral *détente*. Don't talk of her too much; it seems to bring her back. She'll come back in plenty of time."

Madame Merle, in fact, had come back before it was too late — too late, I mean, to recover whatever advantage she might have lost. But meantime, if, as I have said, she was sensibly different, Isabel's feelings were also not quite the same. Her consciousness of the situation was as acute as of old, but it was much less satisfying. A dissatisfied mind, whatever else it may miss, is rarely in want of reasons; they bloom as thick as buttercups in June. The fact of Madame Merle's having had a hand in Gilbert Osmond's marriage ceased to be one of her titles to consideration; it might have been written, after all, that there was not so much to thank her for. As time went on there was less and less, and Isabel once said to herself that perhaps without her these things would not have been. That reflection indeed was instantly stifled; she knew an immediate horror at having made it. "Whatever happens to me let me not be unjust," she said; "let me bear my burdens myself and not shift them upon others!" This disposition was tested, eventually, by that ingenious apology for her present conduct which Madame Merle saw fit to make and of which I have given a sketch; for there was something irritating — there was almost an air of mockery — in her neat discriminations and clear convictions. In Isabel's mind to-day there was nothing clear; there was a confusion of regrets, a complication of fears. She felt helpless as she turned away from her friend, who had just made the statements I have quoted: Madame Merle knew so little what she was thinking of! She was herself moreover so unable to explain. Jealous of her — jealous of her with Gilbert? The idea just then suggested no near reality. She almost wished jealousy had been possible; it would have made in a manner for refreshment. Was n't it in a manner one of the symptoms of happiness? Madame Merle, however, was wise, so wise that she might have been pretending to know Isabel better than Isabel knew herself. This young woman had always been fertile in resolutions — many of them of an elevated character; but at no period had they flourished (in the privacy of her heart) more richly than to-day. It is true that they all had a family likeness; they might have been summed up in the determination that if she was to be unhappy it should not be by a fault of her own. Her poor winged spirit had always had a great desire to do its best, and it had not as yet been seriously discouraged. It wished, therefore, to hold fast to justice — not to pay itself by petty revenges. To associate Madame Merle with its disappointment would be a petty revenge — especially as the pleasure to be derived from that would be perfectly insincere. It might feed her sense of bitterness, but it would not loosen her bonds. It was impossible to pretend that she had not acted with her eyes open; if ever a girl was a free agent she had been. A girl in love was doubtless not a free agent; but the sole source of her mistake had been within herself. There had been no plot, no snare; she had looked and considered and chosen.

When a woman had made such a mistake, there was only one way to repair it — just immensely (oh, with the highest grandeur!) to accept it. One folly was enough, especially when it was to last for ever; a second one would not much set it off. In this vow of reticence there was a certain nobleness which kept Isabel going; but Madame Merle had been right, for all that, in taking her precautions.

One day about a month after Ralph Touchett's arrival in Rome Isabel came back from a walk with Pansy. It was not only a part of her general determination to be just that she was at present very thankful for Pansy — it was also a part of her tenderness for things that were pure and weak. Pansy was dear to her, and there was nothing else in her life that had the rightness of the young creature's attachment or the sweetness of her own clearness about it. It was like a soft presence — like a small hand in her own; on Pansy's part it was more than an affection — it was a kind of ardent coercive faith. On her own side her sense of the girl's dependence was more than a pleasure; it operated as a definite reason when motives threatened to fail her. She had said to herself that we must take our duty where we find it, and that we must look for it as much as possible. Pansy's sympathy was a direct admonition; it seemed to say that here was an opportunity, not eminent perhaps, but unmistakeable. Yet an opportunity for what Isabel could hardly have said; in general, to be more for the child than the child was able to be for herself. Isabel could have smiled, in these days, to remember that her little companion had once been ambiguous, for she now perceived that Pansy's ambiguities were simply her own grossness of vision. She had been unable to believe any one could care so much — so extraordinarily much — to please. But since then she had seen this delicate faculty in operation, and now she knew what to think of it. It was the whole creature — it was a sort of genius. Pansy had no pride to interfere with it, and though she was constantly extending her conquests she took no credit for them. The two were constantly together; Mrs. Osmond was rarely seen without her stepdaughter. Isabel liked her company; it had the effect of one's carrying a nosegay composed all of the same flower. And then not to neglect Pansy, not under any provocation to neglect her — this she had made an article of religion. The young girl had every appearance of being happier in Isabel's society than in that of any one save her father, whom she admired with an intensity justified by the fact that, as paternity was an exquisite pleasure to Gilbert Osmond, he had always been luxuriously mild. Isabel knew how Pansy liked to be with her and how she studied the means of pleasing her. She had decided that the best way of pleasing her was negative, and consisted in not giving her trouble — a conviction which certainly could have had no reference to trouble already existing. She was therefore ingeniously passive and almost imaginatively docile; she was careful even to moderate the eagerness with which she assented to Isabel's propositions and which might have implied that she could have thought otherwise. She never interrupted, never asked social questions, and though she delighted in approbation, to the point of turning pale when it came to her, never held out her hand for it. She only looked toward it wistfully — an attitude which, as she grew older, made her eyes the prettiest in the world. When during the second winter at Palazzo Roccanera she began to go to parties, to dances, she always, at a reasonable hour, lest Mrs. Osmond should be tired, was the first to propose departure. Isabel appreciated the sacrifice of the late dances, for she knew her little companion had a passionate pleasure in this exercise, taking her steps to the music like a conscientious fairy. Society, moreover, had no drawbacks for her; she liked even the tiresome parts — the heat of ball-rooms, the dulness of dinners, the crush at the door, the awkward waiting for the carriage. During the day, in this vehicle, beside her stepmother, she sat in a small fixed, appreciative posture, bending forward and faintly smiling, as if she had been taken to drive for the first time.

On the day I speak of they had been driven out of one of the gates of the city and at the end of half an hour had left the carriage to await them by the roadside while they walked away over the short grass of the Campagna, which even in the winter months is sprinkled with delicate flowers. This was almost a daily habit with Isabel, who was fond of a walk and had a swift length of step, though not so swift a one as on her first coming to Europe. It was not the form of exercise that Pansy loved best, but she liked it, because she liked everything; and she moved with a shorter undulation beside her father's wife, who afterwards, on their return to Rome, paid a tribute to her preferences by making the circuit of the Pincian or the Villa Borghese. She had gathered a handful of flowers in a sunny hollow, far from the walls of Rome, and on reaching Palazzo Roccanera she went straight to her room, to put them into water. Isabel passed into the drawing-room, the one she herself usually occupied, the second in order from the large ante-chamber which was entered from the staircase and in which even Gilbert Osmond's rich devices had not been able to correct a look of rather grand nudity. Just beyond the threshold of the drawing-room she stopped short, the reason for her doing so being that she had received an impression. The impression had, in strictness, nothing unprecedented; but she felt it as something new, and the soundlessness of her step gave her time to take in the scene before she interrupted it. Madame Merle was there in her bonnet, and Gilbert Osmond was talking to her; for a minute they were unaware she had come in. Isabel had often seen that before, certainly; but what she had not seen, or at least had not noticed, was that their colloquy had for the moment converted itself into a sort of familiar silence, from which she instantly perceived that her entrance would startle them. Madame Merle was standing on the rug, a little way from the fire; Osmond was in a deep chair, leaning back and looking at her. Her head was erect, as usual, but her eyes were bent on his. What struck Isabel first was that he was sitting while Madame Merle stood; there was an anomaly in this that arrested her. Then she perceived that they had arrived at a desultory pause in their exchange of ideas and were musing, face to face, with the freedom of old friends who sometimes exchange ideas without uttering them. There was nothing to shock in this; they were old friends in fact. But the thing made an image, lasting only a moment, like a sudden flicker of light. Their relative positions, their absorbed mutual gaze, struck her as something detected. But it was all over by the time she had fairly seen it. Madame Merle had seen her and had welcomed her without moving; her husband, on the other hand, had instantly jumped up. He presently murmured something about wanting a walk and, after having asked their visitor to excuse him, left the room.

"I came to see you, thinking you would have come in; and as you had n't I waited for you," Madame Merle said.

"Did n't he ask you to sit down?" Isabel asked with a smile.

Madame Merle looked about her. "Ah, it 's very true; I was going away."

"You must stay now."

"Certainly. I came for a reason; I 've something on my mind."

"I 've told you that before," Isabel said — "that it takes something extraordinary to bring you to this house."

"And you know what I 've told *you;* that whether I come or whether I stay away, I 've always the same motive — the affection I bear you."

"Yes, you 've told me that."

"You look just now as if you did n't believe it," said Madame Merle.

"Ah," Isabel answered, "the profundity of your motives, that's the last thing I doubt!"

"You doubt sooner of the sincerity of my words."

Isabel shook her head gravely. "I know you've always been kind to me."

"As often as you would let me. You don't always take it; then one has to let you alone. It's not to do you a kindness, however, that I've come to-day; it's quite another affair. I've come to get rid of a trouble of my own — to make it over to you. I've been talking to your husband about it."

"I'm surprised at that; he does n't like troubles."

"Especially other people's; I know very well. But neither do you, I suppose. At any rate, whether you do or not, you must help me. It's about poor Mr. Rosier."

"Ah," said Isabel reflectively, "it's his trouble then, not yours."

"He has succeeded in saddling me with it. He comes to see me ten times a week, to talk about Pansy."

"Yes, he wants to marry her. I know all about it."

Madame Merle hesitated. "I gathered from your husband that perhaps you did n't."

"How should he know what I know? He has never spoken to me of the matter."

"It's probably because he does n't know how to speak of it."

"It's nevertheless the sort of question in which he's rarely at fault."

"Yes, because as a general thing he knows perfectly well what to think. To-day he does n't."

"Have n't you been telling him?" Isabel asked.

Madame Merle gave a bright, voluntary smile. "Do you know you're a little dry?"

"Yes; I can't help it. Mr. Rosier has also talked to me."

"In that there's some reason. You're so near the child."

"Ah," said Isabel, "for all the comfort I've given him! If you think me dry, I wonder what *he* thinks."

"I believe he thinks you can do more than you have done."

"I can do nothing."

"You can do more at least than I. I don't know what mysterious connection he may have discovered between me and Pansy; but he came to me from the first, as if I held his fortune in my hand. Now he keeps coming back, to spur me up, to know what hope there is, to pour out his feelings."

"He's very much in love," said Isabel.

"Very much — for him."

"Very much for Pansy, you might say as well."

Madame Merle dropped her eyes a moment. "Don't you think she's attractive?"

' "The dearest little person possible — but very limited."

"She ought to be all the easier for Mr. Rosier to love. Mr. Rosier's not unlimited."

"No," said Isabel, "he has about the extent of one's pocket-handkerchief — the small ones with lace borders." Her humour had lately turned a good deal to sarcasm, but in a moment she was ashamed of exercising it on so innocent an object as Pansy's suitor. "He's very kind, very honest," she presently added; "and he's not such a fool as he seems."

"He assures me that she delights in him," said Madame Merle.

"I don't know; I've not asked her."

"You've never sounded her a little?"

"It's not my place; it's her father's."

"Ah, you're too literal!" said Madame Merle.

"I must judge for myself."

Madame Merle gave her smile again. "It isn't easy to help you."

"To help me?" said Isabel very seriously. "What do you mean?"

"It's easy to displease you. Don't you see how wise I am to be careful? I notify you, at any rate, as I notified Osmond, that I wash my hands of the love-affairs of Miss Pansy and Mr. Edward Rosier. *Je n'y peux rien, moi!* I can't talk to Pansy about him. Especially," added Madame Merle, "as I don't think him a paragon of husbands."

Isabel reflected a little; after which, with a smile, "You don't wash your hands then!" she said. After which again she added in another tone: "You can't —you're too much interested."

Madame Merle slowly rose; she had given Isabel a look as rapid as the intimation that had gleamed before our heroine a few moments before. Only this time the latter saw nothing. "Ask him the next time, and you'll see."

"I can't ask him; he has ceased to come to the house. Gilbert has let him know that he's not welcome."

"Ah yes," said Madame Merle, "I forgot that

— though it's the burden of his lamentation. He
says Osmond has insulted him. All the same," she
went on, "Osmond does n't dislike him so much
as he thinks." She had got up as if to close the
conversation, but she lingered, looking about her, and
had evidently more to say. Isabel perceived this
and even saw the point she had in view; but Isabel
also had her own reasons for not opening the way.

"That must have pleased him, if you've told
him," she answered, smiling.

"Certainly I've told him; as far as that goes
I've encouraged him. I've preached patience, have
said that his case is n't desperate if he'll only hold
his tongue and be quiet. Unfortunately he has taken
it into his head to be jealous."

"Jealous?"

"Jealous of Lord Warburton, who, he says, is
always here."

Isabel, who was tired, had remained sitting; but
at this she also rose. "Ah!" she exclaimed simply,
moving slowly to the fireplace. Madame Merle observed her as she passed and while she stood a moment before the mantel-glass and pushed into its
place a wandering tress of hair.

"Poor Mr. Rosier keeps saying there's nothing
impossible in Lord Warburton's falling in love with
Pansy," Madame Merle went on.

Isabel was silent a little; she turned away from
the glass. "It's true — there's nothing impossible,"
she returned at last, gravely and more gently.

"So I've had to admit to Mr. Rosier. So, too,
your husband thinks."

"That I don't know."

"Ask him and you'll see."

"I shall not ask him," said Isabel.

"Pardon me; I forgot you had pointed that out. Of course," Madame Merle added, "you've had infinitely more observation of Lord Warburton's behaviour than I."

"I see no reason why I shouldn't tell you that he likes my stepdaughter very much."

Madame Merle gave one of her quick looks again. "Likes her, you mean — as Mr. Rosier means?"

"I don't know how Mr. Rosier means; but Lord Warburton has let me know that he's charmed with Pansy."

"And you've never told Osmond?" This observation was immediate, precipitate; it almost burst from Madame Merle's lips.

Isabel's eyes rested on her. "I suppose he'll know in time; Lord Warburton has a tongue and knows how to express himself."

Madame Merle instantly became conscious that she had spoken more quickly than usual, and the reflection brought the colour to her cheek. She gave the treacherous impulse time to subside and then said as if she had been thinking it over a little: "That would be better than marrying poor Mr. Rosier."

"Much better, I think."

"It would be very delightful; it would be a great marriage. It's really very kind of him."

"Very kind of him?"

"To drop his eyes on a simple little girl."

"I don't see that."

"It's very good of you. But after all, Pansy Os-mond —"

"After all, Pansy Osmond's the most attractive person he has ever known!" Isabel exclaimed.

Madame Merle stared, and indeed she was justly bewildered. "Ah, a moment ago I thought you seemed rather to disparage her."

"I said she was limited. And so she is. And so's Lord Warburton."

"So are we all, if you come to that. If it's no more than Pansy deserves, all the better. But if she fixes her affections on Mr. Rosier I won't admit that she deserves it. That will be too perverse."

"Mr. Rosier's a nuisance!" Isabel cried abruptly.

"I quite agree with you, and I'm delighted to know that I'm not expected to feed his flame. For the future, when he calls on me, my door shall be closed to him." And gathering her mantle together Madame Merle prepared to depart. She was checked, however, on her progress to the door, by an inconsequent request from Isabel.

"All the same, you know, be kind to him."

She lifted her shoulders and eyebrows and stood looking at her friend. "I don't understand your contradictions! Decidedly I shan't be kind to him, for it will be a false kindness. I want to see her married to Lord Warburton."

"You had better wait till he asks her."

"If what you say's true, he'll ask her. Especially," said Madame Merle in a moment, "if you make him."

"If I make him?"

"It's quite in your power. You've great influence with him."

Isabel frowned a little. "Where did you learn that?"

"Mrs. Touchett told me. Not you — never!" said Madame Merle, smiling.

"I certainly never told you anything of the sort."

"You *might* have done so — so far as opportunity went — when we were by way of being confidential with each other. But you really told me very little; I've often thought so since."

Isabel had thought so too, and sometimes with a certain satisfaction. But she did n't admit it now — perhaps because she wished not to appear to exult in it. "You seem to have had an excellent informant in my aunt," she simply returned.

"She let me know you had declined an offer of marriage from Lord Warburton, because she was greatly vexed and was full of the subject. Of course I think you've done better in doing as you did. But if you would n't marry Lord Warburton yourself, make him the reparation of helping him to marry some one else."

Isabel listened to this with a face that persisted in not reflecting the bright expressiveness of Madame Merle's. But in a moment she said, reasonably and gently enough: "I should be very glad indeed if, as regards Pansy, it could be arranged." Upon which her companion, who seemed to regard this as a speech of good omen, embraced her more tenderly than might have been expected and triumphantly withdrew.

XLI

Osmond touched on this matter that evening for the first time; coming very late into the drawing-room, where she was sitting alone. They had spent the evening at home, and Pansy had gone to bed; he himself had been sitting since dinner in a small apartment in which he had arranged his books and which he called his study. At ten o'clock Lord Warburton had come in, as he always did when he knew from Isabel that she was to be at home; he was going somewhere else and he sat for half an hour. Isabel, after asking him for news of Ralph, said very little to him, on purpose; she wished him to talk with her stepdaughter. She pretended to read; she even went after a little to the piano; she asked herself if she might n't leave the room. She had come little by little to think well of the idea of Pansy's becoming the wife of the master of beautiful Lockleigh, though at first it had not presented itself in a manner to excite her enthusiasm. Madame Merle, that afternoon, had applied the match to an accumulation of inflammable material. When Isabel was unhappy she always looked about her — partly from impulse and partly by theory — for some form of positive exertion. She could never rid herself of the sense that unhappiness was a state of disease — of suffering as opposed to doing. To "do" — it hardly

173

mattered what—would therefore be an escape, perhaps in some degree a remedy. Besides, she wished to convince herself that she had done everything possible to content her husband; she was determined not to be haunted by visions of his wife's limpness under appeal. It would please him greatly to see Pansy married to an English nobleman, and justly please him, since this nobleman was so sound a character. It seemed to Isabel that if she could make it her duty to bring about such an event she should play the part of a good wife. She wanted to be that; she wanted to be able to believe sincerely, and with proof of it, that she had been that. Then such an undertaking had other recommendations. It would occupy her, and she desired occupation. It would even amuse her, and if she could really amuse herself she perhaps might be saved. Lastly, it would be a service to Lord Warburton, who evidently pleased himself greatly with the charming girl. It was a little "weird" he should — being what he was; but there was no accounting for such impressions. Pansy might captivate any one — any one at least but Lord Warburton. Isabel would have thought her too small, too slight, perhaps even too artificial for that. There was always a little of the doll about her, and that was not what he had been looking for. Still, who could say what men ever were looking for? They looked for what they found; they knew what pleased them only when they saw it. No theory was valid in such matters, and nothing was more unaccountable or more natural than anything else. If he had cared for *her* it might seem odd he should care for Pansy, who was so different; but he had not cared for her so much as he had supposed. Or if he had, he had completely got over it, and it was natural that, as that affair had failed, he should think something of quite another sort might succeed. Enthusiasm, as I say, had not come at first to Isabel, but it came to-day and made her feel almost happy. It was astonishing what happiness she could still find in the idea of procuring a pleasure for her husband. It was a pity, however, that Edward Rosier had crossed their path!

At this reflection the light that had suddenly gleamed upon that path lost something of its brightness. Isabel was unfortunately as sure that Pansy thought Mr. Rosier the nicest of all the young men — as sure as if she had held an interview with her on the subject. It was very tiresome she should be so sure, when she had carefully abstained from informing herself; almost as tiresome as that poor Mr. Rosier should have taken it into his own head. He was certainly very inferior to Lord Warburton. It was not the difference in fortune so much as the difference in the men; the young American was really so light a weight. He was much more of the type of the useless fine gentleman than the English nobleman. It was true that there was no particular reason why Pansy should marry a statesman; still, if a statesman admired her, that was his affair, and she would make a perfect little pearl of a peeress.

It may seem to the reader that Mrs. Osmond had grown of a sudden strangely cynical, for she ended by saying to herself that this difficulty could probably be arranged. An impediment that was embodied in poor Rosier could not anyhow present itself as a dangerous one; there were always means of levelling secondary obstacles. Isabel was perfectly aware that she had not taken the measure of Pansy's tenacity, which might prove to be inconveniently great; but she inclined to see her as rather letting go, under suggestion, than as clutching under deprecation — since she had certainly the faculty of assent developed in a very much higher degree than that of protest. She would cling, yes, she would cling; but it really mattered to her very little what she clung to. Lord Warburton would do as well as Mr. Rosier — especially as she seemed quite to like him; she had expressed this sentiment to Isabel without a single reservation; she had said she thought his conversation most interesting — he had told her all about India. His manner to Pansy had been of the rightest and easiest — Isabel noticed that for herself, as she also observed that he talked to her not in the least in a patronising way, reminding himself of her youth and simplicity, but quite as if she understood his subjects with that sufficiency with which she followed those of the fashionable operas. This went far enough for attention to the music and the barytone. He was careful only to be kind — he was as kind as he had been to another fluttered young chit at Gardencourt. A girl might well be touched by that; she remembered how she herself had been touched, and said to herself that if she had been as simple as Pansy the impression would have been deeper still. She had not been simple when she refused him; that operation had been as complicated as, later, her acceptance of Osmond had been. Pansy, however, in spite of *her* simplicity, really did understand, and was glad that Lord Warburton should talk to her, not about her partners and bouquets, but about the state of Italy, the condition of the peasantry, the famous grist-tax, the *pellagra*, his impressions of Roman society. She looked at him, as she drew her needle through her tapestry, with sweet submissive eyes, and when she lowered them she gave little quiet oblique glances at his person, his hands, his feet, his clothes, as if she were considering him. Even his person, Isabel might have reminded her, was better than Mr. Rosier's. But Isabel contented herself at such moments with wondering where this gentleman was; he came no more at all to Palazzo Roccanera. It was surprising, as I say, the hold it had taken of her — the idea of assisting her husband to be pleased.

It was surprising for a variety of reasons which I shall presently touch upon. On the evening I speak of, while Lord Warburton sat there, she had been on the point of taking the great step of going out of the room and leaving her companions alone. I say the great step, because it was in this light that Gilbert Osmond would have regarded it, and Isabel was trying as much as possible to take her husband's view. She succeeded after a fashion, but she fell short of the point I mention. After all she could n't rise to it; something held her and made this impossible. It was not exactly that it would be base or insidious; for women as a general thing practise such manœuvres with a perfectly good conscience, and Isabel was instinctively much more true than false to the common genius of her sex. There was a vague doubt that interposed — a sense that she was not quite sure. So she remained in the drawing-room, and after a while Lord Warburton went off to his party, of which he promised to give Pansy a full account on the morrow. After he had gone she wondered if she had prevented something which would have happened if she had absented herself for a quarter of an hour; and then she pronounced — always mentally — that when their distinguished visitor should wish her to go away he would easily find means to let her know it. Pansy said nothing whatever about him after he had gone, and Isabel studiously said nothing, as she had taken a vow of reserve until after he should have declared himself. He was a little longer in coming to this than might seem to accord with the description he had given Isabel of his feelings. Pansy went to bed, and Isabel had to admit that she could not now guess what her stepdaughter was thinking of. Her transparent little companion was for the moment not to be seen through.

She remained alone, looking at the fire, until, at the end of half an hour, her husband came in. He moved about a while in silence and then sat down; he looked at the fire like herself. But she now had transferred her eyes from the flickering flame in the chimney to Osmond's face, and she watched him while he kept his silence. Covert observation had become a habit with her; an instinct, of which it is not an exaggeration to say that it was allied to that of self-defence, had made it habitual. She wished as much as possible to know his thoughts, to know what he would say, beforehand, so that she might prepare her answer. Preparing answers had not been her strong point of old; she had rarely in this respect got further than thinking afterwards of clever things she might have said. But she had learned caution — learned it in a measure from her husband's very countenance. It was the same face she had looked into with eyes equally earnest perhaps, but less penetrating, on the terrace of a Florentine villa; except that Osmond had grown slightly stouter since his marriage. He still, however, might strike one as very distinguished.

"Has Lord Warburton been here?" he presently asked.

"Yes, he stayed half an hour."

"Did he see Pansy?"

"Yes; he sat on the sofa beside her."

"Did he talk with her much?"

"He talked almost only to her."

"It seems to me he's attentive. Isn't that what you call it?"

"I don't call it anything," said Isabel; "I've waited for you to give it a name."

"That's a consideration you don't always show," Osmond answered after a moment.

"I've determined, this time, to try and act as you'd like. I've so often failed of that."

Osmond turned his head slowly, looking at her. "Are you trying to quarrel with me?"

"No, I'm trying to live at peace."

"Nothing's more easy; you know I don't quarrel myself."

"What do you call it when you try to make me angry?" Isabel asked.

"I don't try; if I've done so it has been the most natural thing in the world. Moreover I'm not in the least trying now."

Isabel smiled. "It does n't matter. I've determined never to be angry again."

"That's an excellent resolve. Your temper is n't good."

"No — it's not good." She pushed away the book she had been reading and took up the band of tapestry Pansy had left on the table.

"That's partly why I've not spoken to you about this business of my daughter's," Osmond said, designating Pansy in the manner that was most frequent with him. "I was afraid I should encounter opposition — that you too would have views on the subject. I've sent little Rosier about his business."

"You were afraid I'd plead for Mr. Rosier? Have n't you noticed that I've never spoken to you of him?"

"I've never given you a chance. We've so little conversation in these days. I know he was an old friend of yours."

"Yes; he's an old friend of mine." Isabel cared little more for him than for the tapestry that she held in her hand; but it was true that he was an old friend and that with her husband she felt a desire not to

extenuate such ties. He had a way of expressing contempt for them which fortified her loyalty to them,
even when, as in the present case, they were in themselves insignificant. She sometimes felt a sort of passion of tenderness for memories which had no other
merit than that they belonged to her unmarried life.
"But as regards Pansy," she added in a moment,
"I've given him no encouragement."

"That's fortunate," Osmond observed.

"Fortunate for me, I suppose you mean. For him
it matters little."

"There's no use talking of him," Osmond said.
"As I tell you, I've turned him out."

"Yes; but a lover outside's always a lover. He's
sometimes even more of one. Mr. Rosier still has
hope."

"He's welcome to the comfort of it! My daughter
has only to sit perfectly quiet to become Lady Warburton."

"Should you like that?" Isabel asked with a simplicity which was not so affected as it may appear.
She was resolved to assume nothing, for Osmond
had a way of unexpectedly turning her assumptions
against her. The intensity with which he would like
his daughter to become Lady Warburton had been
the very basis of her own recent reflections. But
that was for herself; she would recognise nothing
until Osmond should have put it into words; she
would not take for granted with him that he thought
Lord Warburton a prize worth an amount of effort
that was unusual among the Osmonds. It was Gilbert's constant intimation that for him nothing in

life was a prize; that he treated as from equal to equal with the most distinguished people in the world, and that his daughter had only to look about her to pick out a prince. It cost him therefore a lapse from consistency to say explicitly that he yearned for Lord Warburton and that if this nobleman should escape his equivalent might not be found; with which moreover it was another of his customary implications that he was never inconsistent. He would have liked his wife to glide over the point. But strangely enough, now that she was face to face with him and although an hour before she had almost invented a scheme for pleasing him, Isabel was not accommodating, would not glide. And yet she knew exactly the effect on his mind of her question: it would operate as an humiliation. Never mind; he was terribly capable of humiliating *her* — all the more so that he was also capable of waiting for great opportunities and of showing sometimes an almost unaccountable indifference to small ones. Isabel perhaps took a small opportunity because she would not have availed herself of a great one.

Osmond at present acquitted himself very honourably. "I should like it extremely; it would be a great marriage. And then Lord Warburton has another advantage: he's an old friend of yours. It would be pleasant for him to come into the family. It's very odd Pansy's admirers should all be your old friends."

"It's natural that they should come to see me. In coming to see me they see Pansy. Seeing her it's natural they should fall in love with her."

"So I think. But you're not bound to do so."

"If she should marry Lord Warburton I should be very glad," Isabel went on frankly. "He's an excellent man. You say, however, that she has only to sit perfectly still. Perhaps she won't sit perfectly still. If she loses Mr. Rosier she may jump up!"

Osmond appeared to give no heed to this; he sat gazing at the fire. "Pansy would like to be a great lady," he remarked in a moment with a certain tenderness of tone. "She wishes above all to please," he added.

"To please Mr. Rosier, perhaps."

"No, to please me."

"Me too a little, I think," said Isabel.

"Yes, she has a great opinion of you. But she'll do what I like."

"If you're sure of that, it's very well," she went on.

"Meantime," said Osmond, "I should like our distinguished visitor to speak."

"He has spoken — to me. He has told me it would be a great pleasure to him to believe she could care for him."

Osmond turned his head quickly, but at first he said nothing. Then, "Why did n't you tell me that?" he asked sharply.

"There was no opportunity. You know how we live. I 've taken the first chance that has offered."

"Did you speak to him of Rosier?"

"Oh yes, a little."

"That was hardly necessary."

"I thought it best he should know, so that, so that —" And Isabel paused.

"So that what?"

"So that he might act accordingly."

"So that he might back out, do you mean?"

"No, so that he might advance while there's yet time."

"That's not the effect it seems to have had."

"You should have patience," said Isabel. "You know Englishmen are shy."

"This one's not. He was not when he made love to *you*."

She had been afraid Osmond would speak of that; it was disagreeable to her. "I beg your pardon; he was extremely so," she returned.

He answered nothing for some time; he took up a book and fingered the pages while she sat silent and occupied herself with Pansy's tapestry. "You must have a great deal of influence with him," Osmond went on at last. "The moment you really wish it you can bring him to the point."

This was more offensive still; but she felt the great naturalness of his saying it, and it was after all extremely like what she had said to herself. "Why should I have influence?" she asked. "What have I ever done to put him under an obligation to me?"

"You refused to marry him," said Osmond with his eyes on his book.

"I must not presume too much on that," she replied.

He threw down the book presently and got up,

184

standing before the fire with his hands behind him. "Well, I hold that it lies in your hands. I shall leave it there. With a little good-will you may manage it. Think that over and remember how much I count on you." He waited a little, to give her time to answer; but she answered nothing, and he presently strolled out of the room.

XLII

She had answered nothing because his words had put the situation before her and she was absorbed in looking at it. There was something in them that suddenly made vibrations deep, so that she had been afraid to trust herself to speak. After he had gone she leaned back in her chair and closed her eyes ; and for a long time, far into the night and still further, she sat in the still drawing-room, given up to her meditation. A servant came in to attend to the fire, and she bade him bring fresh candles and then go to bed. Osmond had told her to think of what he had said; and she did so indeed, and of many other things. The suggestion from another that she had a definite influence on Lord Warburton — this had given her the start that accompanies unexpected recognition. Was it true that there was something still between them that might be a handle to make him declare himself to Pansy — a susceptibility, on his part, to approval, a desire to do what would please her ? Isabel had hitherto not asked herself the question, because she had not been forced; but now that it was directly presented to her she saw the answer, and the answer frightened her. Yes, there was something — something on Lord Warburton's part. When he had first come to Rome she believed the link that united them to be completely snapped; but little by little she had been reminded that it had yet a palpable existence. It was as thin as a hair, but there were moments when she seemed to hear it vibrate. For herself nothing was changed; what she once thought of him she always thought; it was needless this feeling should change; it seemed to her in fact a better feeling than ever. But he? had he still the idea that she might be more to him than other women? Had he the wish to profit by the memory of the few moments of intimacy through which they had once passed? Isabel knew she had read some of the signs of such a disposition. But what were his hopes, his pretensions, and in what strange way were they mingled with his evidently very sincere appreciation of poor Pansy? Was he in love with Gilbert Osmond's wife, and if so what comfort did he expect to derive from it? If he was in love with Pansy he was not in love with her stepmother, and if he was in love with her stepmother he was not in love with Pansy. Was she to cultivate the advantage she possessed in order to make him commit himself to Pansy, knowing he would do so for her sake and not for the small creature's own — was this the service her husband had asked of her? This at any rate was the duty with which she found herself confronted — from the moment she admitted to herself that her old friend had still an uneradicated predilection for her society. It was not an agreeable task; it was in fact a repulsive one. She asked herself with dismay whether Lord Warburton were pretending to be in love with Pansy in order to cultivate another satisfaction and what might be called other chances. Of this refinement of duplicity she presently acquitted him; she preferred to believe him in perfect good faith. But if his admiration for Pansy were a delusion this was scarcely better than its being an affectation. Isabel wandered among these ugly possibilities until she had completely lost her way; some of them, as she suddenly encountered them, seemed ugly enough. Then she broke out of the labyrinth, rubbing her eyes, and declared that her imagination surely did her little honour and that her husband's did him even less. Lord Warburton was as disinterested as he need be, and she was no more to him than she need wish. She would rest upon this till the contrary should be proved; proved more effectually than by a cynical intimation of Osmond's.

Such a resolution, however, brought her this evening but little peace, for her soul was haunted with terrors which crowded to the foreground of thought as quickly as a place was made for them. What had suddenly set them into livelier motion she hardly knew, unless it were the strange impression she had received in the afternoon of her husband's being in more direct communication with Madame Merle than she suspected. That impression came back to her from time to time, and now she wondered it had never come before. Besides this, her short interview with Osmond half an hour ago was a striking example of his faculty for making everything wither that he touched, spoiling everything for her that he looked at. It was very well to undertake to give him a proof of loyalty; the real fact was that the knowledge of his expecting a thing raised a presumption against it. It was as if he had had the evil eye; as if his presence were a blight and his favour a misfortune. Was the fault in himself, or only in the deep mistrust she had conceived for him? This mistrust was now the clearest result of their short married life; a gulf had opened between them over which they looked at each other with eyes that were on either side a declaration of the deception suffered. It was a strange opposition, of the like of which she had never dreamed — an opposition in which the vital principle of the one was a thing of contempt to the other. It was not her fault — she had practised no deception; she had only admired and believed. She had taken all the first steps in the purest confidence, and then she had suddenly found the infinite vista of a multiplied life to be a dark, narrow alley with a dead wall at the end. Instead of leading to the high places of happiness, from which the world would seem to lie below one, so that one could look down with a sense of exaltation and advantage, and judge and choose and pity, it led rather downward and earthward, into realms of restriction and depression where the sound of other lives, easier and freer, was heard as from above, and where it served to deepen the feeling of failure. It was her deep distrust of her husband — this was what darkened the world. That is a sentiment easily indicated, but not so easily explained, and so composite in its character that much time and still more suffering had been needed to bring it to its actual perfection. Suffering, with Isabel, was an active condition; it was not a chill, a stupor, a despair; it was a passion of thought, of speculation, of response to every pressure. She flattered herself

that she had kept her failing faith to herself, however,
—that no one suspected it but Osmond. Oh, he knew
it, and there were times when she thought he enjoyed
it. It had come gradually — it was not till the first
year of their life together, so admirably intimate at
first, had closed that she had taken the alarm. Then
the shadows had begun to gather; it was as if Osmond deliberately, almost malignantly, had put the
lights out one by one. The dusk at first was vague
and thin, and she could still see her way in it. But
it steadily deepened, and if now and again it had occasionally lifted there were certain corners of her prospect that were impenetrably black. These shadows
were not an emanation from her own mind: she was
very sure of that; she had done her best to be just
and temperate, to see only the truth. They were a
part, they were a kind of creation and consequence,
of her husband's very presence. They were not his
misdeeds, his turpitudes; she accused him of nothing
— that is but of one thing, which was *not* a crime.
She knew of no wrong he had done; he was not violent, he was not cruel: she simply believed he hated
her. That was all she accused him of, and the miserable part of it was precisely that it was not a crime,
for against a crime she might have found redress.
He had discovered that she was so different, that she
was not what he had believed she would prove to be.
He had thought at first he could change her, and
she had done her best to be what he would like. But
she was, after all, herself — she could n't help that;
and now there was no use pretending, wearing a
mask or a dress, for he knew her and had made up

his mind. She was not afraid of him; she had no apprehension he would hurt her; for the ill-will he bore her was not of that sort. He would if possible never give her a pretext, never put himself in the wrong. Isabel, scanning the future with dry, fixed eyes, saw that he would have the better of her there. She would give him many pretexts, she would often put herself in the wrong. There were times when she almost pitied him; for if she had not deceived him in intention she understood how completely she must have done so in fact. She had effaced herself when he first knew her; she had made herself small, pretending there was less of her than there really was. It was because she had been under the extraordinary charm that he, on his side, had taken pains to put forth. He was not changed; he had not disguised himself, during the year of his courtship, any more than she. But she had seen only half his nature then, as one saw the disk of the moon when it was partly masked by the shadow of the earth. She saw the full moon now — she saw the whole man. She had kept still, as it were, so that he should have a free field, and yet in spite of this she had mistaken a part for the whole.

Ah, she had been immensely under the charm! It had not passed away; it was there still: she still knew perfectly what it was that made Osmond delightful when he chose to be. He had wished to be when he made love to her, and as she had wished to be charmed it was not wonderful he had succeeded. He had succeeded because he had been sincere; it never occurred to her now to deny him that. He admired her — he had told her why: because she was the most imaginative woman he had known. It might very well have been true; for during those months she had imagined a world of things that had no substance. She had had a more wondrous vision of him, fed through charmed senses and oh such a stirred fancy! — she had not read him right. A certain combination of features had touched her, and in them she had seen the most striking of figures. That he was poor and lonely and yet that somehow he was noble — that was what had interested her and seemed to give her her opportunity. There had been an indefinable beauty about him — in his situation, in his mind, in his face. She had felt at the same time that he was helpless and ineffectual, but the feeling had taken the form of a tenderness which was the very flower of respect. He was like a sceptical voyager strolling on the beach while he waited for the tide, looking seaward yet not putting to sea. It was in all this she had found her occasion. She would launch his boat for him; she would be his providence; it would be a good thing to love him. And she had loved him, she had so anxiously and yet so ardently given herself — a good deal for what she found in him, but a good deal also for what she brought him and what might enrich the gift. As she looked back at the passion of those full weeks she perceived in it a kind of maternal strain — the happiness of a woman who felt that she was a contributor, that she came with charged hands. But for her money, as she saw to-day, she would never have done it. And then her mind wandered off to poor Mr. Touchett, sleeping under English turf, the beneficent author of infinite woe! For this was the fantastic fact. At bottom her money had been a burden, had been on her mind, which was filled with the desire to transfer the weight of it to some other conscience, to some more prepared receptacle. What would lighten her own conscience more effectually than to make it over to the man with the best taste in the world? Unless she should have given it to a hospital there would have been nothing better she could do with it; and there was no charitable institution in which she had been as much interested as in Gilbert Osmond. He would use her fortune in a way that would make her think better of it and rub off a certain grossness attaching to the good luck of an unexpected inheritance. There had been nothing very delicate in inheriting seventy thousand pounds; the delicacy had been all in Mr. Touchett's leaving them to her. But to marry Gilbert Osmond and bring him such a portion — in that there would be delicacy for her as well. There would be less for him — that was true; but that was his affair, and if he loved her he would n't object to her being rich. Had he not had the courage to say he was glad she was rich?

Isabel's cheek burned when she asked herself if she had really married on a factitious theory, in order to do something finely appreciable with her money. But she was able to answer quickly enough that this was only half the story. It was because a certain ardour took possession of her — a sense of the earnestness of his affection and a delight in his personal qualities. He was better than any one else. This supreme conviction had filled her life for months, and enough of it still remained to prove to her that she could not have done otherwise. The finest — in the sense of being the subtlest — manly organism she had ever known had become her property, and the recognition of her having but to put out her hands and take it had been originally a sort of act of devotion. She had not been mistaken about the beauty of his mind; she knew that organ perfectly now. She had lived with it, she had lived *in* it almost — it appeared to have become her habitation. If she had been captured it had taken a firm hand to seize her; that reflection perhaps had some worth. A mind more ingenious, more pliant, more cultivated, more trained to admirable exercises, she had not encountered; and it was this exquisite instrument she had now to reckon with. She lost herself in infinite dismay when she thought of the magnitude of *his* deception. It was a wonder, perhaps, in view of this, that he did n't hate her more. She remembered perfectly the first sign he had given of it — it had been like the bell that was to ring up the curtain upon the real drama of their life. He said to her one day that she had too many ideas and that she must get rid of them. He had told her that already, before their marriage; but then she had not noticed it: it had come back to her only afterwards. This time she might well have noticed it, because he had really meant it. The words had been nothing superficially; but when in the light of deepening experience she had looked into them they had then appeared portentous. He had really meant it — he would have liked her to have nothing of her own but her pretty appearance. She had known she had too many ideas; she had more even than he had supposed, many more than she had expressed to him when he had asked her to marry him. Yes, she *had* been hypocritical; she had liked him so much. She had too many ideas for herself; but that was just what one married for, to share them with some one else. One could n't pluck them up by the roots, though of course one might suppress them, be careful not to utter them. It had not been this, however, his objecting to her opinions; this had been nothing. She had no opinions — none that she would not have been eager to sacrifice in the satisfaction of feeling herself loved for it. What he had meant had been the whole thing — her character, the way she felt, the way she judged. This was what she had kept in reserve; this was what he had not known until he had found himself — with the door closed behind, as it were — set down face to face with it. She had a certain way of looking at life which he took as a personal offence. Heaven knew that now at least it was a very humble, accommodating way! The strange thing was that she should not have suspected from the first that his own had been so different. She had thought it so large, so enlightened, so perfectly that of an honest man and a gentleman. Had n't he assured her that he had no superstitions, no dull limitations, no prejudices that had lost their freshness? Had n't he all the appearance of a man living in the open air of the world, indifferent to small considerations, caring only for truth and knowledge and believing that two intelligent people ought to look for them together and, whether they found them or not, find at least some happiness in the search ? He had told her he loved the conventional; but there was a sense in which this seemed a noble declaration. In that sense, that of the love of harmony and order and decency and of all the stately offices of life, she went with him freely, and his warning had contained nothing ominous. But when, as the months had elapsed, she had followed him further and he had led her into the mansion of his own habitation, then, *then* she had seen where she really was.

She could live it over again, the incredulous terror with which she had taken the measure of her dwelling. Between those four walls she had lived ever since; they were to surround her for the rest of her life. It was the house of darkness, the house of dumbness, the house of suffocation. Osmond's beautiful mind gave it neither light nor air; Osmond's beautiful mind indeed seemed to peep down from a small high window and mock at her. Of course it had not been physical suffering; for physical suffering there might have been a remedy. She could come and go; she had her liberty; her husband was perfectly polite. He took himself so seriously; it was something appalling. Under all his culture, his cleverness, his amenity, under his good-nature, his facility, his knowledge of life, his egotism lay hidden like a serpent in a bank of flowers. She had taken him seriously, but she had not taken him so seriously as that. How could she — especially when she had known him better ? She was to think of him as he thought of himself — as the first gentleman in Europe. So it was that she had thought of him at first, and that indeed was the reason she had married him. But when she began to see what it implied she drew back; there was more in the bond than she had meant to put her name to. It implied a sovereign contempt for every one but some three or four very exalted people whom he envied, and for everything in the world but half a dozen ideas of his own. That was very well; she would have gone with him even there a long distance; for he pointed out to her so much of the baseness and shabbiness of life, opened her eyes so wide to the stupidity, the depravity, the ignorance of mankind, that she had been properly impressed with the infinite vulgarity of things and of the virtue of keeping one's self unspotted by it. But this base, ignoble world, it appeared, was after all what one was to live for; one was to keep it for ever in one's eye, in order not to enlighten or convert or redeem it, but to extract from it some recognition of one's own superiority. On the one hand it was despicable, but on the other it afforded a standard. Osmond had talked to Isabel about his renunciation, his indifference, the ease with which he dispensed with the usual aids to success; and all this had seemed to her admirable. She had thought it a grand indifference, an exquisite independence. But indifference was really the last of his qualities; she had never seen any one who thought so much of others. For herself, avowedly, the world had always interested her and the study of her fellow creatures been her constant passion. She would have been willing, however, to renounce all her curiosities and sympathies for the sake of a personal life, if the person concerned had only been able to make her believe it was a gain! This at least was her present conviction; and the thing certainly would have been easier than to care for society as Osmond cared for it.

He was unable to live without it, and she saw that he had never really done so; he had looked at it out of his window even when he appeared to be most detached from it. He had his ideal, just as she had tried to have hers; only it was strange that people should seek for justice in such different quarters. His ideal was a conception of high prosperity and propriety, of the aristocratic life, which she now saw that he deemed himself always, in essence at least, to have led. He had never lapsed from it for an hour; he would never have recovered from the shame of doing so. That again was very well; here too she would have agreed; but they attached such different ideas, such different associations and desires, to the same formulas. Her notion of the aristocratic life was simply the union of great knowledge with great liberty; the knowledge would give one a sense of duty and the liberty a sense of enjoyment. But for Osmond it was altogether a thing of forms, a conscious, calculated attitude. He was fond of the old, the consecrated, the transmitted; so was she, but she pretended to do what she chose with it. He had an immense esteem for tradition; he had told her once that the best thing in the world was to have it, but that if one was so unfortunate as not to have it one must immediately proceed to make it. She knew that he meant by this that she had n't it, but that he was better off; though from what source he had derived his traditions she never learned. He had a very large collection of them, however; that was very certain, and after a little she began to see. The great thing was to act in accordance with them; the great thing not only for him but for her. Isabel had an undefined conviction that to serve for another person than their proprietor traditions must be of a thoroughly superior kind; but she nevertheless assented to this intimation that she too must march to the stately music that floated down from unknown periods in her husband's past; she who of old had been so free of step, so desultory, so devious, so much the reverse of processional. There were certain things they must do, a certain posture they must take, certain people they must know and not know. When she saw this rigid system close about her, draped though it was in pictured tapestries, that sense of darkness and suffocation of which I have spoken took possession of her; she seemed shut up with an odour of mould and decay. She had resisted of course; at first very humorously, ironically, tenderly; then, as the situation grew more serious, eagerly, passionately, pleadingly. She had pleaded the cause of freedom, of doing as they chose, of not caring for the aspect and denomination of their life — the cause of other instincts and longings, of quite another ideal.

Then it was that her husband's personality, touched as it never had been, stepped forth and stood erect. The things she had said were answered only by his scorn, and she could see he was ineffably ashamed of her. What did he think of her — that she was base, vulgar, ignoble? He at least knew now that she had no traditions! It had not been in his prevision of things that she should reveal such flatness; her sentiments were worthy of a radical newspaper or a Unitarian preacher. The real offence, as she ultimately perceived, was her having a mind of her own at all. Her mind was to be his — attached to his own like a small garden-plot to a deer-park. He would rake the soil gently and water the flowers; he would weed the beds and gather an occasional nose-gay. It would be a pretty piece of property for a proprietor already far-reaching. He did n't wish her to be stupid. On the contrary, it was because she was clever that she had pleased him. But he expected her intelligence to operate altogether in his favour, and so far from desiring her mind to be a blank he had flattered himself that it would be richly receptive. He had expected his wife to feel with him and for him, to enter into his opinions, his ambitions, his preferences; and Isabel was obliged to confess that this was no great insolence on the part of a man so accomplished and a husband originally at least so tender. But there were certain things she could never take in. To begin with, they were hideously unclean. She was not a daughter of the Puritans, but for all that she believed in such a thing as chastity and even as decency. It would appear that Osmond was far from doing anything of the sort; some of his traditions made her push back her skirts. Did all women have lovers? Did they all lie and even the best have their price? Were there only three or four that did n't deceive their husbands? When Isabel heard such things she felt a greater scorn for them than for the gossip of a village parlour — a scorn that kept its freshness in a very tainted air. There was the taint of her sister-in-law: did her husband judge only by the Countess Gemini? This lady very often lied, and she had practised deceptions that were not simply verbal. It was enough to find these facts assumed among Osmond's traditions — it was enough without giving them such a general extension. It was her scorn of his assumptions, it was this that made him draw himself up. He had plenty of contempt, and it was proper his wife should be as well furnished; but that she should turn the hot light of her disdain upon his own conception of things — this was a danger he had not allowed for. He believed he should have regulated her emotions before she came to it; and Isabel could easily imagine how his ears had scorched on his discovering he had been too confident. When one had a wife who gave one that sensation there was nothing left but to hate her.

She was morally certain now that this feeling of hatred, which at first had been a refuge and a refreshment, had become the occupation and comfort of his life. The feeling was deep, because it was sincere; he had had the revelation that she could after all dispense with him. If to herself the idea was startling, if it presented itself at first as a kind of infidelity, a capacity for pollution, what infinite effect might it not be expected to have had upon *him*? It was very simple; he despised her; she had no traditions and the moral horizon of a Unitarian minister. Poor

Isabel, who had never been able to understand Unitarianism! This was the certitude she had been living with now for a time that she had ceased to measure. What was coming — what was before them? That was her constant question. What would he do — what ought *she* to do? When a man hated his wife what did it lead to? She did n't hate him, that she was sure of, for every little while she felt a passionate wish to give him a pleasant surprise. Very often, however, she felt afraid, and it used to come over her, as I have intimated, that she had deceived him at the very first. They were strangely married, at all events, and it was a horrible life. Until that morning he had scarcely spoken to her for a week; his manner was as dry as a burned-out fire. She knew there was a special reason; he was displeased at Ralph Touchett's staying on in Rome. He thought she saw too much of her cousin — he had told her a week before it was indecent she should go to him at his hotel. He would have said more than this if Ralph's invalid state had not appeared to make it brutal to denounce him; but having had to contain himself had only deepened his disgust. Isabel read all this as she would have read the hour on the clock-face; she was as perfectly aware that the sight of her interest in her cousin stirred her husband's rage as if Osmond had locked her into her room — which she was sure was what he wanted to do. It was her honest belief that on the whole she was not defiant, but she certainly could n't pretend to be indifferent to Ralph. She believed he was dying at last and that she should never see him again, and this gave her a tenderness for him that she had never known before. Nothing was a pleasure to her now; how could anything be a pleasure to a woman who knew that she had thrown away her life? There was an everlasting weight on her heart — there was a livid light on everything. But Ralph's little visit was a lamp in the darkness; for the hour that she sat with him her ache for herself became somehow her ache for *him*. She felt to-day as if he had been her brother. She had never had a brother, but if she had and she were in trouble and he were dying, he would be dear to her as Ralph was. Ah yes, if Gilbert was jealous of her there was perhaps some reason; it did n't make Gilbert look better to sit for half an hour with Ralph. It was not that they talked of him — it was not that she complained. His name was never uttered between them. It was simply that Ralph was generous and that her husband was not. There was something in Ralph's talk, in his smile, in the mere fact of his being in Rome, that made the blasted circle round which she walked more spacious. He made her feel the good of the world; he made her feel what might have been. He was after all as intelligent as Osmond — quite apart from his being better. And thus it seemed to her an act of devotion to conceal her misery from him. She concealed it elaborately; she was perpetually, in their talk, hanging out curtains and arranging screens. It lived before her again — it had never had time to die — that morning in the garden at Florence when he had warned her against Osmond. She had only to close her eyes to see the place, to hear his voice, to feel the warm, sweet air. How could he have known? What a mystery, what a wonder of wisdom! As intelligent as Gilbert? He was much more intelligent — to arrive at such a judgement as that. Gilbert had never been so deep, so just. She had told him then that from her at least he should never know if he was right; and this was what she was taking care of now. It gave her plenty to do; there was passion, exaltation, religion in it. Women find their religion sometimes in strange exercises, and Isabel at present, in playing a part before her cousin, had an idea that she was doing him a kindness. It would have been a kindness perhaps if he had been for a single instant a dupe. As it was, the kindness consisted mainly in trying to make him believe that he had once wounded her greatly and that the event had put him to shame, but that, as she was very generous and he was so ill, she bore him no grudge and even considerately forbore to flaunt her happiness in his face. Ralph smiled to himself, as he lay on his sofa, at this extraordinary form of consideration; but he forgave her for having forgiven him. She did n't wish him to have the pain of knowing she was unhappy: that was the great thing, and it did n't matter that such knowledge would rather have righted him.

For herself, she lingered in the soundless saloon long after the fire had gone out. There was no danger of her feeling the cold; she was in a fever. She heard the small hours strike, and then the great ones, but her vigil took no heed of time. Her mind, assailed by visions, was in a state of extraordinary activity, and her visions might as well come to her there, where she sat up to meet them, as on her pillow, to make a mockery of rest. As I have said, she believed she was not defiant, and what could be a better proof of it than that she should linger there half the night, trying to persuade herself that there was no reason why Pansy should n't be married as you would put a letter in the post-office? When the clock struck four she got up; she was going to bed at last, for the lamp had long since gone out and the candles burned down to their sockets. But even then she stopped again in the middle of the room and stood there gazing at a remembered vision — that of her husband and Madame Merle unconsciously and familiarly associated.

XLIII

THREE nights after this she took Pansy to a great
party, to which Osmond, who never went to dances,
did not accompany them. Pansy was as ready for
a dance as ever; she was not of a generalising turn
and had not extended to other pleasures the inter-
dict she had seen placed on those of love. If she was
biding her time or hoping to circumvent her father she
must have had a prevision of success. Isabel thought
this unlikely; it was much more likely that Pansy
had simply determined to be a good girl. She had
never had such a chance, and she had a proper esteem for chances. She carried herself no less atten-
tively than usual and kept no less anxious an eye
upon her vaporous skirts; she held her bouquet very
tight and counted over the flowers for the twentieth
time. She made Isabel feel old; it seemed so long
since she had been in a flutter about a ball. Pansy,
who was greatly admired, was never in want of partners, and very soon after their arrival she gave Isabel,
who was not dancing, her bouquet to hold. Isabel
had rendered her this service for some minutes when
she became aware of the near presence of Edward
Rosier. He stood before her; he had lost his affable
smile and wore a look of almost military resolution.
The change in his appearance would have made
Isabel smile if she had not felt his case to be at
bottom a hard one: he had always smelt so much

more of heliotrope than of gunpowder. He looked at her a moment somewhat fiercely, as if to notify her he was dangerous, and then dropped his eyes on her bouquet. After he had inspected it his glance softened and he said quickly: "It's all pansies; it must be hers!"

Isabel smiled kindly. "Yes, it's hers; she gave it to me to hold."

"May I hold it a little, Mrs. Osmond?" the poor young man asked.

"No, I can't trust you; I'm afraid you would n't give it back."

"I'm not sure that I should; I should leave the house with it instantly. But may I not at least have a single flower?"

Isabel hesitated a moment, and then, smiling still, held out the bouquet. "Choose one yourself. It's frightful what I'm doing for you."

"Ah, if you do no more than this, Mrs. Osmond!" Rosier exclaimed with his glass in one eye, carefully choosing his flower.

"Don't put it into your button-hole," she said. "Don't for the world!"

"I should like her to see it. She has refused to dance with me, but I wish to show her that I believe in her still."

"It's very well to show it to her, but it's out of place to show it to others. Her father has told her not to dance with you."

"And is that all *you* can do for me? I expected more from you, Mrs. Osmond," said the young man in a tone of fine general reference. "You know our acquaintance goes back very far — quite into the days of our innocent childhood."

"Don't make me out too old," Isabel patiently answered. "You come back to that very often, and I've never denied it. But I must tell you that, old friends as we are, if you had done me the honour to ask me to marry you I should have refused you on the spot."

"Ah, you don't esteem me then. Say at once that you think me a mere Parisian trifler!"

"I esteem you very much, but I'm not in love with you. What I mean by that, of course, is that I'm not in love with you for Pansy."

"Very good; I see. You pity me — that's all." And Edward Rosier looked all round, inconsequently, with his single glass. It was a revelation to him that people shouldn't be more pleased; but he was at least too proud to show that the deficiency struck him as general.

Isabel for a moment said nothing. His manner and appearance had not the dignity of the deepest tragedy; his little glass, among other things, was against that. But she suddenly felt touched; her own unhappiness, after all, had something in common with his, and it came over her, more than before, that here, in recognisable, if not in romantic form, was the most affecting thing in the world — young love struggling with adversity. "Would you really be very kind to her?" she finally asked in a low tone.

He dropped his eyes devoutly and raised the little flower that he held in his fingers to his lips. Then he looked at her. "You pity me; but don't you pity *her* a little?"

"I don't know; I'm not sure. She'll always enjoy life."

"It will depend on what you call life!" Mr. Rosier effectively said. "She won't enjoy being tortured."

"There'll be nothing of that."

"I'm glad to hear it. She knows what she's about You'll see."

"I think she does, and she'll never disobey her father. But she's coming back to me," Isabel added, "and I must beg you to go away."

Rosier lingered a moment till Pansy came in sight on the arm of her cavalier; he stood just long enough to look her in the face. Then he walked away, holding up his head; and the manner in which he achieved this sacrifice to expediency convinced Isabel he was very much in love.

Pansy, who seldom got disarranged in dancing, looking perfectly fresh and cool after this exercise, waited a moment and then took back her bouquet. Isabel watched her and saw she was counting the flowers; whereupon she said to herself that decidedly there were deeper forces at play than she had recognised. Pansy had seen Rosier turn away, but she said nothing to Isabel about him; she talked only of her partner, after he had made his bow and retired; of the music, the floor, the rare misfortune of having already torn her dress. Isabel was sure, however, she had discovered her lover to have abstracted a flower; though this knowledge was not needed to account for the dutiful grace with which she responded to the appeal of her next partner. That perfect amenity under acute constraint was part of a larger system. She was again led forth by a flushed young man, this time carrying her bouquet; and she had not been absent many minutes when Isabel saw Lord Warburton advancing through the crowd. He presently drew near and bade her good-evening; she had not seen him since the day before. He looked about him, and then "Where's the little maid?" he asked. It was in this manner that he had formed the harmless habit of alluding to Miss Osmond.

"She's dancing," said Isabel. "You'll see her somewhere."

He looked among the dancers and at last caught Pansy's eye. "She sees me, but she won't notice me," he then remarked. "Are you not dancing?"

"As you see, I'm a wall-flower."

"Won't you dance with me?"

"Thank you; I'd rather you should dance with the little maid."

"One need n't prevent the other — especially as she's engaged."

"She's not engaged for everything, and you can reserve yourself. She dances very hard, and you'll be the fresher."

"She dances beautifully," said Lord Warburton, following her with his eyes. "Ah, at last," he added, "she has given me a smile." He stood there with his handsome, easy, important physiognomy; and as Isabel observed him it came over her, as it had done before, that it was strange a man of his mettle should take an interest in a little maid. It struck her as a great incongruity; neither Pansy's small fascinations, nor his own kindness, his good-nature, not even his need for amusement, which was extreme and constant, were sufficient to account for it. "I should like to dance with you," he went on in a moment, turning back to Isabel; "but I think I like even better to talk with you."

"Yes, it's better, and it's more worthy of your dignity. Great statesmen ought n't to waltz."

"Don't be cruel. Why did you recommend me then to dance with Miss Osmond?"

"Ah, that's different. If you danced with her it would look simply like a piece of kindness — as if you were doing it for her amusement. If you dance with me you'll look as if you were doing it for your own."

"And pray have n't I a right to amuse myself?"

"No, not with the affairs of the British Empire on your hands."

"The British Empire be hanged! You're always laughing at it."

"Amuse yourself with talking to me," said Isabel.

"I'm not sure it's really a recreation. You're too pointed; I've always to be defending myself. And you strike me as more than usually dangerous to-night. Will you absolutely not dance?"

"I can't leave my place. Pansy must find me here."

He was silent a little. "You're wonderfully good to her," he said suddenly.

Isabel stared a little and smiled. "Can you imagine one's not being?"

"No indeed. I know how one is charmed with her. But you must have done a great deal for her."

"I've taken her out with me," said Isabel, smiling still. "And I've seen that she has proper clothes."

"Your society must have been a great benefit to her. You've talked to her, advised her, helped her to develop."

"Ah yes, if she isn't the rose she has lived near it."

She laughed, and her companion did as much; but there was a certain visible preoccupation in his face which interfered with complete hilarity. "We all try to live as near it as we can," he said after a moment's hesitation.

Isabel turned away; Pansy was about to be restored to her, and she welcomed the diversion. We know how much she liked Lord Warburton; she thought him pleasanter even than the sum of his merits warranted; there was something in his friendship that appeared a kind of resource in case of indefinite need; it was like having a large balance at the bank. She felt happier when he was in the room; there was something reassuring in his approach; the sound of his voice reminded her of the beneficence of nature. Yet for all that it didn't suit her that he should be too near her, that he should take too much of her good-will for granted. She was afraid of that; she averted herself from it; she wished he wouldn't. She felt that if he should come too near, as it were, it might be in her to flash out and bid him keep his distance. Pansy came back to Isabel with another rent in her skirt, which was the inevitable consequence of the first and which she displayed to Isabel with serious eyes. There were too many gentlemen in uniform; they wore those dreadful spurs, which were fatal to the dresses of little maids. It hereupon became apparent that the resources of women are innumerable. Isabel devoted herself to Pansy's desecrated drapery; she fumbled for a pin and repaired the injury; she smiled and listened to her account of her adventures. Her attention, her sympathy were immediate and active; and they were in direct proportion to a sentiment with which they were in no way connected — a lively conjecture as to whether Lord Warburton might be trying to make love to her. It was not simply his words just then; it was others as well; it was the reference and the continuity. This was what she thought about while she pinned up Pansy's dress. If it were so, as she feared, he was of course unwitting; he himself had not taken account of his intention. But this made it none the more auspicious, made the situation none less impossible. The sooner he should get back into right relations with things the better. He immediately began to talk to Pansy — on whom it was certainly mystifying to see that he dropped a smile of chastened devotion. Pansy replied, as usual, with a little air of conscientious aspiration; he had to bend toward her a good deal in conversation, and her eyes, as usual, wandered up and down his robust person as if he had offered it to her for exhibition. She always seemed a little frightened; yet her fright was not of the painful character that suggests dislike; on the contrary, she looked as if she knew that he knew she liked him. Isabel left them together a little and wandered toward a friend whom she saw near and with whom she talked till the music of the following dance began, for which she knew Pansy to be also engaged. The girl joined her presently, with a little fluttered flush, and Isabel, who scrupulously took Osmond's view of his daughter's complete dependence, consigned her, as a precious and momentary loan, to her appointed partner. About all this matter she had her own imaginations, her own reserves; there were moments when Pansy's extreme adhesiveness made each of them, to her sense, look foolish. But Osmond had given her a sort of tableau of her position as his daughter's duenna, which consisted of gracious alternations of concession and contraction; and there were directions of his which she liked to think she obeyed to the letter. Perhaps, as regards some of them, it was because her doing so appeared to reduce them to the absurd.

After Pansy had been led away, she found Lord Warburton drawing near her again. She rested her eyes on him steadily; she wished she could sound his thoughts. But he had no appearance of confusion. "She has promised to dance with me later," he said.

"I'm glad of that. I suppose you've engaged her for the cotillion."

At this he looked a little awkward. "No, I did n't ask her for that. It's a quadrille."

"Ah, you're not clever!" said Isabel almost

angrily. "I told her to keep the cotillion in case you should ask for it."

"Poor little maid, fancy that!" And Lord Warburton laughed frankly. "Of course I will if you like."

"If I like? Oh, if you dance with her only because I like it — !"

"I'm afraid I bore her. She seems to have a lot of young fellows on her book."

Isabel dropped her eyes, reflecting rapidly; Lord Warburton stood there looking at her and she felt his eyes on her face. She felt much inclined to ask him to remove them. She did n't do so, however; she only said to him, after a minute, with her own raised: "Please let me understand."

"Understand what?"

"You told me ten days ago that you'd like to marry my stepdaughter. You've not forgotten it!"

"Forgotten it? I wrote to Mr. Osmond about it this morning."

"Ah," said Isabel, "he did n't mention to me that he had heard from you."

Lord Warburton stammered a little. "I — I did n't send my letter."

"Perhaps you forgot *that*."

"No, I was n't satisfied with it. It's an awkward sort of letter to write, you know. But I shall send it to-night."

"At three o'clock in the morning?"

"I mean later, in the course of the day."

"Very good. You still wish then to marry her?"

"Very much indeed."

"Are n't you afraid that you 'll bore her ?" And as her companion stared at this enquiry Isabel added: "If she can't dance with you for half an hour how will she be able to dance with you for life ?"

"Ah," said Lord Warburton readily, "I 'll let her dance with other people! About the cotillion, the fact is I thought that you — that you —"

"That I would do it with you? I told you I 'd do nothing."

"Exactly; so that while it 's going on I might find some quiet corner where we may sit down and talk."

"Oh," said Isabel gravely, "you 're much too considerate of me."

When the cotillion came Pansy was found to have engaged herself, thinking, in perfect humility, that Lord Warburton had no intentions. Isabel recommended him to seek another partner, but he assured her that he would dance with no one but herself. As, however, she had, in spite of the remonstrances of her hostess, declined other invitations on the ground that she was not dancing at all, it was not possible for her to make an exception in Lord Warburton's favour.

"After all I don't care to dance," he said; "it 's a barbarous amusement: I 'd much rather talk." And he intimated that he had discovered exactly the corner he had been looking for — a quiet nook in one of the smaller rooms, where the music would come to them faintly and not interfere with conversation. Isabel had decided to let him carry out his idea; she wished to be satisfied. She wandered away from the ball-room with him, though she knew her husband desired she should not lose sight of his daughter. It was with his daughter's *prétendant*, however; that would make it right for Osmond. On her way out of the ball-room she came upon Edward Rosier, who was standing in a doorway, with folded arms, looking at the dance in the attitude of a young man without illusions. She stopped a moment and asked him if he were not dancing.

"Certainly not, if I can't dance with *her!*" he answered.

"You had better go away then," said Isabel with the manner of good counsel.

"I shall not go till she does!" And he let Lord Warburton pass without giving him a look.

This nobleman, however, had noticed the melancholy youth, and he asked Isabel who her dismal friend was, remarking that he had seen him somewhere before.

"It's the young man I've told you about, who's in love with Pansy."

"Ah yes, I remember. He looks rather bad."

"He has reason. My husband won't listen to him."

"What's the matter with him?" Lord Warburton enquired. "He seems very harmless."

"He hasn't money enough, and he isn't very clever."

Lord Warburton listened with interest; he seemed struck with this account of Edward Rosier. "Dear me; he looked a well-set-up young fellow."

"So he is, but my husband's very particular."

"Oh, I see." And Lord Warburton paused a moment. "How much money has he got?" he then ventured to ask.

"Some forty thousand francs a year."

"Sixteen hundred pounds? Ah, but that's very good, you know."

"So I think. My husband, however, has larger ideas."

"Yes; I've noticed that your husband has very large ideas. Is he really an idiot, the young man?"

"An idiot? Not in the least; he's charming. When he was twelve years old I myself was in love with him."

"He doesn't look much more than twelve to-day," Lord Warburton rejoined vaguely, looking about him. Then with more point, "Don't you think we might sit here?" he asked.

"Wherever you please." The room was a sort of boudoir, pervaded by a subdued, rose-coloured light; a lady and gentleman moved out of it as our friends came in. "It's very kind of you to take such an interest in Mr. Rosier," Isabel said.

"He seems to me rather ill-treated. He had a face a yard long. I wondered what ailed him."

"You're a just man," said Isabel. "You've a kind thought even for a rival."

Lord Warburton suddenly turned with a stare. "A rival! Do you call him my rival?"

"Surely — if you both wish to marry the same person."

"Yes — but since he has no chance!"

"I like you, however that may be, for putting yourself in his place. It shows imagination."

"You like me for it?" And Lord Warburton looked at her with an uncertain eye. "I think you mean you're laughing at me for it."

"Yes, I'm laughing at you a little. But I like you as somebody to laugh at."

"Ah well, then, let me enter into his situation a little more. What do you suppose one could do for him?"

"Since I have been praising your imagination I'll leave you to imagine that yourself," Isabel said. "Pansy too would like you for that."

"Miss Osmond? Ah, she, I flatter myself, likes me already."

"Very much, I think."

He waited a little; he was still questioning her face. "Well then, I don't understand you. You don't mean that she cares for him?"

"Surely I've told you I thought she did."

A quick blush sprang to his brow. "You told me she would have no wish apart from her father's, and as I've gathered that he would favour me —!" He paused a little and then suggested "Don't you see?" through his blush.

"Yes, I told you she has an immense wish to please her father, and that it would probably take her very far."

"That seems to me a very proper feeling," said Lord Warburton.

"Certainly; it's a very proper feeling." Isabel remained silent for some moments; the room continued empty; the sound of the music reached them with its richness softened by the interposing apartments. Then at last she said: "But it hardly strikes me as the sort of feeling to which a man would wish to be indebted for a wife."

"I don't know; if the wife's a good one and he thinks she does well!"

"Yes, of course you must think that."

"I do; I can't help it. You call that very British, of course."

"No, I don't. I think Pansy would do wonderfully well to marry you, and I don't know who should know it better than you. But you're not in love."

"Ah, yes I am, Mrs. Osmond!"

Isabel shook her head. "You like to think you are while you sit here with me. But that's not how you strike me."

"I'm not like the young man in the doorway. I admit that. But what makes it so unnatural? Could any one in the world be more loveable than Miss Osmond?"

"No one, possibly. But love has nothing to do with good reasons."

"I don't agree with you. I'm delighted to have good reasons."

"Of course you are. If you were really in love you would n't care a straw for them."

"Ah, really in love — really in love!" Lord Warburton exclaimed, folding his arms, leaning back his head and stretching himself a little. "You must remember that I'm forty-two years old. I won't pretend I'm as I once was."

"Well, if you're sure," said Isabel, "it's all right."

He answered nothing; he sat there, with his head

back, looking before him. Abruptly, however, he changed his position; he turned quickly to his friend. "Why are you so unwilling, so sceptical?"

She met his eyes, and for a moment they looked straight at each other. If she wished to be satisfied she saw something that satisfied her; she saw in his expression the gleam of an idea that she was uneasy on her own account — that she was perhaps even in fear. It showed a suspicion, not a hope, but such as it was it told her what she wanted to know. Not for an instant should he suspect her of detecting in his proposal of marrying her step-daughter an implication of increased nearness to herself, or of thinking it, on such a betrayal, ominous. In that brief, extremely personal gaze, however, deeper meanings passed between them than they were conscious of at the moment.

"My dear Lord Warburton," she said, smiling, "you may do, so far as I'm concerned, whatever comes into your head."

And with this she got up and wandered into the adjoining room, where, within her companion's view, she was immediately addressed by a pair of gentlemen, high personages in the Roman world, who met her as if they had been looking for her. While she talked with them she found herself regretting she had moved; it looked a little like running away — all the more as Lord Warburton did n't follow her. She was glad of this, however, and at any rate she was satisfied. She was so well satisfied that when, in passing back into the ball-room, she found Edward Rosier still planted in the doorway, she stopped and spoke to him again. "You did right not to go away. I've some comfort for you."

"I need it," the young man softly wailed, "when I see you so awfully thick with *him!*"

"Don't speak of him; I'll do what I can for you. I'm afraid it won't be much, but what I can I'll do."

He looked at her with gloomy obliqueness. "What has suddenly brought you round?"

"The sense that you are an inconvenience in doorways!" she answered, smiling as she passed him. Half an hour later she took leave, with Pansy, and at the foot of the staircase the two ladies, with many other departing guests, waited a while for their carriage. Just as it approached Lord Warburton came out of the house and assisted them to reach their vehicle. He stood a moment at the door, asking Pansy if she had amused herself; and she, having answered him, fell back with a little air of fatigue. Then Isabel, at the window, detaining him by a movement of her finger, murmured gently: "Don't forget to send your letter to her father!"

XLIV

THE Countess Gemini was often extremely bored
— bored, in her own phrase, to extinction. She had
not been extinguished, however, and she struggled
bravely enough with her destiny, which had been
to marry an unaccommodating Florentine who insisted upon living in his native town, where he enjoyed such consideration as might attach to a gentleman whose talent for losing at cards had not
the merit of being incidental to an obliging disposition. The Count Gemini was not liked even by those
who won from him; and he bore a name which, having a measurable value in Florence, was, like the
local coin of the old Italian states, without currency
in other parts of the peninsula. In Rome he was
simply a very dull Florentine, and it is not remarkable that he should not have cared to pay frequent
visits to a place where, to carry it off, his dulness
needed more explanation than was convenient. The
Countess lived with her eyes upon Rome, and it was
the constant grievance of her life that she had not
an habitation there. She was ashamed to say how
seldom she had been allowed to visit that city; it
scarcely made the matter better that there were other
members of the Florentine nobility who never had
been there at all. She went whenever she could; that
was all she could say. Or rather not all, but all she

said she could say. In fact she had much more to say about it, and had often set forth the reasons why she hated Florence and wished to end her days in the shadow of Saint Peter's. They are reasons, however, that do not closely concern us, and were usually summed up in the declaration that Rome, in short, was the Eternal City and that Florence was simply a pretty little place like any other. The Countess apparently needed to connect the idea of eternity with her amusements. She was convinced that society was infinitely more interesting in Rome, where you met celebrities all winter at evening parties. At Florence there were no celebrities; none at least that one had heard of. Since her brother's marriage her impatience had greatly increased; she was so sure his wife had a more brilliant life than herself. She was not so intellectual as Isabel, but she was intellectual enough to do justice to Rome — not to the ruins and the catacombs, not even perhaps to the monuments and museums, the church ceremonies and the scenery; but certainly to all the rest. She heard a great deal about her sister-in-law and knew perfectly that Isabel was having a beautiful time. She had indeed seen it for herself on the only occasion on which she had enjoyed the hospitality of Palazzo Roccanera. She had spent a week there during the first winter of her brother's marriage, but she had not been encouraged to renew this satisfaction. Osmond did n't want her — that she was perfectly aware of; but she would have gone all the same, for after all she did n't care two straws about Osmond. It was her husband who would n't let her, and the money question was always a trouble. Isabel had been very nice; the Countess, who had liked her sister-in-law from the first, had not been blinded by envy to Isabel's personal merits. She had always observed that she got on better with clever women than with silly ones like herself; the silly ones could never understand her wisdom, whereas the clever ones — the really clever ones — always understood her silliness. It appeared to her that, different as they were in appearance and general style, Isabel and she had somewhere a patch of common ground that they would set their feet upon at last. It was not very large, but it was firm, and they should both know it when once they had really touched it. And then she lived, with Mrs. Osmond, under the influence of a pleasant surprise; she was constantly expecting that Isabel would "look down" on her, and she as constantly saw this operation postponed. She asked herself when it would begin, like fire-works, or Lent, or the opera season; not that she cared much, but she wondered what kept it in abeyance. Her sister-in-law regarded her with none but level glances and expressed for the poor Countess as little contempt as admiration. In reality Isabel would as soon have thought of despising her as of passing a moral judgement on a grasshopper. She was not indifferent to her husband's sister, however; she was rather a little afraid of her. She wondered at her; she thought her very extraordinary. The Countess seemed to her to have no soul; she was like a bright rare shell, with a polished surface and a remarkably pink lip, in which something would rattle when you shook it. This rattle was apparently the Countess's spiritual principle, a little loose nut that tumbled about inside of her. She was too odd for disdain, too anomalous for comparisons. Isabel would have invited her again (there was no question of inviting the Count); but Osmond, after his marriage, had not scrupled to say frankly that Amy was a fool of the worst species — a fool whose folly had the irrepressibility of genius. He said at another time that she had no heart; and he added in a moment that she had given it all away — in small pieces, like a frosted wedding-cake. The fact of not having been asked was of course another obstacle to the Countess's going again to Rome; but at the period with which this history has now to deal she was in receipt of an invitation to spend several weeks at Palazzo Roccanera. The proposal had come from Osmond himself, who wrote to his sister that she must be prepared to be very quiet. Whether or no she found in this phrase all the meaning he had put into it I am unable to say; but she accepted the invitation on any terms. She was curious, moreover; for one of the impressions of her former visit had been that her brother had found his match. Before the marriage she had been sorry for Isabel, so sorry as to have had serious thoughts — if any of the Countess's thoughts were serious — of putting her on her guard. But she had let that pass, and after a little she was reassured. Osmond was as lofty as ever, but his wife would not be an easy victim. The Countess was not very exact at measurements, but it seemed to her that if Isabel should draw herself up she would be the taller spirit of the two. What she wanted to learn now was whether Isabel had drawn herself up; it would give her immense pleasure to see Osmond over-topped.

Several days before she was to start for Rome a servant brought her the card of a visitor — a card with the simple superscription "Henrietta C. Stack-pole." The Countess pressed her finger-tips to her forehead; she did n't remember to have known any such Henrietta as that. The servant then remarked that the lady had requested him to say that if the Countess should not recognise her name she would know her well enough on seeing her. By the time she appeared before her visitor she had in fact re-minded herself that there was once a literary lady at Mrs. Touchett's; the only woman of letters she had ever encountered — that is the only modern one, since she was the daughter of a defunct poetess. She recognised Miss Stackpole immediately, the more so that Miss Stackpole seemed perfectly unchanged; and the Countess, who was thoroughly good-natured, thought it rather fine to be called on by a person of that sort of distinction. She wondered if Miss Stack-pole had come on account of her mother — whether she had heard of the American Corinne. Her mother was not at all like Isabel's friend; the Countess could see at a glance that this lady was much more contemporary; and she received an impression of the improvements that were taking place — chiefly in distant countries — in the character (the profes-sional character) of literary ladies. Her mother had been used to wear a Roman scarf thrown over a pair of shoulders timorously bared of their tight black velvet (oh the old clothes!) and a gold laurel-wreath set upon a multitude of glossy ringlets. She had spoken softly and vaguely, with the accent of her "Creole" ancestors, as she always confessed; she sighed a great deal and was not at all enterprising. But Henrietta, the Countess could see, was always closely buttoned and compactly braided; there was something brisk and business-like in her appearance; her manner was almost conscientiously familiar. It was as impossible to imagine her ever vaguely sighing as to imagine a letter posted without its address. The Countess could not but feel that the correspondent of the *Interviewer* was much more in the movement than the American Corinne. She explained that she had called on the Countess because she was the only person she knew in Florence, and that when she visited a foreign city she liked to see something more than superficial travellers. She knew Mrs. Touchett, but Mrs. Touchett was in America, and even if she had been in Florence Henrietta would not have put herself out for her, since Mrs. Touchett was not one of her admirations.

"Do you mean by that that I am?" the Countess graciously asked.

"Well, I like you better than I do her," said Miss Stackpole. "I seem to remember that when I saw you before you were very interesting. I don't know whether it was an accident or whether it's your usual style. At any rate I was a good deal struck with what you said. I made use of it afterwards in print."

"Dear me!" cried the Countess, staring and half-alarmed; "I had no idea I ever said anything remarkable! I wish I had known it at the time."

"It was about the position of woman in this city," Miss Stackpole remarked. "You threw a good deal of light upon it."

"The position of woman's very uncomfortable. Is that what you mean? And you wrote it down and published it?" the Countess went on. "Ah, do let me see it!"

"I'll write to them to send you the paper if you like," Henrietta said. "I did n't mention your name; I only said a lady of high rank. And then I quoted your views."

The Countess threw herself hastily backward, tossing up her clasped hands. "Do you know I'm rather sorry you did n't mention my name? I should have rather liked to see my name in the papers. I forget what my views were; I have so many! But I'm not ashamed of them. I'm not at all like my brother — I suppose you know my brother? He thinks it a kind of scandal to be put in the papers; if you were to quote him he'd never forgive you."

"He need n't be afraid; I shall never refer to him," said Miss Stackpole with bland dryness. "That's another reason," she added, "why I wanted to come to see you. You know Mr. Osmond married my dearest friend."

"Ah, yes; you were a friend of Isabel's. I was trying to think what I knew about you."

"I'm quite willing to be known by that," Henrietta declared. "But that is n't what your brother likes to know me by. He has tried to break up my relations with Isabel."

"Don't permit it," said the Countess.

"That's what I want to talk about. I'm going to Rome."

"So am I!" the Countess cried. "We'll go together."

"With great pleasure. And when I write about my journey I'll mention you by name as my companion."

The Countess sprang from her chair and came and sat on the sofa beside her visitor. "Ah, you must send me the paper! My husband won't like it, but he need never see it. Besides, he does n't know how to read."

Henrietta's large eyes became immense. "Does n't know how to read? May I put that into my letter?"

"Into your letter?"

"In the *Interviewer*. That's my paper."

"Oh yes, if you like; with his name. Are you going to stay with Isabel?"

Henrietta held up her head, gazing a little in silence at her hostess. "She has not asked me. I wrote to her I was coming, and she answered that she would engage a room for me at a *pension*. She gave no reason."

The Countess listened with extreme interest. "The reason's Osmond," she pregnantly remarked.

"Isabel ought to make a stand," said Miss Stackpole. "I'm afraid she has changed a great deal. I told her she would."

"I'm sorry to hear it; I hoped she would have her own way. Why does n't my brother like you?" the Countess ingenuously added.

"I don't know and I don't care. He's perfectly welcome not to like me; I don't want every one to like me; I should think less of myself if some people did. A journalist can't hope to do much good unless he gets a good deal hated; that's the way he knows how his work goes on. And it's just the same for a lady. But I did n't expect it of Isabel."

"Do you mean that she hates you?" the Countess enquired.

"I don't know; I want to see. That's what I'm going to Rome for."

"Dear me, what a tiresome errand!" the Countess exclaimed.

"She does n't write to me in the same way; it's easy to see there's a difference. If you know anything," Miss Stackpole went on, "I should like to hear it beforehand, so as to decide on the line I shall take."

The Countess thrust out her under lip and gave a gradual shrug. "I know very little; I see and hear very little of Osmond. He does n't like me any better than he appears to like you."

"Yet you're not a lady correspondent," said Henrietta pensively.

"Oh, he has plenty of reasons. Nevertheless they've invited me — I'm to stay in the house!" And the Countess smiled almost fiercely; her exultation, for the moment, took little account of Miss Stackpole's disappointment.

This lady, however, regarded it very placidly. "I should n't have gone if she *had* asked me. That is I think I should n't ; and I 'm glad I had n't to make up my mind. It would have been a very difficult question. I should n't have liked to turn away from her, and yet I should n't have been happy under her roof. A *pension* will suit me very well. But that 's not all."

"Rome 's very good just now," said the Countess; "there are all sorts of brilliant people. Did you ever hear of Lord Warburton ?"

"Hear of him ? I know him very well. Do you consider him very brilliant ?" Henrietta enquired.

"I don't know him, but I 'm told he 's extremely *grand seigneur*. He 's making love to Isabel."

"Making love to her ?"

"So I 'm told; I don't know the details," said the Countess lightly. "But Isabel 's pretty safe."

Henrietta gazed earnestly at her companion; for a moment she said nothing. "When do you go to Rome ?" she enquired abruptly.

"Not for a week, I 'm afraid."

"I shall go to-morrow," Henrietta said. "I think I had better not wait."

"Dear me, I 'm sorry; I 'm having some dresses made. I 'm told Isabel receives immensely. But I shall see you there; I shall call on you at your *pension*." Henrietta sat still — she was lost in thought; and suddenly the Countess cried: "Ah, but if you don't go with me you can't describe our journey!"

Miss Stackpole seemed unmoved by this consideration; she was thinking of something else and presently expressed it. "I 'm not sure that I understand you about Lord Warburton."

"Understand me? I mean he 's very nice, that 's all."

"Do you consider it nice to make love to married women?" Henrietta enquired with unprecedented distinctness.

The Countess stared, and then with a little violent laugh: "It 's certain all the nice men do it. Get married and you 'll see!" she added.

"That idea would be enough to prevent me," said Miss Stackpole. "I should want my own husband; I should n't want any one else's. Do you mean that Isabel's guilty — guilty — ?" And she paused a little, choosing her expression.

"Do I mean she 's guilty? Oh dear no, not yet, I hope. I only mean that Osmond 's very tiresome and that Lord Warburton, as I hear, is a great deal at the house. I 'm afraid you 're scandalised."

"No, I 'm just anxious," Henrietta said.

"Ah, you 're not very complimentary to Isabel! You should have more confidence. I 'll tell you," the Countess added quickly: "if it will be a comfort to you I engage to draw him off."

Miss Stackpole answered at first only with the deeper solemnity of her gaze. "You don't understand me," she said after a while. "I have n't the idea you seem to suppose. I 'm not afraid for Isabel — in that way. I 'm only afraid she 's unhappy — that 's what I want to get at."

The Countess gave a dozen turns of the head; she

looked impatient and sarcastic. "That may very well be; for my part I should like to know whether Osmond is." Miss Stackpole had begun a little to bore her.

"If she's really changed that must be at the bottom of it," Henrietta went on.

"You'll see; she'll tell you," said the Countess.

"Ah, she may *not* tell me — that's what I'm afraid of!"

"Well, if Osmond isn't amusing himself — in his own old way — I flatter myself I shall discover it," the Countess rejoined.

"I don't care for that," said Henrietta.

"I do immensely! If Isabel's unhappy I'm very sorry for her, but I can't help it. I might tell her something that would make her worse, but I can't tell her anything that would console her. What did she go and marry him for? If she had listened to me she'd have got rid of him. I'll forgive her, however, if I find she has made things hot for him! If she has simply allowed him to trample upon her I don't know that I shall even pity her. But I don't think that's very likely. I count upon finding that if she's miserable she has at least made *him* so."

Henrietta got up; these seemed to her, naturally, very dreadful expectations. She honestly believed she had no desire to see Mr. Osmond unhappy; and indeed he could not be for her the subject of a flight of fancy. She was on the whole rather disappointed in the Countess, whose mind moved in a narrower circle than she had imagined, though with a capacity for coarseness even there. "It will be better if they love each other," she said for edification.

"They can't. He can't love any one."

"I presumed that was the case. But it only aggravates my fear for Isabel. I shall positively start to-morrow."

"Isabel certainly has devotees," said the Countess, smiling very vividly. "I declare I don't pity her."

"It may be I can't assist her," Miss Stackpole pursued, as if it were well not to have illusions.

"You can have wanted to, at any rate; that's something. I believe that's what you came from America for," the Countess suddenly added.

"Yes, I wanted to look after her," Henrietta said serenely.

Her hostess stood there smiling at her with small bright eyes and an eager-looking nose; with cheeks into each of which a flush had come. "Ah, that's very pretty — *c'est bien gentil!* Isn't it what they call friendship?"

"I don't know what they call it. I thought I had better come."

"She's very happy — she's very fortunate," the Countess went on. "She has others besides." And then she broke out passionately. "She's more fortunate than I! I'm as unhappy as she — I've a very bad husband; he's a great deal worse than Osmond. And I've no friends. I thought I had, but they're gone. No one, man or woman, would do for me what you've done for her."

Henrietta was touched; there was nature in this bitter effusion. She gazed at her companion a mo-

ment, and then: "Look here, Countess, I'll do anything for you that you like. I'll wait over and travel
with you."

"Never mind," the Countess answered with a
quick change of tone: "only describe me in the newspaper!"

Henrietta, before leaving her, however, was obliged
to make her understand that she could give no ficti-
tious representation of her journey to Rome. Miss
Stackpole was a strictly veracious reporter. On
quitting her she took the way to the Lung' Arno,
the sunny quay beside the yellow river where the
bright-faced inns familiar to tourists stand all in a
row. She had learned her way before this through
the streets of Florence (she was very quick in such
matters), and was therefore able to turn with great
decision of step out of the little square which forms
the approach to the bridge of the Holy Trinity. She
proceeded to the left, toward the Ponte Vecchio, and
stopped in front of one of the hotels which overlook
that delightful structure. Here she drew forth a
small pocket-book, took from it a card and a pencil
and, after meditating a moment, wrote a few words.
It is our privilege to look over her shoulder, and if
we exercise it we may read the brief query: "Could
I see you this evening for a few moments on a very
important matter?" Henrietta added that she should
start on the morrow for Rome. Armed with this
little document she approached the porter, who now
had taken up his station in the doorway, and asked
if Mr. Goodwood were at home. The porter replied,
as porters always reply, that he had gone out about

twenty minutes before; whereupon Henrietta presented her card and begged it might be handed him on his return. She left the inn and pursued her course along the quay to the severe portico of the Uffizi, through which she presently reached the entrance of the famous gallery of paintings. Making her way in, she ascended the high staircase which leads to the upper chambers. The long corridor, glazed on one side and decorated with antique busts, which gives admission to these apartments, presented an empty vista in which the bright winter light twinkled upon the marble floor. The gallery is very cold and during the midwinter weeks but scantily visited. Miss Stackpole may appear more ardent in her quest of artistic beauty than she has hitherto struck us as being, but she had after all her preferences and admirations. One of the latter was the little Correggio of the Tribune — the Virgin kneeling down before the sacred infant, who lies in a litter of straw, and clapping her hands to him while he delightedly laughs and crows. Henrietta had a special devotion to this intimate scene — she thought it the most beautiful picture in the world. On her way, at present, from New York to Rome, she was spending but three days in Florence, and yet reminded herself that they must not elapse without her paying another visit to her favourite work of art. She had a great sense of beauty in all ways, and it involved a good many intellectual obligations. She was about to turn into the Tribune when a gentleman came out of it; whereupon she gave a little exclamation and stood before Caspar Goodwood.

"I've just been at your hotel," she said. "I left a card for you."

"I'm very much honoured," Caspar Goodwood answered as if he really meant it.

"It was not to honour you I did it; I've called on you before and I know you don't like it. It was to talk to you a little about something."

He looked for a moment at the buckle in her hat. "I shall be very glad to hear what you wish to say."

"You don't like to talk with me," said Henrietta. "But I don't care for that; I don't talk for your amusement. I wrote a word to ask you to come and see me; but since I've met you here this will do as well."

"I was just going away," Goodwood stated; "but of course I'll stop." He was civil, but not enthusiastic.

Henrietta, however, never looked for great professions, and she was so much in earnest that she was thankful he would listen to her on any terms. She asked him first, none the less, if he had seen all the pictures.

"All I want to. I've been here an hour."

"I wonder if you've seen my Correggio," said Henrietta. "I came up on purpose to have a look at it." She went into the Tribune and he slowly accompanied her.

"I suppose I've seen it, but I did n't know it was yours. I don't remember pictures — especially that sort." She had pointed out her favourite work, and he asked her if it was about Correggio she wished to talk with him.

"No," said Henrietta, "it's about something less harmonious!" They had the small, brilliant room, a splendid cabinet of treasures, to themselves; there was only a custode hovering about the Medicean Venus. "I want you to do me a favour," Miss Stackpole went on.

Caspar Goodwood frowned a little, but he expressed no embarrassment at the sense of not looking eager. His face was that of a much older man than our earlier friend. "I'm sure it's something I shan't like," he said rather loudly.

"No, I don't think you'll like it. If you did it would be no favour."

"Well, let's hear it," he went on in the tone of a man quite conscious of his patience.

"You may say there's no particular reason why you should do me a favour. Indeed I only know of one: the fact that if you'd let me I'd gladly do *you* one." Her soft, exact tone, in which there was no attempt at effect, had an extreme sincerity; and her companion, though he presented rather a hard surface, could n't help being touched by it. When he was touched he rarely showed it, however, by the usual signs; he neither blushed, nor looked away, nor looked conscious. He only fixed his attention more directly; he seemed to consider with added firmness. Henrietta continued therefore disinterestedly, without the sense of an advantage. "I may say now, indeed—it seems a good time — that if I've ever annoyed you (and I think sometimes I have) it's because I knew I was willing to suffer annoyance for you. I've troubled you—doubtless. But I'd *take* trouble for you."

Goodwood hesitated. "You're taking trouble now."

"Yes, I am — some. I want you to consider whether it's better on the whole that you should go to Rome."

"I thought you were going to say that!" he answered rather artlessly.

"You *have* considered it then?"

"Of course I have, very carefully. I've looked all round it. Otherwise I should n't have come so far as this. That's what I stayed in Paris two months for. I was thinking it over."

"I'm afraid you decided as you liked. You decided it was best because you were so much attracted."

"Best for whom, do you mean?" Goodwood demanded.

"Well, for yourself first. For Mrs. Osmond next."

"Oh, it won't do *her* any good! I don't flatter myself that."

"Won't it do her some harm? — that's the question."

"I don't see what it will matter to her. I'm nothing to Mrs. Osmond. But if you want to know, I do want to see her myself."

"Yes, and that's why you go."

"Of course it is. Could there be a better reason?"

"How will it help you? — that's what I want to know," said Miss Stackpole.

"That's just what I can't tell you. It's just what I was thinking about in Paris."

"It will make you more discontented."

"Why do you say 'more' so?" Goodwood asked rather sternly. "How do you know I'm discontented?"

"Well," said Henrietta, hesitating a little, "you seem never to have cared for another."

"How do you know what I care for?" he cried with a big blush. "Just now I care to go to Rome."

Henrietta looked at him in silence, with a sad yet luminous expression. "Well," she observed at last, "I only wanted to tell you what I think; I had it on my mind. Of course you think it's none of my business. But nothing is any one's business, on that principle."

"It's very kind of you; I'm greatly obliged to you for your interest," said Caspar Goodwood. "I shall go to Rome and I shan't hurt Mrs. Osmond."

"You won't hurt her, perhaps. But will you help her? — that's the real issue."

"Is she in need of help?" he asked slowly, with a penetrating look.

"Most women always are," said Henrietta, with conscientious evasiveness and generalising less hopefully than usual. "If you go to Rome," she added, "I hope you'll be a true friend — not a selfish one!" And she turned off and began to look at the pictures.

Caspar Goodwood let her go and stood watching her while she wandered round the room; but after a moment he rejoined her. "You've heard something about her here," he then resumed. "I should like to know what you've heard."

Henrietta had never prevaricated in her life, and, though on this occasion there might have been a fitness in doing so, she decided, after thinking some minutes, to make no superficial exception. "Yes, I've heard," she answered; "but as I don't want you to go to Rome I won't tell you."

"Just as you please. I shall see for myself," he said. Then inconsistently, for him, "You've heard she's unhappy!" he added.

"Oh, you won't see that!" Henrietta exclaimed.

"I hope not. When do you start?"

"To-morrow, by the evening train. And you?"

Goodwood hung back; he had no desire to make his journey to Rome in Miss Stackpole's company. His indifference to this advantage was not of the same character as Gilbert Osmond's, but it had at this moment an equal distinctness. It was rather a tribute to Miss Stackpole's virtues than a reference to her faults. He thought her very remarkable, very brilliant, and he had, in theory, no objection to the class to which she belonged. Lady correspondents appeared to him a part of the natural scheme of things in a progressive country, and though he never read their letters he supposed that they ministered somehow to social prosperity. But it was this very eminence of their position that made him wish Miss Stackpole didn't take so much for granted. She took for granted that he was always ready for some allusion to Mrs. Osmond; she had done so when they met in Paris, six weeks after his arrival in Europe, and she had repeated the assumption with every successive opportunity. He had no wish whatever

to allude to Mrs. Osmond; he was *not* always thinking of her; he was perfectly sure of that. He was the
most reserved, the least colloquial of men, and this
enquiring authoress was constantly flashing her lantern into the quiet darkness of his soul. He wished
she did n't care so much; he even wished, though it
might seem rather brutal of him, that she would
leave him alone. In spite of this, however, he just
now made other reflections — which show how
widely different, in effect, his ill-humour was from
Gilbert Osmond's. He desired to go immediately
to Rome; he would have liked to go alone, in the
night-train. He hated the European railway-carriages, in which one sat for hours in a vise, knee to
knee and nose to nose with a foreigner to whom one
presently found one's self objecting with all the added
vehemence of one's wish to have the window open;
and if they were worse at night even than by day, at
least at night one could sleep and dream of an American saloon-car. But he could n't take a night-train
when Miss Stackpole was starting in the morning; it
struck him that this would be an insult to an unpro-
tected woman. Nor could he wait until after she had
gone unless he should wait longer than he had patience for. It would n't do to start the next day. She
worried him; she oppressed him; the idea of spending the day in a European railway-carriage with her
offered a complication of irritations. Still, she was a
lady travelling alone; it was his duty to put himself
out for her. There could be no two questions about
that; it was a perfectly clear necessity. He looked
extremely grave for some moments and then said,

wholly without the flourish of gallantry but in a tone of extreme distinctness, "Of course if you're going to-morrow I'll go too, as I may be of assistance to you."

"Well, Mr. Goodwood, I should hope so!" Henrietta returned imperturbably.

XLV

I HAVE already had reason to say that Isabel knew her husband to be displeased by the continuance of Ralph's visit to Rome. That knowledge was very present to her as she went to her cousin's hotel the day after she had invited Lord Warburton to give a tangible proof of his sincerity; and at this moment, as at others, she had a sufficient perception of the sources of Osmond's opposition. He wished her to have no freedom of mind, and he knew perfectly well that Ralph was an apostle of freedom. It was just because he was this, Isabel said to herself, that it was a refreshment to go and see him. It will be perceived that she partook of this refreshment in spite of her husband's aversion to it, that is partook of it, as she flattered herself, discreetly. She had not as yet undertaken to act in direct opposition to his wishes; he was her appointed and inscribed master; she gazed at moments with a sort of incredulous blankness at this fact. It weighed upon her imagination, however; constantly present to her mind were all the traditionary decencies and sanctities of marriage. The idea of violating them filled her with shame as well as with dread, for on giving herself away she had lost sight of this contingency in the perfect belief that her husband's intentions were as generous as her own. She seemed to see, none the less, the rapid approach of the day when she should have to take back something she had solemnly bestown. Such a ceremony would be odious and monstrous; she tried to shut her eyes to it meanwhile. Osmond would do nothing to help it by beginning first; he would put that burden upon her to the end. He had not yet formally forbidden her to call upon Ralph; but she felt sure that unless Ralph should very soon depart this prohibition would come. How could poor Ralph depart? The weather as yet made it impossible. She could perfectly understand her husband's wish for the event; she did n't, to be just, see how he *could* like her to be with her cousin. Ralph never said a word against him, but Osmond's sore, mute protest was none the less founded. If he should positively interpose, if he should put forth his authority, she would have to decide, and that would n't be easy. The prospect made her heart beat and her cheeks burn, as I say, in advance; there were moments when, in her wish to avoid an open rupture, she found herself wishing Ralph would start even at a risk. And it was of no use that, when catching herself in this state of mind, she called herself a feeble spirit, a coward. It was not that she loved Ralph less, but that almost anything seemed preferable to repudiating the most serious act — the single sacred act — of her life. That appeared to make the whole future hideous. To break with Osmond once would be to break for ever; any open acknowledgement of irreconcilable needs would be an admission that their whole attempt had proved a failure. For them there could be no condonement, no compromise, no easy forgetfulness, no formal readjustment. They had attempted only one thing, but that one thing was to have been exquisite. Once they missed it nothing else would do; there was no conceivable substitute for that success. For the moment, Isabel went to the Hôtel de Paris as often as she thought well; the measure of propriety was in the canon of taste, and there could n't have been a better proof that morality was, so to speak, a matter of earnest appreciation. Isabel's application of that measure had been particularly free to-day, for in addition to the general truth that she could n't leave Ralph to die alone she had something important to ask of him. This indeed was Gilbert's business as well as her own.

She came very soon to what she wished to speak of. "I want you to answer me a question. It's about Lord Warburton."

"I think I guess your question," Ralph answered from his arm-chair, out of which his thin legs protruded at greater length than ever.

"Very possibly you guess it. Please then answer it."

"Oh, I don't say I can do that."

"You're intimate with him," she said; "you've a great deal of observation of him."

"Very true. But think how he must dissimulate!"

"Why should he dissimulate? That's not his nature."

"Ah, you must remember that the circumstances are peculiar," said Ralph with an air of private amusement.

"To a certain extent — yes. But is he really in love?"

"Very much, I think. I can make that out."

"Ah!" said Isabel with a certain dryness.

Ralph looked at her as if his mild hilarity had been touched with mystification. "You say that as if you were disappointed."

Isabel got up, slowly smoothing her gloves and eyeing them thoughtfully. "It's after all no business of mine."

"You're very philosophic," said her cousin. And then in a moment: "May I enquire what you're talking about?"

Isabel stared. "I thought you knew. Lord Warburton tells me he wants, of all things in the world, to marry Pansy. I've told you that before, without eliciting a comment from you. You might risk one this morning, I think. Is it your belief that he really cares for her?"

"Ah, for Pansy, no!" cried Ralph very positively.

"But you said just now he did."

Ralph waited a moment. "That he cared for you, Mrs. Osmond."

Isabel shook her head gravely. "That's nonsense, you know."

"Of course it is. But the nonsense is Warburton's, not mine."

"That would be very tiresome." She spoke, as she flattered herself, with much subtlety.

"I ought to tell you indeed," Ralph went on, "that to me he has denied it."

"It's very good of you to talk about it together! Has he also told you that he's in love with Pansy?"

"He has spoken very well of her — very properly. He has let me know, of course, that he thinks she would do very well at Lockleigh."

"Does he really think it?"

"Ah, what Warburton really thinks — !" said Ralph.

Isabel fell to smoothing her gloves again; they were long, loose gloves on which she could freely expend herself. Soon, however, she looked up, and then, "Ah, Ralph, you give me no help!" she cried abruptly and passionately.

It was the first time she had alluded to the need for help, and the words shook her cousin with their violence. He gave a long murmur of relief, of pity, of tenderness; it seemed to him that at last the gulf between them had been bridged. It was this that made him exclaim in a moment: "How unhappy you must be!"

He had no sooner spoken than she recovered her self-possession, and the first use she made of it was to pretend she had not heard him. "When I talk of your helping me I talk great nonsense," she said with a quick smile. "The idea of my troubling you with my domestic embarrassments! The matter's very simple; Lord Warburton must get on by himself. I can't undertake to see him through."

"He ought to succeed easily," said Ralph.

Isabel debated. "Yes — but he has not always succeeded."

"Very true. You know, however, how that always surprised me. Is Miss Osmond capable of giving us a surprise?"

"It will come from him, rather. I seem to see that after all he'll let the matter drop."

"He'll do nothing dishonourable," said Ralph.

"I'm very sure of that. Nothing can be more honourable than for him to leave the poor child alone. She cares for another person, and it's cruel to attempt to bribe her by magnificent offers to give him up."

"Cruel to the other person perhaps — the one she cares for. But Warburton isn't obliged to mind that."

"No, cruel to her," said Isabel. "She would be very unhappy if she were to allow herself to be persuaded to desert poor Mr. Rosier. That idea seems to amuse you; of course you're not in love with him. He has the merit — for Pansy — of being in love with Pansy. She can see at a glance that Lord Warburton isn't."

"He'd be very good to her," said Ralph.

"He has been good to her already. Fortunately, however, he has not said a word to disturb her. He could come and bid her good-bye to-morrow with perfect propriety."

"How would your husband like that?"

"Not at all; and he may be right in not liking it. Only he must obtain satisfaction himself."

"Has he commissioned you to obtain it?" Ralph ventured to ask.

"It was natural that as an old friend of Lord Warburton's — an older friend, that is, than Gilbert — I should take an interest in his intentions."

"Take an interest in his renouncing them, you mean?"

Isabel hesitated, frowning a little. "Let me understand. Are you pleading his cause?"

"Not in the least. I'm very glad he should n't become your stepdaughter's husband. It makes such a very queer relation to you!" said Ralph, smiling. "But I'm rather nervous lest your husband should think you have n't pushed him enough."

Isabel found herself able to smile as well as he. "He knows me well enough not to have expected me to push. He himself has no intention of pushing, I presume. I'm not afraid I shall not be able to justify myself!" she said lightly.

Her mask had dropped for an instant, but she had put it on again, to Ralph's infinite disappointment. He had caught a glimpse of her natural face and he wished immensely to look into it. He had an almost savage desire to hear her complain of her husband — hear her say that she should be held accountable for Lord Warburton's defection. Ralph was certain that this was her situation; he knew by instinct, in advance, the form that in such an event Osmond's displeasure would take. It could only take the meanest and cruellest. He would have liked to warn Isabel of it — to let her see at least how he judged for her and how he knew. It little mattered that Isabel would know much better; it was for his own satisfaction more than for hers that he longed to show her he was not deceived. He tried and tried again to make her betray Osmond; he felt cold-blooded, cruel, dishonourable almost, in doing so. But it scarcely mattered, for he only failed. What had she come for then, and why did she seem almost to offer him a chance to violate their tacit convention? Why did she ask him his advice if she gave him no liberty to answer her? How could they talk of her domestic embarrassments, as it pleased her humorously to designate them, if the principal factor was not to be mentioned? These contradictions were themselves but an indication of her trouble, and her cry for help, just before, was the only thing he was bound to consider. "You'll be decidedly at variance, all the same," he said in a moment. And as she answered nothing, looking as if she scarce understood, "You'll find yourselves thinking very differently," he continued.

"That may easily happen, among the most united couples!" She took up her parasol; he saw she was nervous, afraid of what he might say. "It's a matter we can hardly quarrel about, however," she added; "for almost all the interest is on his side. That's very natural. Pansy's after all his daughter — not mine." And she put out her hand to wish him good-bye.

Ralph took an inward resolution that she should n't leave him without his letting her know that he knew everything: it seemed too great an opportunity to lose. "Do you know what his interest will make him say?" he asked as he took her hand. She shook her head, rather dryly — not discouragingly — and he went on. "It will make him say that your want of zeal is owing to jealousy." He stopped a moment; her face made him afraid.

"To jealousy?"

"To jealousy of his daughter."

She blushed red and threw back her head. "You're not kind," she said in a voice that he had never heard on her lips.

"Be frank with me and you'll see," he answered.

But she made no reply; she only pulled her hand out of his own, which he tried still to hold, and rapidly withdrew from the room. She made up her mind to speak to Pansy, and she took an occasion on the same day, going to the girl's room before dinner. Pansy was already dressed; she was always in advance of the time: it seemed to illustrate her pretty patience and the graceful stillness with which she could sit and wait. At present she was seated, in her fresh array, before the bed-room fire; she had blown out her candles on the completion of her toilet, in accordance with the economical habits in which she had been brought up and which she was now more careful than ever to observe; so that the room was lighted only by a couple of logs. The rooms in Palazzo Roccanera were as spacious as they were numerous, and Pansy's virginal bower was an immense chamber with a dark, heavily-timbered ceiling. Its diminutive mistress, in the midst of it, appeared but a speck of humanity, and as she got up, with quick deference, to welcome Isabel, the latter was more than ever struck with her shy sincerity. Isabel had a difficult task — the only thing was to perform it as simply as possible. She felt bitter and angry, but she warned

herself against betraying this heat. She was afraid
even of looking too grave, or at least too stern; she
was afraid of causing alarm. But Pansy seemed to
have guessed she had come more or less as a con-
fessor; for after she had moved the chair in which
she had been sitting a little nearer to the fire and
Isabel had taken her place in it, she kneeled down
on a cushion in front of her, looking up and resting
her clasped hands on her stepmother's knees. What
Isabel wished to do was to hear from her own lips
that her mind was not occupied with Lord Warburton; but if she desired the assurance she felt herself
by no means at liberty to provoke it. The girl's father
would have qualified this as rank treachery; and
indeed Isabel knew that if Pansy should display the
smallest germ of a disposition to encourage Lord
Warburton her own duty was to hold her tongue. It
was difficult to interrogate without appearing to suggest; Pansy's supreme simplicity, an innocence even
more complete than Isabel had yet judged it, gave
to the most tentative enquiry something of the effect
of an admonition. As she knelt there in the vague
firelight, with her pretty dress dimly shining, her
hands folded half in appeal and half in submission,
her soft eyes, raised and fixed, full of the seriousness
of the situation, she looked to Isabel like a childish
martyr decked out for sacrifice and scarcely presum-
ing even to hope to avert it. When Isabel said to
her that she had never yet spoken to her of what
might have been going on in relation to her getting
married, but that her silence had not been indifference
or ignorance, had only been the desire to leave her at

liberty, Pansy bent forward, raised her face nearer and nearer, and with a little murmur which evidently expressed a deep longing, answered that she had greatly wished her to speak and that she begged her to advise her now.

"It's difficult for me to advise you," Isabel returned. "I don't know how I can undertake that. That's for your father; you must get his advice and, above all, you must act on it."

At this Pansy dropped her eyes; for a moment she said nothing. "I think I should like your advice better than papa's," she presently remarked.

"That's not as it should be," said Isabel coldly. "I love you very much, but your father loves you better."

"It isn't because you love me — it's because you're a lady," Pansy answered with the air of saying something very reasonable. "A lady can advise a young girl better than a man."

"I advise you then to pay the greatest respect to your father's wishes."

"Ah yes," said the child eagerly, "I must do that."

"But if I speak to you now about your getting married it's not for your own sake, it's for mine," Isabel went on. "If I try to learn from you what you expect, what you desire, it's only that I may act accordingly."

Pansy stared, and then very quickly, "Will you do everything I want?" she asked.

"Before I say yes I must know what such things are."

Pansy presently told her that the only thing she wanted in life was to marry Mr. Rosier. He had asked her and she had told him she would do so if her papa would allow it. Now her papa would n't allow it.

"Very well then, it's impossible," Isabel pronounced.

"Yes, it's impossible," said Pansy without a sigh and with the same extreme attention in her clear little face.

"You must think of something else then," Isabel went on; but Pansy, sighing at this, told her that she had attempted that feat without the least success.

"You think of those who think of you," she said with a faint smile. "I know Mr. Rosier thinks of me."

"He ought not to," said Isabel loftily. "Your father has expressly requested he should n't."

"He can't help it, because he knows I think of *him.*"

"You should n't think of him. There's some excuse for him, perhaps; but there's none for you."

"I wish you would try to find one," the girl exclaimed as if she were praying to the Madonna.

"I should be very sorry to attempt it," said the Madonna with unusual frigidity. "If you knew some one else was thinking of you, would you think of him?"

"No one can think of me as Mr. Rosier does; no one has the right."

"Ah, but I don't admit Mr. Rosier's right!" Isabel hypocritically cried.

Pansy only gazed at her, evidently much puzzled; and Isabel, taking advantage of it, began to represent to her the wretched consequences of disobeying her father. At this Pansy stopped her with the assurance that she would never disobey him, would never marry without his consent. And she announced, in the serenest, simplest tone, that, though she might never marry Mr. Rosier, she would never cease to think of him. She appeared to have accepted the idea of eternal singleness; but Isabel of course was free to reflect that she had no conception of its meaning. She was perfectly sincere; she was prepared to give up her lover. This might seem an important step toward taking another, but for Pansy, evidently, it failed to lead in that direction. She felt no bitterness toward her father; there was no bitterness in her heart; there was only the sweetness of fidelity to Edward Rosier, and a strange, exquisite intimation that she could prove it better by remaining single than even by marrying him.

"Your father would like you to make a better marriage," said Isabel. "Mr. Rosier's fortune is not at all large."

"How do you mean better — if that would be good enough? And I have myself so little money; why should I look for a fortune?"

"Your having so little is a reason for looking for more." With which Isabel was grateful for the dimness of the room; she felt as if her face were hideously insincere. It was what she was doing for Osmond; it was what one had to do for Osmond! Pansy's solemn eyes, fixed on her own, almost embarrassed her; she was ashamed to think she had made so light of the girl's preference.

"What should you like me to do?" her companion softly demanded.

The question was a terrible one, and Isabel took refuge in timorous vagueness. "To remember all the pleasure it's in your power to give your father."

"To marry some one else, you mean — if he should ask me?"

For a moment Isabel's answer caused itself to be waited for; then she heard herself utter it in the stillness that Pansy's attention seemed to make. "Yes — to marry some one else."

The child's eyes grew more penetrating; Isabel believed she was doubting her sincerity, and the impression took force from her slowly getting up from her cushion. She stood there a moment with her small hands unclasped and then quavered out: "Well, I hope no one will ask me!"

"There has been a question of that. Some one else would have been ready to ask you."

"I don't think he can have been ready," said Pansy.

"It would appear so — if he had been sure he'd succeed."

"If he had been sure? Then he wasn't ready!"

Isabel thought this rather sharp; she also got up and stood a moment looking into the fire. "Lord Warburton has shown you great attention," she resumed; "of course you know it's of him I speak." She found herself, against her expectation, almost placed in the position of justifying herself; which led her to introduce this nobleman more crudely than she had intended.

"He has been very kind to me, and I like him very much. But if you mean that he'll propose for me I think you're mistaken."

"Perhaps I am. But your father would like it extremely."

Pansy shook her head with a little wise smile. "Lord Warburton won't propose simply to please papa."

"Your father would like you to encourage him," Isabel went on mechanically.

"How can I encourage him?"

"I don't know. Your father must tell you that."

Pansy said nothing for a moment; she only continued to smile as if she were in possession of a bright assurance. "There's no danger — no danger!" she declared at last.

There was a conviction in the way she said this, and a felicity in her believing it, which conduced to Isabel's awkwardness. She felt accused of dishonesty, and the idea was disgusting. To repair her self-respect she was on the point of saying that Lord Warburton had let her know that there *was* a danger. But she didn't; she only said — in her embarrassment rather wide of the mark — that he surely had been most kind, most friendly.

"Yes, he has been very kind," Pansy answered. "That's what I like him for."

"Why then is the difficulty so great?"

"I've always felt sure of his knowing that I don't want — what did you say I should do? — to encourage him. He knows I don't want to marry, and he wants me to know that he therefore won't trouble me. That's the meaning of his kindness. It's as if he said to me: 'I like you very much, but if it does n't please you I 'll never say it again.' I think that's very kind, very noble," Pansy went on with deepening positiveness. "That is all we 've said to each other. And he does n't care for me either. Ah no, there's no danger."

Isabel was touched with wonder at the depths of perception of which this submissive little person was capable; she felt afraid of Pansy's wisdom — began almost to retreat before it. "You must tell your father that," she remarked reservedly.

"I think I 'd rather not," Pansy unreservedly answered.

"You ought n't to let him have false hopes."

"Perhaps not; but it will be good for me that he should. So long as he believes that Lord Warburton intends anything of the kind you say, papa won't propose any one else. And that will be an advantage for me," said the child very lucidly.

There was something brilliant in her lucidity, and it made her companion draw a long breath. It relieved this friend of a heavy responsibility. Pansy had a sufficient illumination of her own, and Isabel felt that she herself just now had no light to spare from her small stock. Nevertheless it still clung to her that she must be loyal to Osmond, that she was on her honour in dealing with his daughter. Under the influence of this sentiment she threw out another suggestion before she retired — a suggestion with which it seemed to her that she should have done her utmost. "Your father takes for granted at least that you would like to marry a nobleman."

Pansy stood in the open doorway; she had drawn back the curtain for Isabel to pass. "I think Mr. Rosier looks like one!" she remarked very gravely.

XLVI

Lord Warburton was not seen in Mrs. Osmond's drawing-room for several days, and Isabel could n't fail to observe that her husband said nothing to her about having received a letter from him. She could n't fail to observe, either, that Osmond was in a state of expectancy and that, though it was not agreeable to him to betray it, he thought their distinguished friend kept him waiting quite too long. At the end of four days he alluded to his absence.

"What has become of Warburton? What does he mean by treating one like a tradesman with a bill?'

"I know nothing about him," Isabel said. "I saw him last Friday at the German ball. He told me then that he meant to write to you."

"He has never written to me."

"So I supposed, from your not having told me."

"He's an odd fish," said Osmond comprehensively. And on Isabel's making no rejoinder he went on to enquire whether it took his lordship five days to indite a letter. "Does he form his words with such difficulty?"

"I don't know," Isabel was reduced to replying. "I've never had a letter from him."

"Never had a letter? I had an idea that you were at one time in intimate correspondence."

She answered that this had not been the case, and

let the conversation drop. On the morrow, however, coming into the drawing-room late in the afternoon, her husband took it up again.

"When Lord Warburton told you of his intention of writing what did you say to him?" he asked.

She just faltered. "I think I told him not to forget it."

"Did you believe there was a danger of that?"

"As you say, he's an odd fish."

"Apparently he has forgotten it," said Osmond. "Be so good as to remind him."

"Should you like me to write to him?" she demanded.

"I've no objection whatever."

"You expect too much of me."

"Ah yes, I expect a great deal of you."

"I'm afraid I shall disappoint you," said Isabel.

"My expectations have survived a good deal of disappointment."

"Of course I know that. Think how I must have disappointed myself! If you really wish hands laid on Lord Warburton you must lay them yourself."

For a couple of minutes Osmond answered nothing; then he said: "That won't be easy, with you working against me."

Isabel started; she felt herself beginning to tremble. He had a way of looking at her through half-closed eyelids, as if he were thinking of her but scarcely saw her, which seemed to her to have a wonderfully cruel intention. It appeared to recognise her as a disagreeable necessity of thought, but to ignore her for the time as a presence. That effect had never been so marked as now. "I think you accuse me of something very base," she returned.

"I accuse you of not being trustworthy. If he does n't after all come forward it will be because you 've kept him off. I don't know that it 's base: it is the kind of thing a woman always thinks she may do. I 've no doubt you 've the finest ideas about it."

"I told you I would do what I could," she went on.

"Yes, that gained you time."

It came over her, after he had said this, that she had once thought him beautiful. "How much you must want to make sure of him!" she exclaimed in a moment.

She had no sooner spoken than she perceived the full reach of her words, of which she had not been conscious in uttering them. They made a comparison between Osmond and herself, recalled the fact that she had once held this coveted treasure in her hand and felt herself rich enough to let it fall. A momentary exultation took possession of her — a horrible delight in having wounded him; for his face instantly told her that none of the force of her exclamation was lost. He expressed nothing otherwise, however; he only said quickly: "Yes, I want it immensely."

At this moment a servant came in to usher a visitor, and he was followed the next by Lord Warburton, who received a visible check on seeing Osmond. He looked rapidly from the master of the house to the mistress; a movement that seemed to denote a reluctance to interrupt or even a perception of ominous conditions. Then he advanced, with his English address, in which a vague shyness seemed to offer itself as an element of good-breeding; in which the only defect was a difficulty in achieving transitions. Osmond was embarrassed; he found nothing to say; but Isabel remarked, promptly enough, that they had been in the act of talking about their visitor. Upon this her husband added that they had n't known what was become of him — they had been afraid he had gone away. "No," he explained, smiling and looking at Osmond; "I'm only on the point of going." And then he mentioned that he found himself suddenly recalled to England: he should start on the morrow or the day after. "I'm awfully sorry to leave poor Touchett!" he ended by exclaiming.

For a moment neither of his companions spoke; Osmond only leaned back in his chair, listening. Isabel did n't look at him; she could only fancy how he looked. Her eyes were on their visitor's face, where they were the more free to rest that those of his lordship carefully avoided them. Yet Isabel was sure that had she met his glance she would have found it expressive. "You had better take poor Touchett with you," she heard her husband say, lightly enough, in a moment.

"He had better wait for warmer weather," Lord Warburton answered. "I should n't advise him to travel just now."

He sat there a quarter of an hour, talking as if he might not soon see them again — unless indeed they should come to England, a course he strongly recommended. Why should n't they come to England in the autumn ? — that struck him as a very happy thought. It would give him such pleasure to do what he could for them — to have them come and spend a month with him. Osmond, by his own admission, had been to England but once; which was an absurd state of things for a man of his leisure and intelligence. It was just the country for him — he would be sure to get on well there. Then Lord Warburton asked Isabel if she remembered what a good time she had had there and if she did n't want to try it again. Did n't she want to see Gardencourt once more ? Gardencourt was really very good. Touchett did n't take proper care of it, but it was the sort of place you could hardly spoil by letting it alone. Why did n't they come and pay Touchett a visit ? He surely must have asked them. Had n't asked them ? What an ill-mannered wretch! — and Lord Warburton promised to give the master of Gardencourt a piece of his mind. Of course it was a mere accident; he would be delighted to have them. Spending a month with Touchett and a month with himself, and seeing all the rest of the people they must know there, they really would n't find it half bad. Lord Warburton added that it would amuse Miss Osmond as well, who had told him that she had never been to England and whom he had assured it was a country she deserved to see. Of course she did n't need to go to England to be admired — that was her fate everywhere; but she would be an immense success there, she certainly would, if that was any inducement. He asked if she were not at home: could n't he say good-bye ? Not that he liked good-byes — he always funked them. When he left England the other

day he had n't said good-bye to a two-legged creature. He had had half a mind to leave Rome without
troubling Mrs. Osmond for a final interview. What
could be more dreary than final interviews? One
never said the things one wanted — one remembered
them all an hour afterwards. On the other hand one
usually said a lot of things one should n't, simply from
a sense that one had to say something. Such a sense
was upsetting; it muddled one's wits. He had it at
present, and that was the effect it produced on him.
If Mrs. Osmond did n't think he spoke as he ought
she must set it down to agitation; it was no light thing
to part with Mrs. Osmond. He was really very sorry
to be going. He had thought of writing to her instead
of calling — but he would write to her at any rate, to
tell her a lot of things that would be sure to occur
to him as soon as he had left the house. They must
think seriously about coming to Lockleigh.

If there was anything awkward in the conditions
of his visit or in the announcement of his departure
it failed to come to the surface. Lord Warburton
talked about his agitation; but he showed it in no
other manner, and Isabel saw that since he had determined on a retreat he was capable of executing it gallantly. She was very glad for him; she liked him
quite well enough to wish him to appear to carry a
thing off. He would do that on any occasion —,not
from impudence but simply from the habit of success;
and Isabel felt it out of her husband's power to frus-
trate this faculty. A complex operation, as she sat
there, went on in her mind. On one side she listened
to their visitor; said what was proper to him; read,

more or less, between the lines of what he said himself; and wondered how he would have spoken if he
had found her alone. On the other she had a perfect consciousness of Osmond's emotion. She felt almost sorry for him; he was condemned to the sharp
pain of loss without the relief of cursing. He had
had a great hope, and now, as he saw it vanish into
smoke, he was obliged to sit and smile and twirl his
thumbs. Not that he troubled himself to smile very
brightly; he treated their friend on the whole to
as vacant a countenance as so clever a man could
very well wear. It was indeed a part of Osmond's
cleverness that he could look consummately uncom-
promised. His present appearance, however, was
not a confession of disappointment; it was simply
a part of Osmond's habitual system, which was to be
inexpressive exactly in proportion as he was really intent. He had been intent on this prize from the first;
but he had never allowed his eagerness to irradiate
his refined face. He had treated his possible son-in-
law as he treated every one — with an air of being
interested in him only for his own advantage, not for
any profit to a person already so generally, so perfectly provided as Gilbert Osmond. He would give
no sign now of an inward rage which was the result
of a vanished prospect of gain — not the faintest nor
subtlest. Isabel could be sure of that, if it was any
satisfaction to her. Strangely, very strangely, it was a
satisfaction; she wished Lord Warburton to triumph
before her husband, and at the same time she wished
her husband to be very superior before Lord Warburton. Osmond, in his way, was admirable; he had,

like their visitor, the advantage of an acquired habit. It was not that of succeeding, but it was something almost as good — that of not attempting. As he leaned back in his place, listening but vaguely to the other's friendly offers and suppressed explanations — as if it were only proper to assume that they were addressed essentially to his wife — he had at least (since so little else was left him) the comfort of thinking how well he personally had kept out of it, and how the air of indifference, which he was now able to wear, had the added beauty of consistency. It was something to be able to look as if the leave-taker's movements had no relation to his own mind. The latter did well, certainly; but Osmond's performance was in its very nature more finished. Lord Warburton's position was after all an easy one; there was no reason in the world why he should n't leave Rome. He had had beneficent inclinations, but they had stopped short of fruition; he had never committed himself, and his honour was safe. Osmond appeared to take but a moderate interest in the proposal that they should go and stay with him and in his allusion to the success Pansy might extract from their visit. He murmured a recognition, but left Isabel to say that it was a matter requiring grave consideration. Isabel, even while she made this remark, could see the great vista which had suddenly opened out in her husband's mind, with Pansy's little figure marching up the middle of it.

Lord Warburton had asked leave to bid good-bye to Pansy, but neither Isabel nor Osmond had made any motion to send for her. He had the air of giving out that his visit must be short; he sat on a small chair, as if it were only for a moment, keeping his hat in his hand. But he stayed and stayed; Isabel wondered what he was waiting for. She believed it was not to see Pansy; she had an impression that on the whole he would rather not see Pansy. It was of course to see herself alone — he had something to say to her. Isabel had no great wish to hear it, for she was afraid it would be an explanation, and she could perfectly dispense with explanations. Osmond, however, presently got up, like a man of good taste to whom it had occurred that so inveterate a visitor might wish to say just the last word of all to the ladies. "I've a letter to write before dinner," he said; "you must excuse me. I'll see if my daughter's disengaged, and if she is she shall know you're here. Of course when you come to Rome you'll always look us up. Mrs. Osmond will talk to you about the English expedition: she decides all those things."

The nod with which, instead of a hand-shake, he wound up this little speech was perhaps rather a meagre form of salutation; but on the whole it was all the occasion demanded. Isabel reflected that after he left the room Lord Warburton would have no pretext for saying, "Your husband's very angry"; which would have been extremely disagreeable to her. Nevertheless, if he had done so, she would have said: "Oh, don't be anxious. He does n't hate *you*: it's me that he hates!"

It was only when they had been left alone together that her friend showed a certain vague awkwardness — sitting down in another chair, handling two or three of the objects that were near him. "I hope he'll make

Miss Osmond come," he presently remarked. " I want very much to see her."

"I'm glad it's the last time," said Isabel.

"So am I. She does n't care for me."

"No, she does n't care for you."

"I don't wonder at it," he returned. Then he added with inconsequence: "You'll come to England, won't you?"

"I think we had better not."

"Ah, you owe me a visit. Don't you remember that you were to have come to Lockleigh once, and you never did?"

"Everything's changed since then," said Isabel.

"Not changed for the worse, surely — as far as we're concerned. To see you under my roof" — and he hung fire but an instant — "would be a great satisfaction."

She had feared an explanation; but that was the only one that occurred. They talked a little of Ralph, and in another moment Pansy came in, already dressed for dinner and with a little red spot in either cheek. She shook hands with Lord Warburton and stood looking up into his face with a fixed smile — a smile that Isabel knew, though his lordship probably never suspected it, to be near akin to a burst of tears.

"I'm going away," he said. "I want to bid you good-bye."

"Good-bye, Lord Warburton." Her voice perceptibly trembled.

"And I want to tell you how much I wish you may be very happy."

"Thank you, Lord Warburton," Pansy answered.

He lingered a moment and gave a glance at Isabel. "You ought to be very happy — you've got a guardian angel."

"I'm sure I shall be happy," said Pansy in the tone of a person whose certainties were always cheerful.

"Such a conviction as that will take you a great way. But if it should ever fail you, remember — remember — " And her interlocutor stammered a little. "Think of me sometimes, you know!" he said with a vague laugh. Then he shook hands with Isabel in silence, and presently he was gone.

When he had left the room she expected an effusion of tears from her stepdaughter; but Pansy in fact treated her to something very different.

"I think you *are* my guardian angel!" she exclaimed very sweetly.

Isabel shook her head. "I'm not an angel of any kind. I'm at the most your good friend."

"You're a very good friend then — to have asked papa to be gentle with me."

"I've asked your father nothing," said Isabel, wondering.

"He told me just now to come to the drawing-room, and then he gave me a very kind kiss."

"Ah," said Isabel, "that was quite his own idea!"

She recognised the idea perfectly; it was very characteristic, and she was to see a great deal more of it. Even with Pansy he couldn't put himself the least in the wrong. They were dining out that day, and after their dinner they went to another entertainment; so that it was not till late in the evening that Isabel saw

him alone. When Pansy kissed him before going to
bed he returned her embrace with even more than his
usual munificence, and Isabel wondered if he meant
it as a hint that his daughter had been injured by the
machinations of her stepmother. It was a partial
expression, at any rate, of what he continued to expect
of his wife. She was about to follow Pansy, but he
remarked that he wished she would remain; he had
something to say to her. Then he walked about the
drawing-room a little, while she stood waiting in her
cloak.

"I don't understand what you wish to do," he said
in a moment. "I should like to know — so that I
may know how to act."

"Just now I wish to go to bed. I'm very tired."

"Sit down and rest; I shall not keep you long.
Not there — take a comfortable place." And he
arranged a multitude of cushions that were scattered
in picturesque disorder upon a vast divan. This was
not, however, where she seated herself; she dropped
into the nearest chair. The fire had gone out; the
lights in the great room were few. She drew her
cloak about her; she felt mortally cold. "I think
you're trying to humiliate me," Osmond went on.
"It's a most absurd undertaking."

"I haven't the least idea what you mean," she
returned.

"You've played a very deep game; you've
managed it beautifully."

"What is it that I've managed?"

"You've not quite settled it, however; we shall
see him again." And he stopped in front of her, with

his hands in his pockets, looking down at her thoughtfully, in his usual way, which seemed meant to let her know that she was not an object, but only a rather disagreeable incident, of thought.

"If you mean that Lord Warburton's under an obligation to come back you're wrong," Isabel said. "He's under none whatever."

"That's just what I complain of. But when I say he'll come back I don't mean he'll come from a sense of duty."

"There's nothing else to make him. I think he has quite exhausted Rome."

"Ah no, that's a shallow judgement. Rome's inexhaustible." And Osmond began to walk about again. "However, about that perhaps there's no hurry," he added. "It's rather a good idea of his that we should go to England. If it were not for the fear of finding your cousin there I think I should try to persuade you."

"It may be that you'll not find my cousin," said Isabel.

"I should like to be sure of it. However, I shall be as sure as possible. At the same time I should like to see his house, that you told me so much about at one time: what do you call it? — Gardencourt. It must be a charming thing. And then, you know, I've a devotion to the memory of your uncle: you made me take a great fancy to him. I should like to see where he lived and died. That indeed is a detail. Your friend was right. Pansy ought to see England."

"I've no doubt she would enjoy it," said Isabel.

"But that's a long time hence; next autumn's far off," Osmond continued; "and meantime there are things that more nearly interest us. Do you think me so very proud?" he suddenly asked.

"I think you very strange."

"You don't understand me."

"No, not even when you insult me."

"I don't insult you; I'm incapable of it. I merely speak of certain facts, and if the allusion's an injury to you the fault's not mine. It's surely a fact that you have kept all this matter quite in your own hands."

"Are you going back to Lord Warburton?" Isabel asked. "I'm very tired of his name."

"You shall hear it again before we've done with it."

She had spoken of his insulting her, but it suddenly seemed to her that this ceased to be a pain. He was going down — down; the vision of such a fall made her almost giddy: that was the only pain. He was too strange, too different; he did n't touch her. Still, the working of his morbid passion was extraordinary, and she felt a rising curiosity to know in what light he saw himself justified. "I might say to you that I judge you 've nothing to say to me that's worth hearing," she returned in a moment. "But I should perhaps be wrong. There's a thing that would be worth my hearing — to know in the plainest words of what it is you accuse me."

"Of having prevented Pansy's marriage to Warburton. Are those words plain enough?"

"On the contrary, I took a great interest in it. I

told you so; and when you told me that you counted on me — that I think was what you said — I accepted the obligation. I was a fool to do so, but I did it."

"You pretended to do it, and you even pretended reluctance to make me more willing to trust you. Then you began to use your ingenuity to get him out of the way."

"I think I see what you mean," said Isabel.

"Where's the letter you told me he had written me?" her husband demanded.

"I have n't the least idea; I have n't asked him."

"You stopped it on the way," said Osmond.

Isabel slowly got up; standing there in her white cloak, which covered her to her feet, she might have represented the angel of disdain, first cousin to that of pity. "Oh, Gilbert, for a man who was so fine —!" she exclaimed in a long murmur.

"I was never so fine as you. You've done everything you wanted. You've got him out of the way without appearing to do so, and you've placed me in the position in which you wished to see me — that of a man who has tried to marry his daughter to a lord, but has grotesquely failed."

"Pansy does n't care for him. She's very glad he's gone," Isabel said.

"That has nothing to do with the matter."

"And he does n't care for Pansy."

"That won't do; you told me he did. I don't know why you wanted this particular satisfaction," Osmond continued; "you might have taken some other. It does n't seem to me that I've been presumptuous — that I have taken too much for granted. I've been very modest about it, very quiet. The idea did n't originate with me. He began to show that he liked her before I ever thought of it. I left it all to you."

"Yes, you were very glad to leave it to me. After this you must attend to such things yourself."

He looked at her a moment; then he turned away. "I thought you were very fond of my daughter."

"I've never been more so than to-day."

"Your affection is attended with immense limitations. However, that perhaps is natural."

"Is this all you wished to say to me?" Isabel asked, taking a candle that stood on one of the tables.

"Are you satisfied? Am I sufficiently disappointed?"

"I don't think that on the whole you're disappointed. You've had another opportunity to try to stupefy me."

"It's not that. It's proved that Pansy can aim high."

"Poor little Pansy!" said Isabel as she turned away with her candle.

XLVII

It was from Henrietta Stackpole that she learned
how Caspar Goodwood had come to Rome; an
event that took place three days after Lord Warburton's departure. This latter fact had been preceded
by an incident of some importance to Isabel — the
temporary absence, once again, of Madame Merle,
who had gone to Naples to stay with a friend, the
happy possessor of a villa at Posilippo. Madame
Merle had ceased to minister to Isabel's happiness,
who found herself wondering whether the most discreet of women might not also by chance be the most
dangerous. Sometimes, at night, she had strange
visions; she seemed to see her husband and her
friend — his friend — in dim, indistinguishable combination. It seemed to her that she had not done with
her; this lady had something in reserve. Isabel's
imagination applied itself actively to this elusive
point, but every now and then it was checked by a
nameless dread, so that when the charming woman
was away from Rome she had almost a consciousness
of respite. She had already learned from Miss Stackpole that Caspar Goodwood was in Europe, Henrietta having written to make it known to her immediately after meeting him in Paris. He himself never
wrote to Isabel, and though he was in Europe she
thought it very possible he might not desire to see
her. Their last interview, before her marriage, had

had quite the character of a complete rupture; if she remembered rightly he had said he wished to take his last look at her. Since then he had been the most discordant survival of her earlier time — the only one in fact with which a permanent pain was associated. He had left her that morning with a sense of the most superfluous of shocks: it was like a collision between vessels in broad daylight. There had been no mist, no hidden current to excuse it, and she herself had only wished to steer wide. He had bumped against her prow, however, while her hand was on the tiller, and — to complete the metaphor — had given the lighter vessel a strain which still occasionally betrayed itself in a faint creaking. It had been horrid to see him, because he represented the only serious harm that (to her belief) she had ever done in the world: he was the only person with an unsatisfied claim on her. She had made him unhappy, she could n't help it; and his unhappiness was a grim reality. She had cried with rage, after he had left her, at — she hardly knew what: she tried to think it had been at his want of consideration. He had come to her with his unhappiness when her own bliss was so perfect; he had done his best to darken the brightness of those pure rays. He had not been violent, and yet there had been a violence in the impression. There had been a violence at any rate in something somewhere; perhaps it was only in her own fit of weeping and in that after-sense of the same which had lasted three or four days.

The effect of his final appeal had in short faded away, and all the first year of her marriage he had dropped out of her books. He was a thankless subject of reference; it was disagreeable to have to think of a person who was sore and sombre about you and whom you could yet do nothing to relieve. It would have been different if she had been able to doubt, even a little, of his unreconciled state, as she doubted of Lord Warburton's; unfortunately it was beyond question, and this aggressive, uncompromising look of it was just what made it unattractive. She could never say to herself that here was a sufferer who had compensations, as she was able to say in the case of her English suitor. She had no faith in Mr. Goodwood's compensations and no esteem for them. A cotton-factory was not a compensation for anything — least of all for having failed to marry Isabel Archer. And yet, beyond that, she hardly knew what he had — save of course his intrinsic qualities. Oh, he was intrinsic enough; she never thought of his even looking for artificial aids. If he extended his business — that, to the best of her belief, was the only form exertion could take with him — it would be because it was an enterprising thing, or good for the business; not in the least because he might hope it would overlay the past. This gave his figure a kind of bareness and bleakness which made the accident of meeting it in memory or in apprehension a peculiar concussion; it was deficient in the social drapery commonly muffling, in an overcivilized age, the sharpness of human contacts. His perfect silence, moreover, the fact that she never heard from him and very seldom heard any mention of him, deepened this impression of his loneliness. She asked Lily for news of him, from time to time; but Lily knew nothing of Boston — her imagination was all bounded on the east by Madison Avenue. As time went on Isabel had thought of him oftener, and with fewer restrictions; she had had more than once the idea of writing to him. She had never told her husband about him — never let Osmond know of his visits to her in Florence; a reserve not dictated in the early period by a want of confidence in Osmond, but simply by the consideration that the young man's disappointment was not her secret but his own. It would be wrong of her, she had believed, to convey it to another, and Mr. Goodwood's affairs could have, after all, little interest for Gilbert. When it had come to the point she had never written to him; it seemed to her that, considering his grievance, the least she could do was to let him alone. Nevertheless she would have been glad to be in some way nearer to him. It was not that it ever occurred to her that she might have married him; even after the consequences of her actual union had grown vivid to her that particular reflection, though she indulged in so many, had not had the assurance to present itself. But on finding herself in trouble he had become a member of that circle of things with which she wished to set herself right. I have mentioned how passionately she needed to feel that her unhappiness should not have come to her through her own fault. She had no near prospect of dying, and yet she wished to make her peace with the world — to put her spiritual affairs in order. It came back to her from time to time that there was an account still to be settled with Caspar, and she saw herself disposed or able to settle it to-day on terms easier for him than ever before. Still, when she learned he was coming to Rome she felt all afraid; it would be more disagreeable for him than for any one else to make out — since he *would* make it out, as over a falsified balance-sheet or something of that sort — the intimate disarray of her affairs. Deep in her breast she believed that he had invested his all in her happiness, while the others had invested only a part. He was one more person from whom she should have to conceal her stress. She was reassured, however, after he arrived in Rome, for he spent several days without coming to see her.

Henrietta Stackpole, it may well be imagined, was much more punctual, and Isabel was largely favoured with the society of her friend. She threw herself into it, for now that she had made such a point of keeping her conscience clear, that was one way of proving she had not been superficial — the more so as the years, in their flight, had rather enriched than blighted those peculiarities which had been humorously criticised by persons less interested than Isabel, and which were still marked enough to give loyalty a spice of heroism. Henrietta was as keen and quick and fresh as ever, and as neat and bright and fair. Her remarkably open eyes, lighted like great glazed railway-stations, had put up no shutters; her attire had lost none of its crispness, her opinions none of their national reference. She was by no means quite unchanged, however; it struck Isabel she had grown vague. Of old she had never been vague; though undertaking many enquiries at once, she had managed to be entire and pointed about each. She had a reason for everything she did; she fairly bristled with motives. Formerly, when she came to Europe it was because she wished to see it, but now, having already seen it, she had no such excuse. She did n't for a moment pretend that the desire to examine decaying civilisations had any-thing to do with her present enterprise; her journey was rather an expression of her independence of the old world than of a sense of further obligations to it. "It 's nothing to come to Europe," she said to Isabel; "it does n't seem to me one needs so many reasons for that. It is something to stay at home; this is much more important." It was not therefore with a sense of doing anything very important that she treated herself to another pilgrimage to Rome; she had seen the place before and carefully inspected it; her present act was simply a sign of familiarity, of her knowing all about it, of her having as good a right as any one else to be there. This was all very well, and Henrietta was restless; she had a perfect right to be restless too, if one came to that. But she had after all a better reason for coming to Rome than that she cared for it so little. Her friend easily recognised it, and with it the worth of the other's fidelity. She had crossed the stormy ocean in midwinter because she had guessed that Isabel was sad. Henrietta guessed a great deal, but she had never guessed so happily as that. Isabel's satisfactions just now were few, but even if they had been more numerous there would still have been some-thing of individual joy in her sense of being justified in having always thought highly of Henrietta. She had made large concessions with regard to her, and had yet insisted that, with all abatements, she was very valuable. It was not her own triumph, however, that she found good; it was simply the relief of confessing to this confidant, the first person to whom she had owned it, that she was not in the least at her ease. Henrietta had herself approached this point with the smallest possible delay, and had accused her to her face of being wretched. She was a woman, she was a sister; she was not Ralph, nor Lord Warburton, nor Caspar Goodwood, and Isabel could speak.

"Yes, I'm wretched," she said very mildly. She hated to hear herself say it; she tried to say it as judicially as possible.

"What does he do to you?" Henrietta asked, frowning as if she were enquiring into the operations of a quack doctor.

"He does nothing. But he does n't like me."

"He's very hard to please!" cried Miss Stackpole. "Why don't you leave him?"

"I can't change that way," Isabel said.

"Why not, I should like to know? You won't confess that you've made a mistake. You're too proud."

"I don't know whether I'm too proud. But I can't publish my mistake. I don't think that's decent. I'd much rather die."

"You won't think so always," said Henrietta.

"I don't know what great unhappiness might bring me to; but it seems to me I shall always be ashamed. One must accept one's deeds. I married him before all the world; I was perfectly free; it was impossible to do anything more deliberate. One can't change that way," Isabel repeated.

"You *have* changed, in spite of the impossibility. I hope you don't mean to say you like him."

Isabel debated. "No, I don't like him. I can tell you, because I'm weary of my secret. But that's enough; I can't announce it on the housetops."

Henrietta gave a laugh. "Don't you think you're rather too considerate?"

"It's not of him that I'm considerate — it's of myself!" Isabel answered.

It was not surprising Gilbert Osmond should not have taken comfort in Miss Stackpole; his instinct had naturally set him in opposition to a young lady capable of advising his wife to withdraw from the conjugal roof. When she arrived in Rome he had said to Isabel that he hoped she would leave her friend the interviewer alone; and Isabel had answered that he at least had nothing to fear from her. She said to Henrietta that as Osmond did n't like her she could n't invite her to dine, but they could easily see each other in other ways. Isabel received Miss Stackpole freely in her own sitting-room, and took her repeatedly to drive, face to face with Pansy, who, bending a little forward, on the opposite seat of the carriage, gazed at the celebrated authoress with a respectful attention which Henrietta occasionally found irritating. She complained to Isabel that Miss Osmond had a little look as if she should remember everything one said. "I don't want to be remembered that way," Miss Stackpole declared; "I consider that my conversation refers only to the moment, like the morning papers. Your stepdaughter, as she sits there, looks as if she kept all the back numbers and would bring them out some day against me." She could not teach herself to think favourably of Pansy, whose absence of initiative, of conversation, of personal claims, seemed to her, in a girl of twenty, unnatural and even uncanny. Isabel presently saw that Osmond would have liked her to urge a little the cause of her friend, insist a little upon his receiving her, so that he might appear to suffer for good manners' sake. Her immediate acceptance of his objections put him too much in the wrong — it being in effect one of the disadvantages of expressing contempt that you cannot enjoy at the same time the credit of expressing sympathy. Osmond held to his credit, and yet he held to his objections — all of which were elements difficult to reconcile. The right thing would have been that Miss Stackpole should come to dine at Palazzo Roccanera once or twice, so that (in spite of his superficial civility, always so great) she might judge for herself how little pleasure it gave him. From the moment, however, that both the ladies were so unaccommodating, there was nothing for Osmond but to wish the lady from New York would take herself off. It was surprising how little satisfaction he got from his wife's friends; he took occasion to call Isabel's attention to it.

"You're certainly not fortunate in your intimates; I wish you might make a new collection," he said to her one morning in reference to nothing visible at the moment, but in a tone of ripe reflection which deprived the remark of all brutal abruptness. "It's as if you had taken the trouble to pick out the people in the world that I have least in common with. Your cousin I have always thought a conceited ass — be-

sides his being the most ill-favoured animal I know.
Then it's insufferably tiresome that one can't tell
him so; one must spare him on account of his health.
His health seems to me the best part of him; it gives
him privileges enjoyed by no one else. If he's so
desperately ill there's only one way to prove it; but
he seems to have no mind for that. I can't say much
more for the great Warburton. When one really
thinks of it, the cool insolence of that performance
was something rare! He comes and looks at one's
daughter as if she were a suite of apartments; he
tries the door-handles and looks out of the windows,
raps on the walls and almost thinks he'll take the
place. Will you be so good as to draw up a lease?
Then, on the whole, he decides that the rooms are
too small; he does n't think he could live on a third
floor; he must look out for a *piano nobile*. And he
goes away after having got a month's lodging in the
poor little apartment for nothing. Miss Stackpole,
however, is your most wonderful invention. She
strikes me as a kind of monster. One has n't a nerve
in one's body that she does n't set quivering. You
know I never have admitted that she's a woman.
Do you know what she reminds me of? Of a new
steel pen — the most odious thing in nature. She
talks as a steel pen writes; are n't her letters, by the
way, on ruled paper? She thinks and moves and
walks and looks exactly as she talks. You may say
that she does n't hurt me, inasmuch as I don't see
her. I don't see her, but I hear her; I hear her all
day long. Her voice is in my ears; I can't get rid
of it. I know exactly what she says, and every in-

flexion of the tone in which she says it. She says charming things about me, and they give you great comfort. I don't like at all to think she talks about me — I feel as I should feel if I knew the footman were wearing my hat."

Henrietta talked about Gilbert Osmond, as his wife assured him, rather less than he suspected. She had plenty of other subjects, in two of which the reader may be supposed to be especially interested. She let her friend know that Caspar Goodwood had discovered for himself that she was unhappy, though indeed her ingenuity was unable to suggest what comfort he hoped to give her by coming to Rome and yet not calling on her. They met him twice in the street, but he had no appearance of seeing them; they were driving, and he had a habit of looking straight in front of him, as if he proposed to take in but one object at a time. Isabel could have fancied she had seen him the day before; it must have been with just that face and step that he had walked out of Mrs. Touchett's door at the close of their last interview. He was dressed just as he had been dressed on that day, Isabel remembered the colour of his cravat; and yet in spite of this familiar look there was a strangeness in his figure too, something that made her feel it afresh to be rather terrible he should have come to Rome. He looked bigger and more overtopping than of old, and in those days he certainly reached high enough. She noticed that the people whom he passed looked back after him; but he went straight forward, lifting above them a face like a February sky.

Miss Stackpole's other topic was very different;
she gave Isabel the latest news about Mr. Bantling.
He had been out in the United States the year before, and she was happy to say she had been able
to show him considerable attention. She did n't
know how much he had enjoyed it, but she would
undertake to say it had done him good; he was n't
the same man when he left as he had been when he
came. It had opened his eyes and shown him that
England was n't everything. He had been very much
liked in most places, and thought extremely simple
— more simple than the English were commonly
supposed to be. There were people who had thought
him affected; she did n't know whether they meant
that his simplicity was an affectation. Some of his
questions were too discouraging; he thought all
the chambermaids were farmers' daughters — or
all the farmers' daughters were chambermaids —
she could n't exactly remember which. He had n't
seemed able to grasp the great school system; it
had been really too much for him. On the whole
he had behaved as if there were too much of everything — as if he' could only take in a small part.
The part he had chosen was the hotel system and
the river navigation. He had seemed really fasci-
nated with the hotels; he had a photograph of every
one he had visited. But the river steamers were his
principal interest; he wanted to do nothing but
sail on the big boats. They had travelled together
from New York to Milwaukee, stopping at the most
interesting cities on the route; and whenever they
started afresh he had wanted to know if they could

go by the steamer. He seemed to have no idea of geography — had an impression that Baltimore was a Western city and was perpetually expecting to arrive at the Mississippi. He appeared never to have heard of any river in America but the Mississippi and was unprepared to recognise the existence of the Hudson, though obliged to confess at last that it was fully equal to the Rhine. They had spent some pleasant hours in the palace-cars; he was always ordering ice-cream from the coloured man. He could never get used to that idea — that you could get ice-cream in the cars. Of course you could n't, nor fans, nor candy, nor anything in the English cars! He found the heat quite overwhelming, and she had told him she indeed expected it was the biggest he had ever experienced. He was now in England, hunting — "hunting round" Henrietta called it. These amusements were those of the American red men; we had left that behind long ago, the pleasures of the chase. It seemed to be generally believed in England that we wore tomahawks and feathers; but such a costume was more in keeping with English habits. Mr. Bantling would not have time to join her in Italy, but when she should go to Paris again he expected to come over. He wanted very much to see Versailles again; he was very fond of the ancient *régime*. They did n't agree about that, but that was what she liked Versailles for, that you could see the ancient *régime* had been swept away. There were no dukes and marquises there now; she remembered on the contrary one day when there were five American families, walking all round. Mr.

Bantling was very anxious that she should take up the subject of England again, and he thought she might get on better with it now; England had changed a good deal within two or three years. He was determined that if she went there he should go to see his sister, Lady Pensil, and that this time the invitation should come to her straight. The mystery about that other one had never been explained.

Caspar Goodwood came at last to Palazzo Roccanera; he had written Isabel a note beforehand, to ask leave. This was promptly granted; she would be at home at six o'clock that afternoon. She spent the day wondering what he was coming for — what good he expected to get of it. He had presented himself hitherto as a person destitute of the faculty of compromise, who would take what he had asked for or take nothing. Isabel's hospitality, however, raised no questions, and she found no great difficulty in appearing happy enough to deceive him. It was her conviction at least that she deceived him, made him say to himself that he had been misinformed. But she also saw, so she believed, that he was not disappointed, as some other men, she was sure, would have been; he had not come to Rome to look for an opportunity. She never found out what he had come for; he offered her no explanation; there could be none but the very simple one that he wanted to see her. In other words he had come for his amusement. Isabel followed up this induction with a good deal of eagerness, and was delighted to have found a formula that would lay the ghost of this gentleman's ancient grievance. If he had come to Rome for his amusement this was exactly what she wanted; for if he cared for amusement he had got over his heartache. If he had got over his heartache everything was as it should be and her responsibilities were at an end. It was true that he took his recreation a little stiffly, but he had never been loose and easy and she had every reason to believe he was satisfied with what he saw. Henrietta was not in his confidence, though he was in hers, and Isabel consequently received no side-light upon his state of mind. He was open to little conversation on general topics; it came back to her that she had said of him once, years before, "Mr. Goodwood speaks a good deal, but he doesn't talk." He spoke a good deal now, but he talked perhaps as little as ever; considering, that is, how much there was in Rome to talk about. His arrival was not calculated to simplify her relations with her husband, for if Mr. Osmond didn't like her friends Mr. Goodwood had no claim upon his attention save as having been one of the first of them. There was nothing for her to say of him but that he was the very oldest; this rather meagre synthesis exhausted the facts. She had been obliged to introduce him to Gilbert; it was impossible she should not ask him to dinner, to her Thursday evenings, of which she had grown very weary, but to which her husband still held for the sake not so much of inviting people as of not inviting them.

To the Thursdays Mr. Goodwood came regularly, solemnly, rather early; he appeared to regard them with a good deal of gravity. Isabel every now and then had a moment of anger; there was something so literal about him; she thought he might know that she did n't know what to do with him. But she could n't call him stupid; he was not that in the least; he was only extraordinarily honest. To be as honest as that made a man very different from most people; one had to be almost equally honest with *him*. She made this latter reflection at the very time she was flattering herself she had persuaded him that she was the most light-hearted of women. He never threw any doubt on this point, never asked her any personal questions. He got on much better with Osmond than had seemed probable. Osmond had a great dislike to being counted on; in such a case he had an irresistible need of disappointing you. It was in virtue of this principle that he gave himself the entertainment of taking a fancy to a perpendicular Bostonian whom he had been depended upon to treat with coldness. He asked Isabel if Mr. Goodwood also had wanted to marry her, and expressed surprise at her not having accepted him. It would have been an excellent thing, like living under some tall belfry which would strike all the hours and make a queer vibration in the upper air. He declared he liked to talk with the great Goodwood; it was n't easy at first, you had to climb up an interminable steep staircase, up to the top of the tower; but when you got there you had a big view and felt a little fresh breeze. Osmond, as we know, had delightful qualities, and he gave Caspar Goodwood the benefit of them all. Isabel could see that Mr. Goodwood thought better of her husband than he had ever wished to; he had given her the impression that morning in Florence of being inaccessible to a good impression. Gilbert asked him repeatedly to dinner, and Mr. Goodwood smoked a cigar with him afterwards and even desired to be shown his collections. Gilbert said to Isabel that he was very original; he was as strong and of as good a style as an English portmanteau, — he had plenty of straps and buckles which would never wear out, and a capital patent lock. Caspar Goodwood took to riding on the Campagna and devoted much time to this exercise; it was therefore mainly in the evening that Isabel saw him. She bethought herself of saying to him one day that if he were willing he could render her a service. And then she added smiling:

"I don't know, however, what right I have to ask a service of you."

"You're the person in the world who has most right," he answered. "I've given you assurances that I've never given any one else."

The service was that he should go and see her cousin Ralph, who was ill at the Hôtel de Paris, alone, and be as kind to him as possible. Mr. Goodwood had never seen him, but he would know who the poor fellow was; if she was not mistaken Ralph had once invited him to Gardencourt. Caspar remembered the invitation perfectly, and, though he was not supposed to be a man of imagination, had enough to put himself in the place of a poor gentleman who lay dying at a Roman inn. He called at the Hôtel de Paris and, on being shown into the presence of the master of Gardencourt, found Miss Stackpole sitting beside his sofa. A singular change had in fact occurred in this lady's relations with Ralph Touchett. She had not been asked by Isabel to go and see him, but on hearing that he was too ill to come out had immediately gone of her own motion. After this she had paid him a daily visit — always under the conviction that they were great enemies. "Oh yes, we 're intimate enemies," Ralph used to say; and he accused her freely — as freely as the humour of it would allow — of coming to worry him to death. In reality they became excellent friends, Henrietta much wondering that she should never have liked him before. Ralph liked her exactly as much as he had always done; he had never doubted for a moment that she was an excellent fellow. They talked about everything and always differed; about everything, that is, but Isabel — a topic as to which Ralph always had a thin forefinger on his lips. Mr. Bantling on the other hand proved a great resource; Ralph was capable of discussing Mr. Bantling with Henrietta for hours. Discussion was stimulated of course by their inevitable difference of view — Ralph having amused himself with taking the ground that the genial ex-guardsman was a regular Machiavelli. Caspar Goodwood could contribute nothing to such a debate; but after he had been left alone with his host he found there were various other matters they could take up. It must be admitted that the lady who had just gone out was not one of these; Caspar granted all Miss Stackpole's merits in advance, but had no further remark to make about her. Neither, after the first allusions, did the two men expatiate upon Mrs. Osmond — a theme in which Goodwood perceived as many dangers as Ralph. He felt very sorry for that unclassable personage; he could n't bear to see a pleasant man, so pleasant for all his queerness, so beyond anything to be done. There was always something to be done, for Goodwood, and he did it in this case by repeating several times his visit to the Hôtel de Paris. It seemed to Isabel that she had been very clever; she had artfully disposed of the superfluous Caspar. She had given him an occupation; she had converted him into a caretaker of Ralph. She had a plan of making him travel northward with her cousin as soon as the first mild weather should allow it. Lord Warburton had brought Ralph to Rome and Mr. Goodwood should take him away. There seemed a happy symmetry in this, and she was now intensely eager that Ralph should depart. She had a constant fear he would die there before her eyes and a horror of the occurrence of this event at an inn, by her door, which he had so rarely entered. Ralph must sink to his last rest in his own dear house, in one of those deep, dim chambers of Gardencourt where the dark ivy would cluster round the edges of the glimmering window. There seemed to Isabel in these days something sacred in Gardencourt; no chapter of the past was more perfectly irrecoverable. When she thought of the months she had spent there the tears rose to her eyes. She flattered herself, as I say, upon her ingenuity, but she had need of all she could muster; for several events occurred which seemed to confront and defy her. The Countess Gemini arrived from Florence — arrived with her trunks, her dresses, her chatter, her falsehoods, her frivolity, the strange, the unholy legend of the number of her lovers. Edward Rosier, who had been away some-where, — no one, not even Pansy, knew where, — reappeared in Rome and began to write her long letters, which she never answered. Madame Merle returned from Naples and said to her with a strange smile : "What on earth did you do with Lord Warburton ?" As if it were any business of hers !

XLVIII

ONE day, toward the end of February, Ralph Touchett made up his mind to return to England. He had his own reasons for this decision, which he was not bound to communicate; but Henrietta Stackpole, to whom he mentioned his intention, flattered herself that she guessed them. She forbore to express them, however; she only said, after a moment, as she sat by his sofa: "I suppose you know you can't go alone?"

"I 've no idea of doing that," Ralph answered. "I shall have people with me."

"What do you mean by 'people'? Servants whom you pay?"

"Ah," said Ralph jocosely, "after all, they 're human beings."

"Are there any women among them?" Miss Stackpole desired to know.

"You speak as if I had a dozen! No, I confess I have n't a soubrette in my employment."

"Well," said Henrietta calmly, "you can't go to England that way. You must have a woman's care."

"I 've had so much of yours for the past fortnight that it will last me a good while."

"You 've not had enough of it yet. I guess I 'll go with you," said Henrietta.

"Go with me?" Ralph slowly raised himself from his sofa.

"Yes, I know you don't like me, but I 'll go with

298

you all the same. It would be better for your health to lie down again."

Ralph looked at her a little; then he slowly relapsed. "I like you very much," he said in a moment.

Miss Stackpole gave one of her infrequent laughs. "You need n't think that by saying that you can buy me off. I 'll go with you, and what is more I 'll take care of you."

"You 're a very good woman," said Ralph.

"Wait till I get you safely home before you say that. It won't be easy. But you had better go, all the same."

Before she left him, Ralph said to her : "Do you really mean to take care of me ?"

"Well, I mean to try."

"I notify you then that I submit. Oh, I submit !" And it was perhaps a sign of submission that a few minutes after she had left him alone he burst into a loud fit of laughter. It seemed to him so inconsequent, such a conclusive proof of his having abdicated all functions and renounced all exercise, that he should start on a journey across Europe under the supervision of Miss Stackpole. And the great oddity was that the prospect pleased him ; he was gratefully, luxuriously passive. He felt even impatient to start ; and indeed he had an immense longing to see his own house again. The end of everything was at hand ; it seemed to him he could stretch out his arm and touch the goal. But he wanted to die at home ; it was the only wish he had left — to extend himself in the large quiet room where he had last seen his father lie, and close his eyes upon the summer dawn.

That same day Caspar Goodwood came to see him, and he informed his visitor that Miss Stackpole had taken him up and was to conduct him back to England. "Ah then," said Caspar, "I'm afraid I shall be a fifth wheel to the coach. Mrs. Osmond has made *me* promise to go with you."

"Good heavens — it's the golden age! You're all too kind."

"The kindness on my part is to her; it's hardly to you."

"Granting that, *she's* kind," smiled Ralph.

"To get people to go with you? Yes, that's a sort of kindness," Goodwood answered without lending himself to the joke. "For myself, however," he added, "I'll go so far as to say that I would much rather travel with you and Miss Stackpole than with Miss Stackpole alone."

"And you'd rather stay here than do either," said Ralph. "There's really no need of your coming. Henrietta's extraordinarily efficient."

"I'm sure of that. But I've promised Mrs. Osmond."

"You can easily get her to let you off."

"She wouldn't let me off for the world. She wants me to look after you, but that isn't the principal thing. The principal thing is that she wants me to leave Rome."

"Ah, you see too much in it," Ralph suggested.

"I bore her," Goodwood went on; "she has nothing to say to me, so she invented that."

"Oh then, if it's a convenience to her I certainly will take you with me. Though I don't see why it should be a convenience," Ralph added in a moment.

"Well," said Caspar Goodwood simply, "she thinks I'm watching her."

"Watching her?"

"Trying to make out if she's happy."

"That's easy to make out," said Ralph. "She's the most visibly happy woman I know."

"Exactly so; I'm satisfied," Goodwood answered dryly. For all his dryness, however, he had more to say. "I've been watching her; I was an old friend and it seemed to me I had the right. She pretends to be happy; that was what she undertook to be; and I thought I should like to see for myself what it amounts to. I've seen," he continued with a harsh ring in his voice, "and I don't want to see any more. I'm now quite ready to go."

"Do you know it strikes me as about time you should?" Ralph rejoined. And this was the only conversation these gentlemen had about Isabel Osmond.

Henrietta made her preparations for departure, and among them she found it proper to say a few words to the Countess Gemini, who returned at Miss Stackpole's *pension* the visit which this lady had paid her in Florence.

"You were very wrong about Lord Warburton," she remarked to the Countess. "I think it right you should know that."

"About his making love to Isabel? My poor lady, he was at her house three times a day. He has left traces of his passage!" the Countess cried.

"He wished to marry your niece; that's why he came to the house."

The Countess stared, and then with an inconsiderate laugh: "Is that the story that Isabel tells? It isn't bad, as such things go. If he wishes to marry my niece, pray why doesn't he do it? Perhaps he has gone to buy the wedding-ring and will come back with it next month, after I'm gone."

"No, he'll not come back. Miss Osmond doesn't wish to marry him."

"She's very accommodating! I knew she was fond of Isabel, but I didn't know she carried it so far."

"I don't understand you," said Henrietta coldly, and reflecting that the Countess was unpleasantly perverse. "I really must stick to my point — that Isabel never encouraged the attentions of Lord Warburton."

"My dear friend, what do you and I know about it? All we know is that my brother's capable of everything."

"I don't know what your brother's capable of," said Henrietta with dignity.

"It's not her encouraging Warburton that I complain of; it's her sending him away. I want particularly to see him. Do you suppose she thought I would make him faithless?" the Countess continued with audacious insistence. "However, she's only keeping him, one can feel that. The house is full of him there; he's quite in the air. Oh yes, he has left traces; I'm sure I shall see him yet."

"Well," said Henrietta after a little, with one of those inspirations which had made the fortune of her

302

letters to the *Interviewer*, "perhaps he'll be more successful with you than with Isabel!"

When she told her friend of the offer she had made Ralph Isabel replied that she could have done nothing that would have pleased her more. It had always been her faith that at bottom Ralph and this young woman were made to understand each other. "I don't care whether he understands me or not," Henrietta declared. "The great thing is that he shouldn't die in the cars."

"He won't do that," Isabel said, shaking her head with an extension of faith.

"He won't if I can help it. I see you want us all to go. I don't know what you want to do."

"I want to be alone," said Isabel.

"You won't be that so long as you've so much company at home."

"Ah, they're part of the comedy. You others are spectators."

"Do you call it a comedy, Isabel Archer?" Henrietta rather grimly asked.

"The tragedy then if you like. You're all looking at me; it makes me uncomfortable."

Henrietta engaged in this act for a while. "You're like the stricken deer, seeking the innermost shade. Oh, you do give me such a sense of helplessness!" she broke out.

"I'm not at all helpless. There are many things I mean to do."

"It's not you I'm speaking of; it's myself. It's too much, having come on purpose, to leave you just as I find you."

"You don't do that; you leave me much refreshed," Isabel said.

"Very mild refreshment — sour lemonade! I want you to promise me something."

"I can't do that. I shall never make another promise. I made such a solemn one four years ago, and I've succeeded so ill in keeping it."

"You've had no encouragement. In this case I should give you the greatest. Leave your husband before the worst comes; that's what I want you to promise."

"The worst? What do you call the worst?"

"Before your character gets spoiled."

"Do you mean my disposition? It won't get spoiled," Isabel answered, smiling. "I'm taking very good care of it. I'm extremely struck," she added, turning away, "with the off-hand way in which you speak of a woman's leaving her husband. It's easy to see you've never had one!"

"Well," said Henrietta as if she were beginning an argument, "nothing is more common in our Western cities, and it's to them, after all, that we must look in the future." Her argument, however, does not concern this history, which has too many other threads to unwind. She announced to Ralph Touchett that she was ready to leave Rome by any train he might designate, and Ralph immediately pulled himself together for departure. Isabel went to see him at the last, and he made the same remark that Henrietta had made. It struck him that Isabel was uncommonly glad to get rid of them all.

For all answer to this she gently laid her hand on

his, and said in a low tone, with a quick smile:
"My dear Ralph —!"

It was answer enough, and he was quite contented.
But he went on in the same way, jocosely, ingenuously: "I've seen less of you than I might, but it's
better than nothing. And then I've heard a great
deal about you."

"I don't know from whom, leading the life you've
done."

"From the voices of the air! Oh, from no one
else; I never let other people speak of you. They
always say you're ' charming,' and that's so flat."

"I might have seen more of you certainly," Isabel
said. "But when one's married one has so much
occupation."

"Fortunately I'm not married. When you come
to see me in England I shall be able to entertain
you with all the freedom of a bachelor." He continued to talk as if they should certainly meet again,
and succeeded in making the assumption appear
almost just. He made no allusion to his term being
near, to the probability that he should not outlast
the summer. If he preferred it so, Isabel was
willing enough ; the reality was sufficiently distinct
without their erecting finger-posts in conversation.
That had been well enough for the earlier time,
though about this, as about his other affairs, Ralph
had never been egotistic. Isabel spoke of his journey, of the stages into which he should divide it, of
the precautions he should take. "Henrietta's my
greatest precaution," he went on. "The conscience
of that woman's sublime."

"Certainly she 'll be very conscientious."

"Will be? She has been! It 's only because she thinks it 's her duty that she goes with me. There 's a conception of duty for you."

"Yes, it 's a generous one," said Isabel, "and it makes me deeply ashamed. I ought to go with you, you know."

"Your husband would n't like that."

"No, he would n't like it. But I might go, all the same."

"I 'm startled by the boldness of your imagination. Fancy my being a cause of disagreement between a lady and her husband!"

"That 's why I don't go," said Isabel simply — yet not very lucidly.

Ralph understood well enough, however. "I should think so, with all those occupations you speak of."

"It is n't that. I 'm afraid," said Isabel. After a pause she repeated, as if to make herself, rather than him, hear the words: "I 'm afraid."

Ralph could hardly tell what her tone meant; it was so strangely deliberate — apparently so void of emotion. Did she wish to do public penance for a fault of which she had not been convicted? or were her words simply an attempt at enlightened self-analysis? However this might be, Ralph could not resist so easy an opportunity. "Afraid of your husband?"

"Afraid of myself!" she said, getting up. She stood there a moment and then added: "If I were afraid of my husband that would be simply my duty. That 's what women are expected to be."

306

"Ah yes," laughed Ralph; "but to make up for it there's always some man awfully afraid of some woman!"

She gave no heed to this pleasantry, but suddenly took a different turn. "With Henrietta at the head of your little band," she exclaimed abruptly, "there will be nothing left for Mr. Goodwood!"

"Ah, my dear Isabel," Ralph answered, "he's used to that. There *is* nothing left for Mr. Goodwood."

She coloured and then observed, quickly, that she must leave him. They stood together a moment; both her hands were in both of his. "You've been my best friend," she said.

"It was for you that I wanted — that I wanted to live. But I'm of no use to you."

Then it came over her more poignantly that she should not see him again. She could not accept that; she could not part with him that way. "If you should send for me I'd come," she said at last.

"Your husband won't consent to that."

"Oh yes, I can arrange it."

"I shall keep that for my last pleasure!" said Ralph.

In answer to which she simply kissed him. It was a Thursday, and that evening Caspar Goodwood came to Palazzo Roccanera. He was among the first to arrive, and he spent some time in conversation with Gilbert Osmond, who almost always was present when his wife received. They sat down together, and Osmond, talkative, communicative, expansive, seemed possessed with a kind of intellectual gaiety. He leaned back with his legs crossed, lounging and chatting, while Goodwood, more restless, but not at all lively, shifted his position, played with his hat, made the little sofa creak beneath him. Osmond's face wore a sharp, aggressive smile; he was as a man whose perceptions have been quickened by good news. He remarked to Goodwood that he was sorry they were to lose him; he himself should particularly miss him. He saw so few intelligent men — they were surprisingly scarce in Rome. He must be sure to come back; there was something very refreshing, to an inveterate Italian like himself, in talking with a genuine outsider.

"I'm very fond of Rome, you know," Osmond said; "but there's nothing I like better than to meet people who haven't that superstition. The modern world's after all very fine. Now you're thoroughly modern and yet are not at all common. So many of the moderns we see are such very poor stuff. If they're the children of the future we're willing to die young. Of course the ancients too are often very tiresome. My wife and I like everything that's really new — not the mere pretence of it. There's nothing new, unfortunately, in ignorance and stupidity. We see plenty of that in forms that offer themselves as a revelation of progress, of light. A revelation of vulgarity! There's a certain kind of vulgarity which I believe is really new; I don't think there ever was anything like it before. Indeed I don't find vulgarity, at all, before the present century. You see a faint menace of it here and there in the last, but to-day the air has grown so dense that delicate things are literally not recognised. Now, we 've *liked you —* !" With which he hesitated a moment, laying his hand gently on Goodwood's knee and smiling with a mixture of assurance and embarrassment. " I 'm going to say something extremely offensive and patronising, but you must let me have the satisfaction of it. We 've liked you because — because you 've reconciled us a little to the future. If there are to be a certain number of people like you — *à la bonne heure!* I 'm talking for my wife as well as for myself, you see. She speaks for me, my wife; why should n't I speak for her? We 're as united, you know, as the candlestick and the snuffers. Am I assuming too much when I say that I think I 've understood from you that your occupations have been — a — commercial? There 's a danger in that, you know; but it 's the way you have escaped that strikes us. Excuse me if my little compliment seems in execrable taste; fortunately my wife does n't hear me. What I mean is that you *might have been* — a — what I was mentioning just now. The whole American world was in a conspiracy to make you so. But you resisted, you 've something about you that saved you. And yet you 're so modern, so modern; the most modern man we know! We shall always be delighted to see you again."

I have said that Osmond was in good humour, and these remarks will give ample evidence of the fact. They were infinitely more personal than he usually cared to be, and if Caspar Goodwood had attended to them more closely he might have thought that the defence of delicacy was in rather odd hands. We may believe, however, that Osmond knew very well what he was about, and that if he chose to use the tone of patronage with a grossness not in his habits he had an excellent reason for the escapade. Goodwood had only a vague sense that he was laying it on somehow; he scarcely knew where the mixture was applied. Indeed he scarcely knew what Osmond was talking about; he wanted to be alone with Isabel, and that idea spoke louder to him than her husband's perfectly-pitched voice. He watched her talking with other people and wondered when she would be at liberty and whether he might ask her to go into one of the other rooms. His humour was not, like Osmond's, of the best; there was an element of dull rage in his consciousness of things. Up to this time he had not disliked Osmond personally; he had only thought him very well-informed and obliging and more than he had supposed like the person whom Isabel Archer would naturally marry. His host had won in the open field a great advantage over him, and Goodwood had too strong a sense of fair play to have been moved to underrate him on that account. He had not tried positively to think well of him; this was a flight of sentimental benevolence of which, even in the days when he came nearest to reconciling himself to what had happened, Goodwood was quite incapable. He accepted him as rather a brilliant personage of the amateurish kind, afflicted with a redundancy of leisure which it amused him to work off in little refinements of conversation. But he only half trusted him; he could never make out why the deuce Osmond should lavish refinements of any sort upon *him*. It made him

suspect that he found some private entertainment in
it, and it ministered to a general impression that his
triumphant rival had in his composition a streak of
perversity. He knew indeed that Osmond could have
no reason to wish him evil; he had nothing to fear
from him. He had carried off a supreme advantage
and could afford to be kind to a man who had lost
everything. It was true that Goodwood had at times
grimly wished he were dead and would have liked to
kill him; but Osmond had no means of knowing this,
for practice had made the younger man perfect in the
art of appearing inaccessible to-day to any violent
emotion. He cultivated this art in order to deceive
himself, but it was others that he deceived first.
He cultivated it, moreover, with very limited success;
of which there could be no better proof than the
deep, dumb irritation that reigned in his soul when
he heard Osmond speak of his wife's feelings as if he
were commissioned to answer for them.

That was all he had had an ear for in what his host
said to him this evening; he had been conscious that
Osmond made more of a point even than usual of re-
ferring to the conjugal harmony prevailing at Palazzo
Roccanera. He had been more careful than ever to
speak as if he and his wife had all things in sweet com-
munity and it were as natural to each of them to say
"we" as to say "I." In all this there was an air of
intention that had puzzled and angered our poor Bostonian, who could only reflect for his comfort that Mrs.
Osmond's relations with her husband were none of his
business. He had no proof whatever that her husband
misrepresented her, and if he judged her by the sur-

face of things was bound to believe that she liked her life. She had never given him the faintest sign of discontent. Miss Stackpole had told him that she had lost her illusions, but writing for the papers had made Miss Stackpole sensational. She was too fond of early news. Moreover, since her arrival in Rome she had been much on her guard; she had pretty well ceased to flash her lantern at him. This indeed, it may be said for her, would have been quite against her conscience. She had now seen the reality of Isabel's situation, and it had inspired her with a just reserve. Whatever could be done to improve it the most useful form of assistance would not be to inflame her former lovers with a sense of her wrongs. Miss Stackpole continued to take a deep interest in the state of Mr. Goodwood's feelings, but she showed it at present only by sending him choice extracts, humorous and other, from the American journals, of which she received several by every post and which she always perused with a pair of scissors in her hand. The articles she cut out she placed in an envelope addressed to Mr. Goodwood, which she left with her own hand at his hotel. He never asked her a question about Isabel: had n't he come five thousand miles to see for himself? He was thus not in the least authorised to think Mrs. Osmond unhappy; but the very absence of authorisation operated as an irritant, ministered to the harshness with which, in spite of his theory that he had ceased to care, he now recognised that, so far as she was concerned, the future had nothing more for him. He had not even the satisfaction of knowing the truth; apparently he could not even be trusted to respect her if she *were* unhappy. He was hopeless, helpless, useless. To this last character she had called his attention by her ingenious plan for making him leave Rome. He had no objection whatever to doing what he could for her cousin, but it made him grind his teeth to think that of all the services she might have asked of him this was the one she had been eager to select. There had been no danger of her choosing one that would have kept him in Rome.

To-night what he was chiefly thinking of was that he was to leave her to-morrow and that he had gained nothing by coming but the knowledge that he was as little wanted as ever. About herself he had gained no knowledge; she was imperturbable, inscrutable, impenetrable. He felt the old bitterness, which he had tried so hard to swallow, rise again in his throat, and he knew there are disappointments that last as long as life. Osmond went on talking; Goodwood was vaguely aware that he was touching again upon his perfect intimacy with his wife. It seemed to him for a moment that the man had a kind of demonic imagination; it was impossible that without malice he should have selected so unusual a topic. But what did it matter, after all, whether he were demonic or not, and whether she loved him or hated him? She might hate him to the death without one's gaining a straw one's self. "You travel, by the by, with Ralph Touchett," Osmond said. "I suppose that means you'll move slowly?"

"I don't know. I shall do just as he likes."

"You're very accommodating. We're immensely obliged to you; you must really let me say it. My wife has probably expressed to you what we feel. Touchett has been on our minds all winter; it has looked more than once as if he would never leave Rome. He ought never to have come; it's worse than an imprudence for people in that state to travel; it's a kind of indelicacy. I would n't for the world be under such an obligation to Touchett as he has been to — to my wife and me. Other people inevitably have to look after him, and every one is n't so generous as you."

"I've nothing else to do," Caspar said dryly.

Osmond looked at him a moment askance. "You ought to marry, and then you'd have plenty to do! It's true that in that case you would n't be quite so available for deeds of mercy."

"Do you find that as a married man you're so much occupied?" the young man mechanically asked.

"Ah, you see, being married 's in itself an occupation. It is n't always active; it's often passive; but that takes even more attention. Then my wife and I do so many things together. We read, we study, we make music, we walk, we drive — we talk even, as when we first knew each other. I delight, to this hour, in my wife's conversation. If you're ever bored take my advice and get married. Your wife indeed may bore you, in that case; but you'll never bore yourself. You'll always have something to say to yourself — always have a subject of reflection."

"I'm not bored," said Goodwood. "I've plenty to think about and to say to myself."

"More than to say to others!" Osmond exclaimed with a light laugh. "Where shall you go next? I mean after you 've consigned Touchett to his natural care-takers — I believe his mother 's at last coming back to look after him. That little lady 's superb ; she neglects her duties with a finish —! Perhaps you 'll spend the summer in England ? "

"I don't know. I 've no plans."

"Happy man! That 's a little bleak, but it 's very free."

"Oh yes, I 'm very free."

"Free to come back to Rome I hope," said Osmond as he saw a group of new visitors enter the room. "Remember that when you do come we count on you! "

Goodwood had meant to go away early, but the evening elapsed without his having a chance to speak to Isabel otherwise than as one of several associated interlocutors. There was something perverse in the inveteracy with which she avoided him; his unquench-able rancour discovered an intention where there was certainly no appearance of one. There was absolutely no appearance of one. She met his eyes with her clear hospitable smile, which seemed almost to ask that he would come and help her to entertain some of her visitors. To such suggestions, however, he opposed but a stiff impatience. He wandered about and waited; he talked to the few people he knew, who found him for the first time rather self-contradictory. This was indeed rare with Caspar Goodwood, though he often contradicted others. There was often music at Pa-lazzo Roccanera, and it was usually very good. Under cover of the music he managed to contain himself; but toward the end, when he saw the people beginning to go, he drew near to Isabel and asked her in a low tone if he might not speak to her in one of the other rooms, which he had just assured himself was empty. She smiled as if she wished to oblige him but found herself absolutely prevented. "I 'm afraid it 's impossible. People are saying good-night, and I must be where they can see me."

"I shall wait till they are all gone then."

She hesitated a moment. "Ah, that will be delightful!" she exclaimed.

And he waited, though it took a long time yet. There were several people, at the end, who seemed tethered to the carpet. The Countess Gemini, who was never herself till midnight, as she said, displayed no consciousness that the entertainment was over; she had still a little circle of gentlemen in front of the fire, who every now and then broke into a united laugh. Osmond had disappeared — he never bade good-bye to people; and as the Countess was extending her range, according to her custom at this period of the evening, Isabel had sent Pansy to bed. Isabel sat a little apart; she too appeared to wish her sister-in-law would sound a lower note and let the last loiterers depart in peace.

"May I not say a word to you now?" Goodwood presently asked her.

She got up immediately, smiling. "Certainly, we 'll go somewhere else if you like." They went together, leaving the Countess with her little circle, and for a moment after they had crossed the threshold neither of them spoke. Isabel would not sit down; she stood in the middle of the room slowly fanning herself;

she had for him the same familiar grace. She seemed to wait for him to speak. Now that he was alone with her all the passion he had never stifled surged into his senses; it hummed in his eyes and made things swim round him. The bright, empty room grew dim and blurred, and through the heaving veil he felt her hover before him with gleaming eyes and parted lips. If he had seen more distinctly he would have perceived her smile was fixed and a trifle forced — that she was frightened at what she saw in his own face. "I suppose you wish to bid me good-bye?" she said.

"Yes — but I don't like it. I don't want to leave Rome," he answered with almost plaintive honesty.

"I can well imagine. It's wonderfully good of you. I can't tell you how kind I think you."

For a moment more he said nothing. "With a few words like that you make me go."

"You must come back some day," she brightly returned.

"Some day? You mean as long a time hence as possible."

"Oh no; I don't mean all that."

"What *do* you mean? I don't understand! But I said I'd go, and I'll go," Goodwood added.

"Come back whenever you like," said Isabel with attempted lightness.

"I don't care a straw for your cousin!" Caspar broke out.

"Is that what you wished to tell me?"

"No, no; I didn't want to tell you anything; I wanted to ask you —" he paused a moment, and

then — "what have you really made of your life?"
he said, in a low, quick tone. He paused again, as
if for an answer; but she said nothing, and he went
on: "I can't understand, I can't penetrate you!
What am I to believe — what do you want me to
think?" Still she said nothing; she only stood looking at him, now quite without pretending to ease.
"I'm told you're unhappy, and if you are I should
like to know it. That would be something for me.
But you yourself say you're happy, and you're
somehow so still, so smooth, so hard. You're completely changed. You conceal everything; I haven't
really come near you."

"You come very near," Isabel said gently, but in
a tone of warning.

"And yet I don't touch you! I want to know the
truth. Have you done well?"

"You ask a great deal."

"Yes — I've always asked a great deal. Of course
you won't tell me. I shall never know if you can help
it. And then it's none of my business." He had
spoken with a visible effort to control himself, to give
a considerate form to an inconsiderate state of mind.
But the sense that it was his last chance, that he
loved her and had lost her, that she would think
him a fool whatever he should say, suddenly gave
him a lash and added a deep vibration to his low
voice. "You're perfectly inscrutable, and that's
what makes me think you've something to hide.
I tell you I don't care a straw for your cousin, but
I don't mean that I don't like him. I mean that it
isn't because I like him that I go away with him.

I'd go if he were an idiot and you should have asked me. If you should ask me I'd go to Siberia to-morrow. Why do you want me to leave the place? You must have some reason for that; if you were as contented as you pretend you are you would n't care. I'd rather know the truth about you, even if it's damnable, than have come here for nothing. That is n't what I came for. I thought I should n't care. I came because I wanted to assure myself that I need n't think of you any more. I have n't thought of anything else, and you're quite right to wish me to go away. But if I must go, there's no harm in my letting myself out for a single moment, is there? If you're really hurt — if *he* hurts you — nothing *I* say will hurt you. When I tell you I love you it's simply what I came for. I thought it was for something else; but it was for that. I should n't say it if I did n't believe I should never see you again. It's the last time — let me pluck a single flower! I've no right to say that, I know; and you've no right to listen. But you don't listen; you never listen, you're always thinking of something else. After this I must go, of course; so I shall at least have a reason. Your asking me is no reason, not a real one. I can't judge by your husband," he went on irrelevantly, almost incoherently; "I don't understand him; he tells me you adore each other. Why does he tell me that? What business is it of mine? When I say that to you, you look strange. But you always look strange. Yes, you've something to hide. It's none of my business — very true. But I love you," said Caspar Goodwood.

As he said, she looked strange. She turned her eyes to the door by which they had entered and raised her fan as if in warning. "You've behaved so well; don't spoil it," she uttered softly.

"No one hears me. It's wonderful what you tried to put me off with. I love you as I've never loved you."

"I know it. I knew it as soon as you consented to go."

"You can't help it — of course not. You would if you could, but you can't, unfortunately. Unfortunately for me, I mean. I ask nothing — nothing, that is, I should n't. But I do ask one sole satisfaction: — that you tell me — that you tell me—!"

"That I tell you what?"

"Whether I may pity you."

"Should you like that?" Isabel asked, trying to smile again.

"To pity you? Most assuredly! That at least would be doing something. I'd give my life to it."

She raised her fan to her face, which it covered all except her eyes. They rested a moment on his. "Don't give your life to it; but give a thought to it every now and then." And with that she went back to the Countess Gemini.

XLIX

MADAME MERLE had not made her appearance at Palazzo Roccanera on the evening of that Thursday of which I have narrated some of the incidents, and Isabel, though she observed her absence, was not surprised by it. Things had passed between them which added no stimulus to sociability, and to appreciate which we must glance a little backward. It has been mentioned that Madame Merle returned from Naples shortly after Lord Warburton had left Rome, and that on her first meeting with Isabel (whom, to do her justice, she came immediately to see) her first utterance had been an enquiry as to the whereabouts of this nobleman, for whom she appeared to hold her dear friend accountable.

"Please don't talk of him," said Isabel for answer; "we've heard so much of him of late."

Madame Merle bent her head on one side a little, protestingly, and smiled at the left corner of her mouth. "You've heard, yes. But you must remember that I've not, in Naples. I hoped to find him here and to be able to congratulate Pansy."

"You may congratulate Pansy still; but not on marrying Lord Warburton."

"How you say that! Don't you know I had set my heart on it?" Madame Merle asked with a great deal of spirit, but still with the intonation of good-humour.

Isabel was discomposed, but she was determined to be good-humoured too. "You should n't have gone to Naples then. You should have stayed here to watch the affair."

"I had too much confidence in you. But do you think it 's too late ? "

"You had better ask Pansy," said Isabel.

"I shall ask her what you 've said to her."

These words seemed to justify the impulse of self-defence aroused on Isabel's part by her perceiving that her visitor's attitude was a critical one. Madame Merle, as we know, had been very discreet hitherto ; she had never criticised; she had been markedly afraid of intermeddling. But apparently she had only reserved herself for this occasion, since she now had a dangerous quickness in her eye and an air of irritation which even her admirable ease was not able to transmute. She had suffered a disappointment which excited Isabel's surprise — our heroine having no knowledge of her zealous interest in Pansy's marriage; and she betrayed it in a manner which quickened Mrs. Osmond's alarm. More clearly than ever before Isabel heard a cold, mocking voice proceed from she knew not where, in the dim void that surrounded her, and declare that this bright, strong, definite, worldly woman, this incarnation of the practical, the personal, the immediate, was a powerful agent in her destiny. She was nearer to her than Isabel had yet discovered, and her nearness was not the charming accident she had so long supposed. The sense of accident indeed had died within her that day when she happened to be struck with the manner in which the wonderful lady and her own husband sat together in private. No definite suspicion had as yet taken its place; but it was enough to make her view this friend with a different eye, to have been led to reflect that there was more intention in her past behaviour than she had allowed for at the time. Ah yes, there had been intention, there had been intention, Isabel said to herself; and she seemed to wake from a long pernicious dream. What was it that brought home to her that Madame Merle's intention had not been good? Nothing but the mistrust which had lately taken body and which married itself now to the fruitful wonder produced by her visitor's challenge on behalf of poor Pansy. There was something in this challenge which had at the very outset excited an answering defiance; a nameless vitality which she could see to have been absent from her friend's professions of delicacy and caution. Madame Merle had been unwilling to interfere, certainly, but only so long as there was nothing to interfere with. It will perhaps seem to the reader that Isabel went fast in casting doubt, on mere suspicion, on a sincerity proved by several years of good offices. She moved quickly indeed, and with reason, for a strange truth was filtering into her soul. Madame Merle's interest was identical with Osmond's: that was enough. "I think Pansy will tell you nothing that will make you more angry," she said in answer to her companion's last remark.

"I'm not in the least angry. I've only a great desire to retrieve the situation. Do you consider that Warburton has left us for ever?"

"I can't tell you; I don't understand you. It's all

over; please let it rest. Osmond has talked to me a great deal about it, and I've nothing more to say or to hear. I've no doubt," Isabel added, "that he'll be very happy to discuss the subject with you."

"I know what he thinks; he came to see me last evening."

"As soon as you had arrived? Then you know all about it and you need n't apply to me for information."

"It is n't information I want. At bottom it's sympathy. I had set my heart on that marriage; the idea did what so few things do — it satisfied the imagination."

"Your imagination, yes. But not that of the persons concerned."

"You mean by that of course that I'm not concerned. Of course not directly. But when one's such an old friend one can't help having something at stake. You forget how long I've known Pansy. You mean, of course," Madame Merle added, "that *you* are one of the persons concerned."

"No; that's the last thing I mean. I'm very weary of it all."

Madame Merle hesitated a little. "Ah yes, your work's done."

"Take care what you say," said Isabel very gravely.

"Oh, I take care; never perhaps more than when it appears least. Your husband judges you severely."

Isabel made for a moment no answer to this; she felt choked with bitterness. It was not the insolence of Madame Merle's informing her that Osmond had been taking her into his confidence as against his wife that struck her most; for she was not quick to believe that this was meant for insolence. Madame Merle was very rarely insolent, and only when it was exactly right. It was not right now, or at least it was not right yet. What touched Isabel like a drop of corrosive acid upon an open wound was the knowledge that Osmond dishonoured her in his words as well as in his thoughts. "Should you like to know how I judge *him?*" she asked at last.

"No, because you'd never tell me. And it would be painful for me to know."

There was a pause, and for the first time since she had known her Isabel thought Madame Merle disagreeable. She wished she would leave her. "Remember how attractive Pansy is, and don't despair," she said abruptly, with a desire that this should close their interview.

But Madame Merle's expansive presence underwent no contraction. She only gathered her mantle about her and, with the movement, scattered upon the air a faint, agreeable fragrance. "I don't despair; I feel encouraged. And I did n't come to scold you; I came if possible to learn the truth. I know you'll tell it if I ask you. It's an immense blessing with you that one can count upon that. No, you won't believe what a comfort I take in it."

"What truth do you speak of?" Isabel asked, wondering.

"Just this: whether Lord Warburton changed his mind quite of his own movement or because you recommended it. To please himself I mean, or to please you. Think of the confidence I must still have in you, in spite of having lost a little of it," Madame Merle continued with a smile, "to ask such a question as that!" She sat looking at her friend, to judge the effect of her words, and then went on: "Now don't be heroic, don't be unreasonable, don't take offence. It seems to me I do you an honour in speaking so. I don't know another woman to whom I would do it. I haven't the least idea that any other woman would tell me the truth. And don't you see how well it is that your husband should know it? It's true that he doesn't appear to have had any tact whatever in trying to extract it; he has indulged in gratuitous suppositions. But that doesn't alter the fact that it would make a difference in his view of his daughter's prospects to know distinctly what really occurred. If Lord Warburton simply got tired of the poor child, that's one thing, and it's a pity. If he gave her up to please you it's another. That's a pity too, but in a different way. Then, in the latter case, you'd perhaps resign yourself to not being pleased — to simply seeing your stepdaughter married. Let him off — let us have him!"

Madame Merle had proceeded very deliberately, watching her companion and apparently thinking she could proceed safely. As she went on Isabel grew pale; she clasped her hands more tightly in her lap. It was not that her visitor had at last thought it the right time to be insolent; for this was not what was most apparent. It was a worse horror than that. "Who are you — what are you?" Isabel murmured. "What have you to do with my husband?" It was strange that for the moment she drew as near to him as if she had loved him.

"Ah then, you take it heroically! I'm very sorry. Don't think, however, that I shall do so."

"What have you to do with me?" Isabel went on.

Madame Merle slowly got up, stroking her muff, but not removing her eyes from Isabel's face. "Everything!" she answered.

Isabel sat there looking up at her, without rising; her face was almost a prayer to be enlightened. But the light of this woman's eyes seemed only a darkness. "Oh misery!" she murmured at last; and she fell back, covering her face with her hands. It had come over her like a high-surging wave that Mrs. Touchett was right. Madame Merle had married her. Before she uncovered her face again that lady had left the room.

Isabel took a drive alone that afternoon; she wished to be far away, under the sky, where she could descend from her carriage and tread upon the daisies. She had long before this taken old Rome into her confidence, for in a world of ruins the ruin of her happiness seemed a less unnatural catastrophe. She rested her weariness upon things that had crumbled for centuries and yet still were upright; she dropped her secret sadness into the silence of lonely places, where its very modern quality detached itself and grew objective, so that as she sat in a sun-warmed angle on a winter's day, or stood in a mouldy church to which no one came, she could almost smile at it and think of its smallness. Small it was, in the large Roman record, and her haunting sense of the continuity of the human lot easily carried her from the less to the greater. She had become deeply, tenderly acquainted with Rome;

it interfused and moderated her passion. But she had grown to think of it chiefly as the place where people had suffered. This was what came to her in the starved churches, where the marble columns, transferred from pagan ruins, seemed to offer her a companionship in endurance and the musty incense to be a compound of long-unanswered prayers. There was no gentler nor less consistent heretic than Isabel; the firmest of worshippers, gazing at dark altar-pictures or clustered candles, could not have felt more intimately the suggestiveness of these objects nor have been more liable at such moments to a spiritual visitation. Pansy, as we know, was almost always her companion, and of late the Countess Gemini, balancing a pink parasol, had lent brilliancy to their equipage; but she still occasionally found herself alone when it suited her mood and where it suited the place. On such occasions she had several resorts; the most accessible of which perhaps was a seat on the low parapet which edges the wide grassy space before the high, cold front of Saint John Lateran, whence you look across the Campagna at the far-trailing outline of the Alban Mount and at that mighty plain, between, which is still so full of all that has passed from it. After the departure of her cousin and his companions she roamed more than usual; she carried her sombre spirit from one familiar shrine to the other. Even when Pansy and the Countess were with her she felt the touch of a vanished world. The carriage, leaving the walls of Rome behind, rolled through narrow lanes where the wild honeysuckle had begun to tangle itself in the hedges, or waited for her in quiet places where the fields lay near, while she strolled further and further over the flower-freckled turf, or sat on a stone that had once had a use and gazed through the veil of her personal sadness at the splendid sadness of the scene — at the dense, warm light, the far gradations and soft confusions of colour, the motionless shepherds in lonely attitudes, the hills where the cloud-shadows had the lightness of a blush.

On the afternoon I began with speaking of, she had taken a resolution not to think of Madame Merle; but the resolution proved vain, and this lady's image hovered constantly before her. She asked herself, with an almost childlike horror of the supposition, whether to this intimate friend of several years the great historical epithet of *wicked* were to be applied. She knew the idea only by the Bible and other literary works; to the best of her belief she had had no personal acquaintance with wickedness. She had desired a large acquaintance with human life, and in spite of her having flattered herself that she cultivated it with some success this elementary privilege had been denied her. Perhaps it was not wicked — in the historic sense — to be even deeply false; for that was what Madame Merle had been — deeply, deeply, deeply. Isabel's Aunt Lydia had made this discovery long before, and had mentioned it to her niece; but Isabel had flattered herself at this time that she had a much richer view of things, especially of the spontaneity of her own career and the nobleness of her own interpretations, than poor stiffly-reasoning Mrs. Touchett. Madame Merle had done what she wanted; she had brought about the union of her two friends; a reflection which could not fail to make it a matter of wonder that she should so much have desired such an event. There were people who had the match-making passion, like the votaries of art for art; but Madame Merle, great artist as she was, was scarcely one of these. She thought too ill of marriage, too ill even of life; she had desired that particular marriage but had not desired others. She had therefore had a conception of gain, and Isabel asked herself where she had found her profit. It took her naturally a long time to discover, and even then her discovery was imperfect. It came back to her that Madame Merle, though she had seemed to like her from their first meeting at Gardencourt, had been doubly affectionate after Mr. Touchett's death and after learning that her young friend had been subject to the good old man's charity. She had found her profit not in the gross device of borrowing money, but in the more refined idea of introducing one of her intimates to the young woman's fresh and ingenuous fortune. She had naturally chosen her closest intimate, and it was already vivid enough to Isabel that Gilbert occupied this position. She found herself confronted in this manner with the conviction that the man in the world whom she had supposed to be the least sordid had married her, like a vulgar adventurer, for her money. Strange to say, it had never before occurred to her; if she had thought a good deal of harm of Osmond she had not done him this particular injury. This was the worst she could think of, and she had been saying to herself that the worst was still to come. A man might marry a woman for her money perfectly well; the thing was often done. But at least he should let her know. She wondered whether, since he had wanted her money, her money would now satisfy him. Would he take her money and let her go? Ah, if Mr. Touchett's great charity would but help her to-day it would be blessed indeed! It was not slow to occur to her that if Madame Merle had wished to do Gilbert a service his recognition to her of the boon must have lost its warmth. What must be his feelings to-day in regard to his too zealous benefactress, and what expression must they have found on the part of such a master of irony? It is a singular, but a characteristic, fact that before Isabel returned from her silent drive she had broken its silence by the soft exclamation: "Poor, poor Madame Merle!"

Her compassion would perhaps have been justified if on this same afternoon she had been concealed behind one of the valuable curtains of time-softened damask which dressed the interesting little *salon* of the lady to whom it referred; the carefully-arranged apartment to which we once paid a visit in company with the discreet Mr. Rosier. In that apartment, towards six o'clock, Gilbert Osmond was seated, and his hostess stood before him as Isabel had seen her stand on an occasion commemorated in this history with an emphasis appropriate not so much to its apparent as to its real importance.

"I don't believe you're unhappy; I believe you like it," said Madame Merle.

"Did I say I was unhappy?" Osmond asked with a face grave enough to suggest that he might have been.

"No, but you don't say the contrary, as you ought in common gratitude."

"Don't talk about gratitude," he returned dryly. "And don't aggravate me," he added in a moment.

Madame Merle slowly seated herself, with her arms folded and her white hands arranged as a support to one of them and an ornament, as it were, to the other. She looked exquisitely calm but impressively sad. "On your side, don't try to frighten me. I wonder if you guess some of my thoughts."

"I trouble about them no more than I can help. I've quite enough of my own."

"That's because they're so delightful."

Osmond rested his head against the back of his chair and looked at his companion with a cynical directness which seemed also partly an expression of fatigue. "You do aggravate me," he remarked in a moment. "I'm very tired."

"*Eh moi donc!*" cried Madame Merle.

"With you it's because you fatigue yourself. With me it's not my own fault."

"When I fatigue myself it's for you. I've given you an interest. That's a great gift."

"Do you call it an interest?" Osmond enquired with detachment.

"Certainly, since it helps you to pass your time."

"The time has never seemed longer to me than this winter."

"You've never looked better; you've never been so agreeable, so brilliant."

"Damn my brilliancy!" he thoughtfully murmured. "How little, after all, you know me!"

"If I don't know you I know nothing," smiled

Madame Merle. "You've the feeling of complete success."

"No, I shall not have that till I've made you stop judging me."

"I did that long ago. I speak from old knowledge. But you express yourself more too."

Osmond just hung fire. "I wish you'd express yourself less!"

"You wish to condemn me to silence? Remember that I've never been a chatterbox. At any rate there are three or four things I should like to say to you first. Your wife does n't know what to do with herself," she went on with a change of tone.

"Pardon me; she knows perfectly. She has a line sharply drawn. She means to carry out her ideas."

"Her ideas to-day must be remarkable."

"Certainly they are. She has more of them than ever."

"She was unable to show me any this morning," said Madame Merle. "She seemed in a very simple, almost in a stupid, state of mind. She was completely bewildered."

"You had better say at once that she was pathetic."

"Ah no, I don't want to encourage you too much."

He still had his head against the cushion behind him; the ankle of one foot rested on the other knee. So he sat for a while. "I should like to know what's the matter with you," he said at last.

"The matter — the matter — !" And here Madame Merle stopped. Then she went on with a sudden outbreak of passion, a burst of summer thunder in a clear sky: "The matter is that I would give my right hand to be able to weep, and that I can't!"

"What good would it do you to weep?"

"It would make me feel as I felt before I knew you."

"If I've dried your tears, that's something. But I've seen you shed them."

"Oh, I believe you'll make me cry still. I mean make me howl like a wolf. I've a great hope, I've a great need, of that. I was vile this morning; I was horrid," she said.

"If Isabel was in the stupid state of mind you mention she probably did n't perceive it," Osmond answered.

"It was precisely my deviltry that stupefied her. I could n't help it; I was full of something bad. Perhaps it was something good; I don't know. You've not only dried up my tears; you've dried up my soul."

"It 's not I then that am responsible for my wife's condition," Osmond said. "It 's pleasant to think that I shall get the benefit of your influence upon her. Don't you know the soul is an immortal principle? How can it suffer alteration?"

"I don't believe at all that it 's an immortal principle. I believe it can perfectly be destroyed. That 's what has happened to mine, which was a very good one to start with; and it 's you I have to thank for it. You're *very* bad," she added with gravity in her emphasis.

"Is this the way we 're to end?" Osmond asked with the same studied coldness.

"I don't know how we're to end. I wish I did! How do bad people end? — especially as to their *common* crimes. You have made me as bad as yourself."

"I don't understand you. You seem to me quite good enough," said Osmond, his conscious indifference giving an extreme effect to the words.

Madame Merle's self-possession tended on the contrary to diminish, and she was nearer losing it than on any occasion on which we have had the pleasure of meeting her. The glow of her eye turned sombre; her smile betrayed a painful effort. "Good enough for anything that I've done with myself? I suppose that's what you mean."

"Good enough to be always charming!" Osmond exclaimed, smiling too.

"Oh God!" his companion murmured; and, sitting there in her ripe freshness, she had recourse to the same gesture she had provoked on Isabel's part in the morning: she bent her face and covered it with her hands.

"Are you going to weep after all?" Osmond asked; and on her remaining motionless he went on: "Have I ever complained to you?"

She dropped her hands quickly. "No, you've taken your revenge otherwise — you have taken it on *her*."

Osmond threw back his head further; he looked a while at the ceiling and might have been supposed to be appealing, in an informal way, to the heavenly powers. "Oh, the imagination of women! It's always vulgar, at bottom. You talk of revenge like a third-rate novelist."

"Of course you have n't complained. You've enjoyed your triumph too much."

"I'm rather curious to know what you call my triumph."

"You've made your wife afraid of you."

Osmond changed his position; he leaned forward, resting his elbows on his knees and looking a while at a beautiful old Persian rug, at his feet. He had an air of refusing to accept any one's valuation of anything, even of time, and of preferring to abide by his own; a peculiarity which made him at moments an irritating person to converse with. "Isabel's not afraid of me, and it's not what I wish," he said at last. "To what do you want to provoke me when you say such things as that?"

"I've thought over all the harm you can do me," Madame Merle answered. "Your wife was afraid of me this morning, but in me it was really you she feared."

"You may have said things that were in very bad taste; I'm not responsible for that. I did n't see the use of your going to see her at all: you're capable of acting without her. I've not made *you* afraid of me that I can see; how then should I have made her? You're at least as brave. I can't think where you've picked up such rubbish; one might suppose you knew me by this time." He got up as he spoke and walked to the chimney, where he stood a moment bending his eye, as if he had seen them for the first time, on the delicate specimens of rare porcelain with which it was covered. He took up a small cup and held it in his hand; then, still holding it and leaning his arm on the mantel, he pursued: "You always see too much in everything; you overdo it; you lose sight of the real. I'm much simpler than you think."

"I think you're very simple." And Madame Merle kept her eye on her cup. "I've come to that with time. I judged you, as I say, of old; but it's only since your marriage that I've understood you. I've seen better what you have been to your wife than I ever saw what you were for me. Please be very careful of that precious object."

"It already has a wee bit of a tiny crack," said Osmond dryly as he put it down. "If you didn't understand me before I married it was cruelly rash of you to put me into such a box. However, I took a fancy to my box myself; I thought it would be a comfortable fit. I asked very little; I only asked that she should like me."

"That she should like you so much!"

"So much, of course; in such a case one asks the maximum. That she should adore me, if you will. Oh yes, I wanted that."

"I never adored you," said Madame Merle.

"Ah, but you pretended to!"

"It's true that you never accused me of being a comfortable fit," Madame Merle went on.

"My wife has declined — declined to do anything of the sort," said Osmond. "If you're determined to make a tragedy of that, the tragedy's hardly for her."

"The tragedy's for me!" Madame Merle exclaimed, rising with a long low sigh but having a glance at the same time for the contents of her mantel-shelf.

"It appears that I'm to be severely taught the disadvantages of a false position."

"You express yourself like a sentence in a copybook. We must look for our comfort where we can find it. If my wife does n't like me, at least my child does. I shall look for compensations in Pansy. Fortunately I have n't a fault to find with her."

"Ah," she said softly, "if I had a child —!"

Osmond waited, and then, with a little formal air, "The children of others may be a great interest!" he announced.

"You're more like a copy-book than I. There's something after all that holds us together."

"Is it the idea of the harm I may do you?" Osmond asked.

"No; it's the idea of the good I may do for you. It's that," Madame Merle pursued, "that made me so jealous of Isabel. I want it to be *my* work," she added, with her face, which had grown hard and bitter, relaxing to its habit of smoothness.

Her friend took up his hat and his umbrella, and after giving the former article two or three strokes with his coat-cuff, "On the whole, I think," he said, "you had better leave it to me."

After he had left her she went, the first thing, and lifted from the mantel-shelf the attenuated coffee-cup in which he had mentioned the existence of a crack; but she looked at it rather abstractedly. "Have I been so vile all for nothing?" she vaguely wailed.

L

As the Countess Gemini was not acquainted with the ancient monuments Isabel occasionally offered to introduce her to these interesting relics and to give their afternoon drive an antiquarian aim. The Countess, who professed to think her sister-in-law a prodigy of learning, never made an objection, and gazed at masses of Roman brickwork as patiently as if they had been mounds of modern drapery. She had not the historic sense, though she had in some directions the anecdotic, and as regards herself the apologetic, but she was so delighted to be in Rome that she only desired to float with the current. She would gladly have passed an hour every day in the damp darkness of the Baths of Titus if it had been a condition of her remaining at Palazzo Roccanera. Isabel, however, was not a severe cicerone; she used to visit the ruins chiefly because they offered an excuse for talking about other matters than the love-affairs of the ladies of Florence, as to which her companion was never weary of offering information. It must be added that during these visits the Countess forbade herself every form of active research; her preference was to sit in the carriage and exclaim that everything was most interesting. It was in this manner that she had hitherto examined the Coliseum, to the infinite regret of her niece, who — with all the respect that she owed her — could not see why she should not descend from the vehicle and enter the building. Pansy had so little chance to ramble that her view of the case was not wholly disinterested; it may be divined that she had a secret hope that, once inside, her parents' guest might be induced to climb to the upper tiers. There came a day when the Countess announced her willingness to undertake this feat — a mild afternoon in March when the windy month expressed itself in occasional puffs of spring. The three ladies went into the Coliseum together, but Isabel left her companions to wander over the place. She had often ascended to those desolate ledges from which the Roman crowd used to bellow applause and where now the wild flowers (when they are allowed) bloom in the deep crevices; and to-day she felt weary and disposed to sit in the despoiled arena. It made an intermission too, for the Countess often asked more from one's attention than she gave in return; and Isabel believed that when she was alone with her niece she let the dust gather for a moment on the ancient scandals of the Arnide. She so remained below therefore, while Pansy guided her undiscriminating aunt to the steep brick staircase at the foot of which the custodian unlocks the tall wooden gate. The great enclosure was half in shadow; the western sun brought out the pale red tone of the great blocks of travertine — the latent colour that is the only living element in the immense ruin. Here and there wandered a peasant or a tourist, looking up at the far sky-line where, in the clear stillness, a multitude of swallows kept circling and plunging. Isabel presently became aware

that one of the other visitors, planted in the middle of
the arena, had turned his attention to her own person
and was looking at her with a certain little poise of
the head which she had some weeks before perceived
to be characteristic of baffled but indestructible
purpose. Such an attitude, to-day, could belong
only to Mr. Edward Rosier; and this gentleman
proved in fact to have been considering the question
of speaking to her. When he had assured himself
that she was unaccompanied he drew near, remarking that though she would not answer his letters
she would perhaps not wholly close her ears to his
spoken eloquence. She replied that her stepdaughter
was close at hand and that she could only give him
five minutes; whereupon he took out his watch and
sat down upon a broken block.

"It's very soon told," said Edward Rosier. "I've
sold all my bibelots!" Isabel gave instinctively an
exclamation of horror; it was as if he had told her
he had had all his teeth drawn. "I've sold them by
auction at the Hôtel Drouot," he went on. "The
sale took place three days ago, and they've telegraphed me the result. It's magnificent."

"I'm glad to hear it; but I wish you had kept
your pretty things."

"I have the money instead — fifty thousand dol-
lars. Will Mr. Osmond think me rich enough now?"

"Is it for that you did it?" Isabel asked gently.

"For what else in the world could it be? That's
the only thing I think of. I went to Paris and made
my arrangements. I could n't stop for the sale; I
could n't have seen them going off; I think it would

have killed me. But I put them into good hands, and they brought high prices. I should tell you I have kept my enamels. Now I have the money in my pocket, and he can't say I'm poor!" the young man exclaimed defiantly.

"He'll say now that you're not wise," said Isabel, as if Gilbert Osmond had never said this before.

Rosier gave her a sharp look. "Do you mean that without my bibelots I'm nothing? Do you mean they were the best thing about me? That's what they told me in Paris; oh they were very frank about it. But they had n't seen *her!*"

"My dear friend, you deserve to succeed," said Isabel very kindly.

"You say that so sadly that it's the same as if you said I should n't." And he questioned her eyes with the clear trepidation of his own. He had the air of a man who knows he has been the talk of Paris for a week and is full half a head taller in consequence, but who also has a painful suspicion that in spite of this increase of stature one or two persons still have the perversity to think him diminutive. "I know what happened here while I was away," he went on. "What does Mr. Osmond expect after she has refused Lord Warburton?"

Isabel debated. "That she'll marry another nobleman."

"What other nobleman?"

"One that he'll pick out."

Rosier slowly got up, putting his watch into his waistcoat-pocket. "You're laughing at some one, but this time I don't think it's at me."

"I did n't mean to laugh," said Isabel. "I laugh very seldom. Now you had better go away."

"I feel very safe!" Rosier declared without moving. This might be; but it evidently made him feel more so to make the announcement in rather a loud voice, balancing himself a little complacently on his toes and looking all round the Coliseum as if it were filled with an audience. Suddenly Isabel saw him change colour; there was more of an audience than he had suspected. She turned and perceived that her two companions had returned from their excursion. "You must really go away," she said quickly.

"Ah, my dear lady, pity me!" Edward Rosier murmured in a voice strangely at variance with the announcement I have just quoted. And then he added eagerly, like a man who in the midst of his misery is seized by a happy thought: "Is that lady the Countess Gemini? I 've a great desire to be presented to her."

Isabel looked at him a moment. "She has no influence with her brother."

"Ah, what a monster you make him out!" And Rosier faced the Countess, who advanced, in front of Pansy, with an animation partly due perhaps to the fact that she perceived her sister-in-law to be engaged in conversation with a very pretty young man.

"I 'm glad you 've kept your enamels!" Isabel called as she left him. She went straight to Pansy, who, on seeing Edward Rosier, had stopped short, with lowered eyes. "We 'll go back to the carriage," she said gently.

"Yes, it 's getting late," Pansy returned more

gently still. And she went on without a murmur, without faltering or glancing back.

Isabel, however, allowing herself this last liberty, saw that a meeting had immediately taken place between the Countess and Mr. Rosier. He had removed his hat and was bowing and smiling; he had evidently introduced himself, while the Countess's expressive back displayed to Isabel's eye a gracious inclination. These facts, none the less, were presently lost to sight, for Isabel and Pansy took their places again in the carriage. Pansy, who faced her stepmother, at first kept her eyes fixed on her lap; then she raised them and rested them on Isabel's. There shone out of each of them a little melancholy ray — a spark of timid passion which touched Isabel to the heart. At the same time a wave of envy passed over her soul, as she compared the tremulous longing, the definite ideal of the child with her own dry despair. "Poor little Pansy!" she affectionately said.

"Oh never mind!" Pansy answered in the tone of eager apology.

And then there was a silence; the Countess was a long time coming. "Did you show your aunt everything, and did she enjoy it?" Isabel asked at last.

"Yes, I showed her everything. I think she was very much pleased."

"And you're not tired, I hope."

"Oh no, thank you, I'm not tired."

The Countess still remained behind, so that Isabel requested the footman to go into the Coliseum and tell her they were waiting. He presently returned with the announcement that the Signora Contessa begged them not to wait — she would come home in a cab!

About a week after this lady's quick sympathies had enlisted themselves with Mr. Rosier, Isabel, going rather late to dress for dinner, found Pansy sitting in her room. The girl seemed to have been awaiting her; she got up from her low chair. "Pardon my taking the liberty," she said in a small voice. "It will be the last — for some time."

Her voice was strange, and her eyes, widely opened, had an excited, frightened look. "You're not going away!" Isabel exclaimed.

"I'm going to the convent."

"To the convent?"

Pansy drew nearer, till she was near enough to put her arms round Isabel and rest her head on her shoulder. She stood this way a moment, perfectly still; but her companion could feel her tremble. The quiver of her little body expressed everything she was unable to say. Isabel nevertheless pressed her. "Why are you going to the convent?"

"Because papa thinks it best. He says a young girl's better, every now and then, for making a little retreat. He says the world, always the world, is very bad for a young girl. This is just a chance for a little seclusion — a little reflexion." Pansy spoke in short detached sentences, as if she could scarce trust herself; and then she added with a triumph of self-control: "I think papa's right; I've been so much in the world this winter."

Her announcement had a strange effect on Isabel;

it seemed to carry a larger meaning than the girl herself knew. "When was this decided?" she asked. "I've heard nothing of it."

"Papa told me half an hour ago; he thought it better it should n't be too much talked about in advance. Madame Catherine's to come for me at a quarter past seven, and I'm only to take two frocks. It's only for a few weeks; I'm sure it will be very good. I shall find all those ladies who used to be so kind to me, and I shall see the little girls who are being educated. I'm very fond of little girls," said Pansy with an effect of diminutive grandeur. "And I'm also very fond of Mother Catherine. I shall be very quiet and think a great deal."

Isabel listened to her, holding her breath; she was almost awe-struck. "Think of *me* sometimes."

"Ah, come and see me soon!" cried Pansy; and the cry was very different from the heroic remarks of which she had just delivered herself.

Isabel could say nothing more; she understood nothing; she only felt how little she yet knew her husband. Her answer to his daughter was a long, tender kiss.

Half an hour later she learned from her maid that Madame Catherine had arrived in a cab and had departed again with the signorina. On going to the drawing-room before dinner she found the Countess Gemini alone, and this lady characterised the incident by exclaiming, with a wonderful toss of the head, "*En voilà, ma chère, une pose!*" But if it was an affectation she was at a loss to see what her husband affected. She could only dimly perceive that he had more traditions than she supposed. It had become her habit to be so careful as to what she said to him that, strange as it may appear, she hesitated, for several minutes after he had come in, to allude to his daughter's sudden departure: she spoke of it only after they were seated at table. But she had forbidden herself ever to ask Osmond a question. All she could do was to make a declaration, and there was one that came very naturally. "I shall miss Pansy very much."

He looked a while, with his head inclined a little, at the basket of flowers in the middle of the table. "Ah yes," he said at last, "I had thought of that. You must go and see her, you know; but not too often. I dare say you wonder why I sent her to the good sisters; but I doubt if I can make you understand. It doesn't matter; don't trouble yourself about it. That's why I had not spoken of it. I did n't believe you would enter into it. But I've always had the idea; I've always thought it a part of the education of one's daughter. One's daughter should be fresh and fair; she should be innocent and gentle. With the manners of the present time she is liable to become so dusty and crumpled. Pansy's a little dusty, a little dishevelled; she has knocked about too much. This bustling, pushing rabble that calls itself society — one should take her out of it occasionally. Convents are very quiet, very convenient, very salutary. I like to think of her there, in the old garden, under the arcade, among those tranquil virtuous women. Many of them are gentlewomen born; several of them are noble. She will have her books and her drawing, she will have her piano. I've made the most liberal arrangements.

There is to be nothing ascetic; there's just to be a certain little sense of sequestration. She'll have time to think, and there's something I want her to think about." Osmond spoke deliberately, reasonably, still with his head on one side, as if he were looking at the basket of flowers. His tone, however, was that of a man not so much offering an explanation as putting a thing into words — almost into pictures — to see, himself, how it would look. He considered a while the picture he had evoked and seemed greatly pleased with it. And then he went on: "The Catholics are very wise after all. The convent is a great institution; we can't do without it; it corresponds to an essential need in families, in society. It's a school of good manners; it's a school of repose. Oh, I don't want to detach my daughter from the world," he added; "I don't want to make her fix her thoughts on any other. This one's very well, as *she* should take it, and she may think of it as much as she likes. Only she must think of it in the right way."

Isabel gave an extreme attention to this little sketch; she found it indeed intensely interesting. It seemed to show her how far her husband's desire to be effective was capable of going — to the point of playing theoretic tricks on the delicate organism of his daughter. She could not understand his purpose, no — not wholly; but she understood it better than he supposed or desired, inasmuch as she was convinced that the whole proceeding was an elaborate mystification, addressed to herself and destined to act upon her imagination. He had wanted to do something sudden and arbitrary, something unexpected and refined; to mark the difference between his sympathies and her own, and show that if he regarded his daughter as a precious work of art it was natural he should be more and more careful about the finishing touches. If he wished to be effective he had succeeded; the incident struck a chill into Isabel's heart. Pansy had known the convent in her childhood and had found a happy home there; she was fond of the good sisters, who were very fond of her, and there was therefore for the moment no definite hardship in her lot. But all the same the girl had taken fright; the impression her father desired to make would evidently be sharp enough. The old Protestant tradition had never faded from Isabel's imagination, and as her thoughts attached themselves to this striking example of her husband's genius — she sat looking, like him, at the basket of flowers — poor little Pansy became the heroine of a tragedy. Osmond wished it to be known that he shrank from nothing, and his wife found it hard to pretend to eat her dinner. There was a certain relief presently, in hearing the high, strained voice of her sister-in-law. The Countess too, apparently, had been thinking the thing out, but had arrived at a different conclusion from Isabel.

"It's very absurd, my dear Osmond," she said, "to invent so many pretty reasons for poor Pansy's banishment. Why don't you say at once that you want to get her out of my way? Have n't you discovered that I think very well of Mr. Rosier? I do indeed; he seems to me *simpaticissimo*. He has made me believe in true love; I never did before! Of course you've made up your mind that with those convictions I'm dreadful company for Pansy."

Osmond took a sip of a glass of wine; he looked perfectly good-humoured. "My dear Amy," he answered, smiling as if he were uttering a piece of gallantry, "I don't know anything about your convictions, but if I suspected that they interfere with mine it would be much simpler to banish *you*."

LI

THE Countess was not banished, but she felt the insecurity of her tenure of her brother's hospitality. A week after this incident Isabel received a telegram from England, dated from Gardencourt and bearing the stamp of Mrs. Touchett's authorship. "Ralph cannot last many days," it ran, "and if convenient would like to see you. Wishes me to say that you must come only if you've not other duties. Say, for myself, that you used to talk a good deal about your duty and to wonder what it was; shall be curious to see whether you've found it out. Ralph is really dying, and there's no other company." Isabel was prepared for this news, having received from Henrietta Stackpole a detailed account of her journey to England with her appreciative patient. Ralph had arrived more dead than alive, but she had managed to convey him to Gardencourt, where he had taken to his bed, which, as Miss Stackpole wrote, he evidently would never leave again. She added that she had really had two patients on her hands instead of one, inasmuch as Mr. Goodwood, who had been of no earthly use, was quite as ailing, in a different way, as Mr. Touchett. Afterwards she wrote that she had been obliged to surrender the field to Mrs. Touchett, who had just returned from America and had promptly given her to understand that she did n't wish any interviewing at Gardencourt. Isabel had

written to her aunt shortly after Ralph came to
Rome, letting her know of his critical condition
and suggesting that she should lose no time in returning to Europe. Mrs. Touchett had telegraphed
an acknowledgement of this admonition, and the only
further news Isabel received from her was the second
telegram I have just quoted.

Isabel stood a moment looking at the latter missive;
then, thrusting it into her pocket, she went straight
to the door of her husband's study. Here she again
paused an instant, after which she opened the door
and went in. Osmond was seated at the table near
the window with a folio volume before him, propped
against a pile of books. This volume was open at
a page of small coloured plates, and Isabel presently
saw that he had been copying from it the drawing
of an antique coin. A box of water-colours and fine
brushes lay before him, and he had already transferred to a sheet of immaculate paper the delicate,
finely-tinted disk. His back was turned toward the
door, but he recognised his wife without looking
round.

"Excuse me for disturbing you," she said.

"When I come to your room I always knock,"
he answered, going on with his work.

"I forgot; I had something else to think of. My
cousin's dying."

"Ah, I don't believe that," said Osmond, looking
at his drawing through a magnifying glass. "He was
dying when we married; he'll outlive us all."

Isabel gave herself no time, no thought, to appreciate the careful cynicism of this declaration; she

simply went on quickly, full of her own intention:
"My aunt has telegraphed for me; I must go to
Gardencourt."

"Why must you go to Gardencourt?" Osmond
asked in the tone of impartial curiosity.

"To see Ralph before he dies."

To this, for some time, he made no rejoinder; he
continued to give his chief attention to his work,
which was of a sort that would brook no negligence.
"I don't see the need of it," he said at last. "He
came to see you here. I did n't like that; I thought
his being in Rome a great mistake. But I tolerated
it because it was to be the last time you should see
him. Now you tell me it's not to have been the
last. Ah, you're not grateful!"

"What am I to be grateful for?"

Gilbert Osmond laid down his little implements,
blew a speck of dust from his drawing, slowly got
up, and for the first time looked at his wife. "For
my not having interfered while he was here."

"Oh yes, I am. I remember perfectly how distinctly you let me know you did n't like it. I was
very glad when he went away."

"Leave him alone then. Don't run after him."

Isabel turned her eyes away from him; they rested
upon his little drawing. "I must go to England,"
she said, with a full consciousness that her tone might
strike an irritable man of taste as stupidly obstinate.

"I shall not like it if you do," Osmond remarked.

"Why should I mind that? You won't like it if
I don't. You like nothing I do or don't do. You
pretend to think I lie."

Osmond turned slightly pale; he gave a cold smile. "That's why you must go then? Not to see your cousin, but to take a revenge on me."

"I know nothing about revenge."

"I do," said Osmond. "Don't give me an occasion."

"You're only too eager to take one. You wish immensely that I would commit some folly."

"I should be gratified in that case if you disobeyed me."

"If I disobeyed you?" said Isabel in a low tone which had the effect of mildness.

"Let it be clear. If you leave Rome to-day it will be a piece of the most deliberate, the most calculated, opposition."

"How can you call it calculated? I received my aunt's telegram but three minutes ago."

"You calculate rapidly; it's a great accomplishment. I don't see why we should prolong our discussion; you know my wish." And he stood there as if he expected to see her withdraw.

But she never moved; she could n't move, strange as it may seem; she still wished to justify herself; he had the power, in an extraordinary degree, of making her feel this need. There was something in her imagination he could always appeal to against her judgement. "You've no reason for such a wish," said Isabel, "and I 've every reason for going. I can't tell you how unjust you seem to me. But I think you know. It's your own opposition that's calculated. It's malignant."

She had never uttered her worst thought to her

husband before, and the sensation of hearing it was evidently new to Osmond. But he showed no surprise, and his coolness was apparently a proof that he had believed his wife would in fact be unable to resist for ever his ingenious endeavour to draw her out. "It's all the more intense then," he answered. And he added almost as if he were giving her a friendly counsel: "This is a very important matter." She recognised that; she was fully conscious of the weight of the occasion; she knew that between them they had arrived at a crisis. Its gravity made her careful; she said nothing, and he went on. "You say I've no reason? I have the very best. I dislike, from the bottom of my soul, what you intend to do. It's dishonourable; it's indelicate; it's indecent. Your cousin is nothing whatever to me, and I'm under no obligation to make concessions to him. I've already made the very handsomest. Your relations with him, while he was here, kept me on pins and needles; but I let that pass, because from week to week I expected him to go. I've never liked him and he has never liked me. That's why you like him — because he hates me," said Osmond with a quick, barely audible tremor in his voice. "I've an ideal of what my wife should do and should not do. She should not travel across Europe alone, in defiance of my deepest desire, to sit at the bedside of other men. Your cousin's nothing to you; he's nothing to us. You smile most expressively when I talk about *us*, but I assure you that *we, we*, Mrs. Osmond, is all I know. I take our marriage seriously; you appear to have found a way of not doing so. I'm not aware that we're divorced or separated; for me we're indissolubly united. You are nearer to me than any human creature, and I'm nearer to you. It may be a disagreeable proximity; it's one, at any rate, of our own deliberate making. You don't like to be reminded of that, I know; but I'm perfectly willing, because — because —" And he paused a moment, looking as if he had something to say which would be very much to the point. "Because I think we should accept the consequences of our actions, and what I value most in life is the honour of a thing!"

He spoke gravely and almost gently; the accent of sarcasm had dropped out of his tone. It had a gravity which checked his wife's quick emotion; the resolution with which she had entered the room found itself caught in a mesh of fine threads. His last words were not a command, they constituted a kind of appeal; and, though she felt that any expression of respect on his part could only be a refinement of egotism, they represented something transcendent and absolute, like the sign of the cross or the flag of one's country. He spoke in the name of something sacred and precious — the observance of a magnificent form. They were as perfectly apart in feeling as two disillusioned lovers had ever been; but they had never yet separated in act. Isabel had not changed; her old passion for justice still abode within her; and now, in the very thick of her sense of her husband's blasphemous sophistry, it began to throb to a tune which for a moment promised him the victory. It came over her that in his wish to preserve appearances he was after all sincere, and that this, as far as it went, was a merit. Ten minutes before she had felt all the joy of irreflective action — a joy to which she had so long been a stranger; but action had been suddenly changed to slow renunciation, transformed by the blight of Osmond's touch. If she must renounce, however, she would let him know she was a victim rather than a dupe. "I know you're a master of the art of mockery," she said. "How can you speak of an indissoluble union — how can you speak of your being contented? Where's our union when you accuse me of falsity? Where's your contentment when you have nothing but hideous suspicion in your heart?"

"It is in our living decently together, in spite of such drawbacks."

"We don't live decently together!" cried Isabel.

"Indeed we don't if you go to England."

"That's very little; that's nothing. I might do much more."

He raised his eyebrows and even his shoulders a little: he had lived long enough in Italy to catch this trick. "Ah, if you've come to threaten me I prefer my drawing." And he walked back to his table, where he took up the sheet of paper on which he had been working and stood studying it.

"I suppose that if I go you'll not expect me to come back," said Isabel.

He turned quickly round, and she could see this movement at least was not designed. He looked at her a little, and then, "Are you out of your mind?" he enquired.

"How can it be anything but a rupture?" she went on; "especially if all you say is true?" She was unable to see how it could be anything but a rupture; she sincerely wished to know what else it might be.

He sat down before his table. "I really can't argue with you on the hypothesis of your defying me," he said. And he took up one of his little brushes again.

She lingered but a moment longer; long enough to embrace with her eye his whole deliberately indifferent yet most expressive figure; after which she quickly left the room. Her faculties, her energy, her passion, were all dispersed again; she felt as if a cold, dark mist had suddenly encompassed her. Osmond possessed in a supreme degree the art of eliciting any weakness. On her way back to her room she found the Countess Gemini standing in the open doorway of a little parlour in which a small collection of heterogeneous books had been arranged. The Countess had an open volume in her hand; she appeared to have been glancing down a page which failed to strike her as interesting. At the sound of Isabel's step she raised her head.

"Ah my dear," she said, "you, who are so literary, do tell me some amusing book to read! Everything here's of a dreariness —! Do you think this would do me any good?"

Isabel glanced at the title of the volume she held out, but without reading or understanding it. "I'm afraid I can't advise you. I've had bad news. My cousin, Ralph Touchett, is dying."

The Countess threw down her book. "Ah, he was so simpatico. I'm awfully sorry for you."

"You would be sorrier still if you knew."

"What is there to know? You look very badly," the Countess added. "You must have been with Osmond."

Half an hour before Isabel would have listened very coldly to an intimation that she should ever feel a desire for the sympathy of her sister-in-law, and there can be no better proof of her present embarrassment than the fact that she almost clutched at this lady's fluttering attention. "I've been with Osmond," she said, while the Countess's bright eyes glittered at her.

"I'm sure then he has been odious!" the Countess cried. "Did he say he was glad poor Mr. Touchett's dying?"

"He said it's impossible I should go to England."

The Countess's mind, when her interests were concerned, was agile; she already foresaw the extinction of any further brightness in her visit to Rome. Ralph Touchett would die, Isabel would go into mourning, and then there would be no more dinner-parties. Such a prospect produced for a moment in her countenance an expressive grimace; but this rapid, picturesque play of feature was her only tribute to disappointment. After all, she reflected, the game was almost played out; she had already overstayed her invitation. And then she cared enough for Isabel's trouble to forget her own, and she saw that Isabel's trouble was deep.

It seemed deeper than the mere death of a cousin, and the Countess had no hesitation in connecting her exasperating brother with the expression of her sister-in-law's eyes. Her heart beat with an almost joyous expectation, for if she had wished to see Osmond overtopped the conditions looked favourable now. Of course if Isabel should go to England she herself would immediately leave Palazzo Roccanera; nothing would induce her to remain there with Osmond. Nevertheless she felt an immense desire to hear that Isabel would go to England. "Nothing's impossible for you, my dear," she said caressingly. "Why else are you rich and clever and good?"

"Why indeed? I feel stupidly weak."

"Why does Osmond say it's impossible?" the Countess asked in a tone which sufficiently declared that she could n't imagine.

From the moment she thus began to question her, however, Isabel drew back; she disengaged her hand, which the Countess had affectionately taken. But she answered this enquiry with frank bitterness. "Because we 're so happy together that we can't separate even for a fortnight."

"Ah," cried the Countess while Isabel turned away, "when I want to make a journey my husband simply tells me I can have no money!"

Isabel went to her room, where she walked up and down for an hour. It may appear to some readers that she gave herself much trouble, and it is certain that for a woman of a high spirit she had allowed herself easily to be arrested. It seemed to her that only now she fully measured the great undertaking of matrimony. Marriage meant that in such a case as this, when one had to choose, one chose as a matter of course for one's husband. "I'm afraid — yes, I'm afraid," she said to herself more than once, stopping short in her walk. But what she was afraid of was not her husband — his displeasure, his hatred, his revenge; it was not even her own later judgement of her conduct — a consideration which had often held her in check; it was simply the violence there would be in going when Osmond wished her to remain. A gulf of difference had opened between them, but nevertheless it was his desire that she should stay, it was a horror to him that she should go. She knew the nervous fineness with which he could feel an objection. What he thought of her she knew, what he was capable of saying to her she had felt; yet they were married, for all that, and marriage meant that a woman should cleave to the man with whom, uttering tremendous vows, she had stood at the altar. She sank down on her sofa at last and buried her head in a pile of cushions.

When she raised her head again the Countess Gemini hovered before her. She had come in all unperceived; she had a strange smile on her thin lips and her whole face had grown in an hour a shining intimation. She lived assuredly, it might be said, at the window of her spirit, but now she was leaning far out. "I knocked," she began, "but you didn't answer me. So I ventured in. I've been looking at you for the last five minutes. You're very unhappy."

"Yes; but I don't think you can comfort me."

"Will you give me leave to try?" And the Countess sat down on the sofa beside her. She continued to smile, and there was something communicative and exultant in her expression. She appeared to have a deal to say, and it occurred to Isabel for the first time that her sister-in-law might say something really human. She made play with her glittering eyes, in which there was an unpleasant fascination. "After all," she soon resumed, "I must tell you, to begin with, that I don't understand your state of mind. You seem to have so many scruples, so many reasons, so many ties. When I discovered, ten years ago, that my husband's dearest wish was to make me miserable — of late he has simply let me alone — ah, it was a wonderful simplification! My poor Isabel, you're not simple enough."

"No, I'm not simple enough," said Isabel.

"There's something I want you to know," the Countess declared — "because I think you ought to know it. Perhaps you do; perhaps you've guessed it. But if you have, all I can say is that I understand still less why you shouldn't do as you like."

"What do you wish me to know?" Isabel felt a foreboding that made her heart beat faster. The Countess was about to justify herself, and this alone was portentous.

But she was nevertheless disposed to play a little with her subject. "In your place I should have guessed it ages ago. Have you never really suspected?"

"I've guessed nothing. What should I have suspected? I don't know what you mean."

"That's because you've such a beastly pure mind. I never saw a woman with such a pure mind!" cried the Countess.

Isabel slowly got up. "You're going to tell me something horrible."

"You can call it by whatever name you will!" And the Countess rose also, while her gathered perversity grew vivid and dreadful. She stood a moment in a sort of glare of intention and, as seemed to Isabel even then, of ugliness; after which she said: "My first sister-in-law had no children."

Isabel stared back at her; the announcement was an anticlimax. "Your first sister-in-law?"

"I suppose you know at least, if one may mention it, that Osmond has been married before! I've never spoken to you of his wife; I thought it might n't be decent or respectful. But others, less particular, must have done so. The poor little woman lived hardly three years and died childless. It was n't till after her death that Pansy arrived."

Isabel's brow had contracted to a frown; her lips were parted in pale, vague wonder. She was trying to follow; there seemed so much more to follow than she could see. "Pansy's not my husband's child then?"

"Your husband's — in perfection! But no one else's husband's. Some one else's wife's. Ah, my good Isabel," cried the Countess, "with you one must dot one's i's!"

"I don't understand. Whose wife's?" Isabel asked.

"The wife of a horrid little Swiss who died — how long? — a dozen, more than fifteen, years ago. He never recognised Miss Pansy, nor, knowing what he was about, would have anything to say to her; and

there was no reason why he should. Osmond did, and
that was better; though he had to fit on afterwards
the whole rigmarole of his own wife's having died in
childbirth, and of his having, in grief and horror, banished the little girl from his sight for as long as possible before taking her home from nurse. His wife had
really died, you know, of quite another matter and in
quite another place: in the Piedmontese mountains,
where they had gone, one August, because her health
appeared to require the air, but where she was suddenly taken worse — fatally ill. The story passed,
sufficiently; it was covered by the appearances so long
as nobody heeded, as nobody cared to look into it. But
of course *I* knew — without researches," the Countess
lucidly proceeded; "as also, you'll understand, without a word said between us — I mean between Osmond and me. Don't you see him looking at me, in
silence, that way, to settle it ? — that is to settle *me* if
I should say anything. I said nothing, right or left —
never a word to a creature, if you can believe that of
me: on my honour, my dear, I speak of the thing
to you now, after all this time, as I've never, never
spoken. It was to be enough for me, from the first,
that the child was my niece — from the moment she
was my brother's daughter. As for her veritable mother —!" But with this Pansy's wonderful aunt
dropped — as, involuntarily, from the impression of
her sister-in-law's face, out of which more eyes might
have seemed to look at her than she had ever had to
meet.

She had spoken no name, yet Isabel could but
check, on her own lips, an echo of the unspoken. She

sank to her seat again, hanging her head. "Why have you told me this?" she asked in a voice the Countess hardly recognised.

"Because I've been so bored with your not knowing. I've been bored, frankly, my dear, with not having told you; as if, stupidly, all this time I could n't have managed! *Ça me dépasse*, if you don't mind my saying so, the things, all round you, that you've appeared to succeed in not knowing. It's a sort of assistance — aid to innocent ignorance — that I've always been a bad hand at rendering; and in this connexion, that of keeping quiet for my brother, my virtue has at any rate finally found itself exhausted. It's not a black lie, moreover, you know," the Countess inimitably added. "The facts are exactly what I tell you."

"I had no idea," said Isabel presently; and looked up at her in a manner that doubtless matched the apparent witlessness of this confession.

"So I believed — though it was hard to believe. Had it never occurred to you that he was for six or seven years her lover?"

"I don't know. Things *have* occurred to me, and perhaps that was what they all meant."

"She has been wonderfully clever, she has been magnificent, about Pansy!" the Countess, before all this view of it, cried.

"Oh, no idea, for me," Isabel went on, "ever *definitely* took that form." She appeared to be making out to herself what had been and what had n't. "And as it is — I don't understand."

She spoke as one troubled and puzzled, yet the poor

Countess seemed to have seen her revelation fall below its possibilities of effect. She had expected to kindle some responsive blaze, but had barely extracted a spark. Isabel showed as scarce more impressed than she might have been, as a young woman of approved imagination, with some fine sinister passage of public history. "Don't you recognise how the child could never pass for *her* husband's? — that is with M. Merle himself," her companion resumed. "They had been separated too long for that, and he had gone to some far country — I think to South America. If she had ever had children — which I'm not sure of — she had lost them. The conditions happened to make it workable, under stress (I mean at so awkward a pinch), that Osmond should acknowledge the little girl. His wife was dead — very true; but she had not been dead too long to put a certain accommodation of dates out of the question — from the moment, I mean, that suspicion was n't started; which was what they had to take care of. What was more natural than that poor Mrs. Osmond, at a distance and for a world not troubling about trifles, should have left behind her, *poverina*, the pledge of her brief happiness that had cost her her life? With the aid of a change of residence — Osmond had been living with her at Naples at the time of their stay in the Alps, and he in due course left it for ever — the whole history was successfully set going. My poor sister-in-law, in her grave, could n't help herself, and the real mother, to save *her* skin, renounced all visible property in the child."

"Ah, poor, poor woman!" cried Isabel, who herewith burst into tears. It was a long time since she had

366

shed any; she had suffered a high reaction from weeping. But now they flowed with an abundance in which the Countess Gemini found only another discomfiture.

"It's very kind of you to pity her!" she discordantly laughed. "Yes indeed, you have a way of your own —!"

"He must have been false to his wife — and so very soon!" said Isabel with a sudden check.

"That's all that's wanting — that you should take up *her* cause!" the Countess went on. "I quite agree with you, however, that it was much too soon."

"But to me, to me —?" And Isabel hesitated as if she had not heard; as if her question — though it was sufficiently there in her eyes — were all for herself.

"To you he has been faithful? Well, it depends, my dear, on what you call faithful. When he married you he was no longer the lover of another woman — *such* a lover as he had been, *cara mia*, between their risks and their precautions, while the thing lasted! That state of affairs had passed away; the lady had repented, or at all events, for reasons of her own, drawn back: she had always had, too, a worship of appearances so intense that even Osmond himself had got bored with it. You may therefore imagine what it was — when he could n't patch it on conveniently to *any* of those he goes in for! But the whole past was between them."

"Yes," Isabel mechanically echoed, "the whole past is between them."

"Ah, this later past is nothing. But for six or seven years, as I say, they had kept it up."

She was silent a little. "Why then did she want him to marry me?"

"Ah my dear, that's her superiority! Because you had money; and because she believed you would be good to Pansy."

"Poor woman — and Pansy who does n't like her!" cried Isabel.

"That's the reason she wanted some one whom Pansy would like. She knows it; she knows everything."

"Will she know that you've told me this?"

"That will depend upon whether you tell her. She's prepared for it, and do you know what she counts upon for her defence? On your believing that I lie. Perhaps you do; don't make yourself uncomfortable to hide it. Only, as it happens this time, I don't. I've told plenty of little idiotic fibs, but they've never hurt any one but myself."

Isabel sat staring at her companion's story as at a bale of fantastic wares some strolling gypsy might have unpacked on the carpet at her feet. "Why did Osmond never marry her?" she finally asked.

"Because she had no money." The Countess had an answer for everything, and if she lied she lied well. "No one knows, no one has ever known, what she lives on, or how she has got all those beautiful things. I don't believe Osmond himself knows. Besides, she would n't have married him."

"How can she have loved him then?"

"She does n't love him in that way. She did at first, and then, I suppose, I suppose, she would have married him; but at that time her husband was living. By the time

M. Merle had rejoined — I won't say his ancestors, because he never had any — her relations with Osmond had changed, and she had grown more ambitious. Besides, she has never had, about him," the Countess went on, leaving Isabel to wince for it so tragically afterwards — "she *had* never had, what you might call any illusions of *intelligence*. She hoped she might marry a great man; that has always been her idea. She has waited and watched and plotted and prayed; but she has never succeeded. I don't call Madame Merle a success, you know. I don't know what she may accomplish yet, but at present she has very little to show. The only tangible result she has ever achieved — except, of course, getting to know every one and staying with them free of expense — has been her bringing you and Osmond together. Oh, she did that, my dear; you need n't look as if you doubted it. I 've watched them for years; I know everything — everything. I 'm thought a great scatterbrain, but I 've had enough application of mind to follow up those two. She hates me, and her way of showing it is to pretend to be for ever defending me. When people say I 've had fifteen lovers she looks horrified and declares that quite half of them were never proved. She has been afraid of me for years, and she has taken great comfort in the vile, false things people have said about me. She has been afraid I 'd expose her, and she threatened me one day when Osmond began to pay his court to you. It was at his house in Florence; do you remember that afternoon when she brought you there and we had tea in the garden ? She let me know then that if I should tell tales two could play at that game. She pretends there's a good deal more to tell about me than about her. It would be an interesting comparison! I don't care a fig what she may say, simply because I know *you* don't care a fig. You can't trouble your head about me less than you do already. So she may take her revenge as she chooses; I don't think she'll frighten you very much. Her great idea has been to be tremendously irreproachable — a kind of full-blown lily — the incarnation of propriety. She has always worshipped that god. There should be no scandal about Cæsar's wife, you know; and, as I say, she has always hoped to marry Cæsar. That was one reason she would n't marry Osmond; the fear that on seeing her with Pansy people would put things together — would even see a resemblance. She has had a terror lest the mother should betray herself. She has been awfully careful; the mother has never done so."

"Yes, yes, the mother has done so," said Isabel, who had listened to all this with a face more and more wan. "She betrayed herself to me the other day, though I did n't recognise her. There appeared to have been a chance of Pansy's making a great marriage, and in her disappointment at its not coming off she almost dropped the mask."

"Ah, that's where she'd dish herself!" cried the Countess. "She has failed so dreadfully that she's determined her daughter shall make it up."

Isabel started at the words "her daughter," which her guest threw off so familiarly. "It seems very wonderful," she murmured; and in this bewildering impression she had almost lost her sense of being personally touched by the story.

"Now don't go and turn against the poor innocent child!" the Countess went on. "She's very nice, in spite of her deplorable origin. I myself have liked Pansy; not, naturally, because she was *hers*, but because she had become yours."

"Yes, she has become mine. And how the poor woman must have suffered at seeing me —!" Isabel exclaimed while she flushed at the thought.

"I don't believe she has suffered; on the contrary, she has enjoyed. Osmond's marriage has given his daughter a great little lift. Before that she lived in a hole. And do you know what the mother thought? That you might take such a fancy to the child that you'd do something for her. Osmond of course could never give her a portion. Osmond was really extremely poor; but of course you know all about that. Ah, my dear," cried the Countess, "why did you ever inherit money?" She stopped a moment as if she saw something singular in Isabel's face. "Don't tell me now that you'll give her a *dot*. You're capable of that, but I would refuse to believe it. Don't try to be too good. Be a little easy and natural and nasty; feel a little wicked, for the comfort of it, once in your life!"

"It's very strange. I suppose I ought to know, but I'm sorry," Isabel said. "I'm much obliged to you."

"Yes, you seem to be!" cried the Countess with a mocking laugh. "Perhaps you are — perhaps you're not. You don't take it as I should have thought."

"How should I take it?" Isabel asked.

"Well, I should say as a woman who has been made use of." Isabel made no answer to this; she only listened, and the Countess went on. "They've always been bound to each other; they remained so even after she broke off — or *he* did. But he has always been more for her than she has been for him. When their little carnival was over they made a bargain that each should give the other complete liberty, but that each should also do everything possible to help the other on. You may ask me how I know such a thing as that. I know it by the way they've behaved. Now see how much better women are than men! She has found a wife for Osmond, but Osmond has never lifted a little finger for *her*. She has worked for him, plotted for him, suffered for him; she has even more than once found money for him; and the end of it is that he's tired of her. She's an old habit; there are moments when he needs her, but on the whole he would n't miss her if she were removed. And, what's more, to-day she knows it. So you need n't be jealous!" the Countess added humorously.

Isabel rose from her sofa again; she felt bruised and scant of breath; her head was humming with new knowledge. "I'm much obliged to you," she repeated. And then she added abruptly, in quite a different tone: "How do you know all this?"

This enquiry appeared to ruffle the Countess more than Isabel's expression of gratitude pleased her. She gave her companion a bold stare, with which, "Let us assume that I've invented it!" she cried. She too, however, suddenly changed her tone and, laying her hand on Isabel's arm, said with the penetration of her sharp bright smile: "Now will you give up your journey?"

Isabel started a little; she turned away. But she felt weak and in a moment had to lay her arm upon the mantel-shelf for support. She stood a minute so, and then upon her arm she dropped her dizzy head, with closed eyes and pale lips.

"I've done wrong to speak — I've made you ill!" the Countess cried.

"Ah, I must see Ralph!" Isabel wailed; not in resentment, not in the quick passion her companion had looked for; but in a tone of far-reaching, infinite sadness.

LII

THERE was a train for Turin and Paris that evening;
and after the Countess had left her Isabel had a rapid
and decisive conference with her maid, who was discreet, devoted and active. After this she thought (except of her journey) only of one thing. She must go
and see Pansy; from her she could n't turn away. She
had not seen her yet, as Osmond had given her to understand that it was too soon to begin. She drove at
five o'clock to a high door in a narrow street in the
quarter of the Piazza Navona, and was admitted by
the portress of the convent, a genial and obsequious
person. Isabel had been at this institution before; she
had come with Pansy to see the sisters. She knew they
were good women, and she saw that the large rooms
were clean and cheerful and that the well-used garden
had sun for winter and shade for spring. But she
disliked the place, which affronted and almost frightened her; not for the world would she have spent a
night there. It produced to-day more than before the
impression of a well-appointed prison; for it was not
possible to pretend Pansy was free to leave it. This
innocent creature had been presented to her in a new
and violent light, but the secondary effect of the revelation was to make her reach out a hand.

The portress left her to wait in the parlour of the
convent while she went to make it known that there
was a visitor for the dear young lady. The parlour

was a vast, cold apartment, with new-looking furniture; a large clean stove of white porcelain, unlighted, a collection of wax flowers under glass, and a series of engravings from religious pictures on the walls. On the other occasion Isabel had thought it less like Rome than like Philadelphia, but to-day she made no reflexions; the apartment only seemed to her very empty and very soundless. The portress returned at the end of some five minutes, ushering in another person. Isabel got up, expecting to see one of the ladies of the sisterhood, but to her extreme surprise found herself confronted with Madame Merle. The effect was strange, for Madame Merle was already so present to her vision that her appearance in the flesh was like suddenly, and rather awfully, seeing a painted picture move. Isabel had been thinking all day of her falsity, her audacity, her ability, her probable suffering; and these dark things seemed to flash with a sudden light as she entered the room. Her being there at all had the character of ugly evidence, of handwritings, of profaned relics, of grim things produced in court. It made Isabel feel faint; if it had been necessary to speak on the spot she would have been quite unable. But no such necessity was distinct to her; it seemed to her indeed that she had absolutely nothing to say to Madame Merle. In one's relations with this lady, however, there were never any absolute necessities; she had a manner which carried off not only her own deficiencies but those of other people. But she was different from usual; she came in slowly, behind the portress, and Isabel instantly perceived that she was not likely to depend upon her habitual resources. For her too

375

the occasion was exceptional, and she had undertaken to treat it by the light of the moment. This gave her a peculiar gravity; she pretended not even to smile, and though Isabel saw that she was more than ever playing a part it seemed to her that on the whole the wonderful woman had never been so natural. She looked at her young friend from head to foot, but not harshly nor defiantly; with a cold gentleness rather, and an absence of any air of allusion to their last meeting. It was as if she had wished to mark a distinction. She had been irritated then, she was reconciled now.

"You can leave us alone," she said to the portress; "in five minutes this lady will ring for you." And then she turned to Isabel, who, after noting what has just been mentioned, had ceased to notice and had let her eyes wander as far as the limits of the room would allow. She wished never to look at Madame Merle again. "You're surprised to find me here, and I'm afraid you're not pleased," this lady went on. "You don't see why I should have come; it's as if I had anticipated you. I confess I've been rather indiscreet — I ought to have asked your permission." There was none of the oblique movement of irony in this; it was said simply and mildly; but Isabel, far afloat on a sea of wonder and pain, could not have told herself with what intention it was uttered. "But I've not been sitting long," Madame Merle continued; "that is I've not been long with Pansy. I came to see her because it occurred to me this afternoon that she must be rather lonely and perhaps even a little miserable. It may be good for a small girl; I know so little about small girls; I can't tell. At any rate it's a little dismal.

Therefore I came — on the chance. I knew of course that you'd come, and her father as well; still, I had not been told other visitors were forbidden. The good woman — what's her name? Madame Catherine — made no objection whatever. I stayed twenty minutes with Pansy; she has a charming little room, not in the least conventual, with a piano and flowers. She has arranged it delightfully; she has so much taste. Of course it's all none of my business, but I feel happier since I've seen her. She may even have a maid if she likes; but of course she has no occasion to dress. She wears a little black frock; she looks so charming. I went afterwards to see Mother Catherine, who has a very good room too; I assure you I don't find the poor sisters at all monastic. Mother Catherine has a most coquettish little toilet-table, with something that looked uncommonly like a bottle of eau-de-Cologne. She speaks delightfully of Pansy; says it's a great happiness for them to have her. She's a little saint of heaven and a model to the oldest of them. Just as I was leaving Madame Catherine the portress came to say to her that there was a lady for the signorina. Of course I knew it must be you, and I asked her to let me go and receive you in her place. She demurred greatly — I must tell you that — and said it was her duty to notify the Mother Superior; it was of such high importance that you should be treated with respect. I requested her to let the Mother Superior alone and asked her how she supposed I would treat you!"

So Madame Merle went on, with much of the brilliancy of a woman who had long been a mistress of the art of conversation. But there were phases and gradations in her speech, not one of which was lost upon Isabel's ear, though her eyes were absent from her companion's face. She had not proceeded far before Isabel noted a sudden break in her voice, a lapse in her continuity, which was in itself a complete drama. This subtle modulation marked a momentous discovery — the perception of an entirely new attitude on the part of her listener. Madame Merle had guessed in the space of an instant that everything was at end between them, and in the space of another instant she had guessed the reason why. The person who stood there was not the same one she had seen hitherto, but was a very different person — a person who knew her secret. This discovery was tremendous, and from the moment she made it the most accomplished of women faltered and lost her courage. But only for that moment. Then the conscious stream of her perfect manner gathered itself again and flowed on as smoothly as might be to the end. But it was only because she had the end in view that she was able to proceed. She had been touched with a point that made her quiver, and she needed all the alertness of her will to repress her agitation. Her only safety was in her not betraying herself. She resisted this, but the startled quality of her voice refused to improve — she could n't help it — while she heard herself say she hardly knew what. The tide of her confidence ebbed, and she was able only just to glide into port, faintly grazing the bottom.

Isabel saw it all as distinctly as if it had been reflected in a large clear glass. It might have been a great moment for her, for it might have been a mo-

ment of triumph. That Madame Merle had lost her
pluck and saw before her the phantom of exposure —
this in itself was a revenge, this in itself was almost
the promise of a brighter day. And for a moment during which she stood apparently looking out of the window, with her back half-turned, Isabel enjoyed that
knowledge. On the other side of the window lay the
garden of the convent; but this is not what she saw;
she saw nothing of the budding plants and the glow-
ing afternoon. She saw, in the crude light of that revelation which had already become a part of experience
and to which the very frailty of the vessel in which it
had been offered her only gave an intrinsic price, the
dry staring fact that she had been an applied handled
hung-up tool, as senseless and convenient as mere
shaped wood and iron. All the bitterness of this knowledge surged into her soul again; it was as if she felt
on her lips the taste of dishonour. There was a moment during which, if she had turned and spoken, she
would have said something that would hiss like a lash.
But she closed her eyes, and then the hideous vision
dropped. What remained was the cleverest woman
in the world standing there within a few feet of her
and knowing as little what to think as the meanest.
Isabel's only revenge was to be silent still — to leave
Madame Merle in this unprecedented situation. She
left her there for a period that must have seemed long
to this lady, who at last seated herself with a movement which was in itself a confession of helplessness.
Then Isabel turned slow eyes, looking down at her.
Madame Merle was very pale; her own eyes covered
Isabel's face. She might see what she would, but her

danger was over. Isabel would never accuse her, never reproach her; perhaps because she never would give her the opportunity to defend herself.

"I'm come to bid Pansy good-bye," our young woman said at last. "I go to England to-night."

"Go to England to-night!" Madame Merle repeated sitting there and looking up at her.

"I'm going to Gardencourt. Ralph Touchett's dying."

"Ah, you'll feel that." Madame Merle recovered herself; she had a chance to express sympathy. "Do you go alone?"

"Yes; without my husband."

Madame Merle gave a low vague murmur; a sort of recognition of the general sadness of things. "Mr. Touchett never liked me, but I'm sorry he's dying. Shall you see his mother?"

"Yes; she has returned from America."

"She used to be very kind to me; but she has changed. Others too have changed," said Madame Merle with a quiet noble pathos. She paused a moment, then added: "And you'll see dear old Gardencourt again!"

"I shall not enjoy it much," Isabel answered.

"Naturally — in your grief. But it's on the whole, of all the houses I know, and I know many, the one I should have liked best to live in. I don't venture to send a message to the people," Madame Merle added; "but I should like to give my love to the place."

Isabel turned away. "I had better go to Pansy. I've not much time."

While she looked about her for the proper egress,

the door opened and admitted one of the ladies of the house, who advanced with a discreet smile, gently rubbing, under her long loose sleeves, a pair of plump white hands. Isabel recognised Madame Catherine, whose acquaintance she had already made, and begged that she would immediately let her see Miss Osmond. Madame Catherine looked doubly discreet, but smiled very blandly and said: "It will be good for her to see you. I'll take you to her myself." Then she directed her pleased guarded vision to Madame Merle.

"Will you let me remain a little?" this lady asked. "It's so good to be here."

"You may remain always if you like!" And the good sister gave a knowing laugh.

She led Isabel out of the room, through several corridors, and up a long staircase. All these departments were solid and bare, light and clean; so, thought Isabel, are the great penal establishments. Madame Catherine gently pushed open the door of Pansy's room and ushered in the visitor; then stood smiling with folded hands while the two others met and embraced.

"She's glad to see you," she repeated; "it will do her good." And she placed the best chair carefully for Isabel. But she made no movement to seat herself; she seemed ready to retire. "How does this dear child look?" she asked of Isabel, lingering a moment.

"She looks pale," Isabel answered.

"That's the pleasure of seeing you. She's very happy. *Elle éclaire la maison*," said the good sister.

Pansy wore, as Madame Merle had said, a little black dress; it was perhaps this that made her look pale. "They're very good to me — they think of everything!" she exclaimed with all her customary eagerness to accommodate.

"We think of you always — you're a precious charge," Madame Catherine remarked in the tone of a woman with whom benevolence was a habit and whose conception of duty was the acceptance of every care. It fell with a leaden weight on Isabel's ears; it seemed to represent the surrender of a personality, the authority of the Church.

When Madame Catherine had left them together Pansy kneeled down and hid her head in her step-mother's lap. So she remained some moments, while Isabel gently stroked her hair. Then she got up, averting her face and looking about the room. "Don't you think I've arranged it well? I've everything I have at home."

"It's very pretty; you're very comfortable." Isabel scarcely knew what she could say to her. On the one hand she could n't let her think she had come to pity her, and on the other it would be a dull mockery to pretend to rejoice with her. So she simply added after a moment: "I've come to bid you good-bye. I'm going to England."

Pansy's white little face turned red. "To England! Not to come back?"

"I don't know when I shall come back."

"Ah, I'm sorry," Pansy breathed with faintness. She spoke as if she had no right to criticise; but her tone expressed a depth of disappointment.

"My cousin, Mr. Touchett, is very ill; he'll probably die. I wish to see him," Isabel said.

"Ah yes; you told me he would die. Of course you must go. And will papa go?"

"No; I shall go alone."

For a moment the girl said nothing. Isabel had often wondered what she thought of the apparent relations of her father with his wife; but never by a glance, by an intimation, had she let it be seen that she deemed them deficient in an air of intimacy. She made her reflexions, Isabel was sure; and she must have had a conviction that there were husbands and wives who were more intimate than that. But Pansy was not indiscreet even in thought; she would as little have ventured to judge her gentle stepmother as to criticise her magnificent father. Her heart may have stood almost as still as it would have done had she seen two of the saints in the great picture in the convent-chapel turn their painted heads and shake them at each other. But as in this latter case she would (for very solemnity's sake) never have mentioned the awful phenomenon, so she put away all knowledge of the secrets of larger lives than her own. "You'll be very far away," she presently went on.

"Yes; I shall be far away. But it will scarcely matter," Isabel explained; "since so long as you're here I can't be called near you."

"Yes, but you can come and see me; though you've not come very often."

"I've not come because your father forbade it. To-day I bring nothing with me. I can't amuse you."

"I'm not to be amused. That's not what papa wishes."

"Then it hardly matters whether I'm in Rome or in England."

"You're not happy, Mrs. Osmond," said Pansy.

"Not very. But it does n't matter."

"That's what I say to myself. What does it matter? But I should like to come out."

"I wish indeed you might."

"Don't leave me here," Pansy went on gently.

Isabel said nothing for a minute; her heart beat fast. "Will you come away with me now?" she asked.

Pansy looked at her pleadingly. "Did papa tell you to bring me?"

"No; it's my own proposal."

"I think I had better wait then. Did papa send me no message?"

"I don't think he knew I was coming."

"He thinks I've not had enough," said Pansy. "But I have. The ladies are very kind to me and the little girls come to see me. There are some very little ones — such charming children. Then my room — you can see for yourself. All that's very delightful. But I've had enough. Papa wished me to think a little — and I've thought a great deal."

"What have you thought?"

"Well, that I must never displease papa."

"You knew that before."

"Yes; but I know it better. I'll do anything — I'll do anything," said Pansy. Then, as she heard her own words, a deep, pure blush came into her face.

Isabel read the meaning of it; she saw the poor girl had been vanquished. It was well that Mr. Edward Rosier had kept his enamels! Isabel looked into her eyes and saw there mainly a prayer to be treated easily. She laid her hand on Pansy's as if to let her know that her look conveyed no diminution of esteem; for the collapse of the girl's momentary resistance (mute and modest thought it had been) seemed only her tribute to the truth of things. She did n't presume to judge others, but she had judged herself; she had seen the reality. She had no vocation for struggling with combinations; in the solemnity of sequestration there was something that overwhelmed her. She bowed her pretty head to authority and only asked of authority to be merciful. Yes; it was very well that Edward Rosier had reserved a few articles!

Isabel got up; her time was rapidly shortening. "Good-bye then. I leave Rome to-night."

Pansy took hold of her dress; there was a sudden change in the child's face. "You look strange; you frighten me."

"Oh, I'm very harmless," said Isabel.

"Perhaps you won't come back?"

"Perhaps not. I can't tell."

"Ah, Mrs. Osmond, you won't leave me!"

Isabel now saw she had guessed everything. "My dear child, what can I do for you?" she asked.

"I don't know — but I'm happier when I think of you."

"You can always think of me."

"Not when you're so far. I'm a little afraid," said Pansy.

"What are you afraid of?"

"Of papa — a little. And of Madame Merle. She has just been to see me."

"You must not say that," Isabel observed.

"Oh, I'll do everything they want. Only if you're here I shall do it more easily."

Isabel considered. "I won't desert you," she said at last. "Good-bye, my child."

Then they held each other a moment in a silent embrace, like two sisters; and afterwards Pansy walked along the corridor with her visitor to the top of the staircase. "Madame Merle has been here," she remarked as they went; and as Isabel answered nothing she added abruptly: "I don't like Madame Merle!"

Isabel hesitated, then stopped. "You must never say that — that you don't like Madame Merle."

Pansy looked at her in wonder; but wonder with Pansy had never been a reason for non-compliance. "I never will again," she said with exquisite gentleness. At the top of the staircase they had to separate, as it appeared to be part of the mild but very definite discipline under which Pansy lived that she should not go down. Isabel descended, and when she reached the bottom the girl was standing above. "You'll come back?" she called out in a voice that Isabel remembered afterwards.

"Yes — I'll come back."

Madame Catherine met Mrs. Osmond below and conducted her to the door of the parlour, outside of which the two stood talking a minute. "I won't go in," said the good sister. "Madame Merle's waiting for you."

At this announcement Isabel stiffened; she was on the point of asking if there were no other egress from the convent. But a moment's reflexion assured her that she would do well not to betray to the worthy nun her desire to avoid Pansy's other friend. Her companion grasped her arm very gently and, fixing her a moment with wise, benevolent eyes, said in French and almost familiarly: "*Eh bien, chère Madame, qu'en pensez-vous?*"

"About my step-daughter? Oh, it would take long to tell you."

"We think it's enough," Madame Catherine distinctly observed. And she pushed open the door of the parlour.

Madame Merle was sitting just as Isabel had left her, like a woman so absorbed in thought that she had not moved a little finger. As Madame Catherine closed the door she got up, and Isabel saw that she had been thinking to some purpose. She had recovered her balance; she was in full possession of her resources. "I found I wished to wait for you," she said urbanely. "But it's not to talk about Pansy."

Isabel wondered what it could be to talk about, and in spite of Madame Merle's declaration she answered after a moment: "Madame Catherine says it's enough."

"Yes; it also seems to me enough. I wanted to ask you another word about poor Mr. Touchett," Madame Merle added. "Have you reason to believe that he's really at his last?"

"I've no information but a telegram. Unfortunately it only confirms a probability."

"I'm going to ask you a strange question," said Madame Merle. "Are you very fond of your cousin?" And she gave a smile as strange as her utterance.

"Yes, I'm very fond of him. But I don't understand you."

She just hung fire. "It's rather hard to explain. Something has occurred to me which may not have occurred to you, and I give you the benefit of my idea. Your cousin did you once a great service. Have you never guessed it?"

"He has done me many services."

"Yes; but one was much above the rest. He made you a rich woman."

"*He* made me —?"

Madame Merle appearing to see herself successful, she went on more triumphantly: "He imparted to you that extra lustre which was required to make you a brilliant match. At bottom it's him you've to thank." She stopped; there was something in Isabel's eyes.

"I don't understand you. It was my uncle's money."

"Yes; it was your uncle's money, but it was your cousin's idea. He brought his father over to it. Ah, my dear, the sum was large!"

Isabel stood staring; she seemed to-day to live in a world illumined by lurid flashes. "I don't know why you say such things. I don't know what you know."

"I know nothing but what I've guessed. But I've guessed that."

Isabel went to the door and, when she had opened it, stood a moment with her hand on the latch. Then she said — it was her only revenge: "I believed it was you I had to thank!"

Madame Merle dropped her eyes; she stood there in a kind of proud penance. "You're very unhappy, I know. But I'm more so."

"Yes; I can believe that. I think I should like never to see you again."

Madame Merle raised her eyes. "I shall go to 'America," she quietly remarked while Isabel passed out.

LIII

IT was not with surprise, it was with a feeling which in other circumstances would have had much of the effect of joy, that as Isabel descended from the Paris Mail at Charing Cross she stepped into the arms, as it were — or at any rate into the hands — of Henrietta Stackpole. She had telegraphed to her friend from Turin, and though she had not definitely said to herself that Henrietta would meet her, she had felt her telegram would produce some helpful result. On her long journey from Rome her mind had been given up to vagueness; she was unable to question the future. She performed this journey with sightless eyes and took little pleasure in the countries she traversed, decked out though they were in the richest freshness of spring. Her thoughts followed their course through other countries — strange-looking, dimly-lighted, pathless lands, in which there was no change of seasons, but only, as it seemed, a perpetual dreariness of winter. She had plenty to think about; but it was neither reflexion nor conscious purpose that filled her mind. Disconnected visions passed through it, and sudden dull gleams of memory, of expectation. The past and the future came and went at their will, but she saw them only in fitful images, which rose and fell by a logic of their own. It was extraordinary the things she remembered. Now that she was in the secret, now that she knew something that so much concerned her and the eclipse of which had made life resemble an attempt to play whist with an imperfect pack of cards, the truth of things, their mutual relations, their meaning, and for the most part their horror, rose before her with a kind of architectural vastness. She remembered a thousand trifles; they started to life with the spontaneity of a shiver. She had thought them trifles at the time; now she saw that they had been weighted with lead. Yet even now they were trifles after all, for of what use was it to her to understand them? Nothing seemed of use to her to-day. All purpose, all intention, was suspended; all desire too save the single desire to reach her much-embracing refuge. Gardencourt had been her starting-point, and to those muffled chambers it was at least a temporary solution to return. She had gone forth in her strength; she would come back in her weakness, and if the place had been a rest to her before, it would be a sanctuary now. She envied Ralph his dying, for if one were thinking of rest that was the most perfect of all. To cease utterly, to give it all up and not know anything more — this idea was as sweet as the vision of a cool bath in a marble tank, in a darkened chamber, in a hot land.

She had moments indeed in her journey from Rome which were almost as good as being dead. She sat in her corner, so motionless, so passive, simply with the sense of being carried, so detached from hope and regret, that she recalled to herself one of those Etruscan figures couched upon the receptacle of their ashes. There was nothing to regret now — that was all over. Not only the time of her folly, but the time of her

repentance was far. The only thing to regret was that
Madame Merle had been so — well, so unimaginable.
Just here her intelligence dropped, from literal in-
ability to say what it was that Madame Merle had
been. Whatever it was it was for Madame Merle
herself to regret it; and doubtless she would do so in
America, where she had announced she was going. It
concerned Isabel no more; she only had an impression
that she should never again see Madame Merle. This
impression carried her into the future, of which from
time to time she had a mutilated glimpse. She saw
herself, in the distant years, still in the attitude of a
woman who had her life to live, and these intimations
contradicted the spirit of the present hour. It might
be desirable to get quite away, really away, further
away than little grey-green England, but this privilege was evidently to be denied her. Deep in her soul
— deeper than any appetite for renunciation — was
the sense that life would be her business for a long
time to come. And at moments there was something
inspiring, almost enlivening, in the conviction. It was
a proof of strength — it was a proof she should some
day be happy again. It could n't be she was to live
only to suffer; she was still young, after all, and a great
many things might happen to her yet. To live only to
suffer — only to feel the injury of life repeated and
enlarged — it seemed to her she was too valuable, too
capable, for that. Then she wondered if it were vain
and stupid to think so well of herself. When had it
even been a guarantee to be valuable? Was n't all history full of the destruction of precious things? Was n't
it much more probable that if one were fine one would

suffer? It involved then perhaps an admission that one had a certain grossness; but Isabel recognised, as it passed before her eyes, the quick vague shadow of a long future. She should never escape; she should last to the end. Then the middle years wrapped her about again and the grey curtain of her indifference closed her in.

Henrietta kissed her, as Henrietta usually kissed, as if she were afraid she should be caught doing it; and then Isabel stood there in the crowd, looking about her, looking for her servant. She asked nothing; she wished to wait. She had a sudden perception that she should be helped. She rejoiced Henrietta had come; there was something terrible in an arrival in London. The dusky, smoky, far-arching vault of the station, the strange, livid light, the dense, dark, pushing crowd, filled her with a nervous fear and made her put her arm into her friend's. She remembered she had once liked these things; they seemed part of a mighty spectacle in which there was something that touched her. She remembered how she walked away from Euston, in the winter dusk, in the crowded streets, five years before. She could not have done that to-day, and the incident came before her as the deed of another person.

"It's too beautiful that you should have come," said Henrietta, looking at her as if she thought Isabel might be prepared to challenge the proposition. "If you had n't — if you had n't; well, I don't know," remarked Miss Stackpole, hinting ominously at her powers of disapproval.

Isabel looked about without seeing her maid. Her

eyes rested on another figure, however, which she felt she had seen before; and in a moment she recognised the genial countenance of Mr. Bantling. He stood a little apart, and it was not in the power of the multitude that pressed about him to make him yield an inch of the ground he had taken — that of abstracting himself discreetly while the two ladies performed their embraces.

"There's Mr. Bantling," said Isabel, gently, irrelevantly, scarcely caring much now whether she should find her maid or not.

"Oh yes, he goes everywhere with me. Come here, Mr. Bantling!" Henrietta exclaimed. Whereupon the gallant bachelor advanced with a smile — a smile tempered, however, by the gravity of the occasion. "Is n't it lovely she has come?" Henrietta asked. "He knows all about it," she added; "we had quite a discussion. He said you would n't, I said you would."

"I thought you always agreed," Isabel smiled in return. She felt she could smile now; she had seen in an instant, in Mr. Bantling's brave eyes, that he had good news for her. They seemed to say he wished her to remember he was an old friend of her cousin — that he understood, that it was all right. Isabel gave him her hand; she thought of him, extravagantly, as a beautiful blameless knight.

"Oh, I always agree," said Mr. Bantling. "But she does n't, you know."

"Did n't I tell you that a maid was a nuisance?" Henrietta enquired. "Your young lady has probably remained at Calais."

"I don't care," said Isabel, looking at Mr. Bantling, whom she had never found so interesting.

"Stay with her while I go and see," Henrietta commanded, leaving the two for a moment together.

They stood there at first in silence, and then Mr. Bantling asked Isabel how it had been on the Channel.

"Very fine. No, I believe it was very rough," she said, to her companion's obvious surprise. After which she added: "You've been to Gardencourt, I know."

"Now how do you know that?"

"I can't tell you — except that you look like a person who has been to Gardencourt."

"Do you think I look awfully sad? It's awfully sad there, you know."

"I don't believe you ever look awfully sad. You look awfully kind," said Isabel with a breadth that cost her no effort. It seemed to her she should never again feel a superficial embarrassment.

Poor Mr. Bantling, however, was still in this inferior stage. He blushed a good deal and laughed, he assured her that he was often very blue, and that when he was blue he was awfully fierce. "You can ask Miss Stackpole, you know. I was at Gardencourt two days ago."

"Did you see my cousin?"

"Only for a little. But he had been seeing people; Warburton had been there the day before. Ralph was just the same as usual, except that he was in bed and that he looks tremendously ill and that he can't speak," Mr. Bantling pursued. "He was awfully jolly and funny all the same. He was just as clever as ever. It's awfully wretched."

Even in the crowded, noisy station this simple picture was vivid. "Was that late in the day?"

"Yes; I went on purpose. We thought you'd like to know."

"I'm greatly obliged to you. Can I go down to-night?"

"Ah, I don't think *she'll* let you go," said Mr. Bantling. "She wants you to stop with her. I made Touchett's man promise to telegraph me to-day, and I found the telegram an hour ago at my club. 'Quiet and easy,' that's what it says, and it's dated two o'clock. So you see you can wait till to-morrow. You must be awfully tired."

"Yes, I'm awfully tired. And I thank you again."

"Oh," said Mr. Bantling, "we were certain you would like the last news." On which Isabel vaguely noted that he and Henrietta seemed after all to agree. Miss Stackpole came back with Isabel's maid, whom she had caught in the act of proving her utility. This excellent person, instead of losing herself in the crowd, had simply attended to her mistress's luggage, so that the latter was now at liberty to leave the station. "You know you're not to think of going to the country to-night," Henrietta remarked to her. "It does n't matter whether there's a train or not. You're to come straight to me in Wimpole Street. There is n't a corner to be had in London, but I 've got you one all the same. It is n't a Roman palace, but it will do for a night."

"I 'll do whatever you wish," Isabel said.

"You'll come and answer a few questions; that's what I wish."

"She does n't say anything about dinner, does she, Mrs. Osmond?" Mr. Bantling enquired jocosely.

Henrietta fixed him a moment with her speculative gaze. "I see you 're in a great hurry to get your own. You'll be at the Paddington Station to-morrow morning at ten."

"Don't come for my sake, Mr. Bantling," said Isabel.

"He'll come for mine," Henrietta declared as she ushered her friend into a cab. And later, in a large dusky parlour in Wimpole Street — to do her justice there had been dinner enough — she asked those questions to which she had alluded at the station. "Did your husband make you a scene about your coming?" That was Miss Stackpole's first enquiry.

"No; I can't say he made a scene."

"He did n't object then?"

"Yes, he objected very much. But it was not what you'd call a scene."

"What was it then?"

"It was a very quiet conversation."

Henrietta for a moment regarded her guest. "It must have been hellish," she then remarked. And Isabel did n't deny that it had been hellish. But she confined herself to answering Henrietta's questions, which was easy, as they were tolerably definite. For the present she offered her no new information. "Well," said Miss Stackpole at last, "I 've only one criticism to make. I don't see why you promised little Miss Osmond to go back."

"I'm not sure I myself see now," Isabel replied. "But I did then."

"If you've forgotten your reason perhaps you won't return."

Isabel waited a moment. "Perhaps I shall find another."

"You'll certainly never find a good one."

"In default of a better my having promised will do," Isabel suggested.

"Yes; that's why I hate it."

"Don't speak of it now. I've a little time. Coming away was a complication, but what will going back be?"

"You must remember, after all, that he won't make you a scene!" said Henrietta with much intention.

"He will, though," Isabel answered gravely. "It won't be the scene of a moment; it will be a scene of the rest of my life."

For some minutes the two women sat and considered this remainder, and then Miss Stackpole, to change the subject, as Isabel had requested, announced abruptly: "I've been to stay with Lady Pensil!"

"Ah, the invitation came at last!"

"Yes; it took five years. But this time she wanted to see me."

"Naturally enough."

"It was more natural than I think you know," said Henrietta, who fixed her eyes on a distant point. And then she added, turning suddenly: "Isabel Archer, I beg your pardon. You don't know why?

Because I criticised you, and yet I 've gone further than you. Mr. Osmond, at least, was born on the other side!"

It was a moment before Isabel grasped her meaning; this sense was so modestly, or at least so ingeniously, veiled. Isabel's mind was not possessed at present with the comicality of things; but she greeted with a quick laugh the image that her companion had raised. She immediately recovered herself, however, and with the right excess of intensity, "Henrietta Stackpole," she asked, "are you going to give up your country?"

"Yes, my poor Isabel, I am. I won't pretend to deny it; I look the fact in the face. I 'm going to marry Mr. Bantling and locate right here in London."

"It seems very strange," said Isabel, smiling now.

"Well yes, I suppose it does. I 've come to it little by little. I think I know what I 'm doing; but I don't know as I can explain."

"One can't explain one's marriage," Isabel answered. "And yours does n't need to be explained. Mr. Bantling is n't a riddle."

"No, he is n't a bad pun — or even a high flight of American humour. He has a beautiful nature," Henrietta went on. "I 've studied him for many years and I see right through him. He 's as clear as the style of a good prospectus. He 's not intellectual, but he appreciates intellect. On the other hand he does n't exaggerate its claims. I sometimes think we do in the United States."

"Ah," said Isabel, "you 're changed indeed! It 's

the first time I 've ever heard you say anything against your native land."

"I only say that we 're too infatuated with mere brain-power ; that, after all, is n't a vulgar fault. But I *am* changed ; a woman has to change a good deal to marry."

"I hope you 'll be very happy. You will at last — over here — see something of the inner life."

Henrietta gave a little significant sigh. "That 's the key to the mystery, I believe. I could n't endure to be kept off. Now I 've as good a right as any one!" she added with artless elation.

Isabel was duly diverted, but there was a certain melancholy in her view. Henrietta, after all, had confessed herself human and feminine, Henrietta whom she had hitherto regarded as a light keen flame, a disembodied voice. It was a disappointment to find she had personal susceptibilities, that she was subject to common passions, and that her intimacy with Mr. Bantling had not been completely original. There was a want of originality in her marrying him — there was even a kind of stupidity; and for a moment, to Isabel's sense, the dreariness of the world took on a deeper tinge. A little later indeed she reflected that Mr. Bantling himself at least was original. But she did n't see how Henrietta could give up her country. She herself had relaxed her hold of it, but it had never been her country as it had been Henrietta's. She presently asked her if she had enjoyed her visit to Lady Pensil.

"Oh yes," said Henrietta, "she did n't know what to make of me."

"And was that very enjoyable?"

"Very much so, because she's supposed to be a master mind. She thinks she knows everything; but she does n't understand a woman of my modern type. It would be so much easier for her if I were only a little better or a little worse. She's so puzzled; I believe she thinks it's my duty to go and do something immoral. She thinks it's immoral that I should marry her brother; but, after all, that is n't immoral enough. And she'll never understand my mixture — never!"

"She's not so intelligent as her brother then," said Isabel. "He appears to have understood."

"Oh no, he has n't!" cried Miss Stackpole with decision. "I really believe that's what he wants to marry me for — just to find out the mystery and the proportions of it. That's a fixed idea — a kind of fascination."

"It's very good in you to humour it."

"Oh well," said Henrietta, "I've something to find out too!" And Isabel saw that she had not renounced an allegiance, but planned an attack. She was at last about to grapple in earnest with England.

Isabel also perceived, however, on the morrow, at the Paddington Station, where she found herself, at ten o'clock, in the company both of Miss Stackpole and Mr. Bantling, that the gentleman bore his perplexities lightly. If he had not found out everything he had found out at least the great point — that Miss Stackpole would not be wanting in initiative. It was evident that in the selection of a wife he had been on his guard against this deficiency.

"Henrietta has told me, and I'm very glad," Isabel said as she gave him her hand.

"I dare say you think it awfully odd," Mr. Bantling replied, resting on his neat umbrella.

"Yes, I think it awfully odd."

"You can't think it so awfully odd as I do. But I've always rather liked striking out a line," said Mr. Bantling serenely.

LIV

Isabel's arrival at Gardencourt on this second occasion was even quieter than it had been on the first. Ralph Touchett kept but a small household, and to the new servants Mrs. Osmond was a stranger ; so that instead of being conducted to her own apartment she was coldly shown into the drawing-room and left to wait while her name was carried up to her aunt. She waited a long time ; Mrs. Touchett appeared in no hurry to come to her. She grew impatient at last ; she grew nervous and scared — as scared as if the objects about her had begun to show for conscious things, watching her trouble with grotesque grimaces. The day was dark and cold ; the dusk was thick in the corners of the wide brown rooms. The house was perfectly still — with a stillness that Isabel remembered ; it had filled all the place for days before the death of her uncle. She left the drawing-room and wandered about — strolled into the library and along the gallery of pictures, where, in the deep silence, her footstep made an echo. Nothing was changed ; she recognised everything she had seen years before ; it might have been only yesterday she had stood there. She envied the security of valuable "pieces" which change by no hair's breadth, only grow in value, while their owners lose inch by inch youth, happiness, beauty ; and she became aware that she was walking about as her aunt had done on the day she had come to see her in

Albany. She was changed enough since then — that had been the beginning. It suddenly struck her that if her Aunt Lydia had not come that day in just that way and found her alone, everything might have been different. She might have had another life and she might have been a woman more blest. She stopped in the gallery in front of a small picture — a charming and precious Bonington — upon which her eyes rested a long time. But she was not looking at the picture ; she was wondering whether if her aunt had not come that day in Albany she would have married Caspar Goodwood.

Mrs. Touchett appeared at last, just after Isabel had returned to the big uninhabited drawing-room. She looked a good deal older, but her eye was as bright as ever and her head as erect ; her thin lips seemed a repository of latent meanings. She wore a little grey dress of the most undecorated fashion, and Isabel wondered, as she had wondered the first time, if her remarkable kinswoman resembled more a queen-regent or the matron of a gaol. Her lips felt very thin indeed on Isabel's hot cheek.

"I've kept you waiting because I've been sitting with Ralph," Mrs. Touchett said. "The nurse had gone to luncheon and I had taken her place. He has a man who's supposed to look after him, but the man's good for nothing ; he's always looking out of the window — as if there were anything to see! I didn't wish to move, because Ralph seemed to be sleeping and I was afraid the sound would disturb him. I waited till the nurse came back· I remembered you knew the house."

"I find I know it better even than I thought; I've been walking everywhere," Isabel answered. And then she asked if Ralph slept much.

"He lies with his eyes closed; he does n't move. But I'm not sure that it's always sleep."

"Will he see me? Can he speak to me?"

Mrs. Touchett declined the office of saying. "You can try him," was the limit of her extravagance. And then she offered to conduct Isabel to her room. "I thought they had taken you there; but it's not my house, it's Ralph's; and I don't know what they do. They must at least have taken your luggage; I don't suppose you've brought much. Not that I care, however. I believe they've given you the same room you had before; when Ralph heard you were coming he said you must have that one."

"Did he say anything else?"

"Ah, my dear, he does n't chatter as he used!" cried Mrs. Touchett as she preceded her niece up the staircase.

It was the same room, and something told Isabel it had not been slept in since she occupied it. Her luggage was there and was not voluminous; Mrs. Touchett sat down a moment with her eyes upon it. "Is there really no hope?" our young woman asked as she stood before her.

"None whatever. There never has been. It has not been a successful life."

"No — it has only been a beautiful one." Isabel found herself already contradicting her aunt; she was irritated by her dryness.

"I don't know what you mean by that; there's no

beauty without health. That is a very odd dress to travel in."

Isabel glanced at her garment. "I left Rome at an hour's notice; I took the first that came."

"Your sisters, in America, wished to know how you dress. That seemed to be their principal interest. I was n't able to tell them — but they seemed to have the right idea: that you never wear anything less than black brocade."

"They think I'm more brilliant than I am; I'm afraid to tell them the truth," said Isabel. "Lily wrote me you had dined with her."

"She invited me four times, and I went once. After the second time she should have let me alone. The dinner was very good; it must have been expensive. Her husband has a very bad manner. Did I enjoy my visit to America? Why should I have enjoyed it? I did n't go for my pleasure."

These were interesting items, but Mrs. Touchett soon left her niece, whom she was to meet in half an hour at the midday meal. For this repast the two ladies faced each other at an abbreviated table in the melancholy dining-room. Here, after a little, Isabel saw her aunt not to be so dry as she appeared, and her old pity for the poor woman's inexpressiveness, her want of regret, of disappointment, came back to her. Unmistakeably she would have found it a blessing to-day to be able to feel a defeat, a mistake, even a shame or two. She wondered if she were not even missing those enrichments of consciousness and privately trying — reaching out for some aftertaste of life, dregs of the banquet; the testimony of pain or the cold recreation of remorse. On the other hand perhaps she was afraid; if she should begin to know remorse at all it might take her too far. Isabel could perceive, however, how it had come over her dimly that she had failed of something, that she saw herself in the future as an old woman without memories. Her little sharp face looked tragical. She told her niece that Ralph had as yet not moved, but that he probably would be able to see her before dinner. And then in a moment she added that he had seen Lord Warburton the day before; an announcement which startled Isabel a little, as it seemed an intimation that this personage was in the neighbourhood and that an accident might bring them together. Such an accident would not be happy; she had not come to England to struggle again with Lord Warburton. She none the less presently said to her aunt that he had been very kind to Ralph; she had seen something of that in Rome.

"He has something else to think of now," Mrs. Touchett returned. And she paused with a gaze like a gimlet.

Isabel saw she meant something, and instantly guessed what she meant. But her reply concealed her guess; her heart beat faster and she wished to gain a moment. "Ah yes—the House of Lords and all that."

"He's not thinking of the Lords; he's thinking of the ladies. At least he's thinking of one of them; he told Ralph he's engaged to be married."

"Ah, to be married!" Isabel mildly exclaimed.

"Unless he breaks it off. He seemed to think Ralph would like to know. Poor Ralph can't go to the wedding, though I believe it's to take place very soon."

"And who's the young lady?"

"A member of the aristocracy ; Lady Flora, Lady Felicia — something of that sort."

"I'm very glad," Isabel said. "It must be a sudden decision."

"Sudden enough, I believe ; a courtship of three weeks. It has only just been made public."

"I'm very glad," Isabel repeated with a larger emphasis. She knew her aunt was watching her — looking for the signs of some imputed soreness, and the desire to prevent her companion from seeing anything of this kind enabled her to speak in the tone of quick satisfaction, the tone almost of relief. Mrs. Touchett of course followed the tradition that ladies, even married ones, regard the marriage of their old lovers as an offence to themselves. Isabel's first care therefore was to show that however that might be in general she was not offended now. But meanwhile, as I say, her heart beat faster ; and if she sat for some moments thoughtful — she presently forgot Mrs. Touchett's observation — it was not because she had lost an admirer. Her imagination had traversed half Europe ; it halted, panting, and even trembling a little, in the city of Rome. She figured herself announcing to her husband that Lord Warburton was to lead a bride to the altar, and she was of course not aware how extremely wan she must have looked while she made this intellectual effort. But at last she collected herself and said to her aunt: "He was sure to do it some time or other."

Mrs. Touchett was silent; then she gave a sharp little shake of the head. "Ah, my dear, you're beyond me!" she cried suddenly. They went on with their luncheon in silence; Isabel felt as if she had heard of Lord Warburton's death. She had known him only as a suitor, and now that was all over. He was dead for poor Pansy; by Pansy he might have lived. A servant had been hovering about; at last Mrs. Touchett requested him to leave them alone. She had finished her meal; she sat with her hands folded on the edge of the table. "I should like to ask you three questions," she observed when the servant had gone.

"Three are a great many."

"I can't do with less; I've been thinking. They're all very good ones."

"That's what I'm afraid of. The best questions are the worst," Isabel answered. Mrs. Touchett had pushed back her chair, and as her niece left the table and walked, rather consciously, to one of the deep windows, she felt herself followed by her eyes.

"Have you ever been sorry you did n't marry Lord Warburton?" Mrs. Touchett enquired.

Isabel shook her head slowly, but not heavily. "No, dear aunt."

"Good. I ought to tell you that I propose to believe what you say."

"Your believing me's an immense temptation," she declared, smiling still.

"A temptation to lie? I don't recommend you to do that, for when I'm misinformed I'm as dangerous as a poisoned rat. I don't mean to crow over you."

"It's my husband who does n't get on with me," said Isabel.

"I could have told him he would n't. I don't call that crowing over *you*," Mrs. Touchett added. "Do you still like Serena Merle?" she went on.

"Not as I once did. But it does n't matter, for she 's going to America."

"To America? She must have done something very bad."

"Yes — very bad."

"May I ask what it is?"

"She made a convenience of me."

"Ah," cried Mrs. Touchett, "so she did of me! She does of every one."

"She 'll make a convenience of America," said Isabel, smiling again and glad that her aunt's questions were over.

It was not till the evening that she was able to see Ralph. He had been dozing all day; at least he had been lying unconscious. The doctor was there, but after a while went away — the local doctor, who had attended his father and whom Ralph liked. He came three or four times a day; he was deeply interested in his patient. Ralph had had Sir Matthew Hope, but he had got tired of this celebrated man, to whom he had asked his mother to send word he was now dead and was therefore without further need of medical advice. Mrs. Touchett had simply written to Sir Matthew that her son disliked him. On the day of Isabel's arrival Ralph gave no sign, as I have related, for many hours; but toward evening he raised himself and said he knew that she had come.

How he knew was not apparent, inasmuch as for fear of exciting him no one had offered the information. Isabel came in and sat by his bed in the dim light; there was only a shaded candle in a corner of the room. She told the nurse she might go — she herself would sit with him for the rest of the evening. He had opened his eyes and recognised her, and had moved his hand, which lay helpless beside him, so that she might take it. But he was unable to speak; he closed his eyes again and remained perfectly still, only keeping her hand in his own. She sat with him a long time — till the nurse came back; but he gave no further sign. He might have passed away while she looked at him; he was already the figure and pattern of death. She had thought him far gone in Rome, and this was worse; there was but one change possible now. There was a strange tranquillity in his face; it was as still as the lid of a box. With this he was a mere lattice of bones; when he opened his eyes to greet her it was as if she were looking into immeasurable space. It was not till midnight that the nurse came back; but the hours, to Isabel, had not seemed long; it was exactly what she had come for. If she had come simply to wait she found ample occasion, for he lay three days in a kind of grateful silence. He recognised her and at moments seemed to wish to speak; but he found no voice. Then he closed his eyes again, as if he too were waiting for something — for something that certainly would come. He was so absolutely quiet that it seemed to her what was coming had already arrived; and yet she never lost the sense that they were still together.

But they were not always together; there were other hours that she passed in wandering through the empty house and listening for a voice that was not poor Ralph's. She had a constant fear; she thought it possible her husband would write to her. But he remained silent, and she only got a letter from Florence and from the Countess Gemini. Ralph, however, spoke at last — on the evening of the third day.

"I feel better to-night," he murmured, abruptly, in the soundless dimness of her vigil; "I think I can say something." She sank upon her knees beside his pillow; took his thin hand in her own; begged him not to make an effort — not to tire himself. His face was of necessity serious — it was incapable of the muscular play of a smile; but its owner apparently had not lost a perception of incongruities. "What does it matter if I'm tired when I've all eternity to rest? There's no harm in making an effort when it's the very last of all. Don't people always feel better just before the end? I've often heard of that; it's what I was waiting for. Ever since you've been here I thought it would come. I tried two or three times; I was afraid you'd get tired of sitting there." He spoke slowly, with painful breaks and long pauses; his voice seemed to come from a distance. When he ceased he lay with his face turned to Isabel and his large unwinking eyes open into her own. "It was very good of you to come," he went on. "I thought you would; but I was n't sure."

"I was not sure either till I came," said Isabel.

"You've been like an angel beside my bed. You know they talk about the angel of death. It's the most beautiful of all. You've been like that; as if you were waiting for me."

"I was not waiting for your death; I was waiting for — for this. This is not death, dear Ralph."

"Not for you — no. There's nothing makes us feel so much alive as to see others die. That's the sensation of life — the sense that we remain. I've had it — even I. But now I'm of no use but to give it to others. With me it's all over." And then he paused. Isabel bowed her head further, till it rested on the two hands that were clasped upon his own. She could n't see him now; but his far-away voice was close to her ear. "Isabel," he went on suddenly, "I wish it were over for you." She answered nothing; she had burst into sobs; she remained so, with her buried face. He lay silent, listening to her sobs; at last he gave a long groan. "Ah, what is it you have done for me?"

"What is it you did for me?" she cried, her now extreme agitation half smothered by her attitude. She had lost all her shame, all wish to hide things. Now he must know; she wished him to know, for it brought them supremely together, and he was beyond the reach of pain. "You did something once — you know it. O Ralph, you've been everything! What have I done for you — what can I do to-day? I would die if you could live. But I don't wish you to live; I would die myself, not to lose you." Her voice was as broken as his own and full of tears and anguish.

"You won't lose me — you'll keep me. Keep me in your heart; I shall be nearer to you than I've ever been. Dear Isabel, life is better; for in life there's love. Death is good — but there's no love."

"I never thanked you — I never spoke — I never was what I should be!" Isabel went on. She felt a passionate need to cry out and accuse herself, to let her sorrow possess her. All her troubles, for the moment, became single and melted together into this present pain. "What must you have thought of me? Yet how could I know? I never knew, and I only know to-day because there are people less stupid than I."

"Don't mind people," said Ralph. "I think I'm glad to leave people."

She raised her head and her clasped hands; she seemed for a moment to pray to him. "Is it true — is it true?" she asked.

"True that you've been stupid? Oh no," said Ralph with a sensible intention of wit.

"That you made me rich — that all I have is yours?"

He turned away his head, and for some time said nothing. Then at last: "Ah, don't speak of that — that was not happy." Slowly he moved his face toward her again, and they once more saw each other. "But for that — but for that —!" And he paused. "I believe I ruined you," he wailed.

She was full of the sense that he was beyond the reach of pain; he seemed already so little of this world. But even if she had not had it she would still have spoken, for nothing mattered now but the only knowledge that was not pure anguish — the knowledge that they were looking at the truth together.

"He married me for the money," she said. She wished to say everything; she was afraid he might die before she had done so.

He gazed at her a little, and for the first time his fixed eyes lowered their lids. But he raised them in a moment, and then, "He was greatly in love with you," he answered.

"Yes, he was in love with me. But he would n't have married me if I had been poor. I don't hurt you in saying that. How can I? I only want you to understand. I always tried to keep you from understanding; but that's all over."

"I always understood," said Ralph.

"I thought you did, and I did n't like it. But now I like it."

"You don't hurt me — you make me very happy." And as Ralph said this there was an extraordinary gladness in his voice. She bent her head again, and pressed her lips to the back of his hand. "I always understood," he continued, "though it was so strange — so pitiful. You wanted to look at life for yourself — but you were not allowed; you were punished for your wish. You were ground in the very mill of the conventional!"

"Oh yes, I've been punished," Isabel sobbed.

He listened to her a little, and then continued: "Was he very bad about your coming?"

"He made it very hard for me. But I don't care."

"It is all over then between you?"

"Oh no; I don't think anything's over."

"Are you going back to him?" Ralph gasped.

"I don't know — I can't tell. I shall stay here as

long as I may. I don't want to think — I need n't
think. I don't care for anything but you, and that 's
enough for the present. It will last a little yet. Here
on my knees, with you dying in my arms, I 'm happier
than I have been for a long time. And I want you
to be happy — not to think of anything sad; only to
feel that I 'm near you and I love you. Why should
there be pain ? In such hours as this what have
we to do with pain ? That 's not the deepest thing;
there 's something deeper."

Ralph evidently found from moment to moment
greater difficulty in speaking; he had to wait longer
to collect himself. At first he appeared to make no
response to these last words; he let a long time elapse.
Then he murmured simply: "You must stay here."

"I should like to stay — as long as seems right."

"As seems right — as seems right ?" He repeated
her words. "Yes, you think a great deal about that."

"Of course one must. You 're very tired," said
Isabel.

"I 'm very tired. You said just now that pain 's
not the deepest thing. No — no. But it 's very deep.
If I could stay —"

"For me you 'll always be here," she softly interrupted. It was easy to interrupt him.

But he went on, after a moment: "It passes, after
all; it 's passing now. But love remains. I don't
know why we should suffer so much. Perhaps I shall
find out. There are many things in life. You 're very
young."

"I feel very old," said Isabel.

"You 'll grow young again. That 's how I see you.

416

I don't believe — I don't believe —" But he stopped again; his strength failed him.

She begged him to be quiet now. "We need n't speak to understand each other," she said.

"I don't believe that such a generous mistake as yours can hurt you for more than a little."

"Oh Ralph, I'm very happy now," she cried through her tears.

"And remember this," he continued, "that if you've been hated you've also been loved. Ah but, Isabel— *adored!*" he just audibly and lingeringly breathed.

"Oh my brother!" she cried with a movement of still deeper prostration.

LV

He had told her, the first evening she ever spent at
Gardencourt, that if she should live to suffer enough
she might some day see the ghost with which the old
house was duly provided. She apparently had ful-
filled the necessary condition; for the next morning,
in the cold, faint dawn, she knew that a spirit was
standing by her bed. She had lain down without
undressing, it being her belief that Ralph would not
outlast the night. She had no inclination to sleep;
she was waiting, and such waiting was wakeful. But
she closed her eyes; she believed that as the night
wore on she should hear a knock at her door. She
heard no knock, but at the time the darkness began
vaguely to grow grey she started up from her pillow
as abruptly as if she had received a summons. It
seemed to her for an instant that he was standing
there — a vague, hovering figure in the vagueness
of the room. She stared a moment; she saw his
white face — his kind eyes; then she saw there was
nothing. She was not afraid; she was only sure.
She quitted the place and in her certainty passed
through dark corridors and down a flight of oaken
steps that shone in the vague light of a hall-window.
Outside Ralph's door she stopped a moment, listening,
but she seemed to hear only the hush that filled it.
She opened the door with a hand as gentle as if she

were lifting a veil from the face of the dead, and saw Mrs. Touchett sitting motionless and upright beside the couch of her son, with one of his hands in her own. The doctor was on the other side, with poor Ralph's further wrist resting in his professional fingers. The two nurses were at the foot between them. Mrs. Touchett took no notice of Isabel, but the doctor looked at her very hard; then he gently placed Ralph's hand in a proper position, close beside him. The nurse looked at her very hard too, and no one said a word; but Isabel only looked at what she had come to see. It was fairer than Ralph had ever been in life, and there was a strange resemblance to the face of his father, which, six years before, she had seen lying on the same pillow. She went to her aunt and put her arm around her; and Mrs. Touchett, who as a general thing neither invited nor enjoyed caresses, submitted for a moment to this one, rising, as might be, to take it. But she was stiff and dry-eyed; her acute white face was terrible.

"Dear Aunt Lydia," Isabel murmured.

"Go and thank God you've no child," said Mrs. Touchett, disengaging herself.

Three days after this a considerable number of people found time, at the height of the London "season," to take a morning train down to a quiet station in Berkshire and spend half an hour in a small grey church which stood within an easy walk. It was in the green burial-place of this edifice that Mrs. Touchett consigned her son to earth. She stood herself at the edge of the grave, and Isabel stood beside her; the sexton himself had not a more practical interest in the scene than Mrs. Touchett. It was a solemn occasion, but neither a harsh nor a heavy one ; there was a certain geniality in the appearance of things. The weather had changed to fair; the day, one of the last of the treacherous May-time, was warm and windless, and the air had the brightness of the hawthorn and the blackbird. If it was sad to think of poor Touchett, it was not too sad, since death, for him, had had no violence. He had been dying so long; he was so ready; everything had been so expected and prepared. There were tears in Isabel's eyes, but they were not tears that blinded. She looked through them at the beauty of the day, the splendour of nature, the sweetness of the old English churchyard, the bowed heads of good friends. Lord Warburton was there, and a group of gentlemen all unknown to her, several of whom, as she afterwards learned, were connected with the bank; and there were others whom she knew. Miss Stackpole was among the first, with honest Mr. Bantling beside her; and Caspar Goodwood, lifting his head higher than the rest — bowing it rather less. During much of the time Isabel was conscious of Mr. Goodwood's gaze ; he looked at her somewhat harder than he usually looked in public, while the others had fixed their eyes upon the churchyard turf. But she never let him see that she saw him; she thought of him only to wonder that he was still in England. She found she had taken for granted that after accompanying Ralph to Gardencourt he had gone away; she remembered how little it was a country that pleased him. He was there, however, very distinctly there; and something in his attitude seemed to say that he was there with a complex intention. She would n't meet his eyes, though there was doubtless sympathy in them; he made her rather uneasy. With the dispersal of the little group he disappeared, and the only person who came to speak to her — though several spoke to Mrs. Touchett — was Henrietta Stackpole. Henrietta had been crying.

Ralph had said to Isabel that he hoped she would remain at Gardencourt, and she made no immediate motion to leave the place. She said to herself that it was but common charity to stay a little with her aunt. It was fortunate she had so good a formula; otherwise she might have been greatly in want of one. Her errand was over; she had done what she had left her husband to do. She had a husband in a foreign city, counting the hours of her absence; in such a case one needed an excellent motive. He was not one of the best husbands, but that did n't alter the case. Certain obligations were involved in the very fact of marriage, and were quite independent of the quantity of enjoyment extracted from it. Isabel thought of her husband as little as might be; but now that she was at a distance, beyond its spell, she thought with a kind of spiritual shudder of Rome. There was a penetrating chill in the image, and she drew back into the deepest shade of Gardencourt. She lived from day to day, postponing, closing her eyes, trying not to think. She knew she must decide, but she decided nothing; her coming itself had not been a decision. On that occasion she had simply started. Osmond gave no sound and now evidently would give none; he would leave it all to her. From Pansy she heard nothing, but that was very simple: her father had told her not to write.

Mrs. Touchett accepted Isabel's company, but offered her no assistance; she appeared to be absorbed in considering, without enthusiasm but with perfect lucidity, the new conveniences of her own situation. Mrs. Touchett was not an optimist, but even from painful occurrences she managed to extract a certain utility. This consisted in the reflexion that, after all, such things happened to other people and not to herself. Death was disagreeable, but in this case it was her son's death, not her own; she had never flattered herself that her own would be disagreeable to any one but Mrs. Touchett. She was better off than poor Ralph, who had left all the commodities of life behind him, and indeed all the security; since the worst of dying was, to Mrs. Touchett's mind, that it exposed one to be taken advantage of. For herself she was on the spot; there was nothing so good as that. She made known to Isabel very punctually — it was the evening her son was buried — several of Ralph's testamentary arrangements. He had told her everything, had consulted her about everything. He left her no money; of course she had no need of money. He left her the furniture of Gardencourt, exclusive of the pictures and books and the use of the place for a year; after which it was to be sold. The money produced by the sale was to constitute an endowment for a hospital for poor persons suffering from the malady of which he died; and of this portion of the will Lord Warburton was appointed executor. The rest of his property, which was to be withdrawn from the bank, was disposed of in various bequests, several of them to those cousins in Vermont to whom his father had already been so bountiful. Then there were a number of small legacies.

"Some of them are extremely peculiar," said Mrs. Touchett; "he has left considerable sums to persons I never heard of. He gave me a list, and I asked then who some of them were, and he told me they were people who at various times had seemed to like him. Apparently he thought you did n't like him, for he has n't left you a penny. It was his opinion that you had been handsomely treated by his father, which I 'm bound to say I think you were — though I don't mean that I ever heard him complain of it. The pictures are to be dispersed; he has distributed them about, one by one, as little keepsakes. The most valuable of the collection goes to Lord Warburton. And what do you think he has done with his library? It sounds like a practical joke. He has left it to your friend Miss Stackpole — 'in recognition of her services to literature.' Does he mean her following him up from Rome? Was that a service to literature? It contains a great many rare and valuable books, and as she can't carry it about the world in her trunk he recommends her to sell it at auction. She will sell it of course at Christie's, and with the proceeds she 'll set up a newspaper. Will that be a service to literature?"

This question Isabel forbore to answer, as it exceeded the little interrogatory to which she had deemed it necessary to submit on her arrival. Besides, she had never been less interested in literature than to-day, as she found when she occasionally took down from the shelf one of the rare and valuable volumes of which Mrs. Touchett had spoken. She was quite unable to read; her attention had never been so little at her command. One afternoon, in the library, about a week after the ceremony in the churchyard, she was trying to fix it for an hour; but her eyes often wandered from the book in her hand to the open window, which looked down the long avenue. It was in this way that she saw a modest vehicle approach the door and perceived Lord Warburton sitting, in rather an uncomfortable attitude, in a corner of it. He had always had a high standard of courtesy, and it was therefore not remarkable, under the circumstances, that he should have taken the trouble to come down from London to call on Mrs. Touchett. It was of course Mrs. Touchett he had come to see, and not Mrs. Osmond; and to prove to herself the validity of this thesis Isabel presently stepped out of the house and wandered away into the park. Since her arrival at Gardencourt she had been but little out of doors, the weather being unfavourable for visiting the grounds. This evening, however, was fine, and at first it struck her as a happy thought to have come out. The theory I have just mentioned was plausible enough, but it brought her little rest, and if you had seen her pacing about you would have said she had a bad conscience. She was not pacified when at the end of a quarter of an hour, finding herself in view of the house, she saw Mrs. Touchett emerge from the portico accompanied by her visitor. Her aunt had evidently proposed to Lord Warburton that they should come in search of her. She was in no humour for visitors and, if she had had a chance, would have drawn back behind one of the great trees. But she saw she had been seen and that nothing was left her but to advance. As the lawn at Gardencourt was a vast expanse this took some time; during which she observed that, as he walked beside his hostess, Lord Warburton kept his hands rather stiffly behind him and his eyes upon the ground. Both persons apparently were silent; but Mrs. Touchett's thin little glance, as she directed it toward Isabel, had even at a distance an expression. It seemed to say with cutting sharpness: "Here's the eminently amenable nobleman you might have married!" When Lord Warburton lifted his own eyes, however, that was not what they said. They only said "This is rather awkward, you know, and I depend upon you to help me." He was very grave, very proper and, for the first time since Isabel had known him, greeted her without a smile. Even in his days of distress he had always begun with a smile. He looked extremely self-conscious.

"Lord Warburton has been so good as to come out to see me," said Mrs. Touchett. "He tells me he did n't know you were still here. I know he's an old friend of yours, and as I was told you were not in the house I brought him out to see for himself."

"Oh, I saw there was a good train at 6.40, that would get me back in time for dinner," Mrs. Touch-

ett's companion rather irrelevantly explained. "I'm
so glad to find you've not gone."

"I'm not here for long, you know," Isabel said
with a certain eagerness.

"I suppose not; but I hope it's for some weeks.
You came to England sooner than — a — than you
thought?"

"Yes, I came very suddenly."

Mrs. Touchett turned away as if she were looking
at the condition of the grounds, which indeed was
not what it should be, while Lord Warburton hesitated a little. Isabel fancied he had been on the point
of asking about her husband — rather confusedly —
and then had checked himself. He continued immit-
igably grave, either because he thought it becoming
in a place over which death had just passed, or for
more personal reasons. If he was conscious of personal reasons it was very fortunate that he had the
cover of the former motive; he could make the most
of that. Isabel thought of all this. It was not that his
face was sad, for that was another matter; but it was
strangely inexpressive.

"My sisters would have been so glad to come if
they had known you were still here — if they had
thought you would see them," Lord Warburton went
on. "Do kindly let them see you before you leave
England."

"It would give me great pleasure; I have such a
friendly recollection of them."

"I don't know whether you would come to Lockleigh for a day or two? You know there's always
that old promise." And his lordship coloured a little

426

as he made this suggestion, which gave his face a somewhat more familiar air. "Perhaps I'm not right in saying that just now; of course you're not thinking of visiting. But I meant what would hardly be a visit. My sisters are to be at Lockleigh at Whitsuntide for five days; and if you could come then — as you say you're not to be very long in England — I would see that there should be literally no one else."

Isabel wondered if not even the young lady he was to marry would be there with her mamma; but she did not express this idea. "Thank you extremely," she contented herself with saying; "I'm afraid I hardly know about Whitsuntide."

"But I have your promise — have n't I? — for some other time."

There was an interrogation in this; but Isabel let it pass. She looked at her interlocutor a moment, and the result of her observation was that — as had happened before — she felt sorry for him. "Take care you don't miss your train," she said. And then she added: "I wish you every happiness."

He blushed again, more than before, and he looked at his watch. "Ah yes, 6.40; I have n't much time, but I've a fly at the door. Thank you very much." It was not apparent whether the thanks applied to her having reminded him of his train or to the more sentimental remark. "Good-bye, Mrs. Osmond; good-bye." He shook hands with her, without meeting her eyes, and then he turned to Mrs. Touchett, who had wandered back to them. With her his parting was equally brief; and in a moment the two ladies saw him move with long steps across the lawn.

"Are you very sure he's to be married?" Isabel asked of her aunt.

"I can't be surer than he; but he seems sure. I congratulated him, and he accepted it."

"Ah," said Isabel, "I give it up!" — while her aunt returned to the house and to those avocations which the visitor had interrupted.

She gave it up, but she still thought of it — thought of it while she strolled again under the great oaks whose shadows were long upon the acres of turf. At the end of a few minutes she found herself near a rustic bench, which, a moment after she had looked at it, struck her as an object recognised. It was not simply that she had seen it before, nor even that she had sat upon it; it was that on this spot something important had happened to her — that the place had an air of association. Then she remembered that she had been sitting there, six years before, when a servant brought her from the house the letter in which Caspar Goodwood informed her that he had followed her to Europe; and that when she had read the letter she looked up to hear Lord Warburton announcing that he should like to marry her. It was indeed an historical, an interesting, bench; she stood and looked at it as if it might have something to say to her. She wouldn't sit down on it now — she felt rather afraid of it. She only stood before it, and while she stood the past came back to her in one of those rushing waves of emotion by which persons of sensibility are visited at odd hours. The effect of this agitation was a sudden sense of being very tired, under the influence of which she overcame her scruples and sank into the rustic seat. I have said that she was restless and unable to occupy herself; and whether or no, if you had seen her there, you would have admired the justice of the former epithet, you would at least have allowed that at this moment she was the image of a victim of idleness. Her attitude had a singular absence of purpose; her hands, hanging at her sides, lost themselves in the folds of her black dress; her eyes gazed vaguely before her. There was nothing to recall her to the house; the two ladies, in their seclusion, dined early and had tea at an indefinite hour. How long she had sat in this position she could not have told you; but the twilight had grown thick when she became aware that she was not alone. She quickly straightened herself, glancing about, and then saw what had become of her solitude. She was sharing it with Caspar Goodwood, who stood looking at her, a few yards off, and whose footfall on the unresonant turf, as he came near, she had not heard. It occurred to her in the midst of this that it was just so Lord Warburton had surprised her of old.

She instantly rose, and as soon as Goodwood saw he was seen he started forward. She had had time only to rise when, with a motion that looked like violence, but felt like — she knew not what, he grasped her by the wrist and made her sink again into the seat. She closed her eyes; he had not hurt her; it was only a touch, which she had obeyed. But there was something in his face that she wished not to see. That was the way he had looked at her the other day in the churchyard; only at present it was worse. He said nothing at first; she only felt him close to her — beside her on the bench and pressingly turned to her. It almost seemed to her that no one had ever been so close to her as that. All this, however, took but an instant, at the end of which she had disengaged her wrist, turning her eyes upon her visitant. "You've frightened me," she said.

"I did n't mean to," he answered, "but if I did a little, no matter. I came from London a while ago by the train, but I could n't come here directly. There was a man at the station who got ahead of me. He took a fly that was there, and I heard him give the order to drive here. I don't know who he was, but I did n't want to come with him; I wanted to see you alone. So I've been waiting and walking about. I've walked all over, and I was just coming to the house when I saw you here. There was a keeper, or some one, who met me; but that was all right, because I had made his acquaintance when I came here with your cousin. Is that gentleman gone? Are you really alone? I want to speak to you." Goodwood spoke very fast; he was as excited as when they had parted in Rome. Isabel had hoped that condition would subside; and she shrank into herself as she perceived that, on the contrary, he had only let out sail. She had a new sensation; he had never produced it before; it was a feeling of danger. There was indeed something really formidable in his resolution. She gazed straight before her; he, with a hand on each knee, leaned forward, looking deeply into her face.

The twilight seemed to darken round them. "I want to speak to you," he repeated; "I've something particular to say. I don't want to trouble you — as I did the other day in Rome. That was of no use; it only distressed you. I could n't help it; I knew I was wrong. But I'm not wrong now; please don't think I am," he went on with his hard, deep voice melting a moment into entreaty. "I came here to-day for a purpose. It's very different. It was vain for me to speak to you then; but now I can help you."

She could n't have told you whether it was because she was afraid, or because such a voice in the darkness seemed of necessity a boon; but she listened to him as she had never listened before; his words dropped deep into her soul. They produced a sort of stillness in all her being; and it was with an effort, in a moment, that she answered him. "How can you help me?" she asked in a low tone, as if she were taking what he had said seriously enough to make the enquiry in confidence.

"By inducing you to trust me. Now I know — to-day I know. Do you remember what I asked you in Rome? Then I was quite in the dark. But to-day I know on good authority; everything's clear to me to-day. It was a good thing when you made me come away with your cousin. He was a good man, a fine man, one of the best; he told me how the case stands for you. He explained everything; he guessed my sentiments. He was a member of your family and he left you — so long as you should be in England — to my care," said Goodwood as if he were making a great point. "Do you know what he said to me the

last time I saw him — as he lay there where he died ?
He said : 'Do everything you can for her; do everything she 'll let you.'"

Isabel suddenly got up. "You had no business to
talk about me!"

"Why not — why not, when we talked in that
way ?" he demanded, following her fast. "And he
was dying — when a man 's dying it 's different."
She checked the movement she had made to leave
him ; she was listening more than ever ; it was true
that he was not the same as that last time. That had
been aimless, fruitless passion, but at present he had
an idea, which she scented in all her being. "But it
does n't matter!" he exclaimed, pressing her still
harder, though now without touching a hem of her
garment. "If Touchett had never opened his mouth
I should have known all the same. I had only to look
at you at your cousin's funeral to see what 's the
matter with you. You can't deceive me any more ;
for God's sake be honest with a man who 's so
honest with you. You 're the most unhappy of women,
and your husband 's the deadliest of fiends."

She turned on him as if he had struck her. "Are
you mad ?" she cried.

"I 've never been so sane; I see the whole thing.
Don't think it 's necessary to defend him. But I won't
say another word against him; I 'll speak only of
you," Goodwood added quickly. "How can you
pretend you 're not heart-broken ? You don't know
what to do — you don't know where to turn. It 's
too late to play a part; did n't you leave all that
behind you in Rome ? Touchett knew all about it,

432

and I knew it too — what it would cost you to come here. It will have cost you your life? Say it will" — and he flared almost into anger: "give me one word of truth! When I know such a horror as that, how can I keep myself from wishing to save you? What would you think of me if I should stand still and see you go back to your reward? 'It's awful, what she'll have to pay for it!' — that's what Touchett said to me. I may tell you that, may n't I? He was such a near relation!" cried Goodwood, making his queer grim point again. "I'd sooner have been shot than let another man say those things to me; but he was different; he seemed to me to have the right. It was after he got home — when he saw he was dying, and when I saw it too. I understand all about it: you're afraid to go back. You're perfectly alone; you don't know where to turn. You can't turn anywhere; you know that perfectly. Now it is therefore that I want you to think of *me*."

"To think of 'you'?" Isabel said, standing before him in the dusk. The idea of which she had caught a glimpse a few moments before now loomed large. She threw back her head a little; she stared at it as if it had been a comet in the sky.

"You don't know where to turn. Turn straight to *me*. I want to persuade you to trust me," Goodwood repeated. And then he paused with his shining eyes. "Why should you go back — why should you go through that ghastly form?"

"To get away from *you!*" she answered. But this expressed only a little of what she felt. The rest was that she had never been loved before. She had believed it, but this was different; this was the hot wind of the desert, at the approach of which the others dropped dead, like mere sweet airs of the garden. It wrapped her about; it lifted her off her feet, while the very taste of it, as of something potent, acrid and strange, forced open her set teeth.

At first, in rejoinder to what she had said, it seemed to her that he would break out into greater violence. But after an instant he was perfectly quiet; he wished to prove he was sane, that he had reasoned it all out. "I want to prevent that, and I think I may, if you'll only for once listen to me. It's too monstrous of you to think of sinking back into that misery, of going to open your mouth to that poisoned air. It's you that are out of your mind. Trust me as if I had the care of you. Why shouldn't we be happy — when it's here before us, when it's so easy? I'm yours for ever — for ever and ever. Here I stand; I'm as firm as a rock. What have you to care about? You've no children; that perhaps would be an obstacle. As it is you've nothing to consider. You must save what you can of your life; you mustn't lose it all simply because you've lost a part. It would be an insult to you to assume that you care for the look of the thing, for what people will say, for the bottomless idiocy of the world. We've nothing to do with all that; we're quite out of it; we look at things as they are. You took the great step in coming away; the next is nothing; it's the natural one. I swear, as I stand here, that a woman deliberately made to suffer is justified in anything in life — in going down into the streets if that will help her! I know how you suffer, and that's why I'm here. We can do absolutely as we please; to whom under the sun do we owe anything? What is it that holds us, what is it that has the smallest right to interfere in such a question as this? Such a question is between ourselves — and to say that is to settle it! Were we born to rot in our misery — were we born to be afraid? I never knew *you* afraid! If you'll only trust me, how little you will be disappointed! The world's all before us — and the world's very big. I know something about that."

Isabel gave a long murmur, like a creature in pain; it was as if he were pressing something that hurt her. "The world's very small," she said at random; she had an immense desire to appear to resist. She said it at random, to hear herself say something; but it was not what she meant. The world, in truth, had never seemed so large; it seemed to open out, all round her, to take the form of a mighty sea, where she floated in fathomless waters. She had wanted help, and here was help; it had come in a rushing torrent. I know not whether she believed everything he said; but she believed just then that to let him take her in his arms would be the next best thing to her dying. This belief, for a moment, was a kind of rapture, in which she felt herself sink and sink. In the movement she seemed to beat with her feet, in order to catch herself, to feel something to rest on.

"Ah, be mine as I'm yours!" she heard her companion cry. He had suddenly given up argument, and his voice seemed to come, harsh and terrible, through a confusion of vaguer sounds.

This however, of course, was but a subjective fact, as the metaphysicians say; the confusion, the noise of waters, all the rest of it, were in her own swimming head. In an instant she became aware of this. "Do me the greatest kindness of all," she panted. "I beseech you to go away!"

"Ah, don't say that. Don't kill me!" he cried.

She clasped her hands; her eyes were streaming with tears. "As you love me, as you pity me, leave me alone!"

He glared at her a moment through the dusk, and the next instant she felt his arms about her and his lips on her own lips. His kiss was like white lightning, a flash that spread, and spread again, and stayed; and it was extraordinarily as if, while she took it, she felt each thing in his hard manhood that had least pleased her, each aggressive fact of his face, his figure, his presence, justified of its intense identity and made one with this act of possession. So had she heard of those wrecked and under water following a train of images before they sink. But when darkness returned she was free. She never looked about her; she only darted from the spot. There were lights in the windows of the house; they shone far across the lawn. In an extraordinarily short time — for the distance was considerable — she had moved through the darkness (for she saw nothing) and reached the door. Here only she paused. She looked all about her; she listened a little; then she put her hand on the latch. She had not known where to turn; but she knew now. There was a very straight path.

Two days afterwards Caspar Goodwood knocked at the door of the house in Wimpole Street in which Henrietta Stackpole occupied furnished lodgings. He had hardly removed his hand from the knocker when the door was opened and Miss Stackpole herself stood before him. She had on her hat and jacket; she was on the point of going out. "Oh, good-morning," he said, "I was in hopes I should find Mrs. Osmond."

Henrietta kept him waiting a moment for her reply; but there was a good deal of expression about Miss Stackpole even when she was silent. "Pray what led you to suppose she was here?"

"I went down to Gardencourt this morning, and the servant told me she had come to London. He believed she was to come to you."

Again Miss Stackpole held him — with an intention of perfect kindness — in suspense. "She came here yesterday, and spent the night. But this morning she started for Rome."

Caspar Goodwood was not looking at her; his eyes were fastened on the doorstep. "Oh, she started — ?" he stammered. And without finishing his phrase or looking up he stiffly averted himself. But he could n't otherwise move.

Henrietta had come out, closing the door behind her, and now she put out her hand and grasped his arm. "Look here, Mr. Goodwood," she said; "just you wait!"

On which he looked up at her — but only to guess, from her face, with a revulsion, that she simply meant he was young. She stood shining at him

437

with that cheap comfort, and it added, on the spot, thirty years to his life. She walked him away with her, however, as if she had given him now the key to patience.

THE END